Book Three of The Malloreon

DEMON LORD OF
KARANDA

By David Eddings
Published by Ballantine Books

THE BELGARIAD
Book One: *Pawn of Prophecy*
Book Two: *Queen of Sorcery*
Book Three: *Magician's Gambit*
Book Four: *Castle of Wizardry*
Book Five: *Enchanters' End Game*

THE MALLOREON
Book One: *Guardians of the West*
Book Two: *King of the Murgos*
Book Three: *Demon Lord of Karanda*
Book Four: *Sorceress of Darshiva**
Book Five: *The Seeress of Kell**

HIGH HUNT

* *Forthcoming*

Book Three of The Malloreon

DEMON LORD OF KARANDA

DAVID EDDINGS

A Del Rey Book

Ballantine Books · New York

A Del Rey Book
Published by Ballantine Books

Copyright © 1988 by David Eddings

Maps by Shelly Shapiro

All rights reserved under International and Pan-American Copyright Con-
ventions. Published in the United States of America by Ballantine Books,
a division of Random House, Inc., New York, and simultaneously in Canada
by Random House of Canada Limited, Toronto.

Library of Congress Cataloging-in-Publication Data

Eddings, David.
  Demon lord of Karanda.

  (The Malloreon : bk. 3)
  "A Del Rey book."
  I. Title. II. Series: Eddings, David.
Malloreon ; bk. 3.
PS3555.D38D46 1988   813'.54   88-47804
ISBN 0-345-33004-8

Design by Holly Johnson

Manufactured in the United States of America

First Edition: September 1988

10 9 8 7 6 5 4 3 2 1

For Patrick Janson-Smith,
a very special friend,
from writer, wife, and Fatso.

At this time I would again like to express my indebtedness to my wife, Leigh Eddings, for her support, her contributions, and her wholehearted collaboration in this ongoing story. Without her help, none of this would have been possible.

I would also like to take this opportunity to thank my editor, Lester del Rey, for his patience and forbearance, as well as for contributions too numerous to mention.

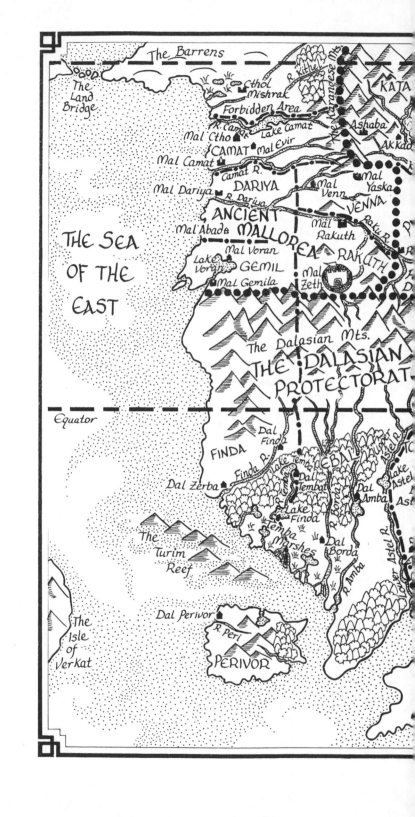

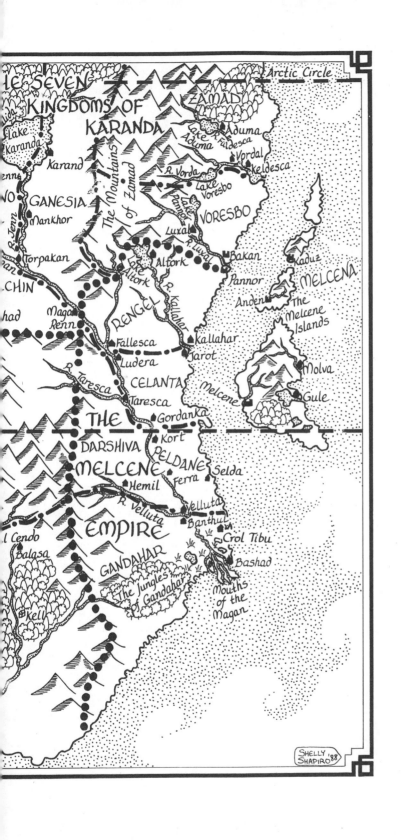

Prologue

Being a brief history of Mallorea and the races that dwell there.
—Digested from *The Chronicles of Angarak*
University of Melcene Press

Tradition places the ancestral home of the Angaraks somewhere off the south coast of present-day Dalasia. Then Torak, Dragon God of Angarak, used the power of the Stone, Cthrag Yaska, in what has come to be called "the cracking of the world." The crust of the earth split, releasing liquid magma from below and letting the waters of the southern ocean in to form the Sea of the East. This cataclysmic process continued for decades before the world gradually assumed its present form.

As a result of this upheaval, the Alorns and their allies were forced to retreat into the unexplored reaches of the western continent, while the Angaraks fled into the wilderness of Mallorea.

Torak had been maimed and disfigured by the Stone, which rebelled at the use to which the God put it, and the Grolim priests were demoralized. Thus leadership fell by default to the military; by the time the Grolims recovered, the military had established *de facto* rule of all Angarak. Lacking their former preeminence, the priests set up an opposing center of power at Mal Yaska, near the tip of the Karandese mountain Range.

At this point, Torak roused himself to prevent the imminent civil war between priesthood and military rule. But he made no move against the military headquarters at Mal Zeth; instead, he marched to the extreme northwest of Malorea Antiqua with a quarter of the Angarak people to build the Holy City of Cthol Mishrak. There he remained, so absorbed by efforts to gain control of Cthrag Yaska that he was oblivious to the fact that the people had largely turned from their previous preoccupation with theological matters. Those with him in Cthol Mishrak were mostly a hysterical fringe of fanatics under the rigid control of Torak's three disciples, Zedar, Ctuchik, and Urvon. These three maintained the old forms in the society of Cthol Mishrak while the rest of Angarak changed.

When the continuing friction between the Church and military finally came to Torak's attention, he summoned the military High Command and the Grolim Hierarchy to Cthol Mishrak and delivered his commands in terms that brooked no demur. Exempting only Mal Yaska and Mal Zeth, all towns and districts were to be ruled jointly by the military and priesthood. The subdued Hierarchy and High Command immediately settled their differences and returned to their separate enclaves. This enforced truce freed the generals to turn their attention to the other peoples living in Mallorea.

The origins of these people are lost in myth, but three races had predated the Angaraks on the continent: the Dalasians of the southwest; the Karands of the north; and the Melcenes of the East. It was to the Karands the military turned its efforts.

The Karands were a warlike race with little patience for cultural niceties. They lived in crude cities where hogs roamed freely in the muddy streets. Traditionally, they were related to the Morindim of the far north of Gar og Nadrak. Both races were given to the practice of demon worship.

At the beginning of the second millenium, roving bands of Karandese brigands had become a serious problem along the eastern frontier, and the Angarak army now moved out of Mal Zeth to the western fringes of the Karandese Kingdom of Pallia. The city of Rakand in southwestern Pallia was sacked and burned, and the inhabitants were taken captives.

At this point, one of the greatest decisions of Angarak history was made. While the Grolims prepared for an orgy of human sacrifice, the generals paused. They had no desire to occupy Pallia, and the difficulties of long-distance communication made the notion unattractive. To the generals, it seemed far better to keep Pallia as a subject kingdom and exact tribute, rather than to occupy a depopulated territory. The Grolims were outraged, but the generals were adamant. Ultimately, both sides agreed to take the matter before Torak for his decision.

Not surprisingly, Torak agreed with the High Command; if the Karands could be converted, he would nearly double the congregation of his Church as well as the size of his army for any future confrontation with the Kings of the West. "Any man who liveth in boundless Mallorea shall bow down and worship me," he told his reluctant missionaries. And to insure their zeal, he sent Urvon to Mal Yaska to oversee the conversion of the Karands. There Urvon established himself as temporal head of the Mallorean Church in pomp and luxury hitherto unknown to the ascetic Grolims.

The army moved against Katakor, Jenno, and Delchin, as well as Pallia. But the missionaries fared poorly as the Karandese magicians conjured up hordes of demons to defend their society. Urvon finally journeyed to Cthol Mishrak to consult with Torak. It is not clear what Torak did, but the Karandese magicians soon discovered that the spells previously used to control the demons were no longer effective. Any magician could now reach into the realms of darkness only at the peril of life and soul.

The conquest of the Karands absorbed the attention of both military and priesthood for the next several centuries, but ultimately the resistance collapsed and Karanda became a subject nation, its peoples generally looked upon as inferiors.

When the army advanced down the Great River Magan against the Melcene Empire, however, it met a sophisticated and technologically superior people. In several disastrous battles, in which Melcene war chariots and elephant cavalry destroyed whole battalions, the Angaraks abandoned their efforts. The Angarak generals made overtures of peace. To their astonishment, the Melcenes quickly agreed to normalize relations and offered to trade horses, which the Angaraks previously lacked. They refused, however, even to discuss the sale of elephants.

The army then turned to Dalasia, which proved to be an easy conquest. The Dalasians were simple farmers and herdsmen with little skill for war. The Angaraks moved into Dalasia and established military protectorates during the next ten years. The priesthood seemed at first equally successful. The Dalasians meekly accepted the forms of Angarak worship. But they were a mystical people, and the Grolims soon discovered that the power of the witches, seers, and prophets remained unbroken. Moreover, copies of the infamous *Mallorean Gospels* still circulated in secret among the Dalasians.

In time, the Grolims might have succeeded in stamping out

the secret Dalasian religion. But then a disaster occurred that was to change forever the complexion of Angarak life. Somehow, the legendary sorcerer Belgarath, accompanied by three Alorns, succeeded in evading all the security measures and came unobserved at night to steal Cthrag Yaska from the iron tower of Torak in the center of Cthol Mishrak. Although pursued, they managed to escape with the stolen Stone to the West.

In furious rage, Torak destroyed his city. Then he ordered that the Murgos, Thulls, and Nadraks be sent to the western borders of the Sea of the East. More than a million lives were lost in the crossing of the northern land bridge, and the society and culture of the Angaraks took long to recover.

Following the dispersal and the destruction of Cthol Mishrak, Torak became almost inaccessible, concentrating totally on various schemes to thwart the growing power of the Kingdoms of the West. The God's neglect gave the military time to exploit fully its now virtually total control of Mallorea and the subject kingdoms.

For many centuries, the uneasy peace between Angaraks and Melcenes continued, broken occasionally only by little wars in which both sides avoided committing their full forces. The two nations eventually established the practice of each sending children of the leaders to be raised by leaders of the other side. This led to a fuller understanding by both, as well as to the growth of a body of cosmopolitan youths that eventually became the norm for the ruling class of the Mallorean Empire.

One such youth was Kallath, the son of a high-ranking Angarak general. Brought up in Melcene, he returned to Mal Zeth to become the youngest man ever to be elevated to the General Staff. Returning to Melcene, he married the daughter of the Melcene Emperor and managed to have himself declared Emperor following the old man's death in 3830. Then, using the Melcene army as a threat, he managed to get himself declared hereditary Commander in Chief of the Angaraks.

The integration of Melcene and Angarak was turbulent. But in time, the Melcene patience won out over Angarak brutality. Unlike other peoples, the Melcenes were ruled by a bureaucracy. And in the end, that bureaucracy proved far more efficient than the Angarak military administration. By 4400, the ascendancy of the bureaucracy was complete. By that time, also, the title of Commander in Chief had been forgotten and the ruler of both peoples was simply the Emperor of Mallorea.

To the sophisticated Melcenes, the worship of Torak remained largely superficial. They accepted the forms out of expediency, but the Grolims were never able to command the abject submission to the Dragon God that had characterized the Angaraks.

Then in 4850, Torak suddenly emerged from his eons of seclusion to appear before the gates of Mal Zeth. Wearing a steel mask to conceal his maimed face, he set aside the Emperor and declared himself Kal Torak, King and God. He immediately began mustering an enormous force to crush the Kingdoms of the West and bring all the world under his domination.

The mobilization that followed virtually stripped Mallorea of able-bodied males. The Angaraks and Karands were marched north to the land bridge, crossing to northermost Gar og Nadrak, and the Dalasians and Melcenes moved to where fleets had been constructed to ferry them across the Sea of the East to southern Cthol Murgos. The northern Malloreans joined with the Nadraks, Thulls, and northern Murgos to strike toward the Kingdoms of Drasnia and Algaria. The second group of Malloreans joined with the southern Murgos and were to march northwesterly. Torak meant to crush the West between the two huge armies.

The southern forces, however, were caught in a freak storm that swept off the Western Sea in the spring of 4875 and that buried them alive in the worst blizzard of recorded history. When it finally abated, the column was mired in fourteen-foot snowdrifts that persisted until early summer. No theory has yet been able to explain this storm, which was clearly not of natural origin. Whatever the cause, the southern army perished. The few survivors who struggled back to the east told tales of horror that were truly unthinkable.

The northern force was also beset by various disasters, but eventually laid siege to Vo Mimbre, where they were completely routed by the combined armies of the West. And there Torak was struck down by the power of Cthrag Yaska (there called the Orb of Aldur) and lay in a coma that was to last centuries, though his body was rescued and taken to a secret hiding place by his disciple Zedar.

In the years following these catastrophes, Mallorean society began to fracture back into its original components of Melcene, Karanda, Dalasia, and the lands of the Angaraks. The Empire was saved only by the emergence of Korzeth as Emperor.

Korzeth was only fourteen when he seized the throne from his aged father. Deceived by his youth, the separatist regions began to declare independence of the imperial throne. Korzeth moved decisively to stem the revolution. He spent the rest of his life on horseback in one of the greatest bloodbaths of history, but when he was done, he delivered a strong and united Mallorea to his successors. Henceforth, the descendants of Korzeth ruled in total and unquestioned power from Mal Zeth.

This continued until the present Emperor, Zakath, ascended the throne. For a time, he gave promise of being an enlightened ruler of Mallorea and the western kingdoms of the Angaraks. But soon there were signs of trouble.

The Murgos were ruled by Taur Urgas, and it was evident that he was both mad and unscrupulously ambitious. He instigated some plot against the young Emperor. It has never been established clearly what form his scheming took. But Zakath discovered that Taur Urgas was behind it and vowed vengeance. This took the form of a bitter war in which Zakath began a campaign to destroy the mad ruler utterly.

It was in the middle of this struggle that the West struck. While the Kings of the West sent an army against the East, Belgarion, the young Overlord of the West and descendant of Belgarath the Sorcerer, advanced on foot across the north and across the land bridge into Mallorea. He was accompanied by Belgarath and a Drasnian and he bore the ancient Sword of Riva, on the pommel of which was Cthrag Yaska, the Orb of Aldur. His purpose was to slay Torak, apparently in response to some prophecy known in the West.

Torak had been emerging from his long coma in the ruins of his ancient city of Cthol Mishrak. Now he roused himself to meet the challenger. But in the confrontation, Belgarion overcame the God and slew him with the Sword, leaving the priesthood of Mallorea in chaos and confusion.

Part One

RAK HAGGA

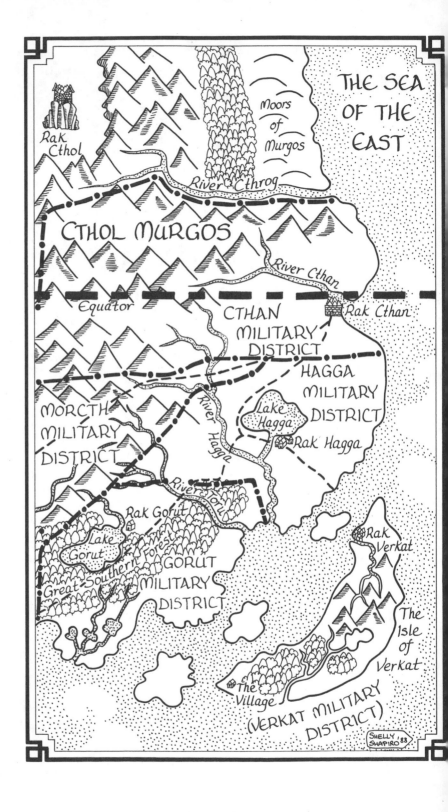

CHAPTER ONE

The first snow of the season settled white and quiet through the breathless air onto the decks of their ship. It was a wet snow with large, heavy flakes that piled up on the lines and rigging, turning the tarred ropes into thick, white cables. The sea was black, and the swells rose and fell without sound. From the stern came the slow, measured beat of a muffled drum that set the stroke for the Mallorean oarsmen. The sifting flakes settled on the shoulders of the sailors and in the folds of their scarlet cloaks as they pulled steadily through the snowy morning. Their breath steamed in the chill dampness as they bent and straightened in unison to the beat of the drum.

Garion and Silk stood at the rail with their cloaks pulled tightly around them, staring somberly out through the filmy snowfall.

"Miserable morning," the rat-faced little Drasnian noted, distastefully brushing snow from his shoulders.

Garion grunted sourly.

"You're in a cheerful humor today."

"I don't really have all that much to smile about, Silk," Garion went back to glowering out at the gloomy black-and-white morning.

Belgarath the Sorcerer came out of the aft cabin, squinted up into the thickly settling snow, and raised the hood of his stout old cloak. Then he came forward along the slippery deck to join them at the rail.

Silk glanced at the red-cloaked Mallorean soldier who had unobstrusively come up on deck behind the old man and who now stood leaning with some show of idleness on the rail several yards aft. "I see that General Atesca is still concerned about your well-being," he said, pointing at the man who had dogged Belgarath's steps since they had sailed out of the harbor at Rak Verkat.

Belgarath threw a quick disgusted glance in the soldier's direction. "Stupidity," he said shortly. "Where does he think I'm going?"

A sudden thought came to Garion. He leaned forward and spoke very quietly. "You know," he said, "we *could* go someplace, at that. We've got a ship here, and a ship goes wherever you point it—Mallorea just as easily as the coast of Hagga."

"It's an interesting notion, Belgarath," Silk agreed.

"There are four of us, Grandfather," Garion pointed out. "You, me, Aunt Pol, and Durnik. I'm sure we wouldn't have much difficulty in taking over this ship. Then we could change course and be halfway to Mallorea before Kal Zakath realized that we weren't coming to Rak Hagga after all." The more he thought about it, the more the idea excited him. "Then we could sail north along the Mallorean coast and anchor in a cove or inlet someplace on the shore of Camat. We'd only be a week or so from Ashaba. We might even be able to get there before Zandramas does." A bleak smile touched his lips. "I'd sort of like to be waiting for her when she gets there."

"It's got some definite possibilities, Belgarath," Silk said. "Could you do it?"

Belgarath scratched thoughtfully at his beard, squinting out into the sifting snow. "It's possible," he admitted. He looked at Garion. "But what do you think we ought to do with all these Mallorean soldiers and the ship's crew, once we get to the coast of Camat? You weren't planning to sink the ship and drown them all, were you, the way Zandramas does when she's finished using people?"

"Of course not!"

"I'm glad to hear that—but then how did you plan to keep them from running to the nearest garrison just as soon as we leave them behind? I don't know about you, but the idea of having a regiment or so of Mallorean troops hot on our heels doesn't excite me all that much."

Garion frowned. "I guess I hadn't thought about that," he admitted.

"I didn't think you had. It's usually best to work your way completely through an idea before you put it into action. It avoids a great deal of spur-of-the-moment patching later on."

"All right," Garion said, feeling slightly embarrassed.

"I know you're impatient, Garion, but impatience is a poor substitute for a well-considered plan."

"Do you mind, Grandfather?" Garion said acidly.

"Besides, it might just be that we're *supposed* to go to Rak Hagga and meet with Kal Zakath. Why would Cyradis turn us over to the Malloreans, after she went to all the trouble of putting *The Book of Ages* into my hands? There's something else going on here, and I'm not sure we want to disrupt things until we find out a little more about them."

The cabin door opened, and General Atesca, the commander of the Mallorean forces occupying the Isle of Verkat,

13

emerged. From the moment they had been turned over to him, Atesca had been polite and strictly correct in all his dealings with them. He had also been very firm about his intention to deliver them personally to Kal Zakath in Rak Hagga. He was a tall, lean man, and his uniform was bright scarlet, adorned with numerous medals and decorations. He carried himself with erect dignity, though the fact that his nose had been broken at some time in the past made him look more like a street brawler than a general in an imperial army. He came up the slush-covered deck, heedless of his highly polished boots. "Good morning, gentlemen," he greeted them with a stiff, military bow. "I trust you slept well?"

"Tolerably," Silk replied.

"It seems to be snowing," the general said, looking about and speaking in the tone of one making small talk for the sake of courtesy.

"I noticed that," Silk said. "How long is it likely to take us to reach Rak Hagga?"

"A few more hours to reach the coast, your Highness, and then a two-day ride to the city."

Silk nodded. "Have you any idea why your Emperor wants to see us?" he asked.

"He didn't say," Atesca answered shortly, "and I didn't think it appropriate to ask. He merely told me to apprehend you and to bring you to him at Rak Hagga. You are all to be treated with utmost courtesy as long as you don't try to escape. If you do that, his Imperial Majesty instructed me to be more firm." His tone as he spoke was neutral, and his face remained expressionless. "I hope you gentlemen will excuse me now," he said. "I have some matters that need my attention." He bowed curtly, turned, and left them.

"He's a gold mine of information, isn't he?" Silk noted dryly. "Most Melcenes love to gossip, but you've got to pry every word out of this one."

"Melcene?" Garion said. "I didn't know that."

Silk nodded. "Atesca's a Melcene name. Kal Zakath has

14

some peculiar ideas about the aristocracy of talent. Angarak officers don't like the idea, but there's not too much they can do about it—if they want to keep their heads."

Garion was not really that curious about the intricacies of Mallorean politics, so he let the matter drop, to return to the subject they had been discussing previously. "I'm not quite clear about what you were saying, Grandfather," he said, "about our going to Rak Hagga, I mean."

"Cyradis believes that she has a choice to make," the old man replied, "and there are certain conditions that have to be met before she can make it. I've got a suspicion that your meeting with Zakath might be one of those conditions."

"You don't actually believe her, do you?"

"I've seen stranger things happen and I always walk very softly around the Seers of Kell."

"I haven't seen anything about a meeting of that kind in the Mrin Codex."

"Neither have I, but there are more things in the world than the Mrin Codex. You've got to keep in mind the fact that Cyradis is drawing on the prophecies of *both* sides, and if the prophecies are equal, they have equal truth. Not only that, Cyradis is probably drawing on some prophecies that only the Seers know about. Wherever this list of preconditions came from, though, I'm fairly certain that she won't let us get to this 'place which is no more' until every item's been crossed off her list."

"Won't *let* us?" Silk said.

"Don't underestimate Cyradis, Silk," Belgarath cautioned. "She's the receptacle of all the power the Dals possess. That means that she can probably do things that the rest of us couldn't even begin to dream of. Let's look at things from a practical point of view, though. When we started out, we were a half a year behind Zandramas and we were planning a very tedious and time-consuming trek across Cthol Murgos—but we kept getting interrupted."

"Tell me about it," Silk said sardonically.

"Isn't it curious that after all these interruptions, we've reached the eastern side of the continent ahead of schedule and cut Zandramas' lead down to a few weeks?"

Silk blinked, and then his eyes narrowed.

"Gives you something to think about, doesn't it?" The old man pulled his cloak more tightly about him and looked around at the settling snow. "Let's go inside," he suggested. "It's really unpleasant out here."

The coast of Hagga was backed by low hills, filmy-looking and white in the thick snowfall. There were extensive salt marshes at the water's edge, and the brown reeds bent under their burden of wet, clinging snow. A black-looking wooden pier extended out across the marshes to deeper water, and they disembarked from the Mallorean ship without incident. At the landward end of the pier a wagon track ran up into the hills, its twin ruts buried in snow.

Sadi the eunuch looked upward with a slightly bemused expression as they rode off the pier and onto the road. He lightly brushed one long-fingered hand across his shaved scalp. "They feel like fairy wings," he smiled.

"What's that?" Silk asked him.

"The snowflakes. I've almost never seen snow before— only when I was visiting a northern kingdom—and I actually believe that this is the first time I've ever been out of doors when it was snowing. It's not too bad, is it?"

Silk gave him a sour look. "The first chance I get, I'll buy you a sled," he said.

Sadi looked puzzled. "Excuse me, Kheldar, but what's a sled?" he asked.

Silk sighed. "Never mind, Sadi. I was only trying to be funny."

At the top of the first hill a dozen or so crosses leaned at various angles beside the road. Hanging from each cross was a skeleton with a few tattered rags clinging to its bleached bones and a clump of snow crowning its vacant-eyed skull.

"One is curious to know the reason for that, General Atesca," Sadi said mildly, pointing at the grim display at the roadside.

"Policy, your Excellency," Atesca replied curtly. "His Imperial Majesty seeks to alienate the Murgos from their king. He hopes to make them realize that Urgit is the cause of their misfortunes."

Sadi shook his head dubiously. "I'd question the reasoning behind that particular policy," he disagreed. "Atrocities seldom endear one to the victims. I've always preferred bribery myself."

"Murgos are accustomed to being treated atrociously." Atesca shrugged. "It's all they understand."

"Why haven't you taken them down and buried them?" Durnik demanded, his face pale and his voice thick with outrage.

Atesca gave him a long, steady look. "Economy, Goodman," he replied. "An empty cross really doesn't prove very much. If we took them down, we'd just have to replace them with fresh Murgos. That gets to be tedious after a while, and sooner or later one starts to run out of people to crucify. Leaving the skeletons there proves our point—and it saves time."

Garion did his best to keep his body between Ce'Nedra and the gruesome object lesson at the side of the road, trying to shield her from that hideous sight. She rode on obliviously, however, her face strangely numb and her eyes blank and unseeing. He threw a quick, questioning glance at Polgara and saw a slight frown on her face. He dropped back and pulled his horse in beside hers. "What's wrong with her?" he asked in a tense whisper.

"I'm not entirely sure, Garion," she whispered back.

"Is it the melancholia again?" There was a sick, sinking feeling in the pit of his stomach.

"I don't think so." Her eyes were narrowed in thought, and she absently pulled the hood of her blue robe forward to

17

cover the white lock in the midnight of her hair. "I'll keep an eye on her."

"What can I do?"

"Stay with her. Try to get her to talk. She might say something to give us some clues."

Ce'Nedra, however, made few responses to Garion's efforts to engage her in conversation, and her answers for the remainder of that snowy day quite frequently had little relevance to either his questions or his observations.

As evening began to settle over the war-ravaged countryside of Hagga, General Atesca called a halt, and his soldiers began to erect several scarlet pavilions in the lee of a fire-blackened stone wall, all that remained of a burned-out village. "We should reach Rak Hagga by late tomorrow afternoon," he advised them. "That large pavilion in the center of the encampment will be yours for the night. My men will bring you your evening meal in a little while. Now, if you'll all excuse me—" He inclined his head briefly, then turned his horse around to supervise his men.

When the soldiers had completed the erection of the pavilions, Garion and his friends dismounted in front of the one Atesca had indicated. Silk looked around at the guard detachment moving into position around the large red tent. "I wish he'd make up his mind," he said irritably.

"I don't quite follow you, Prince Kheldar," Velvet said to him. "Just who should make up his mind?"

"Atesca. He's the very soul of courtesy, but he surrounds us with armed guards."

"The troops might just be there to protect us, Kheldar," she pointed out. "This *is* a war zone, after all."

"Of course," he said dryly, "and cows might fly, too—if they had wings."

"What a fascinating observation," she marveled.

"I wish you wouldn't do that all the time."

"Do what?" Her brown eyes were wide and innocent.

"Forget it."

The supper Atesca's cooks prepared for them was plain, consisting of soldiers' rations and served on tin plates, but it was hot and filling. The interior of the pavilion was heated by charcoal braziers and filled with the golden glow of hanging oil lamps. The furnishings were of a military nature, the kinds of tables and beds and chairs that could be assembled and disassembled rapidly, and the floors and walls were covered with Mallorean carpets dyed a solid red color.

Eriond looked around curiosuly after he had pushed his plate back. "They seem awfully partial to red, don't they?" he noted.

"I think it reminds them of blood," Durnik declared bleakly. "They like blood." He turned to look coldly at the mute Toth. "If you've finished eating, I think we'd prefer it if you left the table," he said in a flat tone.

"That's hardly polite, Durnik," Polgara said reprovingly.

"I wasn't trying to be polite, Pol. I don't see why he has to be with us in the first place. He's a traitor. Why doesn't he go stay with his friends?"

The giant mute rose from the table, his face melancholy. He lifted one hand as if he were about to make one of those obscure gestures with which he and the smith communicated, but Durnik deliberately turned his back on him. Toth sighed and went over to sit unobstrusively in one corner.

"Garion," Ce'Nedra said suddenly, looking around with a worried little frown, "where's my baby?"

He stared at her.

"Where's Geran?" she demanded, her voice shrill.

"Ce'Nedra—" he started.

"I hear him crying. What have you done with him?" She suddenly sprang to her feet and began to dash about the tent, flinging back the curtains that partitioned off the sleeping quarters and yanking back the blankets on each bed. "Help me!" she cried to them. "Help me find my baby!"

Garion crossed the tent quickly to take her by the arm. "Ce'Nedra—"

"No!" she shouted at him. "You've hidden him somewhere! Let me go!" She wrenched herself free of his grasp and began overturning the furniture in her desperate search, sobbing and moaning unintelligibly.

Again Garion tried to restrain her, but she suddenly hissed at him and extended her fingers like talons to claw at his eyes.

"Ce'Nedra! Stop that!"

But she darted around him and bolted out of the pavilion into the snowy night.

As Garion burst through the tent flap in pursuit, he found his way barred by a red-cloaked Mallorean soldier. "You! Get back inside!" the man barked, blocking Garion with the shaft of his spear. Over the guard's shoulder, Garion saw Ce'Nedra struggling with another soldier; without even thinking, he smashed his fist into the face in front of him. The guard reeled backward and fell. Garion leaped over him, but found himself suddenly seized from behind by a half-dozen more men. "Leave her alone!" he shouted at the guard who was cruelly one of the little Queen's arms behind her.

"Get back inside the tent!" a rough voice barked, and Garion found himself being dragged backward step by step toward the tent flap. The soldier holding Ce'Nedra was half lifting, half pushing her back toward the same place. With a tremendous effort, Garion got control of himself and coldly began to draw in his will.

"That will be enough!" Polgara's voice cracked from the doorway to the tent.

The soldiers stopped, looking uncertainly at each other and somewhat fearfully at the commanding presence in the doorway.

"Durnik!" she said then. "Help Garion bring Ce'Nedra back inside."

Garion shook himself free of the restraining hands and he

and Durnik took the violently struggling little Queen from the soldier and pulled her back toward the pavilion.

"Sadi," Polgara said as Durnik and Garion entered the tent with Ce'Nedra between them, "do you have any oret in that case of yours?"

"Certainly, Lady Polgara," the eunuch replied, "but are you sure that oret is appropriate here? I'd be more inclined toward naladium, personally."

"I think we've got more than a case of simple hysteria on our hands, Sadi. I want something strong enough to insure that she doesn't wake up the minute my back's turned."

"Whatever you think best, Lady Polgara." He crossed the carpeted floor, opened his red leather case, and took out a vial of dark blue liquid. Then he went to the table and picked up a cup of water. He looked at her inquiringly.

She frowned. "Make it three drops," she decided.

He gave her a slightly startled look, then gravely measured out the dosage.

It took several moments of combined effort to get Ce'Nedra to drink the contents of the cup. She continued to sob and struggle for several moments, but then her struggles grew gradually weaker, and her sobbing lessened. Finally she closed her eyes with a deep sigh, and her breathing became regular.

"Let's get her to bed," Polgara said, leading the way to one of the curtained-off sleeping chambers.

Garion picked up the tiny form of his sleeping wife and followed. "What's wrong with her, Aunt Pol?" he demanded as he laid her gently on the bed.

"I'm not positive," Polgara replied, covering Ce'Nedra with a rough soldier's blanket. "I'll need more time to pin it down."

"What can we do?"

"Not very much while we're on the road," she admitted candidly. "We'll keep her asleep until we get to Rak Hagga. Once I get her into a more stable situation, I'll be able to work on it. Stay with her. I want to talk with Sadi for a few moments."

Garion sat worriedly by the bed, gently holding his wife's limp little hand while Polgara went back out to consult with the eunuch concerning the various drugs in his case. Then she returned, drawing the drape shut behind her. "He has most of what I need," she reported quietly. "I'll be able to improvise the rest." She touched Garion's shoulder and bent forward. "General Atesca just came in," she whispered to him. "He wants to see you. I wouldn't be too specific about the cause of Ce'Nedra's attack. We can't be sure just how much Zakath knows about our reasons for being here, and Atesca's certain to report everything that hapapens, so watch what you say."

He started to protest.

"You can't do anything here, Garion, and they need you out there. I'll watch her."

"Is she subject to these seizures often?" Atesca was asking as Garion came through the draped doorway.

"She's very high-strung," Silk replied. "Sometimes circumstances get the best of her. Polgara knows what to do."

Atesca turned to face Garion. "Your Majesty," he said in a chilly tone, "I don't appreciate your attacking my soldiers."

"He got in my way, General," Garion replied. "I don't think I hurt him all that much."

"There's a principle involved, your Majesty."

"Yes," Garion agreed, "there is. Give the man my apologies, but advise him not to interfere with me again—particularly when it concerns my wife. I don't really like hurting people, but I can make exceptions when I have to."

Atesca's look grew steely, and the gaze Garion returned was just as bleak. They stared at each other for a long moment. "With all due respect, your Majesty," Atesca said finally, "don't abuse my hospitality again."

"Only if the situation requires it, General."

"I'll instruct my men to prepare a litter for your wife,"

Atesca said then, "and let's plan to get an early start tomorrow. If the Queen is ill, we want to get her to Rak Hagga as soon as possible."

"Thank you, General," Garion replied.

Atesca bowed coldly, then turned and left.

"Wouldn't you say that was a trifle blunt, Belgarion?" Sadi murmured. "We *are* in Atesca's power at the moment."

Garion grunted. "I didn't like his attitude." He looked at Belgarath, whose expression was faintly disapproving. "Well?" he asked.

"I didn't say anything."

"You didn't have to. I could hear you thinking all the way over here."

"Then I don't have to say it, do I?"

The next day dawned cold and raw, but the snow had stopped. Garion rode at the side of Ce'Nedra's horse-borne litter with his face mirroring his concern. The road they followed ran northwesterly past more burned-out villages and shattered towns. The ruins were covered with a thick coating of the clinging wet snow that had fallen the previous day, and each of them was encircled by a ring of those grim, occupied crosses and stakes.

It was about midafternoon when they crested a hill and saw the lead-gray expanse of Lake Hagga stretching far to the north and east; on the near shore was a large, walled city.

"Rak Hagga," Atesca said with a certain relief.

They rode on down the hill toward the city. A brisk wind was blowing in off the lake, whipping their cloaks about them and tossing the manes of their horses.

"All right, gentlemen," Atesca said over his shoulder to his troops, "let's form up and try to look like soldiers." The red-cloaked Malloreans pulled their horses into a double file and straightened in their saddles.

The walls of Rak Hagga had been breached in several places, and the tops of the battlements were chipped and pitted from the storms of steel-tipped arrows that had swept

23

over them. The heavy gates had been burst asunder during the final assault on the city and hung in splinters from their rusty iron hinges.

The guards at the gate drew themselves up and saluted smartly as Atesca led the way into the city. The battered condition of the stone houses within the walls attested to the savagery of the fighting which had ensued when Rak Hagga had fallen. Many of them stood unroofed to the sky, their gaping, soot-blackened windows staring out at the rubble-choked streets. A work gang of sullen Murgos, dragging clanking chains behind them, labored to clear the fallen building stones out of the slushy streets under the watchful eyes of a detachment of Mallorean soldiers.

"You know," Silk said, "that's the first time I've ever seen a Murgo actually work. I didn't think they even knew how."

The headquarters of the Mallorean army in Cthol Murgos was in a large, imposing yellow-brick house near the center of the city. It faced a broad, snowy square, and a marble staircase led up to the main door with a file of red-cloaked Mallorean soldiers lining each side.

"The former residence of the Murgo Military Governor of Hagga," Sadi noted as they drew near the house.

"You've been here before, then?" Silk asked.

"In my youth," Sadi replied. "Rak Hagga has always been the center of the slave trade."

Atesca dismounted and turned to one of his officers. "Captain," he said, "have your men bring the Queen's litter. Tell them to be very careful."

As the rest of them swung down from their mounts, the captain's men unfastened the litter from the saddles of the two horses that had carried it and started up the marble stairs in General Atesca's wake.

Just inside the broad doors stood a polished table, and seated behind it was an arrogant-looking man with angular eyes and an expensive-looking scarlet uniform. Against the far wall stood a row of chairs occupied by bored-looking officials.

"State your business," the officer behind the table said brusquely.

Atesca's face did not change expression as he silently stared at the officer.

"I said to state your business."

"Have the rules changed, Colonel?" Atesca asked in a deceptively mild voice. "Do we no longer rise in the presence of a superior?"

"I'm too busy to jump to my feet for every petty Melcene official from the outlying districts," the colonel declared.

"Captain," Atesca said flatly to his officer, "if the colonel is not on his feet in the space of two heartbeats, would you be so good as to cut his head off for me?"

"Yes, sir," the captain replied, drawing his sword even as the startled colonel jumped to his feet.

"Much better," Atesca told him. "Now, let's begin over again. Do you by chance remember how to salute?"

The colonel saluted smartly, though his face was pale.

"Splendid. We'll make a soldier of you yet. Now, one of the people I was escorting—a lady of high station—fell ill during our journey. I want a warm, comfortable room prepared for her immediately."

"Sir," the colonel protested, "I'm not authorized to do that."

"Don't put your sword away just yet, Captain."

"But, General, the members of his Majesty's household staff make all those decisions. They'll be infuriated if I overstep my bounds."

"I'll explain it to his Majesty, Colonel," Atesca told him. "The circumstances are a trifle unusual, but I'm sure he'll approve."

The colonel faltered, his eyes filled with indecison.

"Do it, colonel! Now!"

"I'll see to it at once, General," the colonel replied, snapping to attention. "You men," he said to the soldiers holding Ce'Nedra's litter, "follow me."

Garion automatically started to follow the litter, but Polgara took his arm firmly. "No, Garion. I'll go with her. There's nothing you can do right now, and I think Zakath's going to want to talk to you. Just be careful of what you say." And she went off down the hallway behind the litter.

"I see that Mallorean society still has its little frictions," Silk said blandly to General Atesca.

"Angaraks," Atesca grunted. "Sometimes they have a little difficulty coping with the modern world. Excuse me, Prince Kheldar. I want to let his Majesty know that we're here." He went to a polished door at the other end of the room and spoke briefly with one of the guards. Then he came back. "The Emperor is being advised of our arrival," he said to them. "I expect that he'll see us in a few moments."

A rather chubby, bald-headed man in a plain, though obviously costly, brown robe and with a heavy gold chain about his neck approached them. "Atesca, my dear fellow," he greeted the general, "they told me that you were stationed at Rak Verkat."

"I have some business with the Emperor, Brador. What are you doing in Cthol Murgos?"

"Cooling my heels," the chubby man replied. "I've been waiting for two days to see Kal Zakath."

"Who's minding the shop at home?"

"I've arranged it so that it more or less runs itself," Brador replied. "The report I have for his Majesty is so vital that I decided to carry it myself."

"What could be so earth-shaking that it would drag the Chief of the Bureau of Internal Affairs away from the comforts of Mal Zeth?"

"I believe that it's time for his Imperial Exaltedness to tear himself away from his amusements here in Cthol Murgos and come back to the capital."

"Careful, Brador," Atesca said with a brief smile. "Your fine-tuned Melcene prejudices are showing."

"Things are getting grim at home, Atesca," Brador said seriously. "I've *got* to talk with the Emperor. Can you help me to get in to see him?"

"I'll see what I can do."

"Thank you, my friend," Brador said, clasping the general's arm. "The whole fate of the empire may depend on my persuading Kal Zakath to come back to Mal Zeth."

"General Atesca," one of the spear-armed guards at the polished door said in a loud voice, "his Imperial Majesty will see you and your prisoners now."

"Very good," Atesca replied ignoring the ominous word "prisoners." He looked at Garion. "The Emperor must be very eager to see you, your Majesty," he noted. "It often takes weeks to gain an audience with him. Shall we go inside?"

CHAPTER TWO

Kal Zakath, the Emperor of boundless Mallorea, lounged in a red-cushioned chair at the far end of a large plain room. The Emperor wore a simple white linen robe, severe and unadorned. Though Garion knew that he was at least in his forties, his hair was untouched by gray and his face was unlined. His eyes, however, betrayed a kind of dead weariness, devoid of any joy or even any interest in life. Curled in his lap lay a common mackerel-striped alley cat, her eyes closed and her forepaws alternately kneading his thigh. Although the Emperor himself wore the simplest of clothes, the guards lining the walls all wore steel breastplates deeply inlaid with gold.

"My Emperor," General Atesca said with a deep bow, "I have the honor to present his Royal Majesty, King Belgarion of Riva."

Garion nodded briefly, and Zakath inclined his head in response. "Our meeting is long overdue, Belgarion," he said in a voice as dead as his eyes. "Your exploits have shaken the world."

"Yours have also made a certain impression, Zakath." Garion had decided even before he had left Rak Verkat that he would not perpetuate the absurdity of the Mallorean's self-bestowed "Kal."

A faint smile touched Zakath's lips. "Ah," he said in a tone which indicated that he saw through Garion's attempt to be subtle. He nodded briefly to the others, and his attention finally fixed itself upon the rumpled untidy form of Garion's grandfather. "And of course you, sir, would be Belgarath," he noted. "I'm a bit surprised to find you so ordinary looking. The Grolims of Mallorea all agree that you're a hundred feet tall—possible two hundred—and that you have horns and a forked tail."

"I'm in disguise," Belgarath replied with aplomb.

Zakath chuckled, though there was little amusement in that almost mechanical sound. Then he looked around with a faint frown. "I seem to note some absences," he said.

"Queen Ce'Nedra fell ill during our journey, your Majesty," Atesca advised him. "Lady Polgara is attending her."

"Ill? Is it serious?"

"It's difficult to say at this point, your Imperial Majesty," Sadi replied unctuously, "but we have given her certain medications, and I have every confidence in Lady Polgara's skill."

Zakath looked at Garion. "You should have sent word on ahead, Belgarion. I have a healer on my personal staff—a Dalasian woman with remarkable gifts. I'll send her to the Queen's chambers at once. Our first concern must be your wife's health."

"Thank you," Garion replied with genuine gratitude.

Zakath touched a bellpull and spoke briefly with the servant who responded immediately to his summons.

"Please," the Emperor said then, "seat yourselves. I have no particular interest in ceremony."

As the guards hastily brought chairs for them, the cat sleeping in Zakath's lap half opened her golden eyes and looked around at them. She rose to her paws, arched her back, and yawned. Then she jumped heavily to the floor with an audible grunt and waddled over to sniff at Eriond's fingers. With a faintly amused look, Zakath watched his obviously pregnant cat make her matronly way across the carpet. "You'll note that my cat has been unfaithful to me—again." He sighed in mock resignation. "It happens fairly frequently, I'm afraid, and she never seems to feel the slightest guilt about it."

The cat jumped up into Eriond's lap, nestled down, and began to purr contentedly.

"You've grown, boy," Zakath said to the young man. "Have they taught you how to talk as yet?"

"I've picked up a few words, Zakath," Eriond said in his clear voice.

"I know the rest of you—by reputation at least," Zakath said then. "Goodman Durnik and I met on the plains of Mishrak ac Thull, and of course I've heard of the Margravine Liselle of Drasnian Intelligence and of Prince Kheldar, who strives to become the richest man in the world."

Velvet's graceful curtsy of acknowledgement was not quite so florid as Silk's grandiose bow.

"And here, of course," the Emperor continued, "is Sadi, Chief Eunuch in the palace of Queen Salmissra."

Sadi bowed with fluid grace. "I must say that your Majesty is remarkable well informed," he said in his contralto voice. "You have read us all like an open book."

"My chief of intelligence tries to keep me informed, Sadi. He may not be as gifted as the inestimable Javelin of Boktor, but he knows about *most* of what's going on in this part of the

30

world. He's mentioned that huge fellow over in the corner, but so far he hasn't been able to discover his name."

"He's called Toth," Eriond supplied. "He's a mute, so we have to do his talking for him."

"And a Dalasian besides," Zakath noted. "A very curious circumstance."

Garion had been closely watching this man. Beneath the polished, urbane exterior, he sensed a kind of subtle probing. The idle greetings, which seemed to be no more than a polite means of putting them at their ease, had a deeper motive behind them. In some obscure way he sensed that Zakath was somehow testing each of them.

The emperor straightened then. "You have an oddly assorted company with you, Belgarion," he said, "and you're a long way from home. I'm curious about your reasons for being here in Cthol Murgos."

"I'm afraid that's a private matter, Zakath."

One of the Emperor's eyebrows rose slightly. "Under the circumstances, that's hardly a satisfactory answer, Belgarion. I can't really take the chance that you're allied with Urgit."

"Would you accept my word that I'm not?"

"Not until I know a bit more about your visit to Rak Urga. Urgit left there quite suddenly—apparently in your company—and reappeared just as suddenly on the plains of Morcth, where he and a young woman led his troops out of an ambush I'd gone to a great deal of trouble to arrange. You'll have to admit that's a peculiar set of circumstances."

"Not when you look at it from a practical standpoint," Belgarath said. "The decision to take Urgit with us was mine. He'd found out who we are, and I didn't want an army of Murgos on our heels. Murgos aren't too bright, but they can be an inconvenience at times.

Zakath looked surprised. "He was your prisoner?"

Belgarath shrugged. "In a manner of speaking."

The Emperor laughed rather wryly. "You could have wrung

31

almost any concession from me if you had just delivered him into my hands, you know. Why did you let him go?"

"We didn't need him anymore," Garion replied. "We'd reached shores of Lake Cthaka, so he really wasn't any kind of threat to us."

Zakath's expression narrowed slightly. "A few other things happened as well, I think," he observed. "Urgit has always been a notorious coward, wholly under the domination of the Grolim Agachak and of his father's generals. But he didn't seem very timid while he was extricating his troops from the trap I'd laid for them, and all the reports filtering out of Rak Urga seem to suggest that he's actually behaving like a king. Did you by any chance have anything to do with that?"

"It's possible, I suppose," Garion answered. "Urgit and I talked a few times, and I told him what he was doing wrong."

Zakath tapped one forefinger against his chin, and his eyes were shrewd. "You may not have made a lion of him, Belgarion," he said, "but at least he's no longer a rabbit." A chill smile touched the Mallorean's lips. "In a way, I'm rather glad about that. I've never taken much satisfaction in hunting rabbits." He shaded his eyes with one hand, although the light in the room was not particularly bright. "But what I can't understand is how you managed to spirit him out of the Drojim Palace and away from the city. He has whole regiments of bodyguards."

"You're overlooking something, Zakath," Belgarath said to him. "We have certain advantages that aren't available to others."

"Sorcery, you mean? Is it really all that reliable?"

"I've had some luck with it from time to time."

Zakath's eyes had become suddenly intent. "They tell me that you're five thousand years old, Belgarath. Is that true?"

"Seven, actually—or a little more. Why do you ask?"

"In all those years, hasn't it ever occurred to you simply to seize power? You could have made yourself king of the world, you know."

Belgarath looked amused. "Why would I want to?" he asked.

"All men want power. It's human nature."

"Has all your power really made you happy?"

"It has certain satisfactions."

"Enough to make up for all the petty distractions that go with it?"

"I can endure those. At least I'm in a position where no one tells me what to do."

"No one tells me what to do either, and I'm not saddled with all those tedious responsibilities." Belgarath straightened. "All right, Zakath, shall we get to the point? What are your intentions concerning us?"

"I haven't really decided that yet." The Emperor looked around at them. "I presume that we can all be civilized about the present situation?"

"How do you mean, civilized?" Garion asked him.

"I'll accept your word that none of you will try to escape or do anything rash. I'm aware that you and a number of your friends have certain specialized talents. I don't want to be forced to take steps to counteract them."

"We have some rather pressing business," Garion replied carefully, "so we can only delay for just so long. For the time being, however, I think we can agree to be reasonable about things."

"Good. We'll have to talk later, you and I, and come to know one another. I've had comfortable quarters prepared for you and your friends, and I know that you're anxious about your wife. Now, I hope you'll excuse me, but I have some of those tedious responsibilities Belgarath mentioned to attend to."

Although the house was very large, it was not, strictly speaking, a palace. It appeared that the Murgo governors-general of Hagga who had ordered it built had not shared the grandiose delusions which afflicted the rulers of Urga, and so the building was more functional than ornate.

"I hope you'll excuse me," General Atesca said to them when they had emerged from the audience chamber. "I'm obliged to deliver a full report to his Majesty—about various matters—and then I must return immediately to Rak Verkat." He looked at Garion. "The circumstances under which we met were not the happiest, your Majesty," he said, "but I hope you won't think too unkindly of me." He bowed rather stiffly and then left them in the care of a member of the Emperor's staff.

The man who led them down a long, dark-paneled hallway toward the center of the house was obviously not an Angarak. He had not the angular eyes nor the stiff, bleak-faced arrogance that marked the men of that race. His cheerful, round face seemed to hint at a Melcene heritage, and Garion remembered that the bureaucracy which controlled most aspects of Mallorean life was made up almost excusively of Melcenes. "His Majesty asked me to assure you that your quarters are not intended to be a prison," the official told them as they approached a heavily barred iron door blocking off one portion of the hallway. "This was a Murgo house before we took the city, and it has certain structural peculiarities. Your rooms are in what once were the women's quarters, and Murgos are fanatically protective of their women. It has to do with their concept of racial purity, I think."

At the moment, Garion had little interest in sleeping arrangements. All his concern was for Ce'Nedra. "Do you happen to know where I might find my wife?" he asked the moonfaced bureaucrat.

"There at the end of this corridor, your Majesty," the Melcene replied, pointing toward a blue-painted door at the far end of the hall.

"Thank you." Garion glanced at the others. "I'll be back in a little while," he told them and strode on ahead.

The room he entered was warm and the lighting subdued. Deep, ornately woven Mallorean carpets covered the floor and soft green velvet drapes covered the tall, narrow windows.

Ce'Nedra lay in a high-posted bed against the wall opposite the door, and Polgara was seated at the bedside, her expression grave.

"Has there been any change?" Garion asked her, softly closing the door behind him.

"Nothing as yet," she replied.

Ce'Nedra's face was pale as she slept with her crimson curls tumbled on her pillow.

"She *is* going to be all right, isn't she?" Garion asked.

"I'm sure of it, Garion."

Another woman sat near the bed. She wore a light green, cowled robe; despite the fact that she was indoors, she had the hood pulled up, partially concealing her face. Ce'Nedra muttered something in a strangely harsh tone and tossed her head restlessly on her pillow. The cowled woman frowned. "Is this her customary voice, Lady Polgara?" she asked.

Polgara looked at her sharply. "No," she replied. "As a matter of fact, it's not."

"Would the drug you gave her in some way affect the sound of her speech?"

"No, it wouldn't. Actually, she shouldn't be making any sounds at all."

"Ah," the woman said. "I think perhaps I understand now." She leaned forward and very gently laid the fingertips of one hand on Ce'Nedra's lips. She nodded then and withdrew her hand. "As I suspected," she murmured.

Polgara also reached out to touch Ce'Nedra's face. Garion heard the faint whisper of her will, and the candle at the bedside flared up slightly, then sank back until its flame was scarcely more than a pinpoint. "I should have guessed," Polgara accused herself.

"What is it?" Garion asked in alarm.

"Another mind is seeking to dominate your wife and to subdue her will, your Majesty," the cowled woman told him. "It's an art sometimes practiced by the Grolims. They discovered it quite by accident during the third age."

35

"This is Andel, Garion," Polgara told him. "Zakath sent her here to help care for Ce'Nedra."

Garion nodded briefly to the hooded woman. "Exactly what do we mean by the word 'dominate'?" he asked.

"You should be more familiar with that than most people, Garion," Polgara said. "I'm sure you remember Asharak the Murgo."

Garion felt a sudden chill, remembering the force of the mind that had from his earliest childhood sought that same control over his awareness. "Drive it out," he pleaded. "Get whomever it is out of her mind."

"Perhaps not quite yet, Garion," Polgara said coldly. "We have an opportunity here. Let's not waste it."

"I don't understand."

"You will, dear," she told him. Then she rose, sat on the edge of the bed and lightly laid one hand on each of Ce'Nedra's temples. The faint whisper came again, stronger this time, and once again the candles all flared and then sank back as if suffocating. "I know you're in there," she said then. "You might as well speak."

Ce'Nedra's expression grew contorted, and she tossed her head back and forth as if trying to escape the hands touching her temples. Polgara's face grew stern, and she implacably kept her hands in place. The pale lock in her hair began to glow, and a strange chill came into the room, seeming to emanate from the bed itself.

Ce'Nedra suddenly screamed.

"Speak!" Polgara commanded. "You cannot flee until I release you, and I will not release you until you speak."

Ce'Nedra's eyes suddenly opened. They were filled with hate. "I do not fear thee, Polgara," she said in a harsh, rasping voice delivered in a peculiar accent.

"And I fear you even less. Now, who are you?"

"Thou knowest me, Polgara."

"Perhaps, but I will have your name from you." There was a long pause, and the surge of Polgara's will grew stronger.

Ce'Nedra screamed again—a scream filled with an agony that made Garion flinch. "Stop!" the harsh voice cried. "I will speak!"

"Say your name," Polgara insisted implacably.

"I am Zandramas."

"So. What do you hope to gain by this?"

An evil chuckle escaped Ce'Nedra's pale lips. "I have already stolen her heart, Polgara—her child. Now I will steal her mind as well. I could easily kill her if I chose, but a dead Queen may be buried and her grave left behind. A mad one, on the other hand, will give thee much to distract thee from thy search for the Sardion."

"I can banish you with a snap of my fingers, Zandramas."

"And I can return just as quickly."

A frosty smile touched Polgara's lips. "You're not nearly as clever as I thought," she said. "Did you actually believe that I twisted your name out of you for my own amusement? Were you ignorant of the power over you that you gave me when you spoke your own name? The power of the name is the most elementary of all. I can keep you out of Ce'Nedra's mind now. There's much more, though. For example, I know now that you're at Ashaba, haunting the bat-infested ruins of the House of Torak like a poor ragged ghost."

A startled gasp echoed through the room.

"I could tell you more, Zandramas, but this is all beginning to bore me." She straightened, her hands still locked to the sides of Ce'Nedra's head. The white lock at her brow flared into incandescence, and the faint whisper became a deafening roar. "Now, begone!" she commanded.

Ce'Nedra moaned, and her face suddenly contorted into an expression of agony. An icy, stinking wind seemed to howl through the room, and the candles and glowing braziers sank even lower until the room was scarcely lit.

"Begone!" Polgara repeated.

An agonized wail escaped Ce'Nedra's lips, and then that wail became disembodied, coming it seemed from the empty air above the bed. The candles went out, and all light ceased to glow out of the braziers. The wailing voice began to fade, moving swiftly until it came to them as no more than a murmur echoing from an unimaginable distance.

"Is Zandramas gone?" Garion asked in a shaking voice.

"Yes," Polgara replied calmly out of the sudden darkness.

"What are we going to say to Ce'Nedra? When she wakes up, I mean."

"She won't remember any of this. Just tell her something vague. Make some light, dear."

Garion fumbled for one of the candles, brushed his sleeve against it, and then deftly caught it before it hit the floor. He was sort of proud of that.

"Don't play with it, Garion. Just light it."

Her tone was so familiar and so commonplace that he began to laugh, and the little surge of his will that he directed at the candle was a stuttering sort of thing. The flame that appeared bobbled and hiccuped at the end of the wick in a soundless golden chortle.

Polgara looked steadily at the giggling candle, then closed her eyes. "Oh, Garion," she sighed in resignation.

He moved about the room relighting the other candles and fanning the braziers back into life. The flames were all quite sedate—except for the original one, which continued to dance and laugh in blithe glee.

Polgara turned to the hooded Dalasian healer. "You're most perceptive, Andel," she said. "That sort of thing is difficult to recognize unless you know precisely what you're looking for."

"The perception was not mine, Lady Polgara," Andel replied. "I was advised by another of the cause of her Majesty's illness."

"Cyradis?"

Andel nodded. "The minds of all our race are joined with hers, for we are but the instruments of the task which lies upon her. Her concern for the Queen's well-being prompted her to intervene." The hooded woman hesitated. "The Holy Seeress also asked me to beg you to intercede with your husband in the matter of Toth. The Goodman's anger is causing that gentle guide extreme anguish, and his pain is also hers. What happened at Verkat had to happen—otherwise the meeting between the Child of Light and the Child of Dark could not come to pass for ages hence."

Polgara nodded gravely. "I thought it might have been something like that. Tell her that I'll speak with Durnik in Toth's behalf."

Andel inclined her head gratefully.

"Garion," Ce'Nedra murmured drowsily, "where are we?"

He turned to her quickly. "Are you all right?" he asked, taking her hand in his.

"Mmmm," she said. "I'm just so very sleepy. What happened—and where are we?"

"We're at Rak Hagga." He threw a quick glance at Polgara, then turned back to the bed. "You just had a little fainting spell is all," he said with a slightly exaggerated casualness. "How are you feeling?"

"I'm fine, dear, but I think I'd like to sleep now." And her eyes went closed. Then she opened them again with a sleepy little frown. "Garion," she murmured, "why is that candle acting like that?"

He kissed her lightly on the cheek. "Don't worry about it, dear," he told her, but she had already fallen fast asleep.

It was well past midnight when Garion was awakened by a light tapping on the door of the room in which he slept. "Who is it?" he asked, half rising in his bed.

"A messenger from the Emperor, your Majesty," a voice replied from the other side of the door. "He instructed me to ask if you would be so good as to join him in his private study."

"Now? In the middle of the night?"

"Such was the Emperor's instruction, your Majesty."

"All right," Garion said, throwing off his blankets and swinging around to put his feet on the cold floor. "Give me a minute or so to get dressed."

"Of course, your Majesty."

Muttering to himself, Garion began to pull on his clothes by the faint light coming from the brazier in the corner. When he was dressed, he splashed cold water on his face and raked his fingers through his sandy hair, trying to push it into some semblance of order. Almost as an afterthought he ducked his head and arm through the strap attached to the sheath of Iron-grip's sword and shrugged it into place across his back. Then he opened the door. "All right," he said to the messenger, "let's go."

Kal Zakath's study was a book-lined room with several leather-upholstered chairs, a large polished table and a crackling fire on the hearth. The Emperor, still clad in plain white linen, sat in a chair at the table, shuffling through a stack of parchment sheets by the light of a single oil lamp.

"You wanted to see me, Zakath?" Garion asked as he entered the room.

"Ah, yes, Belgarion," Zakath said, pushing aside the parchments. "So good of you to come. I understand that your wife is recovering."

Garion nodded. "Thank you again for sending Andel. Her aid was very helpful."

"My pleasure, Belgarion." Zakath reached out and lowered the wick in the lamp until the corners of the room filled with shadows. "I thought we might talk a little," he said.

"Isn't it sort of late?"

"I don't sleep very much, Belgarion. A man can lose a third of his life in sleep. The day is filled with bright lights and distractions; the night is dim and quiet and allows much greater concentration. Please, sit down."

Garion unbuckled his sword and leaned it against a bookcase.

"I'm not really all *that* dangerous, you know," the Emperor said, looking pointedly at the great weapon.

Garion smiled slightly, settling into a chair by the fire. "I didn't bring it because of you, Zakath. It's just a habit. It's not the kind of sword you want to leave lying around."

"I don't think anyone would steal it, Belgarion."

"It *can't* be stolen. I just don't want anybody getting hurt by accidentally touching it."

"Do you mean to say that it's *that* sword?"

Garion nodded. "I'm sort of obliged to take care of it. It's a nuisance most of the time, but there've been a few occasions when I was glad I had it with me."

"What *really* happened at Cthol Mishrak?" Zakath asked suddenly. "I've heard all sorts of stories."

Garion nodded wryly. "So have I. Most of them get the names right, but not very much else. Neither Torak nor I had very much control over what happened. We fought, and I stuck that sword into his chest."

"And he died" Zakath's face was intent.

"Eventually, yes."

"Eventually?"

"He vomited fire first and wept flames. Then he cried out."

"What did he say?"

"'Mother,'" Garion replied shortly. He didn't really want to talk about it.

"What an extraordinary thing for him to do. Whatever happened to his body? I had the entire ruin of Cthol Mishrak searched for him."

"The other Gods came and took it. Do you suppose we could talk about something else? Those particular memories are painful."

"He *was* your enemy."

Garion sighed. "He was also a God, Zakath—and killing a God is a terrible thing to have to do."

"You're a strangely gentle man, Belgarion. I think I respect you more for that than I do for your invincible courage."

41

"I'd hardly say invincible. I was terrified the whole time—and so was Torak, I think. Was there something you really wanted to talk about?"

Zakath leaned back in his chair, tapping thoughtfully at his pursed lips. "You know that eventually you and I will have to confront each other, don't you?"

"No," Garion disagreed. "That's not absolutely certain."

"There can only be one King of the World."

Garion's look grew pained. "I've got enough trouble trying to rule one small island. I've never wanted to be King of the World."

"But I have—and do."

Garion sighed. "Then we probably will fight at that—sooner or later. I don't think the world was intended to be ruled by one man. If you try to do that, I'll have to stop you."

"I am unstoppable, Belgarion."

"So was Torak—or at least he thought so."

"That's blunt enough."

"It helps to avoid a lot of misunderstandings later on. I'd say that you've got enough trouble at home without trying to invade my kingdom—or those of my friends. That's not to mention the stalemate here in Cthol Murgos."

"You're well informed."

"Queen Porenn is a close personal friend. She keeps me advised, and Silk picks up a great deal of information during the course of his busisness dealings."

"Silk?"

"Excuse me. Prince Kheldar, I mean. Silk's a nickname of sorts."

Zakath looked at him steadily. "In some ways we're very much alike, Belgarion, and in other ways very different, but we still do what necessity compels us to do. Frequently, we're at the mercy of events over which we have no control."

"I suppose you're talking about the two Prophecies?"

Zakath laughed shortly. "I don't believe in prophecy. I only believe in power. It's curious, though, that we've both been faced with similar problems of late. You recently had to put down an uprising in Aloria—a group of religious fanatics, I believe. I have something of much the same nature going on in Darshiva. Religion is a constant thorn in the side of any ruler, wouldn't you say?"

"I've been able to work around it—most of the time."

"You've been very lucky then. Torak was neither a good nor kindly God, and his Grolim priesthood is vile. If I weren't busy here in Cthol Murgos, I think I might endear myself to the next thousand or so generations by obliterating every Grolim on the face of the earth."

Garion grinned at him. "What would you say to an alliance with that in mind?" he suggested.

Zakath laughed briefly, and then his face grew somber again. "Does the name Zandramas mean anything to you?" he asked.

Garion edged around that cautiously, not knowing how much information Zakath had about their real reason for being in Cthol Murgos. "I've heard some rumors," he said.

"How about Cthrag Sardius?"

"I've heard of it."

"You're being evasive, Belgarion." Zakath gave him a steady look, then passed his hand wearily across his eyes.

"I think you need some sleep," Garion told him.

"Time for that soon enough—when my work is done."

"That's up to you, I guess."

"How much do you know about Mallorea, Belgarion?"

"I get reports—a little disjointed sometimes, but fairly current."

"No. I mean our past."

"Not too much, I'm afraid. Western historians tried very hard to ignore the fact that Mallorea was even there."

Zakath smiled wryly. "The University of Melcena has the same shortsightedness regarding the West," he noted. "Anyway, over the past several centuries—since the disaster at Vo Mimbre—Mallorean society has become almost completely

43

secular. Torak was bound in sleep, Ctuchik was practicing his perversions here in Cthol Murgos, and Zedar was wandering around the world like a rootless vagabond—what ever happened to him, by the way? I thought he was at Cthol Mishrak."

"He was."

"We didn't find his body."

"He isn't dead."

"He's not?" Zakath looked stunned. "Where is he, then?"

"Beneath the city. Belgarath opened the earth and sealed him up in solid rock under the ruin."

"*Alive?*" Zakath's exclamation came out in a choked gasp.

"There was a certain amount of justification for it. Go on with your story."

Zakath shuddered and then recovered. "With the rest of them out of the way, the only religious figure left in Mallorea was Urvon, and he devoted himself almost exclusively to trying to make his palace at Mal Yaska more opulent than the imperial one at Mal Zeth. Every so often he'd preach a sermon filled with mumbo jumbo and nonsense, but most of the time he seemed to have forgotten Torak entirely. With the Dragon God and his disciples no longer around, the real power of the Grolim Church was gone—oh, the priests babbled about the return of Torak and they all paid lip service to the notion that one day the sleeping God would awaken, but the memory of him grew dimmer and dimmer. The power of the Church grew less and less, while that of the army—which is to say the imperial throne—grew more and more."

"Mallorean politics seem to be very murky," Garion observed.

Zakath nodded. "It's part of our nature, I suppose. At any rate, our society was functioning and moving out of the dark ages—slowly, perhaps, but moving. Then you suddenly appeared out of nowhere and awakend Torak—and just as suddenly put him permanently back to sleep again. That's when all our problems started."

"Shouldn't it have ended them? That's sort of what I had in mind."

"I don't think you grasp the nature of the religious mind, Belgarion. So long as Torak was there—even though he slept—the Grolims and the other hysterics in the empire were fairly placid, secure and comfortable in the belief that one day he would awaken, punish all their enemies, and reassert the absolute authority of the unwashed and stinking priesthood. But when you killed Torak, you destroyed their comfortable sense of security. They were forced to face the fact that without Torak they were nothing. Some of them were so chagrined that they went mad. Others fell into absolute despair. A few, however, began to hammer together a new mythology—something to replace what you had destroyed with a single stroke of that sword over there."

"It wasn't entirely my idea," Garion told him.

"It's results that matter, Belgarion, not intentions. Anyway, Urvon was forced to tear himself away from his quest for opulence and his wallowing in the adoration of the sycophants who surrounded him and get back to business. For a time he was in an absolute frenzy of activity. He resurrected all the moth-eaten old prophecies and twisted and wrenched at them until they seemed to say what he wanted them to say."

"And what was that?"

"He's trying to convince people that a new God will come to rule over Angarak—either a resurrection of Torak himself or some new deity infused with Torak's spirit. He's even got a candidate in mind for this new God of Angarak."

"Oh? Who's that?"

Zakath's expression became amused. "He sees his new God every time he looks in a mirror."

"You're not serious!"

"Oh, yes. Urvon's been trying to convince himself that he's at least a demigod for several centuries now. He'd probably have himself paraded all over Mallorea in a golden chariot—except that he's afraid to leave Mal Yaska. As I understand it, there's a very nasty hunchback who's been hungering to kill him for eons—one of Aldur's disciples, I believe."

Garion nodded. "Beldin," he said. "I've met him."

"Is he really as bad as the stories make him out to be?"

"Probably even worse. I don't think you'd want to be around to watch what he does, if he ever catches up with Urvon."

"I wish him good hunting, but Urvon's not my only problem, I'm afraid. Not long after the death of Torak, certain rumors started coming out of Darshiva. A Grolim priestess—Zandramas by name—also began to predict the coming of a new God."

"I didn't know that she was a Grolim," Garion said with some surprise.

Zakath nodded gravely. "She formerly had a very unsavory reputation in Darshiva. Then the so-called ecstacy of prophecy fell on her, and she was suddenly transformed by it. Now when she speaks, no one can resist her words. She preaches to multitudes and fires them with invincible zeal. Her message of the coming of a new God ran through Darshiva like wildfire and spread into Regel, Voresebo, and Zamad as well. Virtually the entire northeast coast of Mallorea is hers."

"What's the Sardion got to do with all this?" Garion asked.

"I think it's the key to the whole business," Zakath replied. "Both Zandramas and Urvon seem to believe that whoever finds and possesses it is going to win out."

"Agachak—the Hierarch of Rak Urga—believes the same thing," Garion told him.

Zakath nodded moodily. "I suppose I should have realized that. A Grolim is a Grolim—whether he comes from Mallorea or Cthol Murgos."

"It seems to me that maybe you should go back to Mallorea and put things in order."

"No, Belgarion, I won't abandon my campaign here in Cthol Murgos."

"Is personal revenge worth it?"

Zakath looked startled.

"I know why you hated Taur Urgas, but he's dead, and Urgit's not at all like him. I can't really believe that you'd sacrifice your whole empire just for the sake of revenging yourself on a man who can't feel it."

"You know?" Zakath's face looked stricken. "Who told you?"

"Urgit did. He told me the whole story."

"With pride, I expect." Zakath's teeth were clenched, and his face pale.

"No, not really. It was with regret—and with contempt for Taur Urgas. He hated him even more than you do."

"That's hardly possible, Belgarion. To answer your question, yes, I *will* sacrifice my empire—the whole world if need be—to spill out the last drop of the blood of Taur Urgas. I will neither sleep nor rest nor be turned aside from my vengeance, and I will crush whomever stands in my path."

"*Tell him,*" the dry voice in Garion's mind said suddenly.

"*What?*"

"*Tell him the truth about Urgit.*"

"*But—*"

"*Do it, Garion. He needs to know. There are things he has to do, and he won't do them until he puts this obsession behind him.*"

Zakath was looking at him curiously.

"Sorry, just receiving instructions," Garion explained lamely.

"Instructions? From whom?"

"You wouldn't believe it. I was told to give you some information." He drew in a deep breath. "Urgit isn't a Murgo," he said flatly.

"What are you talking about?"

"I said that Urgit isn't a Murgo—at least not entirely. His mother was, of course, but his father was not Taur Urgas."

"You're lying!"

"No, I'm not. We found out about it while we were at the Drojim Palace in Rak Urga. Urgit didn't know about it either."

47

"I don't believe you, Belgarion!" Zakath's face was livid, and he was nearly shouting.

"Taur Urgas is dead," Garion said wearily. "Urgit made sure of that by cutting his throat and burying him head down in his grave. He also claims that he had every one of his brothers—the *real* sons of Taur Urgas—killed to make himself secure on the throne. I don't think there's one drop of Urga blood left in the world."

Zakath's eyes narrowed. "It's a trick. You've allied yourself with Urgit and brought me this absurd lie to save his life."

"Use the Orb, Garion," the voice instructed.

"How?"

"Take it off the pommel of the sword and hold it in your right hand. It'll show Zakath the truths that he needs to know."

Garion rose to his feet. "If I can show you the truth, will you look?" he asked the agitated Mallorean Emperor.

"Look? Look at what?"

Garion walked over to his sword and peeled off the soft leather sleeve covering the hilt. He put his hand on the Orb, and it came free with an audible click. Then he turned back to the man at the table. "I'm not exactly sure how this works," he said. "I'm told that Aldur was able to do it, but I've never tried it for myself. I think you're supposed to look into this." He extended his right arm until the Orb was in front of Zakath's face.

"What is that?"

"You people call it Cthrag Yaska," Garion replied.

Zakath recoiled, his face blanching.

"It won't hurt you—as long as you don't touch it."

The Orb, which for the past months had rather sullenly obeyed Garion's continued instruction to restrain itself, slowly began to pulsate and glow in his hand, bathing Zakath's face in its blue radiance. The Emperor half lifted his hand as if to push the glowing stone aside.

"Don't touch it," Garion warned again. "Just look."

But Zakath's eyes were already locked on the stone as its

blue light grew stronger and stronger. His hands gripped the edge of the table in front of him so tightly that his knuckles grew white. For a long moment he stared into that blue incandescence. Then, slowly, his fingers lost their grip on the table edge and fell back onto the arms of his chair. An expression of agony crossed his face. "They have escaped me," he groaned with tears welling out of his closed eyes, "and I have slaughtered tens of thousands for nothing." The tears began to stream down his contorted face.

"I'm sorry, Zakath," Garion said quietly, lowering his hand. "I can't change what's already happened, but you had to know the truth."

"I cannot thank you for this truth," Zakath said, his shoulders shaking in the storm of his weeping. "Leave me, Belgarion. Take that accursed stone from my sight."

Garion nodded with a great feeling of compassion and shared sorrow. Then he replaced the Orb on the pommel of his sword, re-covered the hilt, and picked up the great weapon. "I'm very sorry, Zakath," he said again, and then he quietly went out of the room, leaving the Emperor of boundless Mallorea alone with his grief.

CHAPTER THREE

"Really, Garion, I'm perfectly fine," Ce'Nedra objected again.

"I'm glad to hear that."

"Then you'll let me get out of bed?"

"No."

"That's not fair," she pouted.

"Would you like a little more tea?" he asked, going to the fireplace, taking up a poker, and swinging out the iron arm from which a kettle was suspended.

"No, I don't," she replied in a sulky little voice. "It smells, and it tastes awful."

"Aunt Pol says that it's very good for you. Maybe if you

drink some more of it, she'll let you get out of bed and sit in a chair for a while." He spooned some of the dried, aromatic leaves from an earthenware pot into a cup, tipped the kettle carefully with the poker, and filled the cup with steaming water.

Ce'Nedra's eyes had momentarily come alight, but narrowed again almost immediately. "Oh, *very* clever, Garion," she said in a voice heavy with sarcasm. "Don't patronize me."

"Of course not," he agreed blandly, setting the cup on the stand beside the bed. "You probably ought to let that steep for a while," he suggested.

"It can steep all year if it wants to. I'm not going to drink it."

He sighed with resignation. "I'm sorry, Ce'Nedra," he said with genuine regret, "but you're wrong. Aunt Pol says that you're supposed to drink a cup of this every other hour. Until she tells me otherwise, that's exactly what you're going to do."

"What if I refuse?" Her tone was belligerent.

"I'm bigger than you are," he reminded her.

Her eyes went wide with shock. "You wouldn't actually *force* me to drink it, would you?"

His expression grew mournful. "I'd really hate to do something like that," he told her.

"But you'd do it, wouldn't you?" she accused.

He tought about it a moment, then nodded. "Probably," he admitted, "if Aunt Pol told me to."

She glared at him. "All right," she said finally. "Give me the stinking tea."

"It doesn't smell all *that* bad, Ce'Nedra."

"Why don't *you* drink it, then?"

"I'm not the one who's been sick."

She proceeded then to tell him—at some length—exactly what she thought of the tea and him and her bed and the room and of the whole world in general. Many of the terms

51

she used were very colorful—even lurid—and some of them were in languages that he didn't recognize.

"What on earth is all the shouting about?" Polgara asked, coming into the room.

"I absolutely *hate* this stuff!" Ce'Nedra declared at the top of her lungs, waving the cup about and spilling most of the contents.

"I wouldn't drink it then," Aunt Pol advised calmly.

"Garion says that if I don't drink it, he'll pour it down my throat."

"Oh. Those were *yesterday's* instructions." Polgara looked at Garion. "Didn't I tell you that they change today?"

"No," he replied. "As a matter of fact, you didn't." He said it in a very level tone. He was fairly proud of that.

"I'm sorry, dear. I must have forgotten."

"When can I get out of bed?" Ce'Nedra demanded.

Polgara gave her a surprised look. "Any time you want, dear," she said. "As a matter of fact, I just came by to ask if you planned to join us for breakfast."

Ce'Nedra sat up in bed, her eyes like hard little stones. She slowly turned an icy gaze upon Garion and then quite deliberately stuck her tongue out at him.

Garion turned to Polgara. "Thanks awfully," he said to her.

"Don't be snide, dear," she murmured. She looked at the fuming little Queen. "Ce'Nedra, weren't you told as a child that sticking out one's tongue is the worst possible form of bad manners?"

Ce'Nedra smiled sweetly. "Why, yes, Lady Polgara, as a matter of fact I was. That's why I only do it on special occasions."

"I think I'll take a walk," Garion said to no one in particular. He went to the door, opened it, and left.

Some days later he lounged in one of the sitting rooms that had been built in the former women's quarters where he and the others were lodged. The room was peculiarly feminine. The furniture was softly cushioned in mauve, and the broad widows had filmy curtains of pale lavender. Beyond the windows lay a snowy garden, totally embraced by the tall wings of this bleak Murgo house. A cheery fire crackled in the half-moon arch of a broad fireplace, and at the far corner of the room an artfully contrived grotto, thick with green fern and moss, flourished about a trickling fountain. Garion sat brooding out at a sunless noon—at an ash-colored sky spitting white pellets that were neither snow nor hail, but something in between—and realized all of a sudden that he was homesick for Riva. It was a peculiar thing to come to grips with here on the opposite end of the world. Always before, the word "homesick" had been associated with Faldor's farm—the kitchen, the broad central courtyard, Durnik's smithy, and all the other dear, treasured memories. Now, suddenly, he missed that storm-lashed coast, the security of that grim fortress hovering above the bleak city lying below, and the mountains, heavy with snow, rising stark white against a black and stormy sky.

There was a faint knock at the door.

"Yes?" Garion said absently, not looking around.

The door opened almost timidly. "Your Majesty?" a vaguely familiar voice said.

Garion turned, looking back over his shoulder. The man was chubby and bald and he wore brown, a plain serviceable color, though his robe was obviously costly, and the heavy gold chain about his neck loudly proclaimed that this was no minor official. Garion frowned slightly. "Haven't we met before?" he asked. "Aren't you General Atesca's friend—uh—"

"Brador, your Majesty," the brown-robed man supplied. "Chief of the Bureau of Internal Affairs."

"Oh, yes. Now I remember. Come in, your Excellency, come in."

"Thank you, your Majesty." Brador came into the room and moved toward the fireplace, extending his hands to its warmth. "Miserable climate." He shuddered.

"You should try a winter in Riva," Garion said, "although it's summer there right now."

Brador looked out the window at the snowy garden. "Strange place, Cthol Murgos," he said. "One's tempted to believe that all of Murgodom is deliberately ugly, and then one comes across a room like this."

"I suspect that the ugliness was to satisfy Ctuchik—and Taur Urgas," Garion replied. "Underneath, Murgos probably aren't much different from the rest of us."

Brador laughed. "That sort of thinking is considered heresy in Mal Zeth," he said.

"The people in Val Alorn feel much the same way." Garion looked at the bureaucrat. "I expect that this isn't just a social call, Brador," he said. "What's on your mind?"

"Your Majesty," Brador said soberly, "I absolutely *have* to speak with the Emperor. Atesca tried to arrange it before he went back to Rak Verkat, but—" He spread his hands helplessly. "Could you possibly speak to him about it? The matter is of the utmost urgency."

"I really don't think there's very much I can do for you, Brador," Garion told him. "Right now I'm probably the last person he'd want to talk to."

"Oh?"

"I told him something that he didn't want to hear."

Brador's shoulders slumped in defeat. "You were my last hope, your Majesty," he said.

"What's the problem?"

Brador hesitated, looking around nervously as if to assure himself that they were alone. "Belgarion," he said then in a very quiet voice, "have you ever seen a demon?"

"A couple of times, yes. It's not the sort of experience I'd care to repeat."

"How much do you know about the Karands?"

"Not a great deal. I've heard that they're related to the Morindim in northern Gar og Nadrak."

"You know more about them than most people, then. Do

you know very much about the religious practices of the Morindim?"

Garion nodded. "They're demon worshippers. It's not a particularly safe form of religion, I've noticed."

Brador's face was bleak. "The Karands share the beliefs and practices of their cousins on the arctic plains of the West," he said. "After they were converted to the worship of Torak, the Grolims tried to stamp out those practices, but they persisted in the mountains and forests." He stopped and looked fearfully around again. "Belgarion," he said, almost in a whisper, "does the name Mengha mean anything to you?"

"No. I don't think so. Who's Mengha?"

"We don't know—at least not for certain. He seems to have come out of the forest to the north of Lake Karanda about six months ago."

"And?"

"He marched—alone—to the gates of Calida in Jenno and called for the surrender of the city. They laughed at him, of course, but then he marked some symbols on the ground. They didn't laugh any more after that." The Melcene bureaucrat's face was gray. "Belgarion, he unloosed a horror on Calida such as man has never seen before. Those symbols he drew on the ground summoned up a host of demons—not one, or a dozen, but a whole army of them. I've talked with survivors of that attack. They're mostly mad—mercifully so, I think—and what happened at Calida was utterly unspeakable."

"An *army* of them?" Garion exclaimed.

Brador nodded. "That's what makes Mengha so dreadfully dangerous. As I'm sure you know, usually when someone summons a demon, sooner or later it gets away from him and kills him, but Mengha appears to have absolute control of all the fiends he raises and he can call them up by the hundreds. Urvon is terrified and he's even begun to experiment with magic himself, hoping to defend Mal Yaska against Mengha. We don't know where Zandramas is, but her apostate Grolim cohorts are desperately striving also to summon up these fiends. Great Gods, Belgarion, help me! This unholy infection will spread out of Mallorea and sweep the world. We'll all be engulfed by howling fiends, and no place, no matter how remote, will provide a haven for the pitiful remnants of mankind. Help me to persuade Kal Zakath that his petty little war here in Cthol Murgos has no real meaning in the face of the horror that's emerging in Mallorea."

Garion gave him a long, steady look, then rose to his feet. "You'd better come with me, Brador," he said quietly. "I think we need to talk with Belgarath."

They found the old sorcerer in the book-lined library of the house, poring over an ancient volume bound in green leather. He set his book aside and listened as Brador repeated what he had told Garion. "Urvon and Zandramas are also engaging in this insanity?" he asked when the Melcene had finished.

Brador nodded. "According to our best information, Ancient One," he replied.

Belgarath slammed his fist down and began to swear. "What are they thinking of?" he burst out, pacing up and down. "Don't they know that UL himself had forbidden this?"

"They're afraid of Mengha," Brador said helplessly. "They feel that they must have some way to protect themselves from his horde of fiends."

"You don't protect yourself from demons by raising more demons," the old man fumed. "If even one of them breaks free, they'll all get loose. Urvon or Zandramas might be able to handle them, but sooner or later some underling is going to make a mistake. Let's go see Zakath."

"I don't think we can get in to see him just now, Grandfather," Garion said dubiously. "He didn't like what I told him about Urgit."

"That's too bad. This is something that won't wait for him to regain his composure. Let's go."

The three of them went quickly through the corridors of

the house to the large antechamber they had entered with General Atesca upon their arrival from Rak Verkat.

"Absolutely impossible," the colonel at the desk beside the main door declared when Belgarath demanded to see the Emperor immediately.

"As you grow older, Colonel," the old man said ominously, "you'll discover just how meaningless the word 'impossible' really is." He raised one hand, gestured somewhat theatrically, and Garion heard and felt the surge of his will.

A number of battle flags mounted on stout poles projected out from the opposite wall perhaps fifteen feet from the floor. The officious colonel vanished from his chair and reappeared precariously astride one of those poles with his eyes bulging and his hands desperately clinging to his slippery perch.

"Where would you like to go next, Colonel?" Belgarath asked him. "As I recall, there's a very tall flagpole out front. I could set you on top of it if you wish."

The colonel stared at him in horror.

"Now, as soon as I bring you down from there, you're going to persuade your Emperor to see us at once. You're going to be very convincing, Colonel—that's unless you want to be a permanent flagpole ornament, of course."

The colonel's face was still pasty white when he emerged from the guarded door leading to the audience chamber, and he flinched violently every time Belgarath moved his hand. "His Majesty consents to see you," he stammered.

Belgarath grunted. "I was almost sure that he would."

Kal Zakath had undergone a noticeable transformation since Garion had last seen him. His white linen robe was wrinkled and stained, and there were dark circles under his eyes. His face was deathly pale, his hair was unkempt, and he was unshaven. Spasmlike tremors ran through his body, and he looked almost too weak to stand. "What do you want?" he demanded in a barely audible voice.

"Are you sick?" Belgarath asked him.

"A touch of fever, I think." Zakath shrugged. "What's so

important that you felt you had to force your way in here to tell me about it?"

"Your empire's collapsing, Zakath," Belgarath told him flatly. "It's time you went home to mend your fences."

Zakath smiled faintly. "Wouldn't that be so very convenient for you?" he said.

"What's going on in Mallorea isn't convenient for anybody. Tell him, Brador."

Nervously, the Melcene bureaucrat delivered his report.

"Demons?" Zakath retorted sceptically. "Oh, come now, Belgarath. Surely you don't expect me to believe that, do you? Do you honestly think that I'll run back to Mallorea to chase shadows and leave you behind to raise an army here in the West to confront me when I return?" The palsylike shaking Garion had noted when they had entered the room seemed to be growing more severe. Zakath's head bobbed and jerked on his neck, and a stream of spittle ran unnoticed from one corner of his mouth.

"You won't be leaving us behind, Zakath," Belgarath replied. "We're going with you. If even a tenth of what Brador says is true, I'm going to have to go to Karanda and stop this Mengha. If he's raising demons, we're *all* going to have to put everything else aside to stop him."

"Absurd!" Zakath declared agitatedly. His eyes were unfocused now, and his weaving and trembling had become so severe that he was unable to control his limbs. "I'm not going to be tricked by a clever old man into—" He suddenly started up from his chair with an animallike cry, clutching at the sides of his head. Then he toppled forward to the floor, twitching and jerking.

Belgarath jumped forward and took hold of the convulsing man's arms. "Quick!" he snapped. "Get something between his teeth before he bites off his tongue!"

Brador grabbed up a sheaf of reports from a nearby table, wadded them up, and jammed them into the frothing Emperor's mouth.

"Garion!" Belgarath barked. "Get Pol—fast!"

Garion started toward the door at a run.

"Wait!" Belgarath said, sniffing suspiciously at the air above the face of the man he was holding down. "Bring Sadi, too. There's a peculiar smell here. Hurry!"

Garion bolted. He ran through the hallways past startled officials and servants and finally burst into the room where Polgara was quietly talking with Ce'Nedra and Velvet. "Aunt Pol!" he shouted, "Come quickly! Zakath just collapsed!" Then he spun, ran a few more steps down the hall, and shouldered open the door to Sadi's room. "We need you," he barked at the startled eunuch. "Come with me."

It took only a few moments for the three of them to return to the polished door in the anteroom.

"What's going on?" the Angarak colonel demanded in a frightened voice, barring their way.

"Your Emperor is sick," Garion told him. "Get out of the way." Roughly he pushed the protesting officer to one side and yanked the door open.

Zakath's convulsions had at least partially subsided, but Belgarath still held him down.

"What is it, father?" Polgara asked, kneeling beside the stricken man.

"He threw a fit."

"The falling sickness?"

"I don't think so. It wasn't quite the same. Sadi, come over here and smell his breath. I'm getting a peculiar odor from him."

Sadi approached cautiously, leaned forward, and sniffed several times. Then he straightened, his face pale. "Thalot," he announced.

"A poison?" Polgara asked him.

Sadi nodded. "It's quite rare."

"Do you have an antidote?"

"No, my lady," he replied. "There isn't an antidote for

thalot. It's always been universally fatal. It's seldom used because it acts very slowly, but no one ever recovers from it."

"Then he's dying?" Garion asked with a sick feeling.

"In a manner of speaking, yes. The convulsions will subside, but they'll recur with increasing frequency. Finally . . ." Sadi shrugged.

"There's no hope at all?" Polgara asked.

"None whatsoever, my lady. About all we can do is make his last few days more comfortable."

Belgarath started to swear. "Quiet him down, Pol," he said. "We need to get him into bed and we can't move him while he's jerking around that way."

She nodded and put one hand on Zakath's forehead. Garion felt the faint surge, and the struggling Emperor grew quiet.

Brador, his face very pale, looked at them. "I don't think we should announce this just yet," he cautioned. "Let's just call it a slight illness for the moment until we can decide what to do. I'll send for a litter."

The room to which the unconscious Zakath was taken was plain to the point of severity. The Emperor's bed was a narrow cot. The only other furniture was a single plain chair and a low chest. The walls were white and unadorned, and a charcoal brazier glowed in one corner. Sadi went back to their chambers and returned with his red case and the canvas sack in which Polgara kept her collection of herbs and remedies. The two of them consulted in low tones while Garion and Brador pushed the litter bearers and curious soldiers from the room. Then they mixed a steaming cup of a pungent-smelling liquid. Sadi raised Zakath's head and held it while Polgara spooned the medicine into his slack-lipped mouth.

The door opened quietly, and the green-robed Dalasian healer, Andel, entered. "I came as soon as I heard," she said. "Is the Emperor's illness serious?"

Polgara looked at her gravely. "Close the door, Andel," she said quietly.

The healer gave her a strange look, then pushed the door shut. "Is it that grave, my lady?"

Polgara nodded. "He's been poisoned," she said. "We don't want word of it to get out just yet."

Andel gasped. "What can I do to help?" she asked coming quickly to the bed.

"Not very much, I'm afraid," Sadi told her.

"Have you given him the antidote yet?"

"There is no antidote."

"There must be. Lady Polgara—"

Polgara sadly shook her head.

"I have failed, then," the hooded woman said in a voice filled with tears. She turned from the bed, her head bowed, and Garion heard a faint murmur that somehow seemed to come from the air above her—a murmur that curiously was not that of a single voice. There was a long silence, and then a shimmering appeared at the foot of the bed. When it cleared, the blindfolded form of Cyradis stood there, one hand slightly extended. "This must not be," she said in her clear, ringing voice. "Use thine art, Lady Polgara. Restore him. Should he die, all our tasks will fail. Bring thy power to bear."

"It won't work, Cyradis," Polgara replied, setting the cup down. "If a poison affects only the blood, I can usually manage to purge it, and Sadi has a whole case full of antidotes. This poison, however, sinks into every particle of the body. It's killing his bones and organs as well as his blood, and there's no way to leech it out."

The shimmering form at the foot of the bed wrung its hands in anguish. "It cannot be so," Cyradis wailed. "Hast thou even applied the sovereign specific?"

Polgara looked up quickly. "Sovereign specific? A universal remedy? I know of no such agent."

"But it doth exist, Lady Polgara. I know not its origins nor its composition, but I have felt its gentle power abroad in the world for some years now."

Polgara looked at Andel, but the healer shook her head helplessly. "I do not know of such a potion, my lady."

"Think, Cyradis," Polgara said urgently. "Anything you can tell us might give us a clue."

The blindfolded Seeress touched the fingertips of one hand lightly to her temple. "Its origins are recent," she said, half to herself. "It came into being less than a score of years ago—some obscure flower, or so it seemeth to me."

"It's hopeless, then," Sadi said. "There are millions of kinds of flowers." He rose and crossed the room to Belgarath. "I think we might want to leave here—almost immediately," he murmured. "At the first suggestion of the word 'poison,' people start looking for the nearest Nyissan—and those associated with him. I think we're in a great deal of danger right now."

"Can you think of *anything* else, Cyradis?" Polgara pressed. "No matter how remote?"

The Seeress struggled with it, her face strained as she reached deeper into her strange vision. Her shoulders finally sagged in defeat. "Nothing," she said. "Only a woman's face."

"Describe it."

"She is tall," the Seeress replied. "Her hair is very dark, but her skin is like marble. Her husband is much involved with horses."

"Adara!" Garion exclaimed, the beautiful face of his cousin suddenly coming before his eyes.

Polgara snapped her fingers. "And Adara's rose!" Then she frowned. "I examined that flower very closely some years back, Cyradis," she said. "Are you absolutely sure? There are some unusual substances in it, but I didn't find any particular medicinal qualities in any of them—either in any distillation or powder."

Cyradis concentrated. "Can healing be accomplished by means of a fragrance, Lady Polgara?"

Polgara's eyes narrowed in thought. "There are some minor remedies that are inhaled," she said doubtfully, "but—"

"There are poisons that can be administered in that fashion, Lady Polgara," Sadi supplied. "The fumes are drawn into the lungs and from there into the heart. Then the blood carries them to every part of the body. It could very well be the only way to neutralize the effects of thalot."

Belgarath's expression had grown intent. "Well, Pol?" he asked.

"It's worth a try, father," she replied. "I've got a few of the flowers. They're dried, but they *might* work."

"Any seeds?"

"A few, yes."

"Seeds?" Andel exclaimed. "Kal Zakath would be months in his grave before any bush could grow and bloom."

The old man chuckled slyly. "Not quite," he said, winking at Polgara. "I have quite a way with plants sometimes. I'm going to need some dirt—and some boxes or tubs to put it in."

Sadi went to the door and spoke briefly with the guards outside. They looked baffled, but a short command from Andel sent them scurrying.

"What is the origin of this strange flower, Lady Polgara?" Cyradis asked curiously, "How is it that thou art so well acquainted with it?"

"Garion made it." Polgara shrugged, looking thoughtfully at Zakath's narrow cot. "I think we'll want the bed out from the wall, father," she said. "I want it surrounded by flowers."

"*Made?*" the Seeress exclaimed.

Polgara nodded. "Created, actually," she said absently. "Do you think it's warm enough in here, father? We're going to want big, healthy blooms, and even at best the flower's a bit puny."

"I did my best," Garion protested.

"Created?" Cyradis' voice was awed. Then she bowed to Garion with profound respect.

63

When the tubs of half-frozen dirt had been placed about the stricken Emperor's bed, smoothed, and dampened with water, Polgara took a small leather pouch from her green canvas sack, removed a pinch of miniscule seeds, and carefully sowed them in the soil.

"All right," Belgarath said, rolling up his sleeves in a workmanlike fashion, "stand back." He bent and touched the dirt in one of the tubs. "You were right, Pol," he muttered. "Just a little too cold." He frowned slightly, and Garion saw his lips move. The surge was not a large one, and the sound of it was little more than a whisper. The damp earth in the tubs began to steam. "That's better," he said. Then he extended his hands out over the narrow cot and the steaming tubs. Again Garion felt the surge and the whisper.

At first nothing seemed to happen, but then tiny specks of green appeared on the top of the dampened dirt. Even as Garion watched those little leaves grow and expand, he remembered where he had seen Belgarath perform this same feat before. As clearly as if he were there, he saw the courtyard before King Korodullin's palace at Vo Mimbre and he saw the apple twig the old man had thrust down between two flagstones expand and reach up toward the old sorcerer's hand as proof to the skeptical Sir Andorig that he was indeed who he said he was.

The pale green leaves had grown darker, and the spindly twigs and tendrils that had at first appeared had already expanded into low bushes.

"Make them vine up across the bed, father," Polgara said critically. "Vines produce more blossoms, and I want a lot of blossoms."

He let out his breath explosively and gave her a look that spoke volumes. "All right," he said finally. "You want vines? Vines it is."

"Is it too much for you, father?" she asked solicitously.

He set his jaw, but did not answer. He did, however, start to sweat. Longer tendrils began to writhe upward like green snakes winding up around the legs of the Emperor's cot and reaching upward to catch the bedframe. Once they had gained that foothold, they seemed to pause while Belgarath caught his breath. "This is harder than it looks," he puffed. Then he concentrated again, and the vines quickly overspread the cot and Kal Zakath's inert body until only his ashen face remained uncovered by them.

"All right," Belgarath said to the plants, "that's far enough. You can bloom now." There was another surge and a peculiar ringing sound.

The tips of all the myriad twiglets swelled, and then those buds began to split, revealing their pale lavender interiors. Almost shyly the lopsided little flowers opened, filling the room with a gentle-seeming fragrance. Garion straightened as he breathed in that delicate odor. For some reason, he suddenly felt very good, and the cares and worries which had beset him for the past several months seemed to fall away.

The slack-faced Zakath stirred slightly, took a breath, and sighed deeply. Polgara laid her fingertips to the side of his neck. "I think it's working, father," she said. "His heart's not laboring so hard now, and his breathing's easier."

"Good," Belgarath replied. "I hate to go through something like that for nothing."

Then the Emperor opened his eyes. The shimmering form of Cyradis hovered anxiously at the foot of his bed. Strangely, he smiled when he saw her, and her shy, answering smile lighted her pale face. Then Zakath sighed once more and closed his eyes again. Garion leaned forward to make sure that the sick man was still breathing. When he looked back toward the foot of the bed, the Seeress of Kell was gone.

CHAPTER FOUR

A warm wind came in off the lake that night, and the wet snow that had blanketed Rak Hagga and the surrounding countryside turned to a dreary slush that sagged and fell from the limbs of the trees in the little garden at the center of the house and slid in sodden clumps from the gray slate roof. Garion and Silk sat near the fire in the mauve-cushioned room, looking out at the garden and talking quietly.

"We'd know a great deal more, if I could get in touch with Yarblek," Silk was saying. The little man was dressed again in the pearl-gray doublet and black hose which he had favored during those years before they had begun this search, although he wore only a few of the costly rings and ornaments which had made him appear so ostentatiously wealthy at that time.

"Isn't he in Gar og Nadrak?" Garion asked. Garion had also discarded his serviceable travel clothing and reverted to his customary silver-trimmed blue.

"It's hard to say exactly where Yarblek is at any given time, Garion. He moves around a great deal; but no matter where he goes, the reports from our people in Mal Zeth, Melcene, and Maga Renn are all forwarded to him. Whatever this Mengha is up to is almost certain to have disrupted trade. I'm sure that our agents have gathered everything they could find out about him and sent it along to Yarblek. Right now my scruffy-looking partner probably knows more about Mengha than Brador's secret police do."

"I don't want to get sidetracked, Silk. Our business is with Zandramas, not Mengha."

"Demons are everybody's business," Silk replied soberly, "but no matter what we decide to do, we have to get to Mallorea first—and that means persuading Zakath that this is serious. Was he listening at all when you told him about Mengha?"

Garion shook his head. "I'm not sure if he even understood what we were telling him. He wasn't altogether rational."

Silk grunted. "When he wakes up, we'll have to try again." A sly grin crossed the little man's face. "I've had a certain amount of luck negotiating with sick people," he said.

"Isn't that sort of contemptible?"

"Of course it is—but it gets results."

Later that morning, Garion and his rat-faced friend stopped by the Emperor's room, ostensibly to inquire about his health. Polgara and Sadi were seated on either side of the bed, and Andel sat quietly in the corner. The vines that had enveloped the narrow cot had been pulled aside, but the air in the room was still heavy with the fragrance of the small, lavender flowers. The sick man was propped into a half-sitting position by pillows, but his eyes were closed as Silk and Garion entered. His cat lay contentedly purring at the foot of the bed.

"How is he?" Garion asked quietly.

"He's been awake a few times," Sadi replied. "There are still some traces of thalot in his extremities, but they seem to be dissipating." The eunuch was picking curiously at one of the small flowers. "I wonder if these would work if they were distilled down to an essence," he mused, "or perhaps an attar. It might be very interesting to wear a perfume that would ward off any poison." He frowned slightly. "And I wonder if they'd be effective against snake venom."

"Have Zith bite someone," Silk suggested. "Then you can test it."

"Would you like to volunteer, Prince Kheldar?"

"Ah, no, Sadi," Silk declined. "Thanks all the same." He looked at the red case lying open on the floor in the corner. "Is she confined, by the way?" he asked nervously.

"She's sleeping," Sadi replied. "She always takes a little nap after breakfast."

Garion looked at the dozing Emperor. "Is he coherent at all—when he's awake, I mean?"

"His mind seems to be clearing," Polgara told him.

"Hysteria and delirium are some of the symptoms brought on by thalot," Sadi said. "Growing rationality is an almost certain sign of recovery."

"Is that you, Belgarion?" Zakath asked almost in a whisper and without opening his eyes.

"Yes," Garion replied. "How are you feeling?"

"Weak. Light-headed—and every muscle in my body screams like an abscessed tooth. Aside from that, I'm fine." He opened his eyes with a wry smile. "What happened? I seem to have lost track of things."

Garion glanced briefly at Polgara, and she nodded. "You were poisoned," he told the sick man.

Zakath looked a bit surprised. "It must not have been a very good one then," he said.

"Actually, it's one of the very best, your Imperial Majesty," Sadi disagreed mildly. "It's always been universally lethal."

"I'm dying then?" Zakath said it with a peculiar kind of satisfaction, almost as if he welcomed the idea. "Ah, well," he sighed. "That should solve many problems."

"I'm very sorry, your Majesty," Silk said with mock regret, "but I think you'll live. Belgarath tampers with the normal course of events from time to time. It's a bad habit he picked up in his youth, but a man needs *some* vices, I suppose."

Zakath smiled weakly. "You're a droll little fellow, Prince Kheldar."

"If you're really keen on dying, though," Silk added outrageously, "we could always wake Zith. One nip from her almost guarantees perpetual slumber."

"Zith?"

"Sadi's pet—a little green snake. She could even curl up at your ear after she bites you and purr you into eternity."

Zakath sighed, and his eyes drooped shut again.

"I think we should let him sleep," Polgara said quietly.

"Not just yet, Lady Polgara," the Emperor said. "I've shunned sleep and the dreams which infest it for so long that it comes unnaturally now."

"You *must* sleep, Kal Zakath," Andel told him. "There are ways to banish evil dreams, and sleep is the greatest healer."

Zakath sighed and shook his head. "I'm afraid you won't be able to banish *these* dreams, Andel." Then he drowned slightly. "Sadi, is hallucination one of the symptoms of the poison I was given?"

"It's possible," the enunuch admitted. "What horrors have you seen?"

"Not a horror," Zakath replied. "I seem to see the face of a young woman. Her eyes are bound with a strip of cloth. A peculiar peace comes over me when I see her face."

"Then it was not an hallucination, Kal Zakath," Andel told him.

"Who is this strange blind child, then?"

69

"My mistress," Andel said proudly. "The face which came to you in your direst hour was the face of Cyradis, the Seeress of Kell, upon whose decision rests the fate of all the world—and of all other worlds as well."

"So great a responsibility to lie upon such slender shoulders," Zakath said.

"It is her task," Andel said simply.

The sick man seemed to fall again into a doze, his lips lightly touched with a peculiar smile. Then his eyes opened again, seemingly more alert now. "Am I healed, Sadi?" he asked the shaved-headed eunuch. "Has your excellent Nyissan poison quite run its course?"

"Oh," Sadi replied speculatively, "I wouldn't say that you're entirely well yet, your Majesty, but I'd guess that you're out of any immediate danger."

"Good," Zakath said crisply, trying to shoulder his way up into a sitting position. Garion reached out to help him. "And has the knave who poisoned me been apprehended yet?"

Sadi shook his head. "Not as far as I know," he answered.

"I think that might be the first order of business, then. I'm starting to feel a little hungry and I'd rather not go through this again. Is the poison common in Cthol Murgos?"

Sadi frowned. "Murgo law forbids poisons and drugs, your Majesty," he replied. "They're a backward sort of people. The Dagashi assassins probably have access to thalot, though."

"You think my poisoner might have been a Dagashi, then?"

Sadi shrugged. "Most assassinations in Cthol Murgos are carried out by the Dagashi. They're efficient and discreet."

Zakath's eyes narrowed in thought. "That would seem to point a finger directly at Urgit, then. The Dagashi are expensive, and Urgit has access to the royal treasury."

Silk grimaced. "No," he declared. "Urgit wouldn't do that. A knife between your shoulder blades maybe, but not poison."

"How can you be so sure, Kheldar?"

"I know him," Silk replied a bit lamely. "He's weak and a little timid, but he wouldn't be a party to a poisoning. It's a contemptible way to resolve political differences."

"Prince Kheldar!" Sadi protested.

"Except in Nyissa, of course," Silk conceded. "One always needs to take quaint local customs into account." He pulled at his long, pointed nose. "I'll admit that Urgit wouldn't grieve too much if you woke up dead some morning," he said to the Mallorean Emperor, "but it's all just a little too pat. If your generals believed that it was Urgit who arranged to have you killed, they'd stay here for the next ten generations trying to obliterate all of Murgodom, wouldn't they?"

"I'd assume so," Zakath said.

"Who would benefit the most by disposing of you and rather effectively making sure that the bulk of your army doesn't return to Mallorea in the foreseeable future? Not Urgit, certainly. More likely it would be somebody in Mallorea who wants a free hand there." Silk squared his shoulders. "Why don't you let Liselle and me do a little snooping around before you lock your mind in stone on this? Obvious things always make me suspicious."

"That's all very well, Kheldar," Zakath said rather testily, "but how can I be sure that my next meal won't have another dose of exotic spices in it?"

"You have at your bedside the finest cook in the world," the rat-faced man said, pointing grandly at Polgara, "and I can absolutely guarantee that she won't poison you. She might turn you into a radish if you offend her, but she'd never poison you."

"All right, Silk, that will do," Polgara told him.

"I'm only paying tribute to your extraordinary gifts, Polgara."

Her eyes grew hard.

"I think that perhaps it might be time for me to be on my way," Silk said to Garion.

"Wise decision," Garion murmured.

The little man turned and quickly left the room.

"Is he really as good as he pretends to be?" Zakath asked curiously.

Polgara nodded. "Between them, Kheldar and Liselle can probably ferret out any secret in the world. Silk doesn't always like it, but they're almost a perfect team. And now, your Majesty, what would you like for breakfast?"

A curious exchange was taking place in the corner. Throughout the previous conversation, Garion had heard a faint, drowsy purr coming from Zith's earthenware bottle. Either the little snake was expressing a general sense of contentment, or it may have been one of the peculiarities of her species to purr while sleeping. Zakath's pregnant, mackerel-striped cat, attracted by that sound, jumped down from the bed and curiously waddled toward Zith's little home. Absently, probably without even thinking about it, she responded to the purr coming from the bottle with one of her own. She sniffed at the bottle, then tentatively touched it with one soft paw. The peculiar duet of purring continued.

Then, perhaps because Sadi had not stoppered the bottle tightly enough or because she had long since devised this simple means of opening her front door, the little snake nudged the cork out of the bottle with her blunt nose. Both creatures continued to purr, although the cat was now obviously afire with curiosity. For a time Zith did not reveal herself, but lurked shyly in her bottle, still purring. Then, cautiously, she poked out her head, her forked tongue flickering as she tested the air.

The cat jumped straight up to a height of about three feet, giving vent to a startled yowl. Zith retreated immediately back into the safety of her house, though she continued to purr.

Warily, but still burning with curiosity, the cat approached the bottle again, moving one foot at a time.

"Sadi," Zakath said, his voice filled with concern.

"There's no immediate danger, your Majesty," the eunuch assured him. "Zith never bites while she's purring."

72

Again the little green snake slid her head out of the bottle. This time the cat recoiled only slightly. Then, curiosity overcoming her natural aversion to reptiles, she continued her slow advance, her nose reaching out toward this remarkable creature. Zith, still purring, also extended her blunt nose. Their noses touched, and both flinched back slightly. Then they cautiously sniffed at each other, the cat with her nose, the snake with her tongue. Both were purring loudly now.

"Astonishing," Sadi murmured. "I think they actually like each other."

"Sadi, please," Zakath said plaintively. "I don't know how you feel about your snake, but I'm rather fond of my cat, and she *is* about to become a mother."

"I'll speak with them, your Majesty," Sadi assured him. "I'm not sure that they'll listen, but I'll definitely speak with them."

Belgarath had once again retired to the library, and Garion found him later that day poring over a large map of northern Mallorea. "Ah," he said, looking up as Garion entered, "there you are. I was just about to send for you. Come over here and look at this."

Garion went to the table.

"The appearance of this Mengha fellow might just work to our advantage, you know."

"I don't quite follow that, Grandfather."

"Zandramas is here at Ashaba, right?" Belgarath stabbed his finger at a spot in the representation of the Karandese mountains.

"Yes," Garion said.

"And Mengha's moving west and south out of Calida, over here." The old man poked at the map again.

"That's what Brador says."

"He's got her blocked off from most of the continent, Garion. She's been very careful here in Cthol Murgos to avoid populated areas. There's no reason to believe that she's going

73

to change once she gets to Mallorea. Urvon's going to be to the south of her at Mal Yaska, and the wastes to the north are virtually impassable—even though it's nearly summer."

"Summer?"

"In the northern half of the world it is."

"Oh. I keep forgetting." Garion peered at the map. "Grandfather, we don't have any idea of where 'the place which is no more' might be. When Zandramas leaves Ashaba, she could go in any direction."

Belgarath squinted at the map. "I don't think so, Garion. In the light of all that's happened in Mallorea—coupled with the fact that by now she knows that we're on her trail—I think she almost *has* to be trying to get back to her power base in Darshiva. Everybody in the world is after her, and she needs help."

"*We* certainly aren't threatening her all that much," Garion said moodily. "We can't even get out of Cthol Murgos."

"That's what I wanted to talk to you about. You've got to persuade Zakath that it's vital for us to leave here and get to Mallorea as quickly as possible."

"Persuade?"

"Just do whatever you have to, Garion. There's a great deal at stake."

"Why me?" Garion said it without thinking.

Belgarath gave him a long, steady look.

"Sorry," Garion muttered. "Forget that I said it."

"All right. I'll do that."

Late that evening, Zakath's cat gave birth to seven healthy kittens while Zith hovered in anxious attendance, warning off all other observers with ominous hisses. Peculiarly, the only person the protective little reptile would allow near the newborn kittens was Velvet.

Garion had little success during the next couple of days in his efforts to steer his conversations with the convalescing Zakath around to the subject of the necessity for returning to Mallorea. The Emperor usually pleaded a lingering weakness as a result of his poisoning, though Garion privately suspected subterfuge on that score, since the man appeared to have more than enough energy for his usual activities and only protested exhaustion when Garion wanted to talk about a voyage.

On the evening of the fourth day, however, he decided to try negotiation one last time before turning to more direct alternatives. He found Zakath seated in the chair near his bed with a book in his hands. The dark circles beneath his eyes had vanished, the trembling had disappeared entirely, and he seemed totally alert. "Ah, Belgarion," he said almost cheerfully, "so good of you to stop by."

"I thought I'd come in and put you to sleep again," Garion replied with slightly exaggerated sarcasm.

"Have I been that obvious?" Zakath asked.

"Yes, as a matter of fact you have. Every time I mention the words 'ship' and 'Mallorea' in the same sentence, your eyes snap shut. Zakath, we've got to talk about this, and time is starting to run out."

Zakath passed one hand across his eyes with some show of weariness.

"Let me put it this way," Garion pressed on. "Belgarath's starting to get impatient. I'm trying to keep our discussions civil, but if he steps in, I can almost guarantee that they're going to turn unpleasant—very quickly."

Zakath lowered his hand, and his eyes narrowed. "That sounds vaguely like a threat, Belgarion."

"No," Garion disagreed. "As a matter of fact, it's in the nature of friendly advice. If you want to stay here in Cthol Murgos, that's up to you, but *we* have to get to Mallorea—and soon."

"And if I choose not to permit you to go?"

"Permit?" Garion laughed. "Zakath, did you grow up in the same world with the rest of us? Have you got even the remotest idea of what you're talking about?"

"I think that concludes this interview, Belgarion," the Emperor said coldly. He rose stiffly to his feet and turned to his bed. As usual, his cat had deposited her mewling little brood in the center of his coverlet and then gone off to nap alone in her wool-lined box in the corner. The irritated Emperor looked with some exasperation at the furry little puddle on his bed. "You have my permission to withdraw, Belgarion," he said over his shoulder. Then he reached down with both hands to scoop up the cluster of kittens.

Zith reared up out of the very center of the furry heap, fixed him with a cold eye, and hissed warningly.

"Torak's teeth!" Zakath swore, jerking his hands away. "This is going too far! Go tell Sadi that I want his accursed snake out of my room immediately!"

"He's taken her out four times already, Zakath," Garion said mildly. "She just keeps crawling back." He suppressed a grin. "Maybe she likes you."

"Are you trying to be funny?"

"Me?"

"Get the snake out of here."

Garion put his hands behind his back. "Not me, Zakath. I'll go get Sadi."

In the hallway outside, however, he encountered Velvet, who was coming toward the Emperor's room with a mysterious smile on her face.

"Do you think you could move Zith?" Garion asked her. "She's in the middle of Zakath's bed with those kittens."

"*You* can move her, Belgarion," the blond girl said, smiling the dimples into her cheeks. "She trusts you."

"I think I'd rather not try that."

The two of them went back into the Emperor's bedchamber.

"Margravine," Zakath greeted her courteously, inclining his head.

She curtsied. "Your Majesty."

"Can you deal with this?" he asked, pointing at the furry pile on his bed with the snake still half-reared out of the center, her eyes alert.

"Of course, your Majesty." She approached the bed, and the snake flickered her tongue nervously. "Oh, *do* stop that, Zith," the blond girl chided. Then she lifted the front of her skirt to form a kind of pouch and began picking up kittens and depositing them in her improvised basket. Last of all she lifted Zith and laid her in the middle. She crossed the room and casually put them all into the box with the mother cat, who opened one golden eye, made room for her kittens and their bright green nursemaid, and promptly went back to sleep.

"Isn't that sweet?" Velvet murmured softly. Then she turned back to Zakath. "Oh, by the way, your Majesty, Kheldar and I managed to find out who it was who poisoned you."

"What?"

She nodded, frowning slightly. "It came as something of a surprise, actually."

The Emperor's eyes had become intent. "You're sure?"

"As sure as one can be in these cases. You seldom find an eyewitness to a poisoning; but he was in the kitchen at the right time, he left right after you fell ill, and we know him by reputation." She smiled at Garion. "Have you noticed how people always tend to remember a man with white eyes?"

"Naradas?" Garion exclaimed.

"Surprising, isn't it?"

"Who's Naradas?" Zakath demanded.

"He works for Zandramas," Garion replied. He frowned. "That doesn't make any sense, Velvet. Why would Zandramas want to kill him? Wouldn't she want to keep him alive?"

She spread her hands. "I don't know, Belgarion—not yet, anyway."

"Velvet?" Zakath asked in puzzlement.

She smiled the dimples into her cheeks again. "Isn't it silly?" She laughed. "I suppose these little nicknames are a form of affection, though. Belgarion's question is to the point, however. Can you think of any reason why Zandramas might want to kill you?"

"Not immediately, but we can wring that answer out of her when I catch her—and I'll make a point of doing that, even if I have to take Cthol Murgos apart stone by stone."

"She isn't here," Garion said absently, still struggling with the whole idea. "She's at Ashaba—in the House of Torak."

Zakath's eyes narrowed suspiciously. "Isn't this convenient, Belgarion?" he said. "I *happen* to get poisoned right after your arrival. Belgarath *happens* to cure me. Kheldar and Liselle *happen* to discover the identity of the poisoner, who *happens* to work for Zandramas, who *happens* to be at Ashaba, which *happens* to be in Mallorea—a place which just *happens* to be where you so desperately want to go. The coincidence staggers the imagination, wouldn't you say?"

"Zakath, you're starting to make me tired," Garion said irritably. "If I decide that I need a boat to get to Mallorea, I'll *take* one. All that's kept me from doing that so far are the manners Lady Polgara drilled into me when I was a boy."

"And how do you propose to leave this house?" Zakath snapped, his temper also starting to rise.

That did it. The rage that came over Garion was totally irrational. It was the result of a hundred delays and stumbling blocks and petty interruptions that had dogged him for almost a year now. He reached over his shoulder, ripped Iron-grip's sword from its sheath, and peeled the concealing leather sleeve from its hilt. He held the great blade before him and literally threw his will at the Orb. The sword exploded into blue flame. "How do I propose to leave this house?" he half shouted at the stunned Emperor. "I'll use *this* for a key. It works sort of like this." He straightened his arm, leveling the blazing sword at the door. "Burst!" he commanded.

Garion's anger was not only irrational, it was also somewhat excessive. He had intended no more than the door—and possibly a part of the doorframe—simply to illustrate to Zakath the intensity of his feeling about the matter. The Orb, however, startled into wakefulness by the sudden jolt of his angry will, had overreacted. The door, certainly, disappeared, dissolving into splinters that blasted out into the hallway. The doorframe also vanished. What Garion had *not* intended, however, was what happened to the wall.

White-faced and shaking, Zakath stumbled back, staring at the hallway outside that had suddenly been revealed and at the rubble that filled it—rubble that had a moment before been the solid, two-foot-thick stone wall of his bedroom.

"My goodness," Velvet murmured mildly.

Knowing that it was silly and melodramatic, but still caught up in that towering, irrational anger, Garion caught the stunned Zakath by the arm with his left hand and gestured with the sword he held in his right. "Now, we're going to go talk with Belgarath," he announced. "We'll go through the hallways *if* you'll give me your word not to call soldiers every time we go around a corner. Otherwise, we'll just cut straight through the house. The library's sort of in that direction, isn't it?" he pointed at one of the still-standing walls with his sword.

"Belgarion," Velvet chided him gently, "now really, that's no way to behave. Kal Zakath has been a very courteous host. I'm sure that now that he understands the situation, he'll be more than happy to cooperate, won't you, your Imperial Majesty?" She smiled winsomely at the Emperor. "We wouldn't want the Rivan King to get *really* angry, now would we? There are so many breakable things about—windows, walls, houses, the city of Rak Hagga—that sort of thing."

They found Belgarath in the library again. He was reading a small scroll, and there was a large tankard at his elbow.

"Something's come up," Garion said shortly as he entered.

"Oh?"

"Velvet tells us that she and Silk found out that it was Naradas who poisoned Zakath."

"Naradas?" the old man blinked. "That's a surprise, isn't it?"

"What's she up to, Grandfather? Zandramas, I mean."

"I'm not sure." Belgarath looked at Zakath. "Who's likely to succeed you if somebody manages to put you to sleep?"

Zakath shrugged. "There are a few distant cousins scattered about—mostly in the Melcene Islands and Celanta. The line of the succession is a little murky."

"Perhaps that's what she has in mind, Belgarath," Velvet said seriously. "If there's any truth in that Grolim Prophecy you found in Rak Hagga, she's got to have an Angarak king with her at the time of the final meeting. A tame king would suit her purposes much better than someone like his Majesty here—some third or fourth cousin she could crown and anoint and proclaim king. Then she could have her Grolims keep an eye on him and deliver him to her at the proper time."

"It's possible, I suppose," he agreed. "I think there may be a bit more to it than that, though. Zandramas has never been that straightforward about anything before."

"I hope you all realize that I haven't the faintest notion of what you're talking about," Zakath said irritably.

"Just how much does he know?" Belgarath asked Garion.

"Not very much, Grandfather."

"All right. Maybe if he does know what's going on, he won't be quite so difficult." He turned to the Mallorean Emperor. "Have you ever heard of the Mrin Codex?" he asked.

"I've heard that it was written by a madman—like most of the other so-called prophecies."

"How about the Child of Light and the Child of Dark?"

"That's part of the standard gibberish used by religious hysterics."

"Zakath, you're going to have to believe in *something*. This is going to be very difficult for you to grasp if you don't."

"Would you settle for a temporary suspension of skepticism?" the Emperor countered.

"Fair enough, I suppose. All right, now, this gets complicated, so you're going to have to pay attention, listen carefully, and stop me if there's anything you don't understand."

The old man then proceeded to sketch in the ancient story of the "accident" that had occurred before the world had begun and the divergence of the two possible courses of the future and of the two consciousnesses which had somehow infused those courses.

"All right," Zakath said. "That's fairly standard theology so far. I've had Grolims preaching to the same nonsense since I was a boy."

Belgarath nodded. "I just wanted to start us off from common ground." He went on then, telling Zakath of the events spanning the eons between the cracking of the world and the Battle of Vo Mimbre.

"Our point of view is somewhat different," Zakath murmured.

"It would be," Belgarath agreed. "All right, there were five hundred years between Vo Mimbre and the theft of the Orb by Zedar the Apostate."

"Recovery," Zakath corrected. "The Orb was stolen from Cthol Mishrak by Iron-grip the thief and by—" He stopped, and his eyes suddenly widened as he stared at the seedy-looking old man.

"Yes," Belgarath said, "I really *was* there, Zakath—and I was there two thousand years before, when Torak originally stole the Orb from my Master."

"I've been sick, Belgarath," the Emperor said weakly, sinking into a chair. "My nerves aren't really up for too many of these shocks."

Belgarath looked at him, puzzled.

"Their Majesties were having a little discussion," Velvet explained brightly. "King Belgarion gave the Emperor a little demonstration of some of the more flamboyant capabilities of the Sword of the Rivan King. The Emperor was quite impressed. So was most everybody else who happened to be in that part of the house."

Belgarath gave Garion a chill look. "Playing again?" he asked.

Garion tried to reply, but there was nothing he could really say.

"All right, let's get on with this," Belgarath continued

briskly. "What happened after the emergence of Garion here is all recent history, so I'm sure you're familiar with it."

"Garion?" Zakath asked.

"A more common—and familiar—form. 'Belgarion' is a bit ostentatious, wouldn't you say?"

"No more so than 'Belgarath.'"

"I've worn 'Belgarath' for almost seven thousand years, Zakath, and I've sort of rubbed off the rough edges and corners. Garion's only been wearing his 'Bel' for a dozen years, and it still squeaks when he turns around too quickly."

Garion felt slightly offended by that.

"Anyway," the old man continued, "after Torak was dead, Garion and Ce'Nedra got married. About a year or so ago, she gave birth to a son. Garion's attention at that time was on the Bear-cult. Someone had tried to kill Ce'Nedra and had succeeded in killing the Rivan Warder."

"I'd heard about that," Zakath said.

"Anyway, he was in the process of stamping out the cult— he stamps quite well once he puts his mind to it—when someone crept into the Citadel at Riva and abducted his infant son—my great-grandson."

"No!" Zakath exclaimed.

"Oh, yes," Belgarath continued grimly. "We thought that it was the cult and marched to Rheon in Drasnia, their headquarters, but it was all a clever ruse. Zandramas had abducted Prince Geran and misdirected us to Rheon. The leader of the cult turned out to be Harakan, one of the henchmen of Urvon—is this coming too fast for you?"

Zakath's face was startled, and his eyes had gone wide again. "No," he said, swallowing hard. "I think I can keep up."

"There isn't too much more. After we discovered our mistakes, we took up the abductor's trail. We know that she's going to Mallorea—to a 'place which is no more.' That's where the Sardion is. We have to stop her, or at least arrive there at the same time. Cyradis believes that when we all arrive at this 'place which is no more,' there's going to be one of those confrontations between the Child of Light and the Child of Dark which have been happening since before the beginning of time—except that this is going to be the last one. She'll choose between them, and that's supposed to be the end of it."

"I'm afraid that it's at that point that my skepticism reasserts itself, Belgarath," Zakath said. "You don't acutally expect me to believe that these two shadowy figures that predate the world are going to arrive at this mysterious place to grapple once more, do you?"

"What makes you think they're shadowy? The spirits that are at the core of the two possible destinies infuse real people to act as their instruments during these meetings. Right now, for example, Zandramas is the Child of Dark. It used to be Torak—until Garion killed him."

"And who's the Child of Light?"

"I thought that would be obvious."

Zakath turned to stare incredulously into Garion's blue eyes. "You?" he gasped.

"That's what they tell me," Garion replied.

CHAPTER FIVE

Kal Zakath, dread Emperor of boundless Mallorea, looked first at Belgarath, then again at Garion, and finally at Velvet. "Why do I feel that I'm losing control of things here?" he asked. "When you people came here, you were more or less my prisoners. Now somehow I'm yours."

"We told you some things you didn't know before, that's all," Belgarath told him.

"Or some things that you've cleverly made up."

"Why would we do that?"

"I can think of any number of reasons. For the sake of argument I'll accept your story about the abduction of Belgarion's son, but don't you see how that makes all your motives completely obvious? You need my aid in your search. All this mystical nonsense, *and* your wild story about Urgit's parentage, could have been designed to divert me from my campaign here in Cthol Murgos and to trick me into returning with you to Mallorea. Everything you've done or said since you've come here could have been directed toward that end."

"Do you really think we'd do that?" Garion asked him.

"Belgarion, if *I* had a son and someone had abducted him, I'd do *anything* to get him back. I sympathize with your situation, but I have my own concerns, and they're here, not in Mallorea. I'm sorry, but the more I think about this, the less of it I believe. I could not have misjudged the world so much. Demons? Prophecies? Magic? Immortal old men? It's all been very entertaining, but I don't believe one word of it."

"Not even what the orb showed you about Urgit?" Garion asked.

"Please, Belgarion, don't treat me like a child." Zakath's lips were twisted into an ironic smile. "Isn't it altogether possible that the poison had already crept into my mind? And isn't it also possible that you, like any other of the charlatans who infest village fairs, used a show of mysterious lights and suggestions to make me see what you wanted me to see?"

"What *do* you believe, Kal Zakath?" Velvet asked him.

"What I can see and touch—and precious little else."

"So great a skepticism," she murmured. "Then you do not accept one single out-of-the-ordinary thing?"

"Not that I can think of, no."

"Not even the peculiar gift of the Seers at Kell? It's been fairly well documented, you know."

He frowned slightly. "Yes," he admitted, "as a matter of fact, it has."

"How can you document a vision?" Garion asked curiously.

"The Grolims were seeking to discredit the Seers," Zakath replied. "They felt that the easiest way to do that was to have these pronouncements about the future written down and then wait to see what happened. The bureaucracy was instructed to keep records. So far, not one of the predictions of the Seers has proven false."

"Then you *do* believe that the Seers have the ability to know things about the past and the present and the future in ways that the rest of us might not completely understand?" Velvet pressed.

Zakath pursed his lips. "All right, Margravine," he said reluctantly, "I'll concede that the Seers have certain abilities that haven't been explained as yet."

"Do you believe that a Seer could lie to you?"

"Good girl," Belgarath murmured approvingly.

"No," Zakath replied after a moment's thought. "A Seer is incapable of lying. Their truthfulness is proverbial."

"Well, then," she said with a dimpled smile, "all you need to do to find out if what we've told you is the truth is to send for a Seer, isn't it?"

"Liselle," Garion protested, "that could take weeks. We don't have that much time."

"Oh," she said, "I don't think it would take all that long, If I remember correctly, Lady Polgara said that Andel summoned Cyradis when his Majesty here lay dying. I'm fairly sure we could persuade her to do it for us again."

"Well, Zakath," Belgarath said. "Will you agree to accept what Cyradis tells you as the truth?"

The Emperor squinted at him suspiciously, searching for some kind of subterfuge. "You've manipulated me into a corner," he accused. He thought about it. "All right, Belgarath," he said finally. "I'll accept whatever Cyradis says as the truth—if you'll agree to do the same."

"Done then," Belgarath said. "Let's send for Andel and get on with this."

As Velvet stepped out into the hall to speak with one of the guards who trailed along behind the Emperor wherever he went, Zakath leaned back in his chair. "I can't believe that I'm even considering all the wild impossibilities you've been telling me," he said.

Garion exchanged a quick look with his grandfather, and then they both laughed.

"Something funny, gentlemen?"

"Just a family joke, Zakath," Belgarath told him. "Garion and I have been discussing the possible and the impossible since he was about nine years old. He was even more stubborn about it than you are."

"It gets easier to accept after the first shock wears off," Garion added. "It's sort of like swimming in very cold water. Once you get numb, it doesn't hurt quite so much."

It was not long until Velvet reentered the room with the hooded Andel at her side.

"I believe you said that the Seeress of Kell is your mistress, Andel," Zakath said to her.

"Yes, she is, your Majesty."

"Can you summon her?"

"Her semblance, your Majesty, if there is need and if she will consent to come."

"I believe there's a need, Andel. Belgarath has told me certain things that I have to have confirmed. I know that Cyradis speaks only the truth. Belgarath, on the other hand, has a more dubious reputation." He threw a rather sly, sidelong glance at the old man.

Belgarath grinned at him and winked.

"I will speak with my mistress, your Majesty," Andel said, "and entreat her to send her semblance here. Should she consent, I beg of you to ask your questions quickly. The effort of reaching half around the world exhausts her, and she is not robust." Then the Dalasian woman knelt reverently and lowered her head, and Garion once again heard that peculiar murmur as of many voices, followed by a long moment of silence. Again there was that same shimmer in the air; when it had cleared, the hooded and blindfolded form of Cyradis stood there.

"We thank you for coming, Holy Seeress," Zakath said to her in an oddly respectful tone of voice. "My guests here have

87

told me certain things that I am loath to believe, but I have agreed to accept whatever you can confirm."

"I will tell thee what I can, Zakath," she replied. "Some things are hidden from me, and some others may not yet be revealed."

"I understand the limitations, Cyradis. Belgarion tells me that Urgit, the King of the Murgos, is not of the blood of Taur Urgas. Is this true?"

"It is," she replied simply. "King Urgit's father was an Alorn."

"Are any of the sons of Taur Urgas still alive?"

"Nay, Zakath. The line of Taur Urgas became extinct some twelve years ago when his last son was strangled in a cellar in Rak Goska upon the command of Oskatat, King Urgit's Seneschal."

Zakath sighed and shook his head sadly. "And so it has ended," he said. "My enemy's line passed unnoticed from this world in a dark cellar—passed so quietly that I could not even rejoice that they were gone, nor curse the ones who stole them from my grasp."

"Revenge is a hollow thing, Zakath."

"It's the only thing I've had for almost thirty years now." He sighed again, then straightened his shoulders. "Did Zandramas really steal Belgarion's son?"

"She did, and now she carries him to the Place Which Is No More."

"And where's that?"

Her face grew very still. "I may not reveal that," she replied finally, "but the Sardion is there."

"Can you tell me what the Sardion is?"

"It is one half of the stone which was divided."

"Is it really all *that* important?"

"In all of Angarak there is no thing of greater worth. The Grolims all know this. Urvon would give all his wealth for it. Zandramas would abandon the adoration of multitudes for it. Mengha would give his soul for it—indeed, he hath done so already in his enlistment of demons to aid him. Even Agachak, Hierarch of Rak Urga, would abandon his ascendancy in Cthol Murgos to possess it."

"How is it that a thing of such value has escaped my notice?"

"Thine eyes are on worldly matters, Zakath. The Sardion is not of this world—no more than the other half of the divided stone is of this world."

"The other half?"

"That which the Angaraks call Cthrag Yaska and the men of the West call the Orb of Aldur. Cthrag Sardius and Cthrag Yaska were sundered in the moment which saw the birth of the opposing necessities."

Zakath's face had grown quite pale, and he clasped his hands tightly in front of him to control their trembling. "It's all true, then?" he asked in a hoarse voice.

"All, Kal Zakath. All."

"Even that Belgarion and Zandramas are the Child of Light and the Child of Dark?"

"Yes, they are." He started to ask her another question, but she raised her hand. "My time is short, Zakath, and I must now reveal something of greater import unto thee. Know that thy life doth approach a momentous crossroads. Put aside thy lust for power and thy hunger for revenge, as they are but childish toys. Return thou even to Mal Zeth to prepare thyself for *thy* part in the meeting which is to come."

"*My* part?" He sounded startled.

"Thy name and thy task are written in the stars."

"And what is this task?"

"I will instruct thee when thou art ready to understand what it is that thou must do. First thou must cleanse thy heart of that grief and remorse which hath haunted thee."

His face grew still, and he sighed. "I'm afraid not, Cyradis," he said. "What you ask is quite impossible."

"Then thou wilt surely die before the seasons turn again. Consider what I have told thee, and consider it well, Emperor of Mallorea. I will speak with thee anon." And then she shimmered and vanished.

Zakath stared at the empty spot where she had stood. His face was pale, and his jaws were set.

"Well, Zakath?" Belgarath said. "Are you convinced?"

The Emperor rose from his chair and began to pace up and down. "This is an absolute absurdity!" he burst out suddenly in an agitated voice.

"I know," Belgarath replied calmly, "but a willingness to believe the absurd is an indication of faith. It might just be that faith is the first step in the preparation Cyradis mentioned."

"It's not that I don't *want* to believe, Belgarath," Zakath said, in a strangely humble tone. "It's just—"

"Nobody said that it was going to be easy," the old man told him. "But you've done things before that weren't easy, haven't you?"

Zakath dropped into his chair again, his eyes lost in thought. "Why me?" he said plaintively. "Why do *I* have to get involved in this?"

Garion suddenly laughed.

Zakath gave him a cold stare.

"Sorry," Garion apologized, "but *I've* been saying 'why me?' since I was about fourteen. Nobody's ever given me a satisfactory answer, but you get used to the injustice of it after a while."

"It's not that I'm trying to avoid any kind of responsibility, Belgarion. It's just that I can't see what possible help I could be. You people are going to track down Zandramas, retrieve your son, and destroy the Sardion. Isn't that about it?"

"It's a little more complicated than that," Belgarath told him. "Destroying the Sardion is going to involve something rather cataclysmic."

"I don't quite follow that. Can't you just wave your hand and make it cease to exist? You *are* a sorcerer, after all—or so they say."

"That's forbidden," Garion said automatically. "You can't unmake things. That's what Ctuchik tried to do, and he destroyed himself."

Zakath frowned and looked at Belgarath. "I thought *you* killed him."

"Most people do." The old man shrugged. "It adds to my reputation, so I don't argue with them." He tugged at one earlobe. "No," he said, "I think we're going to have to see this all the way through to the end. I'm fairly sure that the only way the Sardion can be destroyed is as a result of the final confrontation between the Child of Light and the Child of Dark." He paused, then sat up suddenly, his face intent. "I think Cyradis slipped and gave us something she hadn't intended, though. She said that the Grolim priesthood all desperately wanted the Sardion, and she included Mengha in her list. Wouldn't that seem to indicate that Mengha's also a Grolim?" He looked at Andel. "Is your young mistress subject to these little lapses?"

"Cyradis cannot misspeak herself, Holy Belgarath," the healer replied. "A Seeress does not speak in her own voice, but in the voice of her vision."

"Then she *wanted* us to know that Mengha is—or was—a Grolim, and that the reason he's raising demons is to help him in his search for the Sardion." He thought about it. "There's another rather bleak possibility, too," he added. "It might just be that his demons are using him to get the Sardion for themselves. Maybe that's why they're so docile where he's concerned. Demons by themselves are bad enough, but if the Sardion has the same power as the Orb, we *definitely* don't want it to fall into their hands." He turned to Zakath. "Well?" he said.

"Well what?"

"Are you with us or against us?"

"Isn't that a little blunt?"

"Yes, it is—but it saves time, and time's starting to be a factor."

Zakath sank lower in his chair, his expression unreadable. "I find very little benefit for *me* in this proposed arrangement," he said.

"You get to keep living," Garion reminded him. "Cyradis said that you'll die before spring if you don't take up the task she's going to lay in front of you."

Zakath's faint smile was melancholy, and the dead indifference returned to his eyes. "My life hasn't really been so enjoyable that I'd consider going out of my way to prolong it, Belgarion," he replied.

"Don't you think you're being just a little childish, Zakath?" Garion snapped, his temper starting to heat up again. "You're not accomplishing a single thing here in Cthol Murgos. There's not one solitary drop of Urga blood left for you to spill, and you've got a situation at home that verges on disaster. Are you a King—or an Emperor, or whatever you want to call it—or are you a spoiled child? You refuse to go back to Mal Zeth just because somebody told you that you ought to. You even dig in your heels when someone assures you that you'll die if you don't go back. That's not only childish, it's irrational, and I don't have the time to try to reason with somebody whose wits have deserted him. Well, you can huddle here in Rak Hagga and nurse all your tired old griefs and disappointments until Cyradis' predictions catch up with you, for all I care, but Geran is my son, and I'm going to Mallorea. I've got work to do, and I don't have time to coddle you." He had saved something up for last. "Besides," he added in an insulting, offhand tone, "I don't need you anyway."

Zakath came to his feet, his eyes ablaze. "You go too far!" he roared, slamming his fist down on the table.

"Amazing," Garion said sarcastically. "You *are* alive after all. I thought I might have to step on your foot to get any kind of response out of you. All right, now that you're awake, let's fight."

"What do you mean, fight?" Zakath demanded, his face still flushed with anger. "Fight about what?"

"About whether or not you're going with us to Mallorea."

"Don't be stupid. Of course I'm going with you. What we *are* going to fight about is your incredible lack of common courtesy."

Garion stared at him for a moment and then suddenly doubled over in a gale of helpless laughter.

Zakath's face was still red, and his fists were clenching and unclenching. Then a slightly sheepish expression came over his face, and he, too, began to laugh.

Belgarath let out an explosive breath. "Garion," he said irritably, "let me know when you're going to do something like that. My veins aren't what they used to be."

Zakath wiped at his eyes, though he was still laughing. "How long do you think it might take for you and your friends to get packed?" he asked them.

"Not too long," Garion replied. "Why?"

"I'm suddenly homesick for Mal Zeth. It's spring there now, and the cherry trees are in bloom. You and Ce'Nedra will love Mal Zeth, Garion."

Garion was not entirely sure if the omission of the "Bel" was inadvertent or an overture of friendship. He *was*, however, quite sure that the Emperor of Mallorea was a man of even greater complexity than he had imagined.

"I hope you'll all excuse me now," Zakath said, "but I want to talk with Brador and get a few more details about what's been going on in Karanda. This Mengha he told me about seems to be mounting an open insurrection against the crown, and I've always had a violent prejudice against that sort of thing."

"I can relate to that," Garion agreed blandly.

For the next few days the road between Rak Hagga and the port city of Rak Cthan was thick with imperial messengers. Finally, on a frosty morning when the sun was bright and the sky dark blue and when misty steam rose from the dark waters of Lake Hagga, they set out, riding across a winter-browned plain toward the coast. Garion, his gray Rivan cloak drawn about him, rode at the head of the column with Zakath, who seemed for some reason to be in better spirits than he had been at any time since the two had met. The column which followed them stretched back for miles.

"Vulgar, isn't it?" the Mallorean said wryly, looking back over his shoulder. "I'm absolutely surrounded by parasites and toadies, and they proliferate like maggots in rotten meat."

"If they bother you so much, then why not dismiss them?" Garion suggested.

"I can't. They all have powerful relatives. I have to balance them very carefully—one from this tribe to match the one from that clan. As long as no one family has too many high offices, they spend all their time plotting against each other. That way they don't have the time to plot against me."

"I suppose that's one way to keep things under control."

As the sun moved up through the bright blue winter sky at this nether end of the world, the frost gently dissolved from the long stems of dead grass or fell lightly from the fern and bracken to leave ghostly white imprints of those drooping brown fronds on the short green moss spread beneath.

They paused for a noon meal that was every bit as sumptuous as one that might have been prepared back in Rak Hagga and was served on snowy damask beneath a wide-spread canvas roof. "Adequate, I suppose," Zakath said critically after they had eaten.

"You're overpampered, my lord," Polgara told him. "A hard ride in wet weather and a day or so on short rations would probably do wonders for your appetite."

Zakath gave Garion an amused look. "I thought it was just you," he said, "but this blunt outspokenness seems to be a characteristic of your whole family."

Garion shrugged. "It saves time."

"Forgive my saying this, Belgarion," Sadi interjected, "but what possible interest can an immortal have in time?" He sighed rather mournfully. "Immortality must give one a great deal of satisfaction—watching all one's enemies grow old and die."

"It's much overrated," Belgarath said, leaning back in his chair with a brimming silver tankard. "Sometimes whole centuries go by when one doesn't *have* any enemies and there's nothing to do but watch the years roll by."

Zakath suddenly smiled broadly. "Do you know something?" he said to them all. "I feel better right now than I've felt in over twenty-five years. It's as if a great weight has been lifted from me."

"Probably an aftereffect of the poison," Velvet suggested archly. "Get plenty of rest, and it should pass in a month or so."

"Is the Margravine always like this?" Zakath asked.

"Sometimes she's even worse," Silk replied morosely.

As they emerged from beneath the wide-spread canvas, Garion looked around for his horse, a serviceable roan with a long, hooked nose, but he could not seem to see the animal. Then he suddenly noticed that his saddle and packs were on a different horse, a very large dark gray stallion. Puzzled, he looked at Zakath, who was watching him intently. "What's this?" he asked.

"Just a little token of my unbounded respect, Garion," Zakath said, his eyes alight. "Your roan was an adequate mount, I suppose, but he was hardly a regal animal. A King needs a kingly horse, and I think you'll find that Chretienne can lend himself to any occasion that requires ceremony."

"Chretienne?"

"That's his name. He's been the pride of my stable here in Cthol Murgos. Don't you have a stable at Riva?"

Garion laughed. "My kingdom's an island, Zakath. We're more interested in boats than in horses." He looked at the proud gray standing with his neck arched and with one hoof lightly pawing the earth and was suddenly overcome with gratitude. He clasped the Mallorean Emperor's hand warmly. "This is a magnificent gift, Zakath," he said.

"Of course it is. I'm a magnificent fellow—or hadn't you noticed? Ride him, Garion. Feel the wind in your face and let the thunder of his hooves fill your blood."

"Well," Garion said, trying to control his eagerness, "maybe he and I really ought to get to know each other."

Zakath laughed with delight. "Of course," he said.

Garion approached the big gray horse, who watched him quite calmly.

"I guess we'll be sharing a saddle for a while," he said to the animal. Chretienne nickered and nudged at Garion with his nose.

"He wants to run," Eriond said. "I'll ride with you, if you don't mind. Horse wants to run, too."

"All right," Garion agreed. "Let's go then." He gathered the reins, set his foot in the stirrup, and swung up into the saddle. The gray was running almost before Garion was in place.

It was a new experience. Garion had spent many hours riding—sometimes for weeks on end. He had always taken care of his mounts, as any good Sendar would, but there had never really been any personal attachment before. For him, a horse had simply been a means of conveyance, a way to get from one place to another, and riding had never been a particular source of pleasure. With this great stallion, Chretienne, however, it was altogether different. There was a kind of electric thrill to the feel of the big horse's muscles bunching and flowing beneath him as they ran out across the winter-brown grass toward a rounded hill a mile or so distant, with Eriond and his chestnut stallion racing alongside.

When they reached the hilltop, Garion was breathless and laughing with sheer delight. He reined in, and Chretienne reared, pawing at the air with his hooves, wanting to be off again.

"Now you know, don't you?" Eriond asked with a broad smile.

"Yes," Garion admitted, still laughing, "I guess I do. I wonder how I missed it all these years."

"You have to have the right horse," Eriond told him wisely. He gave Garion a sidelong glance. "You know that you'll never be the same again, don't you?"

"That's all right," Garion replied. "I was getting tired of the old way anyhow." He pointed at a low string of hills outlined against the crisp blue sky a league or so on ahead. "Why don't we go over there and see what's on the other side?" he suggested.

"Why not?" Eriond laughed.

And so they did.

The Emperor's household staff was well organized, and a goodly number of them rode on ahead to prepare their night's encampment at a spot almost precisely halfway to the coast. The column started early the following morning, riding again along a frosty track beneath a deep blue sky. It was late afternoon when they crested a hill to look out over the expanse of the Sea of the East, rolling a dark blue under the winter sun and with smoky-looking cloud banks the color of rust blurring the far horizon. Two dozen ships with their red sails furled stood at anchor in the indented curve of a shallow bay far below, and Garion looked with some puzzlement at Zakath.

"Another symptom of the vulgar ostentation I mentioned." The Emperor shrugged. "I ordered this fleet down here from the port at Cthan. A dozen or so of those ships are here to transport all my hangers-on and toadies—as well as the humbler people who actually do the work. The other dozen are here to escort our royal personages with suitable pomp. You have to have pomp, Garion. Otherwise people might mistake a King or an Emperor for an honest man."

"You're in a whimsical humor this afternoon."

"Maybe it's another of those lingering symptoms Liselle

97

mentioned. We'll sleep on board ship tonight and sail at first light tomorrow."

Garion nodded, touching Chretienne's bowed neck with an odd kind of regret as he handed his reins to a waiting groom.

The vessel to which they were ferried from the sandy beach was opulent. Unlike the cramped cabins on most of the other ships Garion had sailed aboard, the chambers on this one were nearly as large as the rooms in a fair-sized house. It took him a little while to pin down the reason for the difference. The other ships had devoted so little room to cabins because the bulk of the space on board had been devoted to cargo. The only cargo *this* ship customarily carried, however, was the Emperor of Mallorea.

They dined that evening on lobster, served in the low-beamed dining room aboard Zakath's floating palace. So much of Garion's attention for the past week or more had been fixed on the unpredictable Emperor that he had not had much opportunity to talk with his friends. Thus, when they took their places at the table, he rather deliberately sat at the opposite end from the Mallorean. It was with a great deal of relief that he took his seat between Polgara and Durnik, while Ce'Nedra and Velvet diverted the Emperor with sparkling feminine chatter.

"You look tired, Garion," Polgara noted.

"I've been under a certain strain," he replied. "I wish that man wouldn't keep changing every other minute. Every time I think I've got him figured out, he turns into somebody else."

"It's not a good idea to categorize people, dear," she advised placidly, touching his arm. "That's the first sign of fuzzy thinking."

"Are we actually supposed to eat these things?" Durnik asked in a disgusted sort of voice, pointing his knife at the bright red lobster staring up at him from his plate with its claws seemingly at the ready.

"That's what the pliers are for, Durnik," Polgara explained in a peculiarly mild tone. "You have to crack it out of its shell."

He pushed his plate away. "I'm not going to eat something that looks like a big red bug," he declared with uncharacteristic heat. "I draw the line at some things."

"Lobster is a delicacy, Durnik," she said.

He grunted. "Some people eat snails, too."

Her eyes flashed, but then she gained control of her anger and continued to speak to him in that same mild tone. "I'm sure we can have them take it away and bring you something else," she said.

He glared at her.

Garion looked back and forth between the two of them. Then he decided that they had all known each other for far too long to step delicately around any problems. "What's the matter, Durnik?" he asked bluntly. "You're as cross as a badger with a sore nose."

"Nothing," Durnik almost snapped at him.

Garion began to put a few things together. He remembered the plea Andel had made to Aunt Pol concerning Toth. He looked down the table to where the big mute, his eyes lowered to his plate, seemed almost to be trying to make himself invisible. Then he looked back at Durnik, who kept his face stiffly turned away from his former friend. "Oh," he said, "now I think I understand. Aunt Pol told you something you didn't want to hear. Someone you liked very much did something that made you angry. You said some things to him that you wish now you hadn't said. Then you found out that he didn't really have any choice in the matter and that what he did was really right after all. Now you'd like to make friends with him again, but you don't know how. Is that sort of why you're behaving this way—and being so impolite to Aunt Pol?"

Durnik's look was at first stricken. Then his face grew red—then pale. "I don't have to listen to this," he burst out, coming to his feet.

"Oh, sit down, Durnik," Garion told him. "We all love each other too much to behave this way. Instead of being embarrassed and bad-tempered about it, why don't we see what we can do to fix it?"

Durnik tried to meet Garion's eyes, but finally lowered his head, his face flaming. "I treated him badly, Garion," he mumbled, sinking back into his chair again.

"Yes," Garion agreed, "you did. But it was because you didn't understand what he was doing—and why. I didn't understand myself until the day before yesterday—when Zakath finally changed his mind and decided to take us all to Mal Zeth. Cyradis knew that he was going to do that, and that's why she made Toth turn us over to Atesca's men. She *wants* us to get to the Sardion and meet Zandramas, and so she's going to arrange it. Toth will be the one who does what she thinks has to be done to accomplish that. Under the present circumstances, we couldn't find a better friend."

"How can I possibly—I mean, after the way I treated him?"

"Be honest. Admit that you were wrong and apologize."

Durnik's face grew stiff.

"It doesn't have to be in words, Durnik," Garion told his friend patiently. "You and Toth have been talking together without words for months." He looked speculatively up at the low-beamed ceiling. "This is a ship," he noted, "and we're going out onto an ocean. Do you imagine that there might be a few fish out there in all that water?"

Durnik's smile was immediate.

Polgara's sigh, however, was pensive.

The smith looked almost shyly across the table. "How did you say that I'm supposed to get this bug out of its shell, Pol?" he asked, pointing at the angry-looking lobster on his plate.

They sailed northeasterly from the coast of Hagga and soon left winter behind. At some point during the voyage they crossed that imaginary line equidistant from the poles and once again entered the northern half of the world. Durnik and Toth, shyly at first, but then with growing confidence, resumed their friendship and spent their days at the ship's stern, probing the sea with lines, bright-colored lures, and various baits gleaned from the galley.

Zakath's humor continued to remain uncharacteristically sunny, though his discussions with Belgarath and Polgara centered on the nature of demons, a subject about which there was very little to smile. Finally, one day when they had been at sea for about a week, a servant came up to Garion, who stood at the portside rail watching the dance of the wind atop the sparkling waves, and advised him that the Emperor would like to see him. Garion nodded and made his way aft to the cabin where Zakath customarily held audience. Like most of the cabins aboard the floating palace, this one was quite large and ostentatiously decorated. Owing to the broad windows stretching across the ship's stern, the room was bright and airy. The drapes at the sides of the windows were of crimson velvet, and the fine Mallorean carpet was a deep blue. Zakath, dressed as always in plain white linen, sat on a low, leather-upholstered divan at the far end of the cabin, looking out at the whitecaps and the flock of snowy gulls trailing the ship. His cat lay purring in his lap as he absently stroked her ears.

"You wanted to see me, Zakath?" Garion asked as he entered.

"Yes. Come in, Garion," the Mallorean replied. "I haven't seen much of you for the past few days. Are you cross with me?"

"No," Garion said. "You've been busy learning about demons. I don't know that much about them, so I couldn't have added all that much to the discussions." He crossed the cabin, pausing at one point to stoop and unwrap a ferociously playful kitten from around his left ankle.

"They love to pounce." Zakath smiled.

A thought came to Garion, and he looked around warily. "Zith isn't in here, is she?"

Zakath laughed. "No. Sadi's devised a means of keeping her at home." He looked whimsically at Garion. "Is she really as deadly as he says?"

Garion nodded. "She bit a Grolim at Rak Urga," he said. "He was dead in about a half a minute."

Zakath shuddered. "You don't have to tell Sadi about this," he said, "but snakes make my flesh creep."

"Talk to Silk. He could give you a whole dissertation about how much he dislikes them."

"He's a complicated little fellow, isn't he?"

Garion smiled. "Oh, yes. His life is filled with danger and excitement, and so his nerves are as tightly wound as lute strings. He's erratic sometimes, but you get used to that after a while." He looked at the other man critically. "You're looking particularly fit," he noted, sitting down on the other end of the leather couch. "Sea air must agree with you."

"I don't think it's really the air, Garion. I think it has to do with the fact that I've been sleeping eight to ten hours a night."

"Sleep? You?"

"Astonishing, isn't it?" Zakath's face went suddenly quite somber. "I'd rather that this didn't go any further, Garion," he said.

"Of course."

"Urgit told you what happened when I was young?"

Garion nodded. "Yes."

"My habit of not sleeping very much dates from then. A face that had been particularly dear to me haunted my dreams, and sleep became an agony to me."

"That didn't diminish? Not even after some thirty years?"

"Not one bit. I lived in continual grief and guilt and remorse. I lived only to revenge myself on Taur Urgas. Cho-Hag's saber robbed me of that. I had planned a dozen different deaths for the madman—each more horrible than the one before—but he cheated me by dying cleanly in battle."

"No," Garion disagreed. "His death was worse than anything you could possibly have devised. I've talked with Cho-Hag about it. Taur Urgas went totally mad before Cho-Hag killed him, but he lived long enough to realize that he had

102

finally been beaten. He died biting and clawing at the earth in frustration. Being beaten was more than he could bear."

Zakath thought about it. "Yes," he said finally. "That would have been quite dreadful for him, wouldn't it? I think that maybe I'm less disappointed now."

"And was it your discovery that the Urga line is now extinct that finally laid the ghost that's haunted your sleep all these years?"

"No, Garion. I don't think that had anything to do with it. It's just that instead of the face that had always been there before, now I see a different face."

"Oh?"

"A blindfolded face."

"Cyradis? I don't know that I'd recommend thinking about her in that fashion."

"You misunderstand, Garion. She's hardly more than a child, but somehow she's touched my life with more peace and comfort than I've ever known. I sleep like a baby and I walk around all day with this silly euphoria bubbling up in me." He shook his head. "Frankly, I can't stand myself like this, but I can't help it for some reason."

Garion stared out the window, not even seeing the play of sunlight on the waves nor the hovering gulls. Then it came to him so clearly that he knew that it was undeniably true. "It's because you've come to that crossroads in your life that Cyradis mentioned," he said. "You're being rewarded because you've chosen the right fork."

"Rewarded? By whom?"

Garion looked at him and suddenly laughed. "I don't think you're quite ready to accept that information yet," he said. "Could you bring yourself to believe that it's Cyradis who's making you feel good right now?"

"In some vague way, yes."

"It goes a little deeper, but that's a start." Garion looked at the slightly perplexed man before him. "You and I are caught up together in something over which we have absolutely no control," he said seriously. "I've been through it before, so I'll try to cushion the shocks that are in store for you as much as I can. Just try to keep an open mind about a peculiar way of looking at the world." He thought about it some more. "I think that we're going to be working together—at least up to a point—so we might as well be friends." He held out his right hand.

Zakath laughed. "Why not?" he said, taking Garion's hand in a firm grip. "I think we're both as crazy as Taur Urgas, but why not? We're the two most powerful men in the world. We should be deadly enemies, and you propose friendship. Well, why not?" He laughed again delightedly.

"We have much more deadly enemies, Zakath," Garion said gravely, "and all of your armies—and all of mine—won't mean a thing when we get to where we're going."

"And where's that, my young friend?"

"I think it's called 'the place which is no more.'"

"I've been meaning to ask you about that. The whole phrase is a contradiction in terms. How can you go someplace which doesn't exist any more?"

"I don't really know," Garion told him. "I'll tell you when we get there."

Two days later, they arrived at Mal Gemila, a port in southern Mallorea Antiqua, and took to horse. They rode eastward at a canter on a well-maintained highway that crossed a pleasant plain, green with spring. A regiment of red-tunicked cavalrymen cleared the road ahead of them, and their pace left the entourage which usually accompanied the Emperor far behind. There were way stations along the highway—not unlike the Tolnedran hostels dotting the roads in the west—and the imperial guard rather brusquely ejected other guests at these roadside stops to make way for the Emperor and his party.

As they pressed onward, day after day, Garion began slowly to comprehend the true significance of the word "boundless" as it was applied to Mallorea. The plains of Algaria, which had always before seemed incredibly vast, shrank into insignificance. The snowy peaks of the Dalasian mountains, lying to the south of the road they traveled, raked their white talons at the sky. Garion drew in on himself, feeling smaller and smaller the deeper they rode into this vast domain.

Peculiarly, Ce'Nedra seemed to be suffering a similar shrinkage, and she quite obviously did not like it very much. Her comments became increasingly waspish; her observations more acid. She found the loose-fitting garments of the peasantry uncouth. She found fault with the construction of the gangplows that opened whole acres at a time behind patiently plodding herds of oxen. She didn't like the food. Even the water—as clear as crystal, and as cold and sweet as might have sprung from any crevice in the Tolnedran mountains—offended her taste.

Silk, his eyes alight with mischief, rode at her side on the sunny midmorning of the last day of their journey from Mal Gemila. "Beware, your Majesty," he warned her slyly as they neared the crest of a hillside sheathed in pale spring grass so verdant that it almost looked like a filmy green mist. "The first sight of Mal Zeth has sometimes struck the unwary traveler blind. To be safe, why don't you cover one eye with your hand? That way you can preserve at least partial sight."

Her face grew frosty, and she drew herself to her full height in her saddle—a move that might have come off better had she been only slightly taller—and said to him in her most imperious tone, "*We* are not amused, Prince Kheldar, and *we* do not expect to find a barbarian city at the far end of the world a rival to the splendors of Tol Honeth, the only truly imperial city in the—"

And then she stopped—as they all did.

The valley beyond the crest stretched not for miles, but for leagues, and it was filled to overflowing with the city of Mal Zeth. The streets were as straight as tautly stretched strings, and the buildings gleamed—not with marble, for there was not marble enough in all the world to sheath the buildings

105

of this enormous city—but rather with an intensely gleaming, thick white mortar that seemed somehow to shoot light at the eye. It was stupendous.

"It's not much," Zakath said in an exaggeratedly deprecating tone. "Just a friendly little place we like to call home." He looked at Ce'Nedra's stiff, pale little face with an artful expression. "We really should press on, your Majesty," he told her. "It's a half-day's ride to the imperial palace from here."

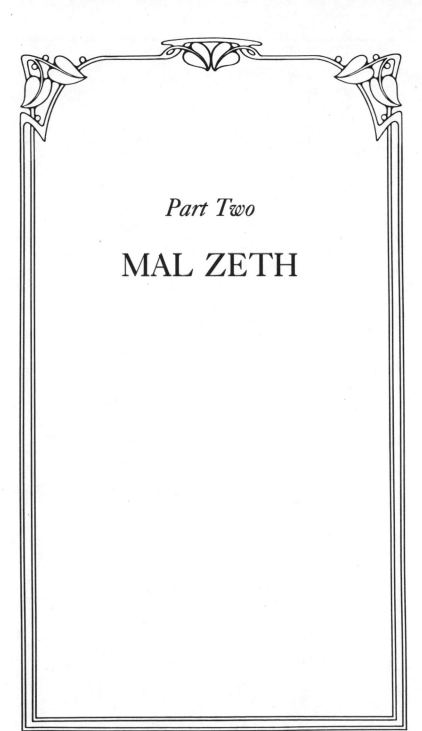

Part Two

MAL ZETH

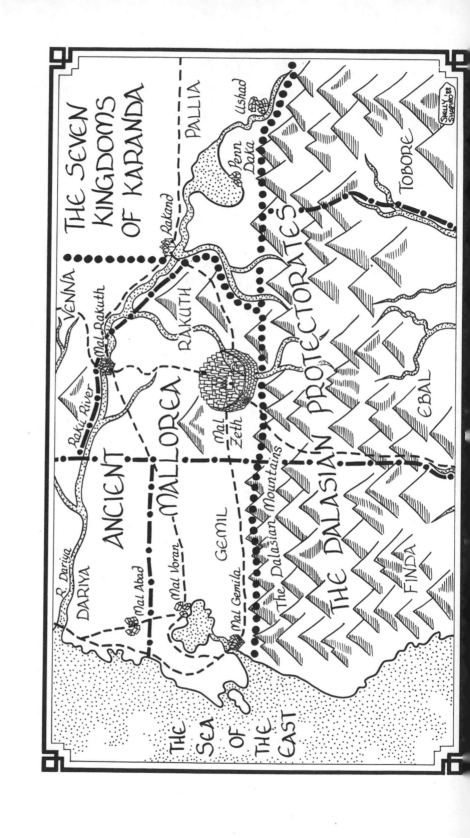

CHAPTER SIX

The gates of Mal Zeth, like those of Tol Honeth, were of bronze, broad and burnished. The city lying within those gates, however, was significantly different from the capital of the Tolnedran Empire. There was a peculiar sameness about the structures, and they were built so tightly against each other that the broad avenues of the city were lined on either side by solid, mortar-covered walls, pierced only by deeply inset, arched doorways with narrow white stairways leading up to the flat rooftops. Here and there, the mortar had crumbled away, revealing the fact that the buildings beneath that coating were constructed of squared-off timbers.

Durnik, who believed that all buildings should be made of stone, noted that fact with a look of disapproval.

As they moved deeper into the city, Garion noticed the almost total lack of windows. "I don't want to seem critical," he said to Zakath, "but isn't your city just a little monotonous?"

Zakath looked at him curiously.

"All the houses are the same, and there aren't very many windows."

"Oh," Zakath smiled, "that's one of the drawbacks of leaving architecture up to the military. They're great believers in uniformity, and windows have no place in military fortifications. Each house has its own little garden, though, and the windows face that. In the summertime, the people spend most of their time in the gardens—or on the rooftops."

"Is the whole city like this?" Durnik asked, looking at the cramped little houses all packed together.

"No, Goodman," the Emperor replied. "This quarter of the city was built for corporals. The streets reserved for officers are a bit more ornate, and those where the privates and workmen live are much shabbier. Military people tend to be very conscious of rank and the appearances that go with it."

A few doors down a side street branching off from the one they followed, a stout, red-faced woman was shrilly berating a scrawny-looking fellow with a hangdog expression as a group of soldiers removed furniture from a house and piled it in a rickety cart. "You had to go and do it, didn't you, Actas?" she demanded. "You had to get drunk and insult your captain. Now what's to become of us? I spent all those years living in those pigsty privates' quarters waiting for you to get promoted, and just when I think things are taking a turn for the better, you have to destroy it all by getting drunk and being reduced to private again."

He mumbled something.

"What was that?"

"Nothing, dear."

"I'm not going to let you forget this, Actas, let me tell you."

"Life does have its little ups and downs, doesn't it?" Sadi murmured as they rode on out of earshot.

"I don't think it's anything to laugh about," Ce'Nedra said with surprising heat. "They're being thrown out of their home over a moment's foolishness. Can't someone do something?"

Zakath gave her an appraising look, then beckoned to one of the red-cloaked officers riding respectfully along behind them. "Find out which unit that man's in," he instructed. "Then go to his captain and tell him that I'd take it as a personal favor if Actas were reinstated in his former rank— on the condition that he stays sober."

"At once, your Majesty." The officer saluted and rode off.

"Why, thank you, Zakath," Ce'Nedra said, sounding a little startled.

"My pleasure, Ce'Nedra." He bowed to her from his saddle. Then he laughed shortly. "I suspect that Actas' wife will see to it that he suffers sufficiently for his misdeeds anyway."

"Aren't you afraid that such acts of compassion might damage your reputation, your Majesty?" Sadi asked him.

"No," Zakath replied. "A ruler must always strive to be unpredictable, Sadi. It keeps the underlings off balance. Besides, an occasional act of charity toward the lower ranks helps to strengthen their loyalty."

"Don't you ever do anything that isn't motivated by politics?" Garion asked him. For some reason, Zakath's flippant explanation of his act irritated him.

"Not that I can think of," Zakath said. "Politics is the greatest game in the world, Garion, but you have to play it all the time to keep your edge."

Silk laughed. "I've said the exact same thing about commerce," he said. "About the only difference I can see is that in commerce you have money as a way of keeping score. How do you keep score in politics?"

Zakath's expression was perculiarly mixed—half amused and half deadly serious. "It's very simple, Kheldar," he said.

"If you're still on the throne at the end of the day, you've won. If you're dead, you've lost—and each day is a complete new game."

Silk gave him a long, speculative look, then looked over at Garion, his fingers moving slightly. —*I need to talk to you— at once—*

Garion nodded briefly, then leaned over in his saddle. He reined in.

"Something wrong?" Zakath asked him.

"I think my cinch is loose," Garion replied, dismounting. "Go on ahead. I'll catch up."

"Here, I'll help you, Garion," Silk offered, also swinging down from his saddle.

"What's this all about?" Garion asked when the Emperor, chatting with Ce'Nedra and Velvet, had ridden out of earshot.

"Be very careful with him, Garion," the little man replied quietly, pretending to check the straps on Garion's saddle. "He let something slip there. He's all smiles and courtesy on the surface, but underneath it all he hasn't really changed all that much."

"Wasn't he just joking?"

"Not even a little. He was deadly serious. He's brought us all to Mal Zeth for reasons that have nothing to do with Mengha or our search for Zandramas. Be on your guard with him. That friendly smile of his can fall off his face without any warning at all." He spoke a little more loudly then. "There," he said, tugging at a strap, "that ought to hold it. Let's catch up with the others."

They rode into a broad square surrounded on all sides by canvas booths dyed in various hues of red, green, blue, and yellow. The square teemed with merchants and citizens, all dressed in varicolored, loose-fitting robes that hung to their heels.

"Where do the common citizens live if the whole city's divided up into sections based on military rank?" Durnik asked.

Brador, the bald, chubby Chief of the Bureau of Internal Affairs, who happened to be riding beside the smith, looked around with a smile. "They all have their ranks, Goodman," he replied, "each according to his individual accomplishments. It's all very rigidly controlled by the Bureau of Promotions. Housing, places of business, suitable marriages— they're all determined by rank."

"Isn't that sort of overregimented?" Durnik asked pointedly.

"Malloreans love to be regimented, Goodman Durnik." Brador laughed. "Angaraks bow automatically to authority; Melcenes have a deep inner need to compartmentalize things; Karands are too stupid to take control of their own destinies; and the Dals—well, nobody knows what the Dals want."

"We aren't really all that different from the people in the West, Durnik," Zakath said back over his shoulder. "In Tolnedra and Sendaria, such matters are determined by economics. People gravitate to the houses and shops and marriages they can afford. We've just formalized it, that's all."

"Tell me, your Majesty," Sadi said, "how is it that your people are so undemonstrative?"

"I don't quite follow you."

"Shouldn't they at least salute as you ride by? You *are* the Emperor, after all."

"They don't recognize me." Zakath shrugged. "The Emperor is a man in crimson robes who rides in a golden carriage, wears a terribly heavy jeweled crown, and is accompanied by at least a regiment of imperial guards all blowing trumpets. I'm just a man in white linen riding through town with a few friends."

Garion thought about that, still mindful of Silk's half-whispered warning. The almost total lack of any kind of self-aggrandizement implicit in Zakath's statement revealed yet another facet of the man's complex personality. He was quite sure that not even King Fulrach of Sendaria, the most modest of all the monarchs of the West, could be quite so self-effacing.

The streets beyond the square were lined with somewhat larger houses than those they had passed near the city gates, and there had been some attempt at ornamentation here. It appeared, however, that Mallorean sculptors had limited talent, and the mortar-cast filigree surmounting the front of each house was heavy and graceless.

"The sergeant's district," Zakath said laconically.

The city seemed to go on forever. At regular intervals there were squares and market places and bazaars, all filled with people wearing the bright, loose-fitting robes that appeared to be the standard Mallorean garb. When they passed the last of the rigidly similar houses of the sergeants and of those civilians of equal rank, they entered a broad belt of trees and lawns where fountains splashed and sparkled in the sunlight and where broad promenades were lined with carefully sculptured green hedges interspersed with cherry trees laden with pink blossoms shimmering in the light breeze.

"How lovely," Ce'Nedra exclaimed.

"We do have some beauty here in Mal Zeth," Zakath told her. "No one—not even an army architect—could make a city this big uniformly ugly."

"The officers' districts aren't quite so severe," Silk told the little Queen.

"You're familiar with Mal Zeth, then, your Highness?" Brador asked.

Silk nodded. "My partner and I have a facility here," he replied. "It's more in the nature of a centralized collection point than an actual business. It's cumbersome doing business in Mal Zeth—too many regulations."

"Might one inquire as to the rank you were assigned?" the moon-faced bureaucrat asked delicately.

"We're generals," Silk said in a rather grandly offhand manner. "Yarblek wanted to be a field marshal, but I didn't think the expense of buying that much rank was really justified."

"Is rank for sale?" Sadi asked.

"In Mal Zeth, everything's for sale," Silk replied. "In most respects it's almost exactly like Tol Honeth."

"Not entirely, Silk," Ce'Nedra said primly.

"Only in the broadest terms, your Imperial Highness," he agreed quickly. "Mal Zeth has never been graced by the presence of a divinely beautiful Imperial Princess, glowing like a precious jewel and shooting beams of her fire back at the sun."

She gave him a hard look, then turned her back on him.

"What did I say?" the little man asked Garion in an injured tone.

"People always suspect you, Silk," Garion told him. "They can never quite be sure that you're not making fun of them. I thought you knew that."

Silk sighed tragically. "Nobody understands me," he complained.

"Oh, I think they do."

The plazas and boulevards beyond the belt of parks and gardens were more grand, and the houses larger and set apart from each other. There was still, however, a stiff similarity about them, a kind of stern sameness that insured that men of equal rank would be assigned to rigidly equal quarters.

Another broad strip of lawns and trees lay beyond the mansions of the generals and their mercantile equivalents, and within that encircling green there arose a fair-sized marble city with its own walls and burnished gates.

"The imperial palace," Zakath said indifferently. He frowned. "What have you done over there?" he asked Brador, pointing at a long row of tall buildings rising near the south wall of the enclosed compound.

Brador coughed delicately. "Those are the bureaucratic offices, your Majesty," he replied in a neutral tone. "You'll recall that you authorized their construction just before the battle of Thull Mardu."

Zakath pursed his lips. "I hadn't expected something on quite such a grand scale," he said.

"There are quite a lot of us, your Majesty," Brador explained, "and we felt that things might be more harmonious if each bureau had its own building." He looked a bit apologetic. "We really *did* need the space," he explained defensively to Sadi. "We were all jumbled together with the military, and very often men from different bureaus had to share the same office. It's really much more efficient this way, wouldn't you say?"

"I think I'd prefer it if you didn't involve me in this discussion, your Excellency," Sadi answered.

"I was merely attempting to draw upon your Excellency's expertise in managing affairs of state."

"Salmissra's palace is somewhat unique," Sadi told him. "We *like* being jumbled together. It gives us greater opportunities for spying and murder and intrigue and the other normal functions of government."

As they approached the gates to the imperial complex, Garion noticed with some surprise that the thick bronze gates had been overlaid with beaten gold, and his thrifty Sendarian heritage recoiled from the thought of such wanton lavishness. Ce'Nedra, however, looked at the priceless gates with undisguised aquisitiveness.

"You wouldn't be able to move them," Silk advised her.

"What?" she said inattentatively.

"The gates. They're much to heavy to steal."

"Shut up, Silk," she said absently, her eyes still appraising the gates.

He began to laugh uproariously, and she looked at him, her green eyes narrowing dangerously.

"I think I'll ride back to see what's keeping Belgarath," the little man said.

"Do," she said. Then she looked at Garion, who was trying to conceal a broad grin. "Something funny?" she asked him.

"No, dear," he replied quickly. "Just enjoying the scenery is all."

The detachment of guards at the gates was not as burnished nor plumed as the ceremonial guards at the gates of Tol Honeth. They wore polished shirts of chain mail over the customary red tunic, baggy breeches tucked into the tops of knee-high boots, red cloaks, and pointed conical helmets. They nonetheless looked very much like soldiers. They greeted Kal Zakath with crisp military salutes, and, as the Emperor passed through the gilded gates, trumpeteers announced his entrance into the imperial compound with a brazen fanfare.

"I've always hated that," the Mallorean ruler said confidentially to Garion. "The sound grates on my ears."

"What irritated me were the people who used to follow me around hoping that I might need something," Garion told him.

"That's convenient sometimes."

Garion nodded. "Sometimes," he agreed, "but it stopped being convenient when one of them threw a knife at my back."

"Really? I thought your people universally adored you."

"It was a misunderstanding. The young man and I had a talk about it, and he promised not to do it any more."

"That's all?" Zakath exclaimed in astonishment. "You didn't have him executed?"

"Of course not. Once he and I understood each other, he turned out to be extraordinarily loyal." Garion sighed sadly. "He was killed at Thull Mardu."

"I'm sorry, Garion," Zakath said. "We all lost friends at Thull Mardu."

The marble-clad buildings inside the imperial complex were a jumble of conflicting architectural styles, ranging from the severely utilitarian to the elaborately ornate. For some reason Garion was reminded of the vast rabbit warren of King Anheg's palace at Val Alorn. Although Zakath's palace did not consist of one single building, the structures were all linked to each other by column-lined promenades and galleries which passed through parklike grounds studded with statues and marble pavilions.

Zakath led them through the confusing maze toward the

middle of the complex, where a single palace stood in splendid isolation, announcing by its expanse and height that it was the center of all power in boundless Mallorea. "The residence of Kallath the Unifier," the Emperor announced with grand irony, "my revered ancestor."

"Isn't it just a bit overdone?" Ce'Nedra asked tartly, still obviously unwilling to concede the fact that Mal Zeth far outstripped her girlhood home.

"Of course it is," the Mallorean replied, "but the ostentation was necessary. Kallath had to demonstrate to the other generals that he outranked them, and in Mal Zeth one's rank is reflected by the size of one's residence. Kallath was an undisguised knave, a usurper and a man of little personal charm, so he had to assert himself in other ways."

"Don't you just love politics?" Velvet said to Ce'Nedra. "It's the only field where the ego is allowed unrestricted play—as long as the treasury holds out."

Zakath laughed. "I should offer you a position in the government, Margravine Liselle," he said. "I think we need an imperial deflator—someone to puncture all our puffed-up self-importance."

"Why, thank you, your Majesty," she said with a dimpled smile. "If it weren't for my commitments to the family business, I might even consider accepting such a post. It sounds like so much fun."

He sighed with mock regret. "Where were you when I needed a wife?"

"Probably in my cradle, your Majesty," she replied innocently.

He winced. "That was unkind," he accused.

"Yes," she agreed. "True, though," she added clinically.

He laughed again and looked at Polgara. "I'm going to steal her from you, my lady," he declared.

"To be your court jester, Kal Zakath?" Liselle asked, her face no longer lightly amused. "To entertain you with clever insults and banter? Ah, no. I don't think so. There's another side to me that I don't think you'd like very much. They call me 'Velvet' and think of me as a soft-winged butterfly, but this particular butterfly has a poisoned sting—as several people have discovered after it was too late."

"Behave, dear," Polgara murmured to her. "And don't give away trade secrets in a moment of pique."

Velvet lowered her eyes. "Yes, Lady Polgara," she replied meekly.

Zakath looked at her, but did not say anything. He swung down from his saddle, and three grooms dashed to his side to take the reins from his hand. "Come along, then," he said to Garion and the others. "I'd like to show you around." He threw a sly glance at Velvet. "I hope that the Margravine will forgive me if I share every home owner's simple pride in his domicile—no matter how modest."

She laughed a golden little laugh.

Garion dismounted and laid an affectionate hand on Chretienne's proud neck. It was with a pang of almost tangible regret that he handed the reins to a waiting groom.

They entered the palace through broad, gilded doors and found themselves in a vaulted rotunda, quite similar in design to the one in the Emperor's palace in Tol Honeth, though this one lacked the marble busts that made Varana's entryway appear vaguely like a mausoleum. A crowd of officials, military and civilian, awaited their Emperor, each with a sheaf of important-looking documents in his hand.

Zakath sighed as he looked at them. "I'm afraid we'll have to postpone the grand tour," he said. "I'm certain that you'll all want to bathe and change anyway—and perhaps rest a bit before we start the customary formalities. Brador, would you be good enough to show our guests to their rooms and arrange to have a light lunch prepared for them?"

"Of course, your Majesty."

"I think the east wing might be pleasant. It's away from all the scurrying through the halls in this part of the palace."

"My very thought, your Majesty."

119

Zakath smiled at them all. "We'll dine together this evening," he promised. Then he smiled ironically. "An intimate little supper with no more than two or three hundred guests." He looked at the nervous officials clustered nearby and made a wry face. "Until this evening, then."

Brador led them through the echoing marble corridors teeming with servants and minor functionaries.

"Big place," Belgarath observed after they had been walking for perhaps ten minutes. The old man had said very little since they had entered the city, but had ridden in his customary half doze, although Garion was quite sure that very little escaped his grandfather's half-closed eyes.

"Yes," Brador agreed with him. "The first Emperor, Kallath, had grandiose notions at times."

Belgarath grunted. "It's a common affliction among rulers. I think it has something to do with insecurity."

"Tell me, Brador," Silk said, "didn't I hear somewhere that the state secret police are under the jurisdiction of your bureau?"

Brador nodded with a deprecating little smile. "It's one of my many responsibilities, Prince Kheldar," he replied. "I need to know what's going on in the empire in order to stay on top of things, so I had to organize a modest little intelligence service—nothing on nearly the scale of Queen Porenn's, however."

"It will grow with time," Velvet assured him. "Those things always do, for some reason."

The east wing of the palace was set somewhat apart from the rest of the buildings in the complex and it embraced a kind of enclosed courtyard or atrium that was green with exotic flowering plants growing about a mirrorlike pool at its center. Jewellike hummingbirds darted from blossom to blossom, adding splashes of vibrant, moving color.

Polgara's eyes came alight when Brador opened the door to the suite of rooms she was to share with Durnik. Just beyond an arched doorway leading from the main sitting room was a large marble tub sunk into the floor with little tendrils of steam rising from it. "Oh, my," she sighed. "Civilization— at last."

"Just try not to get waterlogged, Pol," Belgarath said.

"Of course not, father," she agreed absently, still eyeing the steaming tub with undisguised longing.

"Is it really all that important, Pol?" he asked her.

"Yes, father," she replied. "It really is."

"It's an irrational prejudice against dirt." He grinned at the rest of them. "I've always been sort of fond of dirt myself."

"Quite obviously," she said. Then she stopped. "Incidentally, Old Wolf," she said critically as they all began to file out, "if your room happens to be similarly equipped, you should make use of the facilities yourself."

"Me?"

"You smell, father."

"No, Pol," he corrected. "I stink. *You* smell."

"Whatever. Go wash, father." She was already absently removing her shoes.

"I've gone as much as ten years at a time without a bath," he declared.

"Yes, father," she said. "I know—only the Gods know how well I know. Now," she said in a very businesslike tone, "if you'll all excuse me . . ." She very deliberately began to unbotton the front of her dress.

The suite of rooms to which Garion and Ce'Nedra were led was, if anything, even more opulent than that shared by Durnik and Polgara. As Garion moved about the several large chambers, examining the furnishings, Ce'Nedra went directly toward the bath, her eyes dreamy and her clothes falling to the floor behind her as she went. His wife's tendency toward casual nudity had occasionally shocked Garion in the past. He did not *personally* object to Ce'Nedra's skin. What disturbed him had been that she had seemed oblivious to the fact that sometimes her unclad state was highly inappropriate. He recalled with a shudder the time when he and the Sendarian ambassador had entered the royal apartment at Riva just as Ce'Nedra was in the process of trying on several new undergarments she had received from her dressmaker that very morning. Quite calmly, she had asked the ambassador's opinion of various of the frilly little things, modeling each in turn for him. The ambassador, a staid and proper Sendarian gentleman in his seventies, received more shocks in that ten minutes than he had encountered in the previous half century, and his next dispatch to King Fulrach had plaintively requested that he be relieved of his post.

"Ce'Nedra, aren't you at least going to close the door?" Garion asked her as she tested the water's temperature with a tentative toe.

"That makes it very hard for us to talk, Garion," she replied reasonably as she stepped down into the tub. "I hate to have to shout."

"Oh?" he said. "I hadn't noticed that."

"Be nice," she told him, sinking into the water with a contented sigh. Curiously she began to unstopper and sniff the crystal decanters lined along one side of the tub which contained, Garion assumed, the assorted condiments with which ladies seasoned their bath water. Some of these she restoppered disapprovingly. Others she liberaly sprinkled into her bath. One or two of them she rubbed on herself in various places.

"What if somebody comes in?" Garion asked her pointedly. "Some official or messenger or servant or something?"

"Well, what if they do?"

He stared at her.

"Garion, darling," she said in that same infuriatingly reasonable tone, "if they hadn't intended for the bath to be used, they wouldn't have prepared it, would they?"

Try as he might, he could not find an answer to that question.

She laid her head back in the water, letting her hair fan out around her face. Then she sat up. "Would you like to wash my back for me?" she asked him.

An hour or so later, after an excellent lunch served by efficient servants, Silk stopped by. The little thief had also bathed and changed clothes once again. His pearl-gray doublet was formally elegant, and he once again dripped jewels. His short, scraggly beard had been neatly crimmed, and there was a faint air of exotic perfume lingering about him. "Appearances," he responded to Garion's quizzical look. "One always wants to put one's best foot forward in a new situation."

"Of course," Garion said dryly.

"Belgarath asked me to stop by," the little man continued. "There's a large room upstairs. We're gathering there for a council of war."

"War?"

"Metaphorically speaking, of course."

"Oh. Of course."

The room at the top of a flight of marble stairs to which Silk led Garion and Ce'Nedra was quite large, and there was a thronelike chair on a dais against the back wall. Garion looked about at the lush furnishings and heavy crimson drapes. "This isn't the throne room, is it?" he asked.

"No," Silk replied. "At least not Kal Zakath's official one. It's here to make visiting royalty feel at home. Some kings get nervous when they don't have official-looking surroundings to play in."

"Oh."

Belgarath sat with his mismatched boots up on a polished table. His hair and beard were slightly damp, evidence that, despite his pretended indifference to bathing, he had in fact followed Polgara's instructions. Polgara and Durnik were talking quietly at one side, and Eriond and Toth were nearby. Velvet and Sadi stood looking out the window at the formal garden lying to the east of Zakath's sprawling palace.

"All right," the old sorcerer said, "I guess we're all here now. I think we need to talk."

—I wouldn't say anything too specific— Silk's fingers said in the gestures of the Drasnian secret language. *—It's almost certain that there are a few spies about—*

Belgarath looked at the far wall, his eyes narrowed as he searched it inch by inch for hidden peepholes. He grunted and looked at Polgara.

"I'll look into it, father," she murmured. Her eyes grew distant, and Garion felt the familiar surge. After a moment she nodded and held up three fingers. She concentrated for a moment, and the quality of the surge changed, seeming somehow languorous. Then she straightened and relaxed her will. "It's all right now," she told them calmly. "They fell asleep."

"That was very smooth, Pol," Durnik said admiringly.

"Why, thank you, dear," she smiled, laying her hand on his.

Belgarath put his feet on the floor and leaned forward. "That's one more thing for us all to keep in mind," he said seriously. "We're likely to be watched all the time that we're here in Mal Zeth, so be careful. Zakath's a sceptic, so we can't really be sure just how much of what we've told him he believes. It's altogether possible that he has other things in mind for us. Right now he needs our help in dealing with Mengha, but he still hasn't entirely abandoned his campaign in Cthol Murgos, and he might want to use us to bring the Alorns and the others into that war on his side. He's also got problems with Urvon and Zandramas. We don't have the time to get caught up in internal Mallorean politics. At the moment, though, we're more or less in his power, so let's be careful."

"We can leave any time we need to, Belgarath," Durnik said confidently.

"I'd rather not do it that way unless we have absolutely no other choice," the old man replied. "Zakath's the kind of man who's very likely to grow testy if he's thwarted, and I don't want to have to creep around dodging his soldiers. It takes too much time and it's dangerous. I'll be a lot happier if we can leave Mal Zeth with his blessing—or at least with his consent."

"I want to get to Ashaba before Zandramas has time to escape again," Garion insisted.

"So do I, Garion," his grandfather said, "but we don't know what she's doing there, so we don't know how long she's likely to stay."

"She's been looking for something, father," Polgara told the old man. "I saw that in her mind when I trapped her back in Rak Hagga."

He looked at her thoughtfully. "Could you get any idea of what it was, Pol?"

She shook her head. "Not specifically," she replied. "I think it's information of some kind. She can't go any further until she finds it. I was able to pick that much out of her thoughts."

"Whatever it is has to be well hidden," he said. "Beldin and I took Ashaba apart after the Battle of Vo Mimbre and we didn't find anything out of the ordinary—if you can accept the idea that Torak's house was in any way ordinary."

"Can we be sure that she's still there with my baby?" Ce'Nedra asked intently.

"No, dear," Polgara told her. "She's taken steps to hide her mind from me. She's rather good, actually."

"Even if she's left Ashaba, the Orb can pick up her trail again," Belgarath said. "The chances are pretty good that she hasn't found what she's looking for, and that effectively nails her down at Ashaba. If she has found it, she won't be hard to follow."

"We're going on to Ashaba, then?" Sadi asked. "What I'm getting at is that our concern about Mengha was just a ruse to get us to Mallorea, wasn't it?"

"I think I'm going to need more information before I make any decisions about that. The situation in northern Karanda is serious, certainly, but let's not lose sight of the fact that our primary goal is Zandramas, and she's at Ashaba. Before I can decide anything, though, I need to know more about what's going on here in Mallorea."

"My department," Silk volunteered.

"And mine," Velvet added.

"I might be able to help a bit as well," Sadi noted with a faint smile. He frowned then. "Seriously though, Belgarath," he continued, "you and your family here represent power. I don't think we're going to have much luck at persuading Kal Zakath to let you go willingly—no matter how cordial he may appear on the surface."

The old man nodded glumly. "It might turn out that way after all," he agreed. Then he looked at Silk, Velvet, and Sadi. "Be careful," he cautioned them. "Don't let your instincts run away with you. I need information, but don't stir up any hornets' nests getting it for me." He looked pointedly at Silk. "I hope I've made myself clear about this," he said. "Don't complicate things just for the fun of it."

"Trust me, Belgarath," Silk replied with a bland smile.

"Of course he trusts you, Kheldar," Velvet assured the little man.

Belgarath looked at his impromptu spy network and shook his head. "Why do I get the feeling that I'm going to regret this?" he muttered.

"I'll keep an eye on them, Belgarath," Sadi promised.

"Of course, but who's going to keep an eye on you?"

CHAPTER SEVEN

That evening they were escorted with some ceremony through the echoing halls of Zakath's palace to a banquet hall that appeared to be only slightly smaller than a parade ground. The hall was approached by way of a broad, curved stairway lined on either side with branched candelabra and liveried trumpeteers. The stairway was obviously designed to facilitate grand entrances. Each new arrival was announced by a stirring fanfare and the booming voice of a gray-haired herald so thin that it almost appeared that a lifetime of shouting had worn him down to a shadow.

Garion and his friends waited in a small antechamber while the last of the local dignitaries were announced. The fussy chief of protocol, a small Melcene with an elaborately trimmed brown beard, wanted them to line up in ascending order of rank, but the difficulties involved in assigning precise rank to the members of this strange group baffled him. He struggled with it, manfully trying to decide if Sorcerer outranked King or Imperial Princess until Garion solved his problem for him by leading Ce'Nedra out onto the landing at the top of the stairs.

"Their Royal Majesties, King Belgarion and Queen Ce'Nedra of Riva," the herald declaimed grandly, and the trumpets blared.

Garion, dressed all in blue and with his ivory-gowned Queen on his arm, paused on the marble landing at the top of the stairs to allow the brightly clad throng below the time to gawk at him. The somewhat dramatic pause was not entirely his idea. Ce'Nedra had dug her fingernails into his arm with a grip of steel and hissed, "Stand still!"

It appeared that Zakath also had some leaning toward the theatrical, since the stunned silence which followed the herald's announcement clearly indicated that the Emperor had given orders that the identity of his guests remain strictly confidential until this very moment. Garion was honest enough with himself to admit that the startled buzz which ran through the crowd below was moderately gratifying.

He began down the stairway, but found himself reined in like a restive horse. "Don't run!" Ce'Nedra commanded under her breath.

"Run?" he objected. "I'm barely moving."

"Do it slower, Garion."

He discovered then that his wife had a truly amazing talent. She could speak without moving her lips! Her smile was gracious, though somewhat lofty, but a steady stream of low-voiced commands issued from that smile.

The buzzing murmur that had filled the banquet hall when they had been announced died into a respectful silence when they reached the foot of the stair, and a vast wave of bows and curtsies rippled through the crowd as they moved along the carpeted promenade leading to the slightly elevated platform upon which sat the table reserved for the Emperor and his special guests, domestic and foreign.

Zakath himself, still in his customary white, but wearing a gold circlet artfully hammered into the form of a wreath woven of leaves as a concession to the formality of the occasion, rose from his seat and came to meet them, thereby avoiding that awkward moment when two men of equal rank meet in public. "So good of you to come, my dear," he said, taking Ce'Nedra's hand and kissing it. He sounded for all the world like a country squire or minor nobleman greeting friends from the neighborhood.

"So good of you to invite us," she replied with a whimsical smile.

"You're looking well, Garion," the Mallorean said, extending his hand and still speaking in that offhand and informal manner.

"Tolerable, Zakath," Garion responded, taking his cue from his host. If Zakath wanted to play, Garion felt that he should show him that he could play, too.

"Would you care to join me at the table?" Zakath asked. "We can chat while we wait for the others to arrive."

"Of course," Garion agreed in a deliberately commonplace tone of voice.

When they reached their chairs, however, his curiosity finally got the better of him. "Why are we playing 'just plain folks'?" he asked Zakath as he held Ce'Nedra's chair for her. "This affair's a trifle formal for talking about the weather and asking after each other's health, wouldn't you say?"

"It's baffling the nobility," Zakath replied with aplomb. "Never do the expected, Garion. The hint that we're old, old friends will set them afire with curiosity and make people who thought that they knew everything just a little less sure of themselves." He smiled at Ce'Nedra. "You're positively ravishing tonight, my dear," he told her.

Ce'Nedra glowed then looked archly at Garion. "Why don't you take a few notes, dear?" she suggested. "You could learn a great deal from his Majesty here." She turned back to Zakath. "You're so very kind to say it," she told him, "but my hair is an absolute disaster." Her expression was faintly tragic as she lightly touched her curls with her fingertips. Actually, her hair was stupendous, with a coronet of braids interwoven with strings of pearls and with a cascade of coppery ringlets spilling down across the front of her left shoulder.

During this polite exchange, the others in their party were being introduced. Silk and Velvet caused quite a stir, he in his jewel-encrusted doublet and she in a gown of lavender brocade.

Ce'Nedra sighed enviously. "I wish I could wear that color," she murmured.

"You can wear any color you want to, Ce'Nedra," Garion told her.

"Are you color-blind, Garion?" she retorted. "A girl with red hair can *not* wear lavender."

"If that's all that's bothering you, I can change the color of your hair anytime you want."

"Don't you dare!" she gasped, her hands going protectively to the cascade of auburn curls at her shoulder.

"Just a suggestion, dear."

The herald at the top of the stairs announced Sadi, Eriond, and Toth as a group, obviously having some difficulty with the fact that the boy and the giant had no rank that he could discern. The next presentation, however, filled his voice with awe and his bony limbs with trembling. "Her Grace, the Duchess of Erat," he declaimed, "Lady Polgara the Sorceress." The silence following that announcement was stunned. "And Goodman Durnik of Sendaria," the herald added, "the man with two lives."

Polgara and the smith descended the stairs to the accompaniment of a profound silence.

The bows and curtsies which acknowledged the legendary

couple were so deep as to resemble genuflections before an altar. Polgara, dressed in her customary silver-trimmed blue, swept through the hall with all the regal bearing of an Empress. She wore a mysterious smile, and the fabled white lock at her brow glowed in the candlelight as she and Durnik approached the platform.

Meanwhile, at the top of the stairs, the herald had shrunk back from the next guest, his eyes wide and his face gone quite pale.

"Just say it," Garion heard his grandfather tell the frightened man. "I'm fairly sure that they'll all recognize the name."

The herald stepped to the marble railing at the front of the landing. "Your Majesty," he said falteringly, "My lords and ladies, I have the unexpected honor to present Belgarath the Sorcerer."

A gasp ran through the hall as the old man, dressed in a cowled robe of soft gray wool, stumped down the stairs with no attempt at grace or dignity. The assembled Mallorean notables pulled back from him as he walked toward the table where the others had already joined Zakath.

About halfway to the imperial platform, however, a blond Melcene girl in a low-cut gown caught his eye. She stood stricken with awe, unable to curtsy or even to move as the most famous man in all the world approached her. Belgarath stopped and looked her up and down quite slowly and deliberately, noting with appreciation just how revealing her gown was. A slow, insinuating smile crept across his face, and his blue eyes twinkled outrageously.

"Nice dress," he told her.

She blushed furiously.

He laughed, reached out, and patted her cheek. "There's a good girl," he said.

"Father," Polgara said firmly.

"Coming, Pol." He chuckled and moved along the carpet toward the table. The pretty Melcene girl looked after him, her eyes wide and her hand pressed to the cheek he had touched.

"Isn't he disgusting?" Ce'Nedra muttered.

"It's just the way he is, dear," Garion disagreed. "He doesn't pretend to be anything else. He doesn't have to."

The banquet featured a number of exotic dishes that Garion could not put a name to and several which he did not even know how to eat. A deceptively innocent-looking rice dish was laced with such fiery seasonings that it brought tears to his eyes and sent his hand clutching for his water goblet.

"Belar, Mara, and Nedra!" Durnik choked as he also groped about in search of water. So far as he could remember, it was the first time Garion had ever heard Durnik swear. He did it surprisingly well.

"Piquant," Sadi commented as he calmly continued to eat the dreadful concoction.

"How can you eat that?" Garion demanded in amazement.

Sadi smiled. "You forget that I'm used to being poisoned, Belgarion. Poison tends to toughen the tongue and fireproof the throat."

Zakath had watched their reactions with some amusement. "I should have warned you," he apologized. "The dish comes from Gandahar, and the natives of that region entertain themselves during the rainy season by trying to build bonfires in each other's stomachs. They're elephant trappers, for the most part, and they pride themselves on their courage."

After the extended banquet, the brown-robed Brador approached Garion. "If your Majesty wouldn't mind," he said, leaning forward so that Garion could hear him over the sounds of laughter and sprightly conversation from nearby tables, "there are a number of people who are most eager to meet you."

Garion nodded politely even though he inwardly winced. He had been through this sort of thing before and knew how tedious it usually became. The Chief of the Bureau of Internal Affairs led him down from the platform into the swirl of brightly clad celebrants, pausing occasionally to exchange greetings with various fellow officials and to introduce Garion. Garion braced himself for an hour or two of total boredom. The plump, bald-headed Brador, however, proved to be an entertaining escort. Though he seemed to be engaging Garion in light conversation, he was in fact providing a succinct and often pointed briefing even as they went.

"We'll be talking with the kinglet of Pallia," he murmured as they approached a group of men in tall, conical felt caps who wore leather which had been dyed an unhealthy-looking green color. "He's a fawning bootlicker, a liar, a coward, and absolutely not to be trusted."

"Ah, there you are, Brador," one of the felt-capped men greeted the Melcene with a forced heartiness.

"Your Highness," Brador replied with a florid bow. "I have the honor to present his Royal Majesty, Belgarion of Riva." He turned to Garion. "Your Majesty, this is his Highness, King Warasin of Pallia."

"Your Majesty," Warasin gushed, bowing awkwardly. He was a man with a narrow, pockmarked face, close-set eyes, and a slack-lipped mouth. His hands, Garion noticed, were not particularly clean.

"Your Highness," Garion replied with a slightly distant note.

"I was just telling the members of my court here that I'd have sooner believed that the sun would rise in the north tomorrow than that the Overlord of the West would appear at Mal Zeth."

"The world is full of surprises."

"By the beard of Torak, you're right, Belgarion—you don't mind if I call you Belgarion, do you, your Majesty?"

"Torak didn't have a beard," Garion corrected shortly.

"What?"

"Torak—he didn't have a beard. At least he didn't when I met him."

"When you—" Warasin's eyes suddenly widened. "Are

you telling me that all those stories about what happened at Cthol Mishrak are actually *true?*" he gasped.

"I'm not sure, your Highness," Garion told him. "I haven't heard all the stories yet. It's been an absolute delight meeting you, old boy," he said, clapping the stunned-looking kinglet on the shoulder with exaggerated camaraderie. "It's a shame that we don't have more time to talk. Coming, Brador?" He nodded to the petty king of Pallia, turned, and led the Melcene away.

"You're very skilled, Belgarion," Brador murmured. "Much more so than I would have imagined, considering—" He hesitated.

"Considering the fact that I look like an unlettered country oaf?" Garion supplied.

"I don't know that I'd put it exactly that way."

"Why not?" Garion shrugged. "It's the truth, isn't it? What was pigeyes back there trying to maneuver the conversation around to? It was pretty obvious that he was leading up to something."

"It's fairly simple," Brador replied. "He recognizes your current proximity to Kal Zakath. All power in Mallorea derives from the throne, and the man who has the Emperor's ear is in a unique position. Warasin is currently having a border dispute with the Prince Regent of Delchin and he probably wants you to put in a good word for him." Brador gave him an amused look. "You're in a position right now to make millions, you know."

Garion laughed. "I couldn't carry it, Brador," he said. "I visited the royal treasury at Riva once, and I know how much a million weighs. Who's next?"

"The Chief of the Bureau of Commerce—an unmitigated, unprincipled ass. Like most Bureau Chiefs."

Garion smiled. "And what does *he* want?"

Brador tugged thoughtfully at one earlobe. "I'm not entirely certain. I've been out of the country. Vasca's a devious one, though, so I'd be careful of him."

"I'm always careful, Brador."

The Baron Vasca, Chief of the Bureau of Commerce, was wrinkled and bald. He wore the brown robe that seemed to be almost the uniform of the bureaucracy, and the gold chain of his office seemed almost too heavy for his thin neck. Though at first glance he appeared to be old and frail, his eyes were as alert and shrewd as those of a vulture. "Ah, your Majesty," he said after they had been introduced, "I'm so pleased to meet you at last."

"My pleasure, Baron Vasca," Garion said politely.

They chatted together for some time, and Garion could not detect anything in the baron's conversation that seemed in the least bit out of the ordinary.

"I note that Prince Kheldar of Drasnia is a member of your party," the baron said finally.

"We're old friends. You're acquainted with Kheldar then, Baron?"

"We've had a few dealings together—the customary permits and gratuities, you understand. For the most part, though, he tends to avoid contact with the authorities."

"I've noticed that from time to time," Garion said.

"I was certain that you would have. I won't keep your Majesty. Many others here are eager to meet you, and I wouldn't want to be accused of monopolizing your time. We must talk again soon." The baron turned to the Chief of the Bureau of Internal Affairs. "So good of you to introduce us, my dear Brador," he said.

"It's nothing, my dear Baron," Brador replied. He took Garion by the arm, and they moved away from Vasca.

"What was that all about?" Garion asked.

"I'm not altogether sure," Brador replied, "but whatever he wanted, he seems to have gotten."

"We didn't really say anything."

"I know. That's what worries me. I think I'll have my old friend Vasca watched. He's managed to arouse my curiosity."

During the next couple of hours Garion met two more gaudily dressed petty kings, a fair number of more soberly garbed bureaucrats, and a sprinkling of semi-important nobles and their ladies. Many of them, of course, wanted nothing more than to be seen talking to him so that later they could say in a casual, offhand fashion, "I was talking with Belgarion the other day, and he said—" Others made some point of suggesting that a private conversation might be desirable at some later date. A few even tried to set up specific appointments.

It was rather late when Velvet finally came to his rescue. She approached the place where Garion was trapped by the royal family of Peldane, a stodgy little kinglet in a mustard yellow turban, his simpering, scrawny wife in a pink gown that clashed horribly with her orange hair, and three spoiled royal brats who spent their time whining and hitting each other. "Your Majesty," the blond girl said with a curtsy, "Your wife asks your permission to retire."

"Asks?"

"She's feeling slightly unwell."

Garion gave her a grateful look. "I must go to her at once, then," he said quickly. He turned to the Peldane royalty. "I hope you'll all excuse me," he said to them.

"Of course, Belgarion," the kinglet replied graciously.

"And please convey our regards to your lovely wife," the queenlet added.

The royal brood continued to howl and kick each other.

"You looked a bit harried," Velvet murmured as she led Garion away.

"I could kiss you."

"Now that's an interesting suggestion."

Garion glanced sourly back over his shoulder. "They should drown those three little monsters and raise a litter of puppies instead," he muttered.

"Piglets," she corrected.

He looked at her.

"At least they could sell the bacon," she explained. "That way the effort wouldn't be a total loss."

"Is Ce'Nedra really ill?"

"Of course not. She's made as many conquests as she wants to this evening, that's all. She wants to save a few for future occasions. Now it's time for the grand withdrawal, leaving a horde of disappointed admirers, who were all panting to meet her, crushed with despair."

"That's a peculiar way to look at it."

She laughed affectionately, linking her arm in his. "Not if you're a woman, it's not."

The following morning shortly after breakfast, Garion and Belgarath were summoned to meet with Zakath and Brador in the Emperor's private study. The room was large and comfortable, lined with books and maps and with deeply upholstered chairs clustered about low tables. It was a warm day outside, and the windows stood open, allowing a blossom-scented spring breeze to ruffle the curtains.

"Good morning, gentlemen," Zakath greeted them as they were escorted into the room. "I hope you slept well."

"Once I managed to get Ce'Nedra out of the tub." Garion laughed. "It's just a bit too convenient, I think. Would you believe that she bathed three times yesterday?"

"Mal Zeth is very hot and dusty in the summertime," Zakath said. "The baths make it bearable."

"How does the hot water get to them?" Garion asked curiously. "I haven't seen anyone carrying pails up and down the halls."

"It's piped in under the floors," the Emperor replied. "The artisan who devised the system was rewarded with a baronetcy."

"I hope you don't mind if we steal the idea. Durnik's already making sketches."

"I think it's unhealthy myself," Belgarath said. "Bathing should be done out of doors—in cold water. All this pampering softens people." He looked at Zakath. "I'm sure you didn't

137

ask us here to discuss the philosophical ramifications of bathing, though."

"Not unless you really want to, Belgarath," Zakath replied. He straightened in his chair. "Now that we've all had a chance to rest from our journey, I thought that maybe it was time for us to get to work. Brador's people have made their reports to him, and he's ready to give us his assessment of the current situation in Karanda. Go ahead, Brador."

"Yes, your Majesty." The plump, bald Melcene rose from his chair and crossed to a very large map of the Mallorean continent hanging on the wall. The map was exquisitely colored with blue lakes and rivers, green prairies, darker green forests and brown, white-topped mountains. Instead of simply being dots on the map, the cities were represented by pictures of buildings and fortifications. The Mallorean highway system, Garion noted, was very nearly as extensive as the Tolnedran network in the west.

Brador cleared his throat, fought for a moment with one of Zakath's ferocious kittens for the long pointer he wanted to use, and began. "As I reported to you in Rak Hagga," he said, "a man named Mengha came out of this immense forest to the north of Lake Karanda some six months ago." He tapped the representation of a large belt of trees stretching from the Karandese range to the Mountains of Zamad. "We know very, very little about his background."

"That's not entirely true, Brador," Belgarath disagreed. "Cyradis told us that he's a Grolim priest—or he used to be. That puts us in a position to deduce quite a bit."

"I'd be interested to hear whatever you can come up with," Zakath said.

Belgarath squinted around the room, and his eyes fixed on several full crystal decanters and some polished glasses sitting on a sideboard across the room. "Do you mind?" he asked, pointing at the decanters. "I think better with a glass in my hand."

"Help yourself," Zakath replied.

The old man rose, crossed to the sideboard, and poured himself a glass of ruby-red wine. "Garion?" he asked, holding out the decanter.

"No, thanks all the same, Grandfather."

Belgarath replaced the crystal stopper with a clink and began to pace up and down on the blue carpet. "All right," he said. "We know that demon worship persists in the back country of Karanda, even though the Grolim priests tried to stamp out the practice when the Karands were converted to the worship of Torak in the second millennium. We also know that Mengha was a priest himself. Now, if the Grolims here in Mallorea reacted in the same way that the ones in Cthol Murgos did when they heard about the death of Torak, then we know that they were thoroughly demoralized. The fact that Urvon spent several years scrambling around trying to find prophecies that would hint at the possibility of a justification for keeping the Church intact is fairly good evidence that he was faced with almost universal despair in the ranks of the Grolims." He paused to sip at his wine. "Not bad," he said to Zakath approvingly. "Not bad at all."

"Thank you."

"Now," the old man continued, "there are many possible reactions to religious despair. Some men go mad, some men try to lose themselves in various forms of dissipation, some men refuse to admit the truth and try to keep the old forms alive. A few men, however, go in search of some new kind of religion—usually something the exact opposite of what they believed before. Since the Grolim Church in Karanda had concentrated for eons on eradicating demon worship, it's only logical that a few of the despairing priests would seek out demon-masters in the hope of learning their secrets. Remember, if you can actually control a demon, it gives you a great deal of power, and the hunger for power has always been at the core of the Grolim mentality."

"It does fit together, Ancient One," Brador admitted.

"I thought so myself. All right, Torak is dead, and Mengha

suddenly finds that his theological ground has been cut out from under him. He probably goes through a period of doing all the things that he wasn't allowed to do as a priest—drinking, wenching, that sort of thing. But if you do things to excess, eventually they become empty and unsatisfying. Even debauchery can get boring after a while."

"Aunt Pol will be amazed to hear that you said that," Garion said.

"You just keep it to yourself," Belgarath told him. "Our arguments about my bad habits are the cornerstone of our relationship." He took another sip of his wine. "This is really excellent," he said, holding up the glass to admire the color of the wine in the sunlight. "Now then, here we have Mengha waking up some morning with a screaming headache, a mouth that tastes like a chicken coop, and a fire in his stomach that no amount of water will put out. He has no real reason to go on living. He might even take out his sacrificial gutting knife and set the point against his chest."

"Isn't your speculation going a bit far afield?" Zakath asked.

Belgarath laughed. "I used to be a professional storyteller," he apologized. "I can't stand to let a good story slip by without a few artistic touches. All right, maybe he did or maybe he didn't think about killing himself. The point is that he had reached the absolute rock bottom. That's when the idea of demons came to him. Raising demons is almost as dangerous as being the first man up the scaling ladder during an assault on a fortified city, but Mengha has nothing to lose. So, he journeys into the forest up there, finds a Karandese magician, and somehow persuades him to teach him the art—if that's what you want to call it. It takes him about a dozen years to learn all the secrets."

"How did you arrive at that number?" Brador asked.

Belgarath shrugged. "It's been fourteen years since the death of Torak—or thereabouts. No normal man can seriously mistreat himself for more than a couple of years before he starts to fall apart, so it was probably about twelve years ago that Mengha went in search of a magician to give him instruction. Then, once he's learned all the secrets, he kills his teacher, and—"

"Wait a minute," Zakath objected. "Why would he do that?"

"His teacher knew too much about him, and *he* could also raise demons to send after our defrocked Grolim. Then there's the fact that the arrangement between teacher and pupil in these affairs involves lifetime servitude enforced with a curse. Mengha could not leave his master until the old man was dead."

"How do you know so much about this, Belgarath?" Zakath asked.

"I went through it all among the Morindim a few thousand years ago. I wasn't doing anything very important and I was curious about magic."

"Did you kill your master?"

"No—well, not exactly. When I left him, he sent his familiar demon after me. I took control of it and sent it back to him."

"And it killed him?"

"I assume so. They usually do. Anyway, getting back to Mengha. He arrives at the gates of Calida about six months ago and raises a whole army of demons. Nobody in his right mind raises more than one at a time because they're too difficult to control." He frowned, pacing up and down staring at the floor. "The only thing I can think of is that somehow he's managed to raise a Demon Lord and get it under control."

"Demon Lord?" Garion asked.

"They have rank, too—just as humans do. If Mengha has a grip on a Demon Lord, then it's that creature that's calling up the army of lesser demons." He refilled his glass, looking faintly satisfied with himself. "That's probably fairly close to Mengha's life story," he said, sitting down again.

"A virtuoso performance, Belgarath," Zakath congratulated him.

"Thank you," the old man replied. "I thought so myself." He looked at Brador. "Now that we know him, why don't you tell us what he's been up to?"

Brador once again took his place beside the map, fending off the same kitten with his pointer. "After Mengha took Calida, word of his exploits ran all through Karanda," he began. "It appears that the worship of Torak was never really very firmly ingrained in the Karands to begin with, and about the only thing that kept them in line was their fear of the sacrificial knives of the Grolims."

"Like the Thulls?" Garion suggested.

"Very much so, your Majesty. Once Torak was dead, however, and his Church in disarray, the Karands began to revert. The old shrines began to reappear, and the old rituals came back into practice." Brador shuddered. "Hideous rites," he said. "Obscene."

"Even worse than the Grolim rite of sacrifice?" Garion asked mildly.

"There was some justification for that, Garion," Zakath objected. "It was an honor to be chosen, and the victims went under the knife willingly."

"Not any of them that I ever saw," Garion disagreed.

"We can discuss comparative theology some other time," Belgarath told them. "Go on, Brador."

"Once the Karands heard about Mengha," the Melcene official continued, "they began to flock to Calida to support him and to enlist themselves on the side of the demons. There's always been a subterranean independence movement in the seven kingdoms of Karanda, and many hotheads there believe that the demons offer the best hope of throwing off the yoke of Angarak oppression." He looked at the Emperor. "No offense intended, your Majesty," he murmured.

"None taken, Brador," Zakath assured him.

"Naturally, the little kinglets in Karanda tried to keep their people from joining Mengha. The loss of subjects is always painful to a ruler. The army—our army—was also alarmed by the hordes of Karands flocking to Mengha's banner, and they tried to block off borders and the like. But, since a large portion of the army was in Cthol Murgos with his Majesty here, the troops in Karanda just didn't have the numbers. The Karands either slipped around them or simply overwhelmed them. Mengha's army numbers almost a million by now—ill-equipped and poorly trained, perhaps, but a million is a significant number, even if they're armed with sticks. Not only Jenno but also Ganesia are totally under Mengha's domination, and he's on the verge of overwhelming Katakor. Once he succeeds there, he'll inevitably move on Pallia and Delchin. If he isn't stopped, he'll be knocking on the gates of Mal Zeth by Erastide."

"Is he unleashing his demons in these campaigns?" Belgarath asked intently.

"Not really," Brador replied. "After what happened at Calida, there's no real need for that. The sight of them alone is usually enough to spring open the gates of any city he's taken so far. He's succeeded with remarkably little actual fighting."

The old man nodded. "I sort of thought that might have been the case. A demon is very hard to get back under control once it's tasted blood."

"It's not really the demons that are causing the problems," Brador continued. "Mengha's flooded all the rest of Karanda with his agents, and the stories that they're circulating are whipping previously uncommitted people into a frenzy." He looked at the Emperor. "Would you believe that we actually caught one of his missionaries in the Karandese barracks right here in Mal Zeth?" he said.

Zakath looked up sharply. "How did he get in?" he demanded.

"He disguised himself as a corporal returning from convalescent leave at home," Brador replied. "He'd even gone so far as to give himself a wound to make his story look authentic. It was very believable the way he cursed Murgos."

"What did you do to him?"

"Unfortunately, he didn't survive the questioning," Brador said, frowning. He bent to remove the kitten from around his ankle.

"Unfortunately?"

"I had some interesting plans for him. I take it rather personally when someone manages to circumvent my secret police. It's a matter of professional pride."

"What do you advise, then?" Zakath asked.

Brador began to pace. "I'm afraid that you're going to have to bring the army back from Cthol Murgos, your Majesty," he said. "You can't fight a war on two fronts."

"Absolutely out of the question." Zakath's tone was adamant.

"I don't think we have much choice," Brador told him. "Almost half of the forces left here in Mallorea are of Karandese origin, and it's my considered opinion that to rely upon them in any kind of confrontation with Mengha would be sheer folly."

Zakath's face grew bleak.

"Put it this way, your Majesty," Brador said smoothly. "If you weaken your forces in Cthol Murgos, it's quite possible that you'll lose Rak Cthaka and maybe Rak Gorut, but if you don't bring the army home, you're going to lose Mal Zeth."

Zakath glared at him.

"There's still time to consider the matter, Sire," Brador added in a reasonable tone of voice. "This is only *my* assessment of the situation. I'm sure you'll want confirmation of what I've said from military intelligence, and you'll need to consult with the High Command."

"No," Zakath said bluntly. "The decision is mine." He scowled at the floor. "All right, Brador, we'll bring the army home. Go tell the High Command that I want to see them all at once."

"Yes, your Majesty."

Garion had risen to his feet. "How long will it take to ship your troops back from Cthol Murgos?" he asked with a sinking feeling.

"About three months," Zakath replied.

"I can't wait that long, Zakath."

"I'm very sorry, Garion, but none of us has any choice. Neither you nor I will leave Mal Zeth until the army gets here."

CHAPTER EIGHT

The following morning, Silk came early to the rooms Garion shared with Ce'Nedra. The little man once again wore his doublet and hose, though he had removed most of his jewelry. Over his arm he carried a pair of Mallorean robes, the lightweight, varicolored garments worn by most of the citizens of Mal Zeth. "Would you like to go into the city?" he asked Garion.

"I don't think they'll let us out of the palace."

"I've already taken care of that. Brador gave his permission—provided that we don't try to get away from the people who are going to be following us."

"That's a depressing thought. I hate being followed."

"You get used to it."

"Have you got anything specific in mind, or is this just a sight-seeing tour?"

"I want to stop by our offices here and have a talk with our factor."

Garion gave him a puzzled look.

"The agent who handles things for us here in Mal Zeth."

"Oh. I hadn't heard the word before."

"That's because you aren't in business. Our man here is named Dolmar. He's a Melcene—very efficient, and he doesn't steal too much."

"I'm not sure that I'd enjoy listening to you talk business," Garion said.

Silk looked around furtively. "You might learn all kinds of things, Garion," he said, but his fingers were already moving rapidly.—*Dolmar can give us a report on what's really happening in Karanda*— he gestured.—*I think you'd better come along*—

"Well," Garion said with slightly exaggerated acquiescence, "maybe you're right. Besides, the walls here are beginning to close in on me."

"Here," Silk said, holding out one of the robes, "wear this."

"It's not really cold, Silk."

"The robe isn't to keep you warm. People in western clothing attract a lot of attention on the streets of Mal Zeth, and I don't like being stared at." Silk grinned quickly. "It's very hard to pick pockets when everybody in the street is watching you. Shall we go?"

The robe Garion put on was open at the front and hung straight from his shoulders to his heels. It was a serviceable outer garment with deep pockets at the sides. The material of which it was made was quite thin, and it flowed out behind him as he moved around. He went to the door of the adjoining room. Ce'Nedra was combing her hair, still damp from her morning bath.

"I'm going into the city with Silk," he told her. "Do you need anything?"

She thought about that. "See if you can find me a comb," she said, holding up the one she had been using. "Mine's starting to look a little toothless."

"All right." He turned to leave.

"As long as you're going anyway," she added, "why don't you pick me up a bolt of silk cloth—teal green, if you can find it. I'm told that there's a dressmaker here in the palace with a great deal of skill."

"I'll see what I can do." He turned again.

"And perhaps a few yards of lace—not too ornate, mind. Tasteful."

"Anything else?"

She smiled at him. "Buy me a surprise of some kind. I love surprises."

"A comb, a bolt of teal green silk, a few yards of tasteful lace, and a surprise." He ticked them off on his fingers.

"Get me one of those robes like you're wearing, too."

He waited.

She pursed her lips thoughtfully. "That's all I can think of, Garion, but you and Silk might ask Liselle and Lady Polgara if they need anything."

He sighed.

"It's only polite, Garion."

"Yes, dear. Maybe I'd better make out a list."

Silk's face was blandly expressionless as Garion came back out.

"Well?" Garion asked him.

"I didn't say anything."

"Good."

They started out the door.

"Garion," Ce'Nedra called after him.

"Yes, dear?"

"See if you can find some sweetmeats, too."

Garion went out into the hall behind Silk and firmly closed the door behind him.

"You handle that sort of thing very well," Silk said.

"Practice."

Velvet added several items to Garion's growing list, and Polgara several more. Silk looked at the list as they walked down the long, echoing hallway toward the main part of the palace. "I wonder if Brador would lend us a pack mule," he murmured.

"Quit trying to be funny."

"Would I do that?"

"Why were we talking with our fingers back there?"

"Spies."

"In our private quarters?" Garion was shocked, remembering Ce'Nedra's sometimes aggressive indifference to the way she was dressed—or not dressed—when they were alone.

"Private places are where the most interesting secrets are to be found. No spy ever passes up the opportunity to peek into a bedroom."

"That's disgusting!" Garion exclaimed, his cheeks burning.

"Of course it is. Fairly common practice, though."

They passed through the vaulted rotunda just inside the gold-plated main door of the palace and walked out into a bright spring morning touched with a fragrant breeze.

"You know," Silk said, "I like Mal Zeth. It always smells so good. Our office here is upstairs over a bakery, and some mornings the smells from downstairs almost make me swoon."

There was only the briefest of pauses at the gates of the imperial complex. A curt gesture from one of the pair of unobtrusive men who were following them advised the gate guards that Silk and Garion were to be allowed to pass into the city.

"Policemen do have their uses sometimes," Silk said as they started down a broad boulevard leading away from the palace.

149

The streets of Mal Zeth teemed with people from all over the empire and not a few from the West was well. Garion was a bit surprised to see a sprinkling of Tolnedran mantles among the varicolored robes of the local populace, and here and there were Sendars, Drasnians, and a fair number of Nadraks. There were, however, no Murgos. "Busy place," he noted to Silk.

"Oh, yes. Mal Zeth makes Tol Honeth look like a country fair and Camaar like a village market."

"It's the biggest commercial center in the world, then?"

"No. That's Melcene—of course Melcene concentrates on money instead of goods. You can't even buy a tin pot in Melcene. All you can buy there is money."

"Silk, how can you make any kind of profit buying money with money?"

"It's a little complicated." Silk's eyes narrowed. "Do you know something?" he said. "If you could put your hands on the royal treasury of Riva, I could show you how to double it in six months on Basa Street in Melcene—with a nice commission for the both of us thrown in for good measure."

"You want me to speculate with the royal treasury? I'd have an open insurrection on my hands if anybody ever found out about it."

"That's the secret, Garion. You don't let anybody find out."

"Have you ever had an honest thought in your entire life?"

The little man thought about it. "Not that I recall, no," he replied candidly. "But then, I've got a well-trained mind."

The offices of the commercial empire of Silk and Yarblek here in Mal Zeth were, as the little man had indicated, rather modest and were situated above a busy bakeshop. Access to that second floor was by way of an outside stairway rising out of a narrow side street. As Silk started up those stairs, a certain tension that Garion had not even been aware of seemed to flow out of his friend. "I *hate* not being able to talk freely," he said. "There are so many spies in Mal Zeth that every

150

word you say here is delivered to Brador in triplicate before you get your mouth shut."

"There are bound to be spies around your office, too."

"Of course, but they can't hear anything. Yarblek and I had a solid foot of cork built into the floors, ceilings, and walls."

"Cork?"

"It muffles all sounds."

"Didn't that cost a great deal?"

Silk nodded. "But we made it all back during the first week we were here by managing to keep certain negotiations secret." He reached into an inside pocket and took out a large brass key. "Let's see if I can catch Dolmar with his hands in the cash box," he half whispered.

"Why? You already know that he's stealing from you."

"Certainly I do, but if I can catch him, I can reduce his year-end bonus."

"Why not just pick his pocket?"

Silk tapped the brass key against his cheek as he thought about it. "No," he decided finally. "That's not really good business. A relationship like this is founded on trust."

Garion began to laugh.

"You have to draw the line *somewhere*, Garion." Silk quietly slipped his brass key into the lock and slowly turned it. Then he abruptly shoved the door open and jumped into the room.

"Good morning, Prince Kheldar," the man seated behind a plain table said quite calmly. "I've been expecting you."

Silk looked a bit crestfallen.

The man sitting at the table was a thin Melcene with crafty, close-set eyes, thin lips, and scraggly, mud-brown hair. He had the kind of face that one instantly distrusts.

Silk straightened. "Good morning, Dolmar," he said. "This is Belgarion of Riva."

"Your Majesty." Dolmar rose and bowed.

"Dolmar."

Silk closed the door and pulled a pair of chairs out from the brown, cork-sheathed wall. Although the floor was of ordinary boards, the way that all sounds of walking or moving pieces of furniture were muted testified to the thickness of the cork lying beneath.

"How's business?" Silk asked, seating himself and pushing the other chair to Garion with his foot.

"We're paying the rent," Dolmar replied cautiously.

"I'm sure that the baker downstairs is overjoyed. Specifics, Dolmar. I've been away from Mal Zeth for quite a while. Stun me with how well my investments here are doing."

"We're up fifteen percent from last year."

"That's all?" Silk sounded disappointed.

"We've just made quite a large investment in inventory. If you take the current value of that into account, the number would be much closer to forty percent."

"That's more like it. Why are we accumulating inventory?"

"Yarblek's instructions. He's at Mal Camat right now arranging for ships to take the goods to the west. I expect that he'll be here in a week or so—he and that foulmouthed wench of his." Dolmar stood up, carefully gathered the documents from the table, and crossed to an iron stove sitting in the corner. He bent, opened the stove door, and calmly laid the parchment sheets on the small fire inside.

To Garion's amazement, Silk made no objection to his factor's blatant incendiarism. "We've been looking into the wool market," the Melcene reported as he returned to his now-empty table. "With the growing mobilization, the Bureau of Military Procurement is certain to need wool for uniforms, cloaks, and blankets. If we can buy up options from all the major sheep producers, we'll control the market and perhaps break the stranglehold that the Melcene consortium has on military purchases. If we can just get our foot in the door of the Bureau, I'm sure that we can get a chance to bid on all sorts of contracts."

Silk was pulling at his long, pointed nose, his eyes narrowed in thought. "Beans," he said shortly.

"I beg your pardon?"

"Look into the possibility of tying up this year's bean crop. A soldier can live in a worn-out uniform, but he has to eat. If we control the bean crop—and maybe coarse flour as well— the Bureau of Military Procurement won't have any choice. They'll *have* to come to us."

"Very shrewd, Prince Kheldar."

"I've been around for a while," Silk replied.

"The consortium is meeting this week in Melcene," the factor reported. "They'll be setting the prices of common items. We really want to get our hands on that price list if we can."

"I'm in the palace," Silk said. "Maybe I can pry it out of somebody."

"There's something else you should know, Prince Kheldar. Word has leaked out that the consortium is also going to propose certain regulations to Baron Vasca of the Bureau of Commerce. They'll present them under the guise of protecting the economy, but the fact of the matter is that they're aimed at you and Yarblek. They want to restrict western merchants who gross more than ten million a year to two or three enclaves on the west coast. That wouldn't inconvenience smaller merchants, but it would probably put us out of business."

"Can we bribe someone to put a stop to it?"

"We're already paying Vasca a fortune to leave us alone, but the consortium is throwing money around like water. It's possible that the baron won't stay bribed."

"Let me nose around inside the palace a bit," Silk said, "before you double Vasca's bribe or anything."

"Bribery's the standard procedure, Prince Kheldar."

"I know, but sometimes blackmail works even better." Silk looked over at Garion, then back at his factor. "What do you know about what's happening in Karanda?" he asked.

"Enough to know that it's disastrous for business. All sorts of perfectly respectable and otherwise sensible merchants are closing up their shops and flocking off to Calida to enlist in Mengha's army. Then they march around in circles singing

'Death to the Angaraks' while they wave rusty swords in the air."

"Any chance of selling them weapons?" Silk asked quickly.

"Probably not. There's not enough real money in northern Karanda to make it worthwhile to try to deal with them, and the political unrest has closed down all the mines. The market in gem stones has just about dried up."

Silk nodded glumly. "What's really going on up there, Dolmar?" he asked. "The reports Brador passed on to us were sort of sketchy."

"Mengha arrived at the gates of Calida with demons." The factor shrugged. "The Karands went into hysterics and then fell down in the throes of religious ecstasy."

"Brador told us about certain atrocities," Garion said.

"I expect that the reports he received were a trifle exaggerated, your Majesty," Dolmar replied. "Even the most well trained observer is likely to multiply mutilated corpses lying in the streets by ten. In point of fact, the vast majority of the casualties were either Melcene or Angarak. Mengha's demons rather scrupulously avoided killing Karands—except by accident. The same has held true in every city that he's taken so far." He scratched at his head, his close-set eyes narrowing. "It's really very shrewd, you know. The Karands see Mengha as a liberator and his demons as an invincible spearhead of their army. I can't swear to his *real* motives, but those barbarians up there believe that he's a savior come to sweep Karanda clean of Angaraks and the Melcene bureaucracy. Give him another six months or so, and he'll accomplish what no one has ever been able to do before."

"What's that?" Silk asked.

"Unify all of Karanda."

"Does he use his demons in the assault on every city he takes?" Garion asked, wanting to confirm what Brador had told them.

Dolmar shook his head. "Not any more, your Majesty. After what happened at Calida and several other towns he took early in his campaign, he doesn't really have to. All he's been doing lately is march up to the city. The demons are with him, of course, but they don't have to do anything but stand there looking awful. The Karands butcher all the Angaraks and Melcenes in town, throw open their gates, and welcome him with open arms. Then his demons vanish." He thought a moment. "He always has one particular one of them with him, though— a shadowy sort of creature that doesn't seem to be gigantic the way they're supposed to be. He stands directly behind Mengha's left shoulder at any public appearance."

A sudden thought occurred to Garion. "Are they desecrating Grolim temples?" he asked.

Dolmar blinked. "No," he replied with some surprise, "as a matter of fact, they're not—and they don't seem to be any Grolims among the dead, either. Of course it's possible that Urvon pulled all his Grolims out of Karanda when the trouble started."

"That's unlikely," Garion disagreed. "Mengha's arrival at Calida came without any kind of warning. The Grolims wouldn't have had time to escape." He stared up at the ceiling, thinking hard.

"What is it, Garion?" Silk asked.

"I just had a chilling sort of notion. We know that Mengha's a Grolim, right?"

"I didn't know that," Dolmar said with some surprise.

"We got a bit of inside information," Silk told him. "Go ahead, Garion."

"Urvon spends all of his time in Mal Yaska, doesn't he?"

Silk nodded. "So I've heard. He doesn't want Beldin to catch him out in the open."

"Wouldn't that make him a fairly ineffective leader? All right, then. Let's suppose that Mengha went through his period of despair after the death of Torak and then found a magician to teach him how to raise demons. When he comes back, he offers his former Grolim brethren an alternative to Urvon—along with access to a kind of power they'd never

155

experienced before. A demon in the hands of an illiterate and fairly stupid Karandese magician is one thing, but a demon controlled by a Grolim sorcerer would be much worse, I think. If Mengha is gathering disaffected Grolims around him and training them in the use of magic, we have a *big* problem. I don't think I'd care to face a legion of Chabats, would you?"

Silk shuddered. "Not hardly," he replied fervently.

"He has to be uprooted then," Dolmar said, "and soon."

Garion made a sour face. "Zakath won't move until he gets his army back from Cthol Murgos—about three months from now."

"In three months, Mengha's going to be invincible," the factor told him.

"Then we'll have to move now," Garion said, "with Zakath or without him."

"How do you plan to get out of the city?" Silk asked.

"We'll let Belgarath work that out." Garion looked at Silk's agent. "Can you tell us anything else?" he asked.

Dolmar tugged at his nose in a curious imitation of Silk's habitual gesture. "It's only a rumor," he said.

"Go ahead."

"I've been getting some hints out of Karanda that Mengha's familiar demon is named Nahaz."

"Is that significant?"

"I can't be altogether sure, your Majesty. When the Grolims went into Karanda in the second millennium, they destroyed all traces of Karandese mythology, and no one has ever tried to record what few bits and pieces remained. All that's left is a hazy oral tradition, but the rumors I've heard say that Nahaz was the tribal demon of the original Karands who migrated into the region before the Angaraks came to Mallorea. The Karands follow Mengha not only because he's a political leader, but also because he's resurrected the closest thing they've ever had to a God of their own."

"A Demon Lord?" Garion asked him.

"That's a very good way to describe him, your Majesty. If

the rumors are true, the demon Nahaz has almost unlimited power."

"I was afraid you were going to say that."

Later, when they were back out in the street, Garion looked curiously at Silk. "Why didn't you object when he burned those documents?" he asked.

"It's standard practice." the rat-faced man shrugged. "We never keep anything in writing. Dolmar has everything committed to memory."

"Doesn't that make it fairly easy for him to steal from you?"

"Of course, but he keeps his thievery within reasonable limits. If the Bureau of Taxation got its hands on written records, though, it could be a disaster. Do you want to go back to the palace now?"

Garion took out his list. "No," he said. "We've got to take care of this first." He looked glumly at the sheet. "I wonder how we're going to carry it all."

Silk glanced back over his shoulder at the two unobtrusive spies trailing along behind them. "Help is only a few paces away." He laughed. "As I said before, there are many uses for policemen."

During the next several days, Garion discovered that the imperial palace at Mal Zeth was unlike any court in the West. Since all power rested in Zakath's hands, the bureaucrats and palace functionaries contested with each other for the Emperor's favor and strove with oftentimes wildly complicated plots to discredit their enemies. The introduction of Silk, Velvet, and Sadi into this murky environment added whole new dimensions to palace intrigue. The trio rather casually pointed out the friendship between Garion and Zakath and let it be generally known that they had the Rivan King's complete trust. Then they sat back to await developments.

The officials and courtiers in the imperial palace were quick to grasp the significance and the opportunities implicit in this new route to the Emperor's ear. Perhaps even without formally discussing it, the trio of westerners neatly divided up

the possible spheres of activity. Silk concentrated his attention
on commercial matters, Velvet dabbled in politics, and Sadi
delicately dipped his long-fingered hands into the world of
high-level crime. Though all of them subtly let it be known
that they were susceptible to bribery, they also expressed a
willingness to pass along various requests in exchange for information. Thus, almost by accident, Garion found that he
had a very efficient espionage apparatus at his disposal. Silk
and Velvet manipulated the fears, ambitions, and open greed
of those who contacted them with a musicianlike skill, delicately playing the increasingly nervous officials like well-
tuned instruments. Sadi's methods, derived from his extensive experience in Salmissra's court, were in some instances
even more subtle, but in others, painfully direct. The contents
of his red leather case brought premium prices, and several
high-ranking criminals, men who literally owned whole pla-
toons of bureaucrats and even generals, quite suddenly died
under suspicious circumstances—one of them even toppling
over with a blackened face and bulging eyes in the presence
of the Emperor himself.

Zakath, who had watched the activities of the three with
a certain veiled amusement, drew the line at that point. He
spoke quite firmly with Garion about the matter during their
customary evening meeting on the following day.

"I don't really mind what they're doing, Garion," he said,
idly stroking the head of an orange kitten who lay purring in
his lap. "They're confusing all the insects who scurry around
in the dark corners of the palace, and a confused bug can't
consolidate his position. I like to keep all these petty boot-
lickers frightened and off balance, since it makes it easier to
control them. I really must object to poison, however. It's far
too easy for an unskilled poisoner to make mistakes."

"Sadi could poison one specific person at a banquet with
a hundred guests," Garion assured him.

"I have every confidence in his ability," Zakath agreed,
"but the trouble is that he's not doing the actual poisoning

himself. He's selling his concoctions to rank amateurs. There are *some* people here in the palace that I need. Their identities are general knowledge, and that keeps the daggers out of their entrails. A mistake with some poison, however, could wipe out whole branches of my government. Could you ask him not to sell any more of it here in the palace? I'd speak to him personally, but I don't want it to seem like an official reprimand."

"I'll have a talk with him," Garion promised.

"I'd appreciate it, Garion." The Emperor's eyes grew sly. "Just the poisons, though. I find the effects of some of his other compounds rather amusing. Just yesterday, I saw an eighty-five-year-old general in hot pursuit of a young chambermaid. The old fool hasn't had that kind of thought for a quarter of a century. And the day before that, the Chief of the Bureau of Public Works—a pompus ass who makes me sick just to look at him—tried for a solid half hour in front of dozens of witnesses to walk up the side of a building. I haven't laughed so hard in years."

"Nyissan elixirs do strange things to people." Garion smiled. "I'll ask Sadi to confine his dealings to recreational drugs."

"Recreational drugs," Zakath laughed. "I like that description."

"I've always had a way with words," Garion replied modestly.

The orange kitten rose, yawned, and jumped down from the Emperor's lap. The mackerel-tabby mother cat promptly caught a black and white kitten by the scruff of the neck and deposited it exactly where the orange one had been lying. Then she looked at Zakath's face and meowed questioningly.

"Thank you," Zakath murmured to her.

Satisfied, the cat jumped down, caught the orange kitten, and began to bathe it, holding it down with one paw.

"Does she do that all the time?" Garion asked.

159

Zakath nodded. "She's busy being a mother, but she doesn't want me to get lonely."

"That's considerate of her."

Zakath looked at the black and white kitten in his lap, who had all four paws wrapped around his hand and was gnawing on one of his knuckles in mock ferocity. "I think I could learn to survive without it," he said, wincing.

CHAPTER NINE

The simplest way to avoid the omnipresent spies infesting the imperial palace was to conduct any significant conversations out in the open, and so Garion frequently found himself strolling around the palace grounds with one or more of his companions. On a beautiful spring morning a few days later he walked with Belgarath and Polgara through the dappled shade of a cherry orchard, listening to Velvet's latest report on the political intrigues which seethed through the corridors of Zakath's palace.

"The surprising thing is that Brador is probably aware of most of what's going on," the blond girl told them. "He doesn't *look* all that efficient, but his secret police are everywhere." Velvet was holding a spray of cherry blossoms in front of her face, rather ostentatiously inhaling their fragrance.

"At least they can't hear us out here," Garion said.

"No, but they can *see* us. If I were you, Belgarion, I still wouldn't talk too openly—even out of doors. I happened to come across one industrious fellow yesterday who was busily writing down every word of a conversation being conducted in whispers some fifty yards away."

"That's a neat trick," Belgarath said. "How did he manage it?"

"He's stone-deaf," she replied. "Over the years, he's learned to understand what people are saying by reading the shape of the words from their lips."

"Clever," the old man murmured. "Is that why you're so busily sniffing cherry blossoms?"

She nodded with a dimpled smile. "That and the fact that they have such a lovely fragrance."

He scratched at his beard, his hand covering him mouth. "All right," he said. "What I need is some sort of disruption—something to draw Brador's police off so that we can slip out of Mal Zeth without being followed. Zakath is rock hard on the point of not doing anything until his army gets back from Cthol Murgos, so it's obvious that we're going to have to move without him. Is there anything afoot that might distract all the spies around here?"

"Not really, Ancient One. The petty kinglet of Pallia and the Prince Regent of Delchin are scheming against each other, but that's been going on for years. The old King of Voresebo is trying to get imperial aid in wresting his throne back from his son, who deposed him a year or so ago. Baron Vasca, the Chief of the Bureau of Commerce, is trying to assimilate the Bureau of Military Procurement, but the generals have him stalemated. Those are the major things in the air right now. There are a number of minor plots going on as well, but nothing earthshaking enough to divert the spies who are watching us."

"Can you stir anything up?" Polgara asked, her lips scarcely moving.

"I can try, Lady Polgara," Velvet replied, "but Brador is right on top of everything that's happening here in the palace. I'll talk with Kheldar and Sadi. It's remotely possible that the three of us can engineer something unexpected enough to give us a chance to slip out of the city."

"It's getting fairly urgent, Liselle," Polgara said. "If Zandramas finds what she's looking for at Ashaba, she'll be off again, and we'll wind up trailing along behind her in the same way that we were back in Cthol Murgos."

"I'll see what we can come up with, my lady," Velvet promised.

"Are you going back inside?" Belgarath asked her.

She nodded.

"I'll go with you." He looked around distastefully. "All this fresh air and exercise is a little too wholesome for my taste."

"Walk a bit farther with me, Garion," Polgara said.

"All right."

As Velvet and Belgarath turned back toward the east wing of the palace, Garion and his aunt strolled on along the neatly trimmed green lawn lying beneath the blossom-covered trees. A wren, standing on the topmost twig of a gnarled, ancient tree, sang as if his heart would burst.

"What's he singing about?" Garion asked, suddenly remembering his aunt's unusual affinity for birds.

"He's trying to attract the attention of a female," she replied, smiling gently. "It's that time of year again. He's being very eloquent and making all sorts of promises—most of which he'll break before the summer's over."

He smiled and affectionately put his arm about her shoulders.

She sighed happily. "This is pleasant," she said. "For some reason when we're apart, I still think of you as a little boy. It always sort of surprises me to find that you've grown so tall."

There wasn't too much that he could say to that. "How's Durnik?" he asked. "I almost never see him these days."

"He and Toth and Eriond managed to find a well-stocked trout pond on the southern end of the imperial grounds," she replied with a slightly comical upward roll of her eyes. "They're catching large numbers of fish, but the kitchen staff is beginning to get a bit surly about the whole thing."

"Trust Durnik to find water." Garion laughed. "Is Eriond actually fishing too? That seems a little out of character for him."

"I don't think he's very serious about it. He goes along mostly for Durnik's company, I think—and because he likes to be outside." She paused and then looked directly at him. As so many times in the past, he was suddenly struck to the heart by her luminous beauty. "How has Ce'Nedra been lately?" she asked him.

"She's managed to locate a number of young ladies to keep her company," he replied. "No matter where we go, she's always able to surround herself with companions."

"Ladies like to have other ladies about them, dear," she said. "Men are nice enough, I suppose, but a woman needs other women to talk to. There are so many important things that men just don't understand." Her face grew serious. "There hasn't been any recurrence of what happened in Cthol Murgos, then?" she asked.

"Not so far as I can tell. She seems fairly normal to me. About the only unusual thing I've noticed is that she never talks about Geran any more."

"That could just be her way of protecting herself, Garion. She might not be able to put it into words exactly, but she's aware of the melancholia that came over her at Prolgu, and I'm sure that she realizes that if she gives in to it, she'll be incapacitated. She still thinks about Geran, I'm sure—probably most of the time—but she just won't talk about him." She paused again. "What about the physical side of your marriage?" she asked him directly.

164

Garion blushed furiously and coughed. "Uh—there really hasn't been much opportunity for that sort of thing, Aunt Pol—and I think she has too many other things on her mind."

She pursed her lips thoughtfully. "It's not a good idea just to ignore that, Garion," she told him. "After a while, people grow apart if they don't periodically renew their intimacy."

He coughed again, still blushing. "She doesn't really seem very interested, Aunt Pol."

"That's your fault, dear. All it takes is a little bit of planning and attention to detail."

"You make it sound awfully calculated and cold-blooded."

"Spontaneity is very nice, dear, but there's a great deal of charm to a well-planned seduction, too."

"Aunt Pol!" he gasped, shocked to the core.

"You're an adult, Garion dear," she reminded him, "and that's one of an adult man's responsibilities. Think about it. You can be quite resourceful at times. I'm sure you'll come up with something." She looked out over the sun-washed lawns. "Shall we go back inside now?" she suggested. "I think it's almost lunch time."

That afternoon, Garion once again found himself strolling about the palace grounds, this time accompanied by Silk and Sadi the eunuch. "Belgarath needs a diversion," he told them seriously. "I think he has a plan to get us out of the city, but we've got to shake off all the spies who are watching us for long enough for him to put it into motion." He was busily scratching at his nose as he spoke, his hand covering his mouth.

"Hay fever?" Silk asked him.

"No. Velvet told us that some of Brador's spies are deaf, but that they can tell what you're saying by watching your lips."

"What an extraordinary gift," Sadi murmured. "I wonder if an undeaf man could learn it."

"I can think of some times myself when it might have been useful," Silk agreed, covering his mouth as he feigned a cough. He looked at Sadi. "Can I get an honest answer out of you?" he asked.

"That depends on the question, Kheldar."

"You're aware of the secret language?"

"Of course."

"Do you understand it?"

"I'm afraid not. I've never met a Drasnian who trusted me enough to teach me."

"I wonder why."

Sadi flashed him a quick grin.

"I think we can manage if we cover our mouths when we speak," Garion said.

"Won't that become a little obvious after a while?" Sadi objected.

"What are they going to do? Tell us to stop?"

"Probably not, but we might want to pass on some disinformation sometimes, and if they know that we know about this way of listening, we won't be able to do that." The eunuch sighed about the lost opportunity, then shrugged. "Oh, well," he said.

Garion looked at Silk. "Do you know of anything that's going on that we could use to pull the police off our trail?"

"No, not really," the little man replied. "At the moment the Melcene consortium seems to be concentrating on keeping this year's price list a secret and trying to persuade Baron Vasca that Yarblek and I should be restrained to those enclaves on the west coast. We've got Vasca pretty much in our pockets, though—as long as he stays bribed. There's a great deal of secret maneuvering going on, but I don't think anything is close to coming to a head right now. Even if it did, it probably wouldn't cause a big enough stink to make the secret police abandon their assignment to watch us."

"Why not go right to the top?" Sadi suggested. "I could talk to Brador and see if he's susceptible to bribery."

"I don't think so," Garion said. "He's having us watched

on specific orders from Zakath. I doubt that any amount of money would make him consider risking his head."

"There are other ways to bribe people, Belgarion." Sadi smiled slyly. "I have some things in my case that make people feel *very* good. The only trouble with them is that after you've used them a few times, you have to keep on using them. The pain of stopping is really quite unbearable. I could *own* Brador within the space of a week and make him do anything I told him to do."

Garion felt a sudden surge of profound distaste for the entire notion. "I'd really rather not do that," he said, "or only as a last resort."

"You Alorns have a peculiar notion of morality," the eunuch said, rubbing at his shaved scalp. "You chop people in two without turning a hair, but you get queasy at the idea of poisons or drugs."

"It's a cultural thing, Sadi," Silk told him.

"Have you found anything else that might work to our advantage?" Garion asked.

Sadi considered it. "Not by itself, no," he replied. "A bureaucracy lends itself to endemic corruption, though. There are a number of people in Mallorea who take advantage of that. Caravans have a habit of getting waylaid in the Dalasian Mountains or on the road from Maga Renn. A caravan needs a permit from the Bureau of Commerce, and Vasca has been known on occasion to sell information about departure times and routes to certain robber chiefs. Or, if the price is right, he sells his silence to the merchant barons in Melcene." The eunuch chuckled. "Once he sold information about one single caravan to three separate robber bands. There was a pitched battle on the plains of Delchin, or so I'm told."

Garion's eyes narrowed in thought. "I'm beginning to get the feeling that we might want to concentrate our attention on this Baron Vasca," he said. "Velvet told us that he's *also* trying to take the Bureau of Military Procurement away from the army."

167

"I didn't know that," Silk said with some surprise. "Little Liselle is developing quite rapidly, isn't she?"

"It's the dimples, Prince Kheldar," Sadi said. "I'm almost totally immune to any kind of feminine blandishment, but I have to admit that when she smiles at me, my knees turn to butter. She's absolutely adorable—and totally unscrupulous, of course."

Silk nodded. "Yes," he said. "We're moderately proud of her.

"Why don't you two go look her up?" Garion suggested. "Pool your information about this highly corruptible Baron Vasca. Maybe we can stir something up—something noisy. Open fighting in the halls of the palace might just be the sort of thing we need to cover our escape."

"You have a genuine flair for politics, Belgarion," Sadi said admiringly.

"I'm a quick learner," Garion admitted, "and, of course, I keep company with some very disreputable men."

"Thank you, your Majesty," the eunuch replied with mock appreciation.

Shortly after supper, Garion walked through the halls of the palace for his customary evening conversation with Zakath. As always, a soft-footed secret policeman trailed along some distance behind.

Zakath's mood that evening was pensive—almost approaching the bleak, icy melancholy that had marked him back in Rak Hagga.

"Bad day?" Garion asked him, removing a sleeping kitten from the carpet-covered footstool in front of his chair. Then he leaned back and set his feet on the stool.

Zakath made a sour face. "I've been whittling away at all the work that piled up while I was in Cthol Murgos," he said. "The problem is that now that I'm back, the pile just keeps getting higher."

"I know the feeling," Garion agreed. "When I get back to

Riva, it's probably going to take me a year to clear my desk. Are you open to a suggestion?"

"Suggest away, Garion. Right now, I'll listen to anything." He looked reprovingly at the black and white kitten who was biting his knuckles again. "Not so hard," he murmured, tapping the ferocious little beast on the nose with his forefinger.

The kitten laid back its ears and growled a squeaky little growl at him.

"I'm not trying to be offensive or anything," Garion began cautiously, "but I think you're making the same mistake that Urgit made."

"That's an interesting observation. Go on."

"It seems to me that you need to reorganize your government."

Zakath blinked. "Now, that *is* a major proposal," he said. "I don't get the connection, though. Urgit was a hopeless incompetent—at least he was before you came along and taught him the fundamentals of ruling. What is this mistake that he and I have in common?"

"Urgit's a coward," Garion said, "and probably always will be. You're not a coward—sometimes a bit crazy, maybe, but never a coward. The problem is that you're both making the same mistake. You're trying to make all the decisions yourselves—even the little ones. Even if you stop sleeping altogether, you won't find enough hours in the day to do that."

"So I've noticed. What's the solution?"

"Delegate responsibility. Your Bureau Chiefs and generals are competent—corrupt, I'll grant you, but they know their jobs. Tell them to take care of things and only bring you the major decisions. And tell them that if anything goes wrong, you'll replace them."

"That's not the Angarak way, Garion. The ruler—or Emperor, in this case—has always made all decisions. It's been that way since before the cracking of the world. Torak made every decision in antiquity, and the Emperors of Mallorea have followed that example—no matter what we may have felt about him personally."

"Urgit made the exact same mistake," Garion told him. "What you're both forgetting is that Torak was a God, and his mind and will were unlimited. Human beings can't possibly hope to imitate that sort of thing."

"None of my Bureau Chiefs or generals could be trusted with that kind of authority," Zakath said, shaking his head. "They're almost out of control as it is."

"They'll learn the limits," Garion assured him. "After a few of them have been demoted or dismissed, the rest will get the idea."

Zakath smiled bleakly. "That is also not the Angarak way, Garion. When I make an example of someone, it usually involves the headsman's block."

"That's an internal matter, of course," Garion admitted. "You know your people better than I do, but if a man has talent, you can't really call on him again if you've removed his head, can you? Don't waste talent, Zakath. It's too hard to come by."

"You know something?" Zakath said with a slightly amused look. "They call me the man of ice, but in spite of your mild-seeming behavior, you're even more cold-blooded than I am. You're the most practical man I've ever met."

"I was raised in Sendaria, Zakath," Garion reminded him. "Practicality is a religion there. I learned to run a kingdom from a man named Faldor. A kingdom is very much like a farm, really. Seriously, though, the major goal of any ruler is to keep things from flying apart, and gifted subordinates are too valuable a resourse to waste. I've had to reprimand a few people, but that's as far as it ever went. That way they were still around in case I needed them. You might want to think about that a little bit."

"I'll consider it." Zakath straightened. "By the way," he said, "speaking of corruption in government—"

"Oh? Were we speaking about that?"

"We're about to. My Bureau Chiefs are all more or less dishonest, but your three friends are adding levels of sophistication to the petty scheming and deceit here in the palace that we're not really prepared to cope with."

"Oh?"

"The lovely Margravine Liselle has actually managed to persuade the King of Pallia *and* the Prince Regent of Delchin that she's going to intercede with you in their behalf. Each of them is absolutely convinced that their long-term squabble is about to come out into the open. I don't want them to declare war on each other. I've got trouble in Karanda already."

"I'll have a word with her," Garion promised.

"And Prince Kheldar virtually owns whole floors of the Bureau of Commerce. He's getting more information out of there than I am. The merchants in Melcene gather every year to set prices for just about everything that's sold in Mallorea. It's the most closely guarded secret in the empire, and Kheldar just bought it. He's deliberately undercutting those prices, and he's disrupting our whole economy."

Garion frowned. "He didn't mention that."

"I don't mind his making a reasonable profit—as long as he pays his taxes—but I can't really have him gaining absolute control over all commerce in Mallorea, can I? He *is* an Alorn, after all, and his political loyalties are a little obscure."

"I'll suggest that he moderate his practices a bit. You have to understand Silk, though. I don't believe he even cares about the money. All he's interested in is the game."

"It's still Sadi who concerns me the most, though."

"Oh?"

"He's become rather intensely involved in agriculture."

"Sadi?"

"There's a certain plant that grows wild in the marshes of Camat. Sadi's paying a great deal for it, and one of our prominent bandit chiefs has put all of his men to work harvesting it—and protecting the crop, of course. There have already been some pitched battles up there, I understand."

"A bandit who's harvesting crops is too busy to be robbing travelers on the highways, though," Garion pointed out.

"That's not exactly the point, Garion. I didn't mind so much when Sadi was making a few officials feel good and act foolish, but he's importing this plant into the city by the wagon load and spreading it around through the work force—and the army. I don't care for the idea at all."

"I'll see what I can do to get him to suspend operations," Garion agreed. Then he looked at the Mallorean Emperor through narrowed eyes. "You do realize, though, that if I rein the three of them in, they'll just switch over to something new—and probably just as disruptive. Wouldn't it be better if I just took them out of Mal Zeth entirely?"

Zakath smiled. "Nice try, Garion," he said, "but I don't think so. I think we'll just wait until my army gets back from Cthol Murgos. Then we can all ride out of Mal Zeth together."

"You are the most stubborn man I've ever met," Garion said with some heat. "Can't you get it through your head that time is slipping away from us? This delay could be disastrous—not only for you and me, but for the whole world."

"The fabled meeting between the Child of Light and the Child of Dark again? I'm sorry, Garion, but Zandramas is just going to have to wait for you. I don't want you and Belgarath roaming at will through my empire. I *like* you, Garion, but I don't altogether trust you."

Garion's temper began to heat up. He thrust his jaw out pugnaciously as he rose to his feet. "My patience is starting to wear a little thin, Zakath. I've tried to keep things between us more or less civil, but there *is* a limit, and we're getting rather close to it. I am *not* going to lie around your palace for three months."

"That's where you're wrong," Zakath snapped, also rising to his feet and unceremoniously dumping the surprised kitten to the floor.

Garion ground his teeth together, trying to get his temper under control. "Up to now, I've been polite, but I'd like to remind you about what happened back at Rak Hagga. We can leave here any time we want to, you know."

"And the minute you do, you're going to have three of my regiments right on your heels." Zakath was shouting now.

"Not for very long," Garion replied ominously.

"What are you going to do?" Zakath demanded scornfully. "Turn all my troops into toads or something? No, Garion, I know you well enough to know that you wouldn't do that."

Garion straightened. "You're right," he said, "I wouldn't, but I was thinking of something a bit more elemental. Torak used the Orb to crack the world, remember? I know how it was done and I could do it myself if I had to. Your troops are going to have a great deal of trouble following us if they suddenly run into a trench—ten miles deep and fifty miles wide—stretching all the way across the middle of Mallorea."

"You wouldn't!" Zakath gasped.

"Try me." With a tremendous effort, Garion brought his anger under control. "I think perhaps it's time for us to break this off," he said. "We're starting to shout threats at each other like a pair of schoolboys. Why don't we continue this conversation some other time, after we've both had a chance to cool off a bit?"

He could see a hot retort hovering on Zakath's lips, but then the Emperor also drew himself up and regained his composure, though his face was still pale with anger. "I think perhaps you're right," he said.

Garion nodded curtly and started toward the door.

"Garion," Zakath said then.

"Yes?"

"Sleep well."

"You too." Garion left the room.

Her Imperial Highness, the Princess Ce'Nedra, Queen of Riva and beloved of Belgarion, Overlord of the

West, was feeling pecky. "Pecky" was not a word that her Imperial Highness would normally have used to describe her mood. "Disconsolate" or "out of sorts" might have had a more aristocratic ring, but Ce'Nedra was honest enough with herself privately to admit that "pecky" probably came closer to the mark. She moved irritably from room to room in the luxurious apartment Zakath had provided for her and Garion with the hem of her favorite teal green dressing gown trailing along behind her bare feet. She suddenly wished that breaking a few dishes wouldn't appear quite so unladylike.

A chair got in her way. She almost kicked it, but remembered at the last instant that she was not wearing shoes. Instead she deliberately took the cushion from the chair and set it on the floor. She plumped it a few times, then straightened. She lifted the hem of her dressing gown to her knees, squinted, swung her leg a few times for practice, and then kicked the cushion completely across the room. "There!" She said. "Take that!" For some reason it made her feel a little better.

Garion was away from their rooms at the moment, engaged in his customary evening conversation with Emperor Zakath. Ce'Nedra wished that he were here so that she could pick a fight with him. A nice little fight right now might modify her mood.

She went through a door and looked at the steaming tub sunk in the floor. Perhaps a bath might help. She even went so far as to dip an exploratory toe in the water, then decided against it. She sighed and moved on. She paused for a few moments at the window of the unlighted sitting room that overlooked the verdant atrium at the center of the east wing of the palace. The full moon had risen early that day and stood high in the sky, filling the atrium with its pale, colorless light, and the pool at the center of the private little court reflected back the perfect white circle of the queen of the night. Ce'Nedra stood for quite some time, looking out the window, lost in thought.

The she heard the door open and then slam shut. "Ce'Nedra, where are you?" Garion's voice sounded a trifle testy.

"I'm in here, dear."

"Why are you standing around in the dark?" he asked, coming into the room.

"I was just looking at the moon. Do you realize that it's the same moon that shines down on Tol Honeth—and Riva, too, for that matter?"

"I hadn't really thought about it," he replied shortly.

"Why are you being so grumpy with me?"

"It's not you, Ce'Nedra," he answered apologetically. "I had another fight with Zakath, is all."

"That's getting to be a habit."

"Why is he so unreasonably stubborn?" Garion demanded.

"That's part of the nature of Kings and Emperors, dear."

"What's that supposed to mean?"

"Nothing."

"Do you want something to drink? I think we've still got some of that wine left."

"I don't think so. Not right now."

"Well I do. After my little chat with his pigheaded imperialness, I need something to calm my nerves." He went back out, and she heard the clink of a decanter against the rim of a goblet.

Out in the moon-bright atrium something moved out from the shadows of the tall, broad-leafed trees. It was Silk. He was wearing only his shirt and hose, he had a bath sheet over his shoulder, and he was whistling. He bent at the edge of the pool and dipped his fingers into the water. Then he stood up and began to unbutton his shirt.

Ce'Nedra smiled, drew back behind the drape, and watched as the little man disrobed. Then he stepped down into the pool, shattering the reflected moon into a thousand sparkling fragments. Ce'Nedra continued to watch as he lazily swam back and forth in the moon-dappled water.

Then there was another shadow under the trees, and Liselle came out into the moonlight. She wore a loose-fitting robe, and there was a flower in her hair. The flower was undoubtedly red, but the wan light of the full spring moon leeched away the color, making it appear black against the blond girl's pale hair. "How's the water?" she asked quite calmly. Her voice seemed very close, almost as if she were in the same room with the watching Ce'Nedra.

Silk gave a startled exclamation, then coughed as his mouth and nose filled with water. He spluttered, then recovered his composure. "Not bad," he replied in an unruffled tone.

"Good," Liselle said. She moved to the edge of the pool. "Kheldar, I think it's time that we had a talk."

"Oh? About what?"

"About this." Quite calmly she unbelted her robe and let it fall to the ground about her feet.

She wasn't wearing anything under the robe.

"You seem to have a little difficulty grasping the idea that things change with the passage of time," she continued, diping one foot into the water. Quite deliberately, she pointed at herself. "This is one of those things."

"I noticed that," he said admiringly.

"I'm so glad. I was beginning to be afraid that your eyes might be failing." She stepped down into the pool and stood waist-deep in the water. "Well?" she said then.

"Well what?"

"What do you plan to do about it?" She reached up and took the flower from her hair and carefully laid it on the surface of the pool.

Ce'Nedra darted to the door on silent, bare feet. "Garion!" she called in an urgent whisper. "Come here!"

"Why?"

"Keep your voice down and come here."

He grumbled slightly and came into the darkened room. "What is it?"

176

She pointed at the window with a muffled giggle. "Look!" she commanded in a delighted little whisper.

Garion went to the window and looked out. After a single glance, he quickly averted his eyes. "Oh, my," he said in a strangled whisper.

Ce'Nedra giggled again, came to his side, and burrowed her way under his arm. "Isn't that sweet?" she said softly.

"I'm sure it is," he whispered back, "but I don't think we ought to watch."

"Why not?"

The flower Liselle had laid on the water had floated across the intervening space, and Silk, his expression bemused, picked it up and smelled it. "Yours, I believe," he said, holding it out to the pale-skinned girl sharing the pool with him.

"Why, yes, I believe it is," she replied. "But you haven't answered my question."

"Which question?"

"What are you going to do about this?"

"I'll think of something."

"Good. I'll help you."

Garion firmly reached out and pulled the drape shut.

"Spoilsport," Ce'Nedra pouted.

"Never mind," he told her. "Now come away from the window." He drew her out of the room. "I can't understand what she's up to," he said.

"I thought that was fairly obvious."

"Ce'Nedra!"

"She's seducing him, Garion. She's been in love with him since she was a little girl and she's finally decided to take steps. I'm so happy for her that I could just burst."

He shook his head. "I will *never* understand women," he said. "Just when I think I've got everything worked out, you all get together and change the rules. You wouldn't believe what Aunt Pol said to me just this morning."

"Oh? What was that?"

"She said that I ought to—" He stopped abruptly, his face

177

suddenly going beet red. "Ah—never mind," he added lamely.

"What was it?"

"I'll tell you some other time." He gave her a peculiar look then. It was a look she thought she recognized. "Have you taken your evening bath yet?" he asked with exaggerated casualness.

"Not yet. Why?"

"I thought I might join you—if you don't mind."

Ce'Nedra artfully lowered her lashes. "If you really want to," she said in a girlish voice.

"I'll light some candles in there," he said. "The lamp's a bit bright, don't you think?"

"Whatever you prefer, dear."

"And I think I'll bring in the wine, too. It might help us to relax."

Ce'Nedra felt an exultant little surge of triumph. For some reason her irritability had entirely disappeared. "I think that would be just lovely, dear."

"Well," he said, extending a slightly trembling hand to her, "shall we go in, then?"

"Why don't we?"

CHAPTER TEN

The following morning when they gathered for breakfast, Silk's expression was faintly abstracted as if he had just realized that someone had somehow outbargained him. The little man steadfastly refused to look at Velvet, who kept her eyes demurely on the bowl of strawberries and cream she was eating.

"You seem a trifle out of sorts this morning, Prince Kheldar," Ce'Nedra said to him in an offhand manner, though her eyes sparkled with suppressed mirth. "Whatever is the matter?"

He threw her a quick, suspicious look.

"There, there," she said, fondly patting his hand. "I'm sure that you'll feel much better after breakfast."

"I'm not very hungry," he replied. His voice was just a little sullen. He stood up abruptly. "I think I'll go for a walk," he said.

"But my dear fellow," she protested, "you haven't eaten your strawberries. They're absolutely delicious, aren't they, Liselle?"

"Marvelous," the blond girl agreed with only the faintest hint of her dimples showing.

Silk's scowl deepened, and he marched resolutely toward the door.

"May I have yours, Kheldar?" Velvet called after him. "If you're not going to eat them, that is?"

He slammed the door as he went out, and Ce'Nedra and Velvet exploded into gales of silvery laughter.

"What's this?" Polgara asked them.

"Oh, nothing," Ce'Nedra said, still laughing. "Nothing at all, Lady Polgara. Our Prince Kheldar had a little adventure last night that didn't turn out exactly the way he expected it to."

Velvet gave Ce'Nedra a quick look and flushed slightly. Then she laughed again.

Polgara looked at the giggling pair, and then one of her eyebrows went up. "Oh. I see," she said.

The flush on Velvet's cheeks grew rosier, although she continued to laugh.

"Oh, dear." Polgara sighed.

"Is something wrong, Pol?" Durnik asked her.

She looked at the good, honest man, assessing his strict Sedarian principles. "Just a small complication, Durnik," she replied, "Nothing that can't be managed."

"That's good." He pushed back his bowl. "Do you need me for anything this morning?"

"No, dear," she replied, kissing him.

He returned her kiss and then stood up, looking across the

table at Toth and Eriond, who sat waiting expectantly. "Shall we go then?" he asked them.

The three of them trooped out, their faces alight with anticipation.

"I wonder how long it's going to take them to empty all the fish out of that pond," Polgara mused

"Forever, I'm afraid, Lady Polgara," Sadi told her, popping a strawberry into his mouth. "The grounds keepers restock it every night."

She sighed. "I was afraid of that," she said.

About midmorning, Garion was pacing up and down one of the long, echoing halls. He felt irritable, and a sort of frustrated impatience seemed to weigh him down. The urgent need to get to Ashaba before Zandramas escaped him again was so constantly on his mind now that he could think of almost nothing else. Although they had come up with several possible schemes, Silk, Velvet, and Sadi were still searching for a suitable diversion—something startling enough to draw off Brador's secret policemen so that they could all make good their escape. There was obviously little chance of changing Zakath's mind, and it began to look increasingly as if Garion and his friends were going to have to "do it the other way," as Belgarath sometimes put it. Despite his occasional threats to Zakath, Garion didn't really want to do that. He was quite sure that to do so would permanently end his growing friendship with the strange man who ruled Mallorea. He was honest enough to admit that it was not only the friendship he would regret losing but the political possibilities implicit in the situation as well.

He was about to return to his rooms when a scarlet-liveried servant came up to him. "Your Majesty," the servant said with a deep bow, "Prince Kheldar asked me to find you for him. He'd like to have a word with you."

"Where is he?" Garion asked.

"In the formal garden near the north wall of the complex, your Majesty. There's a half-drunk Nadrak with him—and a woman with a remarkably foul mouth. You wouldn't believe some of the things she said to me."

"I think I know her," Garion replied with a faint smile. "I'd believe it." He turned then and walked briskly through the hallways and out into the palace grounds.

Yarblek had not changed. Though it was pleasantly warm in the neatly manicured formal garden, he nonetheless still wore his shabby felt overcoat and his shaggy fur hat. He was sprawled on a marble bench under a leafy arbor with a broached ale keg conveniently at hand. Vella, as lush as ever, wandered idly among the flower beds, dressed in her tight-fitting Nadrak vest and leather trousers. Her silver-hilted daggers protruded from the tops of her boots and from her belt, and her walk was still that same challenging, sensual strut, a mannerism she had practiced for so long that it was by now automatic and probably even unconscious. Silk sat on the grass near Yarblek's bench, and he, too, held an ale cup.

"I was just about to come looking for you," he said as Garion approached.

The rangy Yarblek squinted at Garion. "Well, well," he said, blinking owlishly, "if it isn't the boy-King of Riva. I see that you're still wearing that big sword of yours."

"It's a habit," Garion shrugged. "You're looking well, Yarblek—aside from being a little drunk, that is."

"I've been cutting down," Yarblek said rather piously. "My stomach isn't what it used to be."

"Did you happen to see Belgarath on your way here?" Silk asked Garion.

"No. Should I have?"

"I sent for him, too. Yarblek's got some information for us, and I want the old man to get it first hand."

Garion looked at Silk's coarse-faced partner. "How long have you been in Mal Zeth?" he asked.

"We got in last night," Yarblek replied, dipping his cup into the ale keg again. "Dolmar told me that you were all here in the palace, so I came by this morning to look you up."

"How long are you going to stay in town?" Silk asked him.

Yarblek tugged at his scraggly beard and squinted up at the arbor. "That's kind of hard to say," he said. "Dolmar picked up *most* of what I need, but I want to nose around the markets a bit. There's a Tolnedran in Boktor who said that he's interested in uncut gem stones. I could pick up a quick fortune on that transaction—particularly if I could sneak the stones past Drasnian customs."

"Don't Queen Porenn's customs agents search your packs pretty thoroughly?" Garion asked him.

"From top to bottom," Yarblek laughed, "And they pat me down as well. They *don't*, however, lay one finger on Vella. They've all learned how quick she is with her daggers. I've made back what I paid for her a dozen times over by hiding little packages here and there in her clothes." He laughed coarsely. "And of course the hiding is sort of fun, too." He belched thunderously. "Par'me," he said.

Belgarath came across the lawn. The old man had resisted all of Zakath's tactful offers of less disreputable raiment, and still wore, defiantly, Garion thought, his stained tunic, patched hose, and mismatched boots. "Well, I see that you finally got here," he said to Yarblek without any preamble.

"I got tied up in Mal Camat," the Nadrak replied. "Kal Zakath is commandeering ships all up and down the west coast to bring his army back from stinking Cthol Murgos. I had to hire boats and hide them in the marshes north of the ruins of Cthol Mishrak." He pointed at the ale keg. "You want some of this?" he asked.

"Naturally. Have you got another cup?"

Yarblek patted here and there at his voluminous coat, reached into an inside pocket, and drew out a squat, dented tankard.

"I like a man who comes prepared."

"A proper host is always ready. Help yourself. Just try not to spill too much." The Nadrak looked at Garion. "How about you?" he asked. "I think I could find another cup."

"No. Thanks anyway, Yarblek. It's a little early for me."

Then a short, gaudily dressed man came around the arbor. His clothes were a riot of frequently conflicting colors. One sleeve was green, the other red. One leg of his hose was striped in pink and yellow and the other covered with large blue polka dots. He wore a tall, pointed cap with a bell attached to the peak. It was not his outrageous clothing that was so surprising, however. What caught Garion's eye first was the fact that the man was quite casually walking on his hands with both feet extended into the air. "Did I hear somebody offer somebody a little drap of somethin' to drink" he asked in a strange, lilting brogue that Garion did not quite recognize.

Yarblek gave the colorful little fellow a sour look and reached inside his coat again.

The acrobat flexed his shoulders, thrusting himself into the air, flipped over in midair, and landed on his feet. He briskly brushed off his hands and came toward Yarblek with an ingratiating smile. His face was nondescript, the kind of face that would be forgotten almost as soon as it was seen, but for some reason, it seemed to Garion to be naggingly familiar.

"Ah, good master Yarblek," the man said to Silk's partner, "I'm sure that yer the kindest man alive. I was near to perishin' of thirst, don't y' know?" He took the cup, dipped into the ale keg, and drank noisily. Then he let out his breath with a gusty sound of appreciation. "'Tis a good brew ye have there, Master Yarblek," he said, dipping again into the keg.

Belgarath had a peculiar expression on his face, partly puzzled but at the same time partially amused.

"He came tagging along when we left Mal Camat," Yarblek told them. "Vella finds him amusing, so I haven't chased him off yet. She turns a little shrill when she doesn't get her own way."

"The name is Feldegast, fine gentlemen," the gaudy little fellow introduce himself with an exaggerated bow. "Feldegast the juggler. I be also an acrobat—as ye've seen fer yerselves—

a comedian of no mean ability, and an accomplished magician. I can baffle yer eyes with me unearthly skill at prestidigitation, don't y' know. I kin also play rousin' tunes on a little wooden whistle—or, if yer mood be melancholy, I kin play ye sad songs on the lute to bring a lump to yer throat and fill yer eyes with sweet, gentle tears. Would ye be wantin' to witness some of me unspeakable talent?"

"Maybe a little later," Belgarath told him, his eyes still a little bemused. "Right now we have some business to discuss."

"Take another cup of ale and go entertain Vella, comedian," Yarblek said to him. "Tell her some more off-color stories."

"'Twill be me eternal delight, good Master Yarblek," the outrageous fellow said grandly. "She's a good strappin' wench with a lusty sense of humor and a fine appreciation fer bawdy stories." He dipped out more ale and then capered across the lawn toward the dark-haired Nadrak girl.

"Disgusting," Yarblek growled, looking after him. "Some of the stories he tells her make *my* ears burn, but the nastier they are, the harder she laughs." He shook his head moodily.

"Let's get down to business," Belgarath said. "We need to know what's going on in Karanda right now."

"That's simple," Yarblek told him. "Mengha, that's what's going on. Mengha and his cursed demons."

"Dolmar filled us in," Silk said. "We know about what happened at Calida and about the way that Karands are flocking in to join his army from all over the seven kingdoms. Is he making any moves toward the south yet?"

"Not that I've heard," Yarblek replied. "He seems to be consolidating things through the north right now. He's whipping all of the Karands into hysteria, though. If Zakath doesn't do something quickly, he's going to have a full-scale revolution on his hands. I can tell you, though, that it's not safe to travel in northern Karanda right now. Mengha's shrieking Karands control everything to the coast of Zamad."

"We have to go to Ashaba," Garion told him.

"I wouldn't advise it," Yarblek said bluntly. "The Karands are picking up some very unsavory habits."

"Oh?" Silk said.

"I'm an Angarak," Yarblek said, "and I've been watching Grolims cut out human hearts to offer to Torak since I was a boy, but what's happening in Karanda turns even *my* stomach. The Karands stake captives out on the ground and then call up their demons. The demons are all getting fat."

"Would you care to be a little more specific?"

"Not really. Use your imagination, Silk. You've been in Morindland. You know what demons eat."

"You're not serious!"

"Oh, yes—and the Karands eat the scraps. As I said—some very unsavory habits. There are also some rumors about the demons breeding with human females."

"That's abominable!" Garion gasped.

"It is indeed," Yarblek agreed with him. "The women usually don't survive their pregnancies, but I've heard of a few live births."

"We have to put a stop to that," Belgarath said bleakly.

"Good luck," Yarblek said. "Me, I'm going back to Gar og Nadrak just as soon as I can get my caravan put together. I'm not going anywhere near Mengha—or the tame demon he keeps on a leash."

"Nahaz?" Garion asked.

"You've heard the name then?"

"Dolmar told us."

"We should probably start with him," Belgarath said. "If we can drive Nahaz back to where he came from, it's likely that the rest of the demons will follow their lord."

"Neat trick," Yarblek grunted.

"I have certain resources," the old man told him. "Once the demons are gone, Mengha won't have anything left but a rag tag army of Karandese fanatics. We'll be able to go on about our business and leave the mopping up to Zakath." He

186

smiled briefly. "That might occupy his mind enough to keep him from breathing down our necks."

Vella was laughing raucously as she and Feldegast the juggler approached the arbor. The little comedian was walking on his hands again—erratically and with his feet waving ludicrously in the air.

"He tells a good story," the lush-bodied Nadrak girl said, still laughing, "but he can't hold his liquor."

"I didn't think he drank all that much," Silk said.

"It wasn't the ale that fuddled him so bad," she replied. She drew a silver flask from under her belt. "I gave him a pull or two at this." Her eyes suddenly sparkled with mischief. "Care to try some, Silk?" she offered, holding out the flask.

"What's in it?" he asked suspiciously.

"Just a little drink we brew in Gar og Nadrak," she said innocently. "It's as mild as mothers' milk." She demonstrated by taking a long drink from the flask.

"Othlass?"

She nodded.

"No thanks." He shuddered. "The last time I drank that, I lost track of a whole week."

"Don't be so chicken-livered, Silk," she told him scornfully. She took another drink. "See? It doesn't hurt a bit." She looked at Garion. "My lord," she said to him. "How's your pretty little wife?"

"She's well, Vella."

"I'm glad to hear that. Have you got her pregnant again yet?"

Garion flushed. "No," he replied.

"You're wasting time, my lord. Why don't you run back to the palace and chase her around the bedroom a time or two?" Then she turned to Belgarath. "Well?" she said to him.

"Well what?"

She smoothly drew one of her knives from her belt. "Would you like to try again?" she asked, turning deliberately so that her well-rounded posterior was available to him.

"Ah, thanks all the same, Vella," he said with a kind of massive dignity, "But it's a bit early."

"That's all right, old man," she said. "I'm ready for you this time. Any time you're in a patting frame of mind, feel free. I sharpened all my knives before we came—especially for you."

"You're too kind."

The drunken Feldegast lurched, tried to regain his balance, and toppled over in an unceremonious heap. When he stumbled to his feet, his plain face was splotched and distorted, and he stood hunched over with his back bowed to the point where he almost looked deformed.

"I think the girl got the best of you, my friend," Belgarath said jovially as he moved quickly to help the inebriated juggler to right himself. "You really ought to straighten up, though. If you stand around bent over like that, you'll tie your insides in knots." Garion saw his grandfather's lips moving slightly as he whispered something to the tipsy entertainer. Then, so faint that it was barely discernible, he felt the surge of the old man's will.

Feldegast straightened, his face buried in his hands. "Oh dear, oh dear, oh dear," he said. "Have y' poisoned me, me girl?" he demanded of Vella. "I can't remember ever bein' taken by the drink so fast." He took his hands away. The splotches and distortion were gone from his face, and he looked as he had before.

"Don't ever try to drink with a Nadrak woman," Belgarath advised him, "particularly when she's the one who brewed the liquor."

"It seems that I heard a snatch of conversation whilst I was entertainin' the wench here. Is it Karanda ye be talkin' about—and the woeful things happenin' there?"

"We were," Belgarath admitted.

"I display me talents betimes in wayside inns and taverns— for pennies and a drink or two, don't y' know—and a great deal of information comes into places like that. Sometimes if ye make a man laugh and be merry, ye kin draw more out of him than ye can with silver or strong drink. As it happened, I was in such a place not long ago—dazzlin' the onlookers with the brilliance of me performance—and happens that whilst I was there, a wayfarer came in from the east. A great brute of a man he was, and he told us the distressful news from Karanda. And after he had eaten and finished more pots of good strong ale than was good for him, I sought him out and questioned him further. A man in me profession can't never know too much about the places where he might be called upon to display his art, don't y' know. This great brute of a man, who should not have feared anythin' that walks, was shakin' and tremblin' like a frightened babe, and he tells me that I should stay out of Karanda as I valued me life. And then he tells me a very strange thing, which I have not yet put the meanin' to. He tells me that the road between Calida and Mal Yaska is thick with messengers goin' to and fro, hither and yon. Isn't that an amazin' thing? How could a man account fer it? But there be strange things goin' on in the world, good masters, and wonders to behold that no man at all could ever begin to imagine."

The juggler's lilting brogue was almost hypnotic in its charm and liquidity, and Garion found himself somehow caught up in the really quite commonplace narrative. He felt a peculiar disappointment as the gaudy little man broke off his story.

"I hope that me tale has brought ye some small entertainment an' enlightenment, good masters," Feldegast said ingratiatingly, his grass-stained hand held out suggestively. "I make me way in the world with me wits and me talents, givin' of them as free as the birds, but I'm always grateful fer little tokens of appreciation, don't y' know."

"Pay him," Belgarath said shortly to Garion.

"What?"

"Give him some money."

Garion sighed and reached for the leather purse at his belt.

"May the Gods all smile down on ye, young master," Feld-egast thanked Garion effusively for the few small coins which changed hands. Then he looked slyly at Vella. "Tell me, me girl," he said, "have ye ever heard the story of the milkmaid and the peddler? I must give ye fair warnin' that it's a naughty little story, and I'd be covered with shame to bring a blush to yer fair cheeks."

"I haven't blushed since I was fourteen," Vella said to him.

"Well then, why don't we go apart a ways, an' I'll see if I can't remedy that? I'm told that blushin' is good fer the complexion."

Vella laughed and followed him back out onto the lawn.

"Silk," Belgarath said brusquely, "I need that diversion— now."

"We don't really have anything put together yet," Silk objected.

"Make something up, then." The old man turned to Yar-blek. "And I don't want you to leave Mal Zeth until I give you the word. I might need you here."

"What's the matter, Grandfather?" Garion asked.

"We have to leave here as quickly as possible."

Out on the lawn, Vella stood wide-eyed and with the palms of her hands pressed to her flaming cheeks.

"Ye'll have to admit that I warned ye, me girl," Feldegast chortled triumphantly. "Which is more than I can say about the deceitful way ye slipped yer dreadful brew into me craw." He looked at her admiringly. "I must say, though, that ye bloom like a red, red rose when ye blush like that, and yer a joy to behold in yer maidenlike confusion. Tell me, have ye by chance heard the one about the shepherdess and the knight-errant?"

Vella fled.

That afternoon, Silk, who normally avoided anything re-motely resembling physical exertion, spent several hours in the leafy atrium in the center of the east wing, busily piling stones across the mouth of the tiny rivulent of fresh, sparkling water which fed the pool at the center of the little garden. Garion watched curiously from the window of his sitting room until he could stand it no longer. He went out into the atrium to confront the sweating little Drasnian. "Are you taking up landscaping as a hobby?" he asked.

"No," Silk replied, mopping his forehead, "just taking a little precaution, is all."

"Precaution against what?"

Silk held up one finger. "Wait," he said gauging the level of the water rising behind his improvised dam. After a moment, the water began to spill over into the pool with a loud gurgling and splashing. "Noisy, isn't it?" he said proudly.

"Won't that make sleep in these surrounding rooms a little hard?" Garion asked.

"It's also going to make listening almost impossible," the little man said smugly. "As soon as it gets dark, why don't you and I and Sadi and Liselle gather here. We need to talk, and my cheerful little waterfall should cover what we say to each other."

"Why after dark?"

Silk slyly laid one finger alongside his long, pointed nose. "So that the night will hide our lips from those police who don't use their ears to listen with."

"That's clever," Garion said.

"Why, yes. I thought so myself." Then Silk made a sour face. "Actually, it was Liselle's idea," he confessed.

Garion smiled. "But she let you do the work."

Silk grunted. "She claimed that she didn't want to break any of her fingernails. I was going to refuse, but she threw her dimples at me, and I gave in."

"She uses those very well, doesn't she? They're more dangerous than your knives."

"Are you trying to be funny, Garion?"

"Would I do that, old friend?"

As the soft spring evening descended over Mal

Zeth, Garion joined his three friends in the dim atrium beside Silk's splashing waterfall.

"Very nice work, Kheldar," Velvet complimented the little man.

"Oh, shut up."

"Why, Kheldar!"

"All right," Garion said, by way of calling the meeting to order, "what have we got that we can work with? Belgarath wants us out of Mal Zeth almost immediately."

"I've been following your advice, Belgarion," Sadi murmured, "and I've been concentrating my attention on Baron Vasca. He's a man of eminent corruption and he has his fingers in so many pies that he sometimes loses track of just who's bribing him at any given moment."

"Exactly what's he up to right now?" Garion asked.

"He's still trying to take over the Bureau of Military Procurement," Velvet reported. "That bureau is controlled by the General Staff, however. It's mostly composed of colonels, but there's a General Bregar serving as Bureau Chief. The colonels aren't *too* greedy, but Bregar has a large payroll. He has to spread quite a bit of money around among his fellow generals to keep Vasca in check."

Garion thought about that. "Aren't you bribing Vasca as well?" he asked Silk.

Silk nodded glumly. "The price is going up, though. The consortium of Melcene merchant barons is laying a lot of money in his path, trying to get him to restrict Yarblek and me to the west coast."

"Can he raise any sort of force? Fighting men, I mean?"

"He has contacts with a fair number of robber chiefs," Sadi replied, "and they have some pretty rough and ready fellows working for them."

"Is there any band operating out of Mal Zeth right now?"

Sadi coughed rather delicately. "I just brought a string of wagons down from Camat," he admitted. "Agricultural products for the most part."

Garion gave him a hard look. "I thought I asked you not to do that any more."

"The crop had already been harvested, Belgarion," the eunuch protested. "It doesn't make sense to just let it rot in the fields, does it?"

"That's sound business thinking, Garion," Silk interceded.

"Anyway," Sadi hurried on, "the band that's handling the harvesting and transport for me is one of the largest in this part of Mallorea—two or three hundred anyway, and I have a goodly number of stout fellows involved in local distribution."

"You did all this in just a few weeks?" Garion was incredulous.

"One makes very little profit by allowing the grass to grow under one's feet," Sadi stated piously.

"Well put," Silk approved.

"Thank you, Prince Kheldar."

Garion shook his head in defeat. "Is there any way you can get your bandits into the palace grounds?"

"Bandits?" Sadi sounded injured.

"Isn't that what they are?"

"I prefer to think of them as entrepreneurs."

"Whatever. Can you get them in?"

"I sort of doubt it, Belgarion. What did you have in mind?"

"I thought we might offer their services to Baron Vasca to help in his forthcoming confrontation with the General Staff."

"Is there going to be a confrontation?" Sadi looked surprised. "I hadn't heard about that."

"That's because we haven't arranged it yet. Vasca's going to find out—probably tomorrow—that his activities have irritated the General Staff, and that they're going to send troops into his offices to arrest him and to dig through his records to find enough incriminating evidence to take to the Emperor."

"That's brilliant," Silk said.

"I liked it—but it won't work unless Vasca's got enough men to hold off a fair number of troops."

"It can still work," Sadi said. "At about the same time that Vasca finds out about his impending arrest, I'll offer him the use of my men. He can bring them into the palace complex under the guise of workmen. All the Bureau Chiefs are continually renovating their offices. It has to do with status, I think."

"What's the plan here, Garion?" Silk asked.

"I want open fighting right here in the halls of the palace. *That* should attract the attention of Brador's policemen."

"He was born to be a King, wasn't he?" Velvet approved. "Only royalty has the ability to devise a deception of that scale."

"Thanks," Garion said dryly. "It's not going to work, though, if Vasca just takes up defensive positions in his bureau offices. We also have to persuade him to strike first. The soldiers won't really be coming after him, so we're going to have to make him start the fight himself. What kind of man is Vasca?"

"Deceitful, greedy, and not really all that bright," Silk replied.

"Can he be pressured into any kind of rashness?"

"Probably not. Bureaucrats tend to be cowardly. I don't think he'd make a move until he sees the soldiers coming."

"I believe I can make him bolder," Sadi said. "I have something very nice in a green vial that would make a mouse attack a lion."

Garion made a face. "I don't much care for that way," he said.

"It's the results that count, Belgarion," Sadi pointed out. "If things are that urgent right now, delicate feelings might be a luxury we can't afford."

"All right," Garion decided. "Do whatever you have to."

"Once things are in motion, I might be able to throw in just a bit of additional confusion," Velvet said. "The King of Pallia and the Prince Regent of Delchin both have sizable retinues, and they're on the verge of open war anyway.

There's also the King of Veresebo, who's so senile that he distrusts everybody. I could probably persuade each of them that any turmoil in the halls is directed at *them* personally. They'd put their men-at-arms into the corridors at the first sound of fighting."

"Now that's got some interesting possibilities," Silk said, rubbing his hands together gleefully. "A five-way brawl in the palace ought to give us all the opportunity we need to leave town."

"And it wouldn't necessarily have to be confined to the palace," Sadi added thoughtfully. "A bit of judicious misdirection could probably spread it out into the city itself. A general riot in the streets would attract quite a bit of attention, wouldn't you say?"

"How long would it take to set it up?" Garion asked.

Silk looked at his partners in crime. "Three days?" he asked them, "Maybe four?"

The both considered it, then nodded.

"That's it then, Garion," Silk said. "Three or four days."

"All right. Do it."

They all turned and started back toward the entrance to the atrium. "Margravine Liselle," Sadi said firmly.

"Yes, Sadi?"

"I'll take my snake back now, if you don't mind."

"Oh, of course, Sadi." She reached into her bodice for Zith.

Silk's face blanched, and he stepped back quickly.

"Something wrong, Kheldar?" she asked innocently.

"Never mind." The little man turned on his heel and went on through the green-smelling evening gesticulating and talking to himself.

CHAPTER ELEVEN

His name was Balsca. He was a rheumy-eyed sea-faring man with bad habits and mediocre skills who hailed from Kaduz, a fish-reeking town on one of the northern Mel-cene Islands. He had signed on as a common deck hand for the past six years aboard a leaky merchantman grandiosely named *The Star of Jarot,* commanded by an irascible peg-leg captain from Celanta who called himself "Woodfoot," a col-orful name which Balsca privately suspected was designed to conceal the captain's true identify from the maritime authorities.

Balsca did not like Captain Woodfoot. Balsca had not liked any ships' officers since he had been summarily flogged ten years back for pilfering grog from ship's stores aboard a ship of the line in the Mallorean navy. Balsca had nursed his grievance from that incident until he had found an opportunity to jump ship, and then he had gone in search of kindlier masters and more understanding officers in the merchant marine.

He had not found them aboard *The Star of Jarot*.

His most recent disillusionment had come about as the result of a difference of views with the ship's bosun, a heavy-fisted rascal from Pannor in Rengel. That altercation had left Balsca without his front teeth, and his vigorous protest to the captain had evoked jeering laughter followed by his being unceremoniously kicked off the quarterdeck by a nail-studded leg constructed of solid oak. The humiliation and the bruises were bad enough, but the splinters which festered for weeks in Balsca's behind made it almost impossible for him to sit down, and sitting down was Balsca's favorite position.

He brooded about it, leaning on the starboard rail well out of Captain Woodfoot's view and staring out at the lead-gray swells surging through the straits of Perivor as *The Star of Jarot* beat her way northwesterly past the swampy coast of the southwestern Dalasian Protectorates and on around the savage breakers engulfing the Turim Reef. By the time they had cleared the reef and turned due north along the desolate coast of Finda, Balsca had concluded that life was going out of its way to treat him unfairly, and that he might be far better off seeking his fortune ashore.

He spent several nights prowling through the cargo hold with a well-shielded lantern until he found the concealed compartment where Woodfoot had hidden a number of small, valuable items that he didn't want to trouble the customs people with. Balsca's patched canvas sea bag picked up a fair amount of weight rather quickly that night.

When *The Star of Jarot* dropped anchor in the harbor of Mal Gemila, Balsca feigned illness and refused his shipmates' suggestion that he go ashore with them for the customary end-of-voyage carouse. He lay instead in his hammock, moaning theatrically. Late during the dog watch, he pulled on his tarred canvas sea coat, the only thing of any value that he owned, picked up his sea bag and went on silent feet up on deck. The solitary watch, as Balsca had anticipated, lay snoring in the scuppers, snuggled up to an earthenware jug; there were no lights in the aft cabins, where Woodfoot and his officers lived in idle luxury; and the moon had already set. A small ship's boat swung on a painter on the starboard side, and Balsca deftly dropped his sea bag into it, swung over the rail, and silently left *The Star of Jarot* forever. He felt no particular regret about that. He did not even pause to mutter a curse at the vessel which had been his home for the past six years. Balsca was a philosophical sort of fellow. Once he had escaped from an unpleasant situation, he no longer held any grudges.

When he reached the docks, he sold the small ship's boat to a beady-eyed man with a missing right hand. Balsca feigned drunkenness during the transaction, and the maimed man— who had undoubtedly had his hand chopped off as punishment for theft—paid him quite a bit more for the boat than would have been the case had the sale taken place in broad daylight. Balsca immediately knew what that meant. He shouldered his sea bag, staggered up the wharf, and began to climb the steep cobblestone street from the harbor. At the first corner, he made a sudden turn to the left and ran like a deer, leaving the surprised press gang the beady-eyed man had sent after him floundering far behind. Balsca was stupid, certainly, but he was no fool.

He ran until he was out of breath and quite some distance from the harbor with all its dangers. He passed a number of alehouses along the way, regretfully perhaps, but there was still business to attend to, and he needed his wits about him.

In a dim little establishment, well hidden up a dank, smelly alleyway, he sold Captain Woodfoot's smuggled treasures, bargaining down to the last copper with the grossly fat woman who ran the place. He even traded his sea coat for a landsman's tunic, and emerged from the alley with all trace of the sea removed from him, except for the rolling gait of a man whose feet have not touched dry land for several months.

He avoided the harbor with its press gangs and cheap grog shops and chose instead a quiet street that meandered past boarded-up warehouses. He followed that until he found a sedate workman's alehouse where a buxom barmaid rather sullenly served him. Her mood, he surmised, was the result of the fact that he was her only customer, and that she had quite obviously intended to close the doors and seek her bed—or someone else's, for all he knew. He jollied her into some semblance of good humor for an hour or so, left a few pennies on the table, and squeezed her ample bottom by way of farewell. Then he lurched into the empty street in search of further adventure.

He found true love under a smoky torch on the corner. Her name, she said, was Elowanda. Balsca suspected that she was not being entirely honest about that, but it was not her name he was interested in. She was quite young and quite obviously sick. She had a racking cough, a hoarse, croaking voice, and her reddened nose ran constantly. She was not particularly clean and she exuded the rank smell of a week or more of dried sweat. Balsca, however, had a sailor's strong stomach and an appetite whetted by six months' enforced abstinence at sea. Elowanda was not very pretty, but she was cheap. After a brief haggle, she led him to a rickety crib in an alley that reeked of moldy sewage. Although he was quite drunk, Balsca grappled with her on a lumpy pallet until dawn was staining the eastern sky.

It was noon when he awoke with a throbbing head. He might have slept longer, but the cry of a baby coming from a wooden box in the corner drove into his ears like a sharp knife. He nudged the pale woman lying beside him, hoping that she would rise and quiet her squalling brat. She moved limply under his hand, her limbs flaccid.

He nudged her again, harder this time. Then he rose up and looked at her. Her stiff face was locked in a dreadful rictus—a hideous grin that made his blood run cold. He suddenly realized that her skin was like clammy ice. He jerked his hand away, swearing under his breath. He reached out gingerly and peeled back one of her eyelids. He swore again.

The woman who had called herself Elowanda was as dead as last week's mackerel.

Balsca rose and quickly pulled on his clothes. He searched the room thoroughly, but found nothing worth stealing except for the few coins he had given the dead woman the previous night. He took those, then glared at the naked corpse lying on the pallet. "Rotten whore!" he said and kicked her once in the side. She rolled limply off the pallet and lay face down on the floor.

Balsca slammed out into the stinking alley, ignoring the wailing baby he had left behind him.

He had a few moments' concern about the possibility of certain social diseases. *Something* had killed Elowanda, and he had not really been all that rough with her. As a precaution, he muttered an old sailors' incantation which was said to be particularly efficacious in warding off the pox; reassured, he went looking for something to drink.

By midafternoon, he was pleasantly drunk and he lurched out of a congenial little wine shop and stopped, swaying slightly, to consider his options. By now Woodfoot would certainly have discovered that his hidden cabinet was empty and that Balsca had jumped ship. Since Woodfoot was a man of limited imagination, he and his officers would certainly be concentrating their search along the waterfront. It would take them some time to realize that their quarry had moved somewhat beyond the sight, if not the smell, of salt water. Balsca prudently decided that if he were to maintain his lead on his vengeful former captain, it was probably time for him to head inland. It occurred to him, moreover, that someone might have seen him with Elowanda, and that her body probably had been found by now. Balsca felt no particular responsibility for her death, but he was by nature slightly shy about talking

with policemen. All in all, he decided, it might just be time
to leave Mal Gemila.

He started out confidently, striding toward the east gate of
the city; but after several blocks, his feet began to hurt. He
loitered outside a warehouse where several workmen were
loading a large wagon. He carefully stayed out of sight until
the work was nearly done, then heartily offered to lend a hand.
He put two boxes on the wagon, then sought out the teamster,
a shaggy-bearded man smelling strongly of mules.

"Where be ye bound, friend?" Balsca asked him as if out
of idle curiosity.

"Mal Zeth," the teamster replied shortly.

"What an amazing coincidence," Balsca exclaimed. "I have
business there myself." In point of fact, Balsca had cared very
little where the teamster and his wagon had been bound. All
he wanted to do was to go inland to avoid Woodfoot or the
police. "What say I ride along with you—for company?"

"I don't get all that lonesome," the teamster said churlishly.

Balsca signed. It was going to be one of *those* days. "I'd be
willing to pay," he offered sadly.

"How much?"

"I don't really have very much."

"Ten coppers," the teamster said flatly.

"Ten? I haven't got that much."

"You'd better start walking then. It's that way."

Balsca sighed and gave in. "All right," he said. "Ten."

"In advance."

"Half now and half when we get to Mal Zeth."

"In advance."

"That's hard."

"So's walking."

Balsca stepped around a corner, reached into an inside
pocket, and carefully counted out the ten copper coins. The
horde he had accumulated as a result of his pilferage aboard
The Star of Jarot had dwindled alarmingly. A number of possibilities occurred to him. He shifted his sheath knife around

201

until it was at his back. If the teamster slept soundly enough and if they stopped for the night in some secluded place, Balsca was quite certain that he could ride into Mal Zeth the proud owner of a wagon and a team of mules—not to mention whatever was in the boxes. Balsca had killed a few men in his time—when it had been safe to do so—and he was not particularly squeamish about cutting throats, if it was worth his while.

The wagon clattered and creaked as it rumbled along the cobbled street in the slanting afternoon sunlight.

"Let's get a few things clear before we start," the teamster said. "I don't like to talk and I don't like having people jabber at me."

"All right."

The teamster reached back and picked up a wicked-looking hatchet out of the wagon bed. "Now," he said, "give me your knife."

"I don't have a knife."

The teamster reined in his mules. "Get out," he said curtly.

"But I paid you?"

"Not enough for me to take any chances with you. Come up with a knife or get out of my wagon."

Balsca glared at him, then at the hatchet. Slowly he drew out his dagger and handed it over.

"Good. I'll give it back to you when we get to Mal Zeth. Oh, by the way, I sleep with one eye open and with this in my fist." He held the hatchet in front of Balsca's face. "If you even come near me while we're on the road, I'll brain you."

Balsca shrank back.

"I'm glad that we understand each other." The teamster shook his reins, and they rumbled out of Mal Gemila.

Balsca was not feeling too well when they reached Mal Zeth. He assumed at first that it was a result of the peculiar swaying motion of the wagon. Though he had never been seasick in all his years as a sailor, he was frequently land-sick.

This time, however, was somewhat different. His stomach, to be sure, churned and heaved, but, unlike his previous bouts of malaise, this time he also found that he was sweating profusely, and his throat was so sore that he could barely swallow. He had alternating bouts of chills and fever, and a foul taste in his mouth.

The surly teamster dropped him off at the main gates of Mal Zeth, idly tossed his dagger at his feet and then squinted at his former passenger. "You don't look so good," he observed. "You ought to go see a physician or something."

Balsca made an indelicate sound. "People die in the hands of physicians," he said, "or if they do manage to get well, they go away with empty purses."

"Suit yourself." The teamster shrugged and drove his wagon into the city without looking back.

Balsca directed a number of muttered curses after him, bent, picked up his knife, and walked into Mal Zeth. He wandered about for a time, trying to get his bearings, then finally accosted a man in a sea coat.

"Excuse me, mate," he said, his voice raspy as a result of his sore throat, "but where's a place where a man can get a good cup of grog at a reasonable price?"

"Try the Red Dog Tavern," the sailor replied. "It's two streets over on the corner."

"Thanks, mate," Balsca said.

"You don't look like you're feeling too good."

"A little touch of a cold, I think." Balsca flashed him a toothless grin. "Nothing that a few cups of grog won't fix."

"That's the honest truth." The sailor laughed his agreement. "It's the finest medicine in the world."

The Red Dog Tavern was a dark grogshop that faintly resembled the forecastle of a ship. It had a low, beamed ceiling of dark wood and portholes instead of windows. The proprietor was a bluff, red-faced man with tattoos on both arms and an exaggerated touch of salt water in his speech. His 'Ahoys' and 'Mateys' began to get on Balsca's nerves after a while, but after three cups of grog, he didn't mind so much. His sore throat eased, his stomach settled down, and the trembling in his hands ceased. He still, however, had a splitting headache. He had two more cups of grog and then fell asleep with his head cradled on his crossed arms.

"Ahoy, mate. Closing time," the Red Dog's proprietor said some time later, shaking his shoulder.

Balsca sat up, blinking. "Must have dropped off for a few minutes," he mumbled hoarsely.

"More like a few hours, matey." The man frowned, then laid his hand on Balsca's forehead. "You're burning up, matey," he said. "You'd better get you to bed."

"Where's a good place to get a cheap room?" Balsca asked, rising unsteadily. His throat hurt worse now than it had before, and his stomach was in knots again.

"Try the third door up the street. Tell them that I sent you."

Balsca nodded, bought a bottle to take with him and surreptitiously filched a rope-scarred marlinespike from the rack beside the door on his way out. "Good tavern," he croaked to the proprietor as he left. "I like the way you've got it fixed up."

The tattooed man nodded proudly. "My own idea," he said. "I thought to myself that a seafaring man might like a homelike sort of place to do his drinking in—even when he's this far from deep water. Come back again."

"I'll do that," Balsca promised.

It took him about a half an hour to find a solitary passerby hurrying home with his head down and his hands jammed into his tunic pockets. Balsca stalked him for a block or so, his rope-soled shoes making no sound on the cobblestones. Then, as the passerby went by the dark mouth of an alleyway, Balsca stepped up behind him and rapped him smartly across the base of the skull with his marlinespike. The man dropped like a poleaxed ox. Balsca had been in enough shipboard fights and tavern brawls to know exactly where and how hard to hit his man. He rolled the fellow over, hit him alongside the head once again just to be on the safe side, and then methodically began to go through the unconscious man's pockets. He found several coins and a stout knife. He put the coins in his pocket, tucked the knife under his broad leather belt, and pulled his victim into the alley out of the light. Then he went on down the street, whistling an old sea song.

He felt much worse the following day. His head throbbed, and his throat was so swollen that he could barely talk. His fever, he was sure, was higher, and his nose ran constantly. It took three pulls on his bottle to quiet his stomach. He knew that he should go out and get something to eat, but the thought of food sickened him. He took another long drink from his bottle, lay back on the dirty bed in the room he had rented, and fell back into a fitful doze.

When he awoke again, it was dark outside, and he was shivering violently. He finished his bottle without gaining any particular relief, then shakily pulled on his clothing, which he absently noted exuded a rank odor, and stumbled down to the street and three doors up to the inviting entrance to the Red Dog.

"By the Gods, matey," the tattooed man said, "ye look positively awful."

"Grog," Balsca croaked. "Grog."

It took nine cups of grog to stem the terrible shaking which had seized him.

Balsca was not counting.

When his money ran out, he staggered into the street and beat a man to death with his marlinespike for six pennies. He lurched on, encountered a fat merchant, and knifed him for his purse. The purse even had some gold in it. He reeled back to the Red Dog and drank until closing time.

"Have a care, matey," the proprietor cautioned him as he thrust him out the door. "There be murdering footpads about, or so I've been told—and the police are as thick as fleas on a mangy dog in the streets and alleys in the neighborhood."

205

Balsca took the jug of grog he had bought back to his shabby room and drank himself into unconsciousness.

He was delirious the following morning and he raved for hours, alternating between drinking from his jug of grog and vomiting on his bed.

It took him until sunset to die. His last words were, "Mother, help me."

When they found him, some days later, he was arched rigidly backward, and his face was fixed in a hideous grin.

Three days later, a pair of wayfarers found the body of a bearded teamster lying in a ditch beside his wagon on the road to Mal Gemila. His body was arched stiffly backward, and his face was locked in a grotesque semblance of a grin. The wayfarers concluded that he had no further need of his team and wagon, and so they stole it. As an afterthought, they also stole his clothes and covered the body with dead leaves. Then they turned the wagon around and rode on back to Mal Zeth.

Perhaps a week after Balsca's largely unnoticed death, a man in a tarred sea coat came staggering into a run-down street in broad daylight. He was raving and clutching at his throat. He lurched along the cobblestone street for perhaps a hundred feet before he collapsed and died. The dreadful grin fixed on his foam-flecked lips gave several onlookers nightmares that night.

The tatooed proprietor of the Red Dog Tavern was found dead in his establishment the following morning. He lay amidst the wreckage of the several tables and chairs he had smashed during his final delirium. His face was twisted into a stiff, hideous grin.

During the course of that day, a dozen more men in that part of the city, all regular patrons of the Red Dog Tavern, also died.

The next day, three dozen more succumbed. The authorities began to take note of the matter.

But by then it was too late. The curious intermingling of classes characteristic of a great city made the confining of the infection to any one district impossible. Servants who lived in that shabby part of town carried the disease into the houses of the rich and powerful. Workmen carried it to construction sites, and their fellow workmen carried it home to other parts of the city. Customers gave it to merchants, who in turn gave it to other customers. The most casual contact was usually sufficient to cause infection.

The dead had at first been numbered in the dozens, but by the end of the week hundreds had fallen ill. The houses of the sick were boarded up despite the weak cries of the inhabitants from within. Grim carts rumbled through the streets, and workmen with camphor-soaked cloths about their lower faces picked up the dead with long hooks. The bodies were stacked in the carts like logs of wood, conveyed to cemeteries, and buried without rites in vast common graves. The streets of Mal Zeth became deserted as the frightened citizens barricaded themselves inside their houses.

There was some concern inside the palace, naturally, but the palace, walled as it was, was remote from the rest of the city. As a further precaution, however, the Emperor ordered that no one be allowed in or out of the compound. Among those locked inside were several hundred workmen who had been hired by Baron Vasca, the Chief of the Bureau of Commerce, to begin the renovations of the bureau offices.

It was about noon on the day after the locking of the palace gates that Garion, Polgara, and Belgarath were summoned to an audience with Zakath. They entered his study to find him gaunt and hollow-eyed, poring over a map of the imperial city. "Come in. Come in," he said when they arrived. They entered and sat down in the chairs he indicated with an absent wave of his hand.

"You look tired," Polgara noted.

"I haven't slept for the past four days," Zakath admitted.

207

He looked wearily at Belgarath. "You say that you're seven thousand years old."

"Approximately, yes."

"You've lived through pestilence before?"

"Several times."

"How long does it usually last?"

"It depends on which disease it is. Some of then run their course in a few months. Others persist until everybody in the region is dead. Pol would know more about that than I would. She's the one with all the medical experience."

"Lady Polgara?" the Emperor appealed to her.

"I'll need to know the symptoms before I can identify the disease," she replied.

Zakath burrowed through the litter of documents on the table in front of him. "Here it is." He picked up a scrap of parchment and read from it. "High fever, nausea, vomiting. Chills, profuse sweating, sore throat, and headache. Finally delirium, followed shortly by death."

She looked at him gravely. "That doesn't sound too good," she said. "Is there anything peculiar about the bodies after they've died?"

"They all have an awful grin on their faces," he told her, consulting his parchment.

She shook her head. "I was afraid of that."

"What is it?"

"A form of plague."

"*Plague?*" His face had gone suddenly pale. "I thought there were swellings on the body with that. This doesn't mention that." He held up the scrap of parchment.

"There are several different varieties of the disease, Zakath. The most common involves the swellings you mentioned. Another attacks the lungs. The one you have here is quite rare, and dreadfully virulent."

"Can it be cured?"

"Not cured, no. Some people manage to survive it, but that's probably the result of mild cases or their body's natural resistance to disease. Some people seem to be immune. They don't catch it no matter how many times they've been exposed."

"What can I do?"

She gave him a steady look. "You won't like this," she told him.

"I like the plague even less."

"Seal up Mal Zeth. Seal the city in the same way that you've sealed the palace."

"You can't be serious!"

"Deadly serious. You have to keep the infection confined to Mal Zeth, and the only way to do that is to prevent people from carrying the disease out of the city to other places." Her face was bleak. "And when I say to seal the city, Zakath, I mean totally. *Nobody* leaves."

"I've got an empire to run, Polgara. I can't seal myself up here and just let it run itself. I have to get messengers in and send orders out."

"Then, inevitably, you will rule an empire of the dead. The symptoms of the disease don't begin to show up until a week or two after the initial infection, but during the last several days of that period, the carrier is already dreadfully contagious. You can catch it from somebody who looks and feels perfectly healthy. If you send out messengers, sooner or later one of them will be infected, and the disease will spread throughout all of Mallorea."

His shoulders slumped in defeat as the full horror of what she was describing struck him. "How many?" he asked quietly.

"I don't quite understand the question."

"How many will die here in Mal Zeth, Polgara?"

She considered it. "Half," she replied, "if you're lucky."

"*Half?*" he gasped. "Polgara, this is the largest city in the world. You're talking about the greatest disaster in the history of mankind."

"I know—and that's only if you're lucky. The death rate could go as high as four-fifths of the population."

He sank his face into his trembling hands. "Is there anything at all that can be done?" he asked in a muffled voice.

"You must burn the dead," she told him. "The best way is just to burn their houses without removing them. That reduces the spread of the disease."

"You'd better have the streets patrolled, too," Belgarath added grimly. "There's bound to be looting, and the looters are going to catch the disease. Send out archers with orders to shoot looters on sight. Then their bodies should be pushed back into the infected houses with long poles and burned along with the bodies already in the houses."

"You're talking about the destruction of Mal Zeth!" Zakath protested violently, starting to his feet.

"No," Polgara disagreed. "We're talking about saving as many of your citizens as possible. You have to steel your heart about this, Zakath. You may eventually have to drive all the heathly citizens out into the fields, surround them with guards to keep them from getting away, and then burn Mal Zeth to the ground."

"That's unthinkable!"

"Perhaps you ought to start thinking about it," she told him. "The alternative could be much, much worse."

CHAPTER TWELVE

"Silk," Garion said urgently, "you've got to stop it."

"I'm sorry, Garion," the little man replied, looking cautiously around the moonlit atrium for hidden spies, "but it's already in motion. Sadi's bandits are inside the palace grounds and they're taking their orders from Vasca. Vasca's so brave now that he's almost ready to confront Zakath himself. General Bregar of the Bureau of Military Procurement knows that something's afoot, so he's surrounded himself with troops. The King of Pallia, the Prince Regent of Delchin, and the old King of Voresebo have armed every one of their retainers. The palace is sealed, and nobody can bring in any outside help—not even Zakath himself. The way things stand right now, one word could set it off."

Garion started to swear, walking around the shadowy atrium and kicking at the short-cropped turf.

"You *did* tell us to go ahead," Silk reminded him.

"Silk, we can't even get out of the palace right now—much less the city. We've stirred up a fight, and now we're going to be caught right in the middle of it."

Silk nodded glumly. "I know," he said.

"I'll have to go to Zakath," Garion said. "Tell him the whole story. He can have his imperial guards disarm everybody."

"If you thought it was hard to come up with a way to get out of the palace, start thinking about how we're going to get out of the imperial dungeon. Zakath's been polite so far, but I don't think his patience—or his hospitality—would extend to this."

Garion grunted.

"I'm afraid that we've outsmarted ourselves," Silk said. He scratched at his head. "I do that sometimes," he added.

"Can you think of *any* way to head it off?"

"I'm afraid not. The whole situation is just too inflammable. Maybe we'd better tell Belgarath."

Garion winced. "He won't be happy."

"He'll be a lot less happy if we don't tell him."

Garion sighed. "I suppose you're right. All right, let's go get it over with."

It took quite some time to locate Belgarath. They finally found him standing at a window in a room high up in the east wing. The window looked out over the palace wall. Beyond that wall fires ranged unchecked in the stricken city. Sheets of sooty flame belched from whole blocks of houses, and a pall of thick smoke blotted out the starry sky. "It's getting out of hand," the old man said. "They should be pulling down houses to make firebreaks, but I think the soldiers are afraid to leave their barracks." He swore. "I hate fires," he said.

"Something's sort of come up," Silk said cautiously, looking around to see if he could locate the spy holes in the walls of the room.

"What is it?"

"Oh, nothing all that much," Silk replied with exaggerated casualness. "We just thought that we'd bring it to your attention, is all." His fingers, however, were twitching and flickering. Even as he spoke quite calmly, improvising some minor problem with the horses for the edification of the spies they all knew were watching and listening, his dancing fingers laid out the entire situation for the old man.

"You *what?*" Belgarath exclaimed, then covered the outburst with a cough.

—*You told us to devise a diversion, Grandfather*— Garion's hands said as Silk continued to ramble on about the horses.

—*A diversion, yes*— Belgarath's fingers replied, —*but not pitched battles inside the palace. What were you thinking of?*—

—*It was the best we could come up with*— Garion replied lamely.

"Let me think about this for a minute," the old man said aloud. He paced back and forth for a while, his hands clasped behind his back and his face furrowed with concentration. "Let's go talk with Durnik," he said finally. "He's more or less in charge of the horses, so we'll need his advice." Just before he turned to lead them from the room, however, his fingers flickered one last time. —*Try not to walk too softly on the way downstairs*— he told them. —*I need to give you some instructions, and wiggling our fingers takes too long*—

As they left the room, Garion and Silk scuffed their feet and brought the heels of their boots down hard on the marble floor to cover Belgarath's whispering voice.

"All right," the old man breathed, scarcely moving his lips as they moved along the corridor toward the stairs leading down. "The situation isn't really irretrievable. Since we can't stop this little brawl you've arranged anyway, let it go ahead and happen. We *will* need the horses, though, so, Garion, I want you to go to Zakath and tell him that we'd like to isolate our mounts from the rest of the stables. Tell him that it's to avoid having them catch the plague.''

"Can horses catch the plague?" Garion whispered in some surprise.

"How should I know? But if *I* don't, you can be sure that Zakath won't either. Silk, you sort of ease around and let everybody know—quietly—that we're just about to leave and to get ready without being too obvious about it.''

"Leave?" Garion's whisper was startled. "Grandfather, do you know a way to get out of the palace—and the city?"

"No, but I know someone who does. Get to Zakath with your request about the horses as quickly as you can. He's got his mind on so many other things right now that he probably won't give you any argument about it.'' He looked at Silk. "Can you give me any kind of idea as to when your little explosion is going to take place?"

"Not really," Silk whispered back, still scuffing his feet on the stairs as they went down. "It could happen at any minute, I suppose."

Belgarath shook his head in disgust. "I think you need to go back to school," he breathed irritably. "*How* to do something is important, yes, but *when* is sometimes even more important.''

"I'll try to remember that.''

"Do. We'd all better hurry, then. We want to be ready when this unscheduled little eruption takes place.''

There were a dozen high-ranking officers with Zakath when Garion was admitted to the large, red-draped room where the Emperor was conferring with his men. "I'll be with you in a bit, Garion," the haggard-looking man said. Then he turned back to his generals. "We *have* to get orders to the troops," he told them. "I need a volunteer to go out into the city.''

The generals looked at each other, scuffing their feet on the thick blue carpet.

"Am I going to have to order someone to go?" Zakath demanded in exasperation.

"Uh—excuse me," Garion interjected mildly, "but why does anybody have to go at all?"

"Because the troops are all sitting on their hands in their barracks while Mal Zeth burns," Zakath snapped. "They have to start tearing down houses to make fire breaks, or we'll lose the whole city. Someone has to order them out."

"Have you got troops posted outside the palace walls?" Garion asked.

"Yes. They have orders to keep the populace away."

"Why not just shout at them from the top of the wall?" Garion suggested. "Tell one of them to go get a colonel or somebody, then yell your orders down to him. Tell him to put the troops to work. Nobody can catch the plague from a hundred yards away—I don't think."

Zakath stared at him and then suddenly began to laugh ruefully. "Why didn't I think of that?" he asked.

"Probably because you weren't raised on a farm," Garion replied. "If you're plowing a different field from the man you want to talk to, you shout back and forth. Otherwise, you do an awful lot of unnecessary walking."

"All right," Zakath said briskly, looking at his generals, "which one of you has the biggest mouth?"

A red-faced officer with a big paunch and snowy white hair grinned suddenly. "In my youth, I could be heard all the way across a parade ground, your Majesty," he said.

"Good. Go see if you can still do it. Get hold of some colonel with a glimmer of intelligence. Tell him to abandon any district that's already burning and to tear down enough houses around the perimeter to keep the fire from spreading. Tell him that there's a generalcy in it for him if he saves at least half of Mal Zeth."

"Provided that he doesn't get the plague and die," one of the other generals muttered.

"That's what soldiers get paid for, gentlemen—taking

215

risks. When the trumpet blows, you're supposed to attack, and I'm blowing the trumpet—right now."

"Yes, your Majesty," they all replied in unison, turned smartly, and marched out.

"That was a clever idea, Garion," Zakath said gratefully. "Thank you." He sprawled wearily in a chair.

"Just common sense." Garion shrugged, also sitting down.

"Kings and Emperors aren't supposed to have common sense. It's too common."

"You're going to have to get some sleep, Zakath," Garion told him seriously. "You look like a man on his last legs."

"Gods," Zakath replied, "I'd give half of Karanda right now for a few hours' sleep—of course, I don't *have* half of Karanda any more."

"Go to bed, then."

"I can't. There's too much to do."

"How much can you do if you collapse from exhaustion? Your generals can take care of things until you wake up. That's what generals are for, isn't it?"

"Maybe." Zakath slumped lower in his chair. He looked across at Garion. "Was there something on your mind?" he asked. "I'm sure this isn't just a social visit."

"Well," Garion said, trying to make it sound only incidental, "Durnik's worried about our horses," he said. "We've talked with Aunt Pol—Lady Polgara—and she's not really sure whether horses can catch plague or not. Durnik wanted me to ask you if it would be all right if we took our animals out of the main stables and picketed them someplace near the east wing where he can keep an eye on them."

"Horses?" Zakath said incredulously. "He's worried about horses at a time like this?"

"You sort of have to understand Durnik," Garion replied. "He's a man who takes his responsibilities very seriously. He looks on it as a duty, and I think we can both appreciate that."

Zakath laughed a tried laugh. "The legendary Sendarian virtues," he said, "duty, rectitude and practicality." He shrugged. "Why not?" he said. "If it makes Goodman Durnik happy, he can stable your horses in the corridors of the east wing if he wants."

"Oh, I don't think he'd want to do that," Garion replied after a moment's thought. "One of the Sendarian virtues you neglected to mention was propriety. Horses don't belong inside the house. Besides," he added, "the marble floors might bruise their hooves."

Zakath smiled weakly. "You're a delight, Garion," he said. "Sometimes you're so serious about the littlest things."

"Big things are made up of little things, Zakath," Garion replied sententiously. He looked at the exhausted man across the table, feeling a peculiar regret at being forced to deceive somebody he genuinely liked. "Are you going to be all right?" he asked.

"I'll survive, I expect," Zakath said. "You see, Garion, one of the big secrets about this world is that the people who desperately cling to life are usually the ones who die. Since I don't really care one way or the other, I'll probably live to be a hundred."

"I wouldn't base any plans on that kind of superstition," Garion told him. Then a thought came to him. "Would it upset you if we locked the doors of the east wing from the inside until this all blows over?" he asked. "I'm not particularly timid about getting sick myself, but I'm sort of concerned about Ce'Nedra and Liselle and Eriond. None of them are really terribly robust, and Aunt Pol said that stamina was one of the things that help people survive the plague."

Zakath nodded. "That's a reasonable request," he agreed, "and really a very good idea. Let's protect the ladies and the boy, if at all possible."

Garion stood up. "You've got to get some sleep," he said.

"I don't think I *can* sleep. There are so many things on my mind just now."

"I'll have someone send Andel to you," Garion suggested. "If she's half as good as Aunt Pol thinks she is, she should

217

be able to give you something that would put a regiment to sleep." He looked at the exhausted man he cautiously considered to be his friend. "I won't be seeing you for a while," he said. "Good luck, and try to take care of yourself, all right?"

"I'll try, Garion. I'll try."

Gravely they shook hands, and Garion turned and quietly left the room.

They were busy for the next several hours. Despite Garion's subterfuges, Brador's secret police dogged their every step. Durnik and Toth and Eriond went to the stables and came back with the horses, trailed closely by the ubiquitous policemen.

"What's holding things up?" Belgarath demanded when they had all gathered once again in the large room at the top of the stairs with its dais and the thronelike chair at one end.

"I'm not sure," Silk replied carefully, looking around. "It's just a matter of time, though."

Then, out on the palace grounds beyond the bolted doors of the east wing, there was the sound of shouting and the thud of running feet, followed by the ring of steel on steel.

"Something seems to be happening," Velvet said clinically.

"It's about time," Belgarath grunted.

"Be nice, Ancient One."

Within their locked-off building there also came the rapid staccato sound of running. The doors leading out into the rest of the palace and to the grounds began to bang open and then slam shut.

"Are they all leaving, Pol?" Belgarath asked.

Her eyes grew distant for a moment. "Yes, father," she said.

The running and slamming continued for several minutes.

"My," Sadi said mildly, "weren't there a lot of them?"

"Will you three stop congratulating yourselves and go bolt those doors again?" Belgarath said.

Silk grinned and slipped out the door. He came back a few minutes later, frowning. "We've got a bit of a problem," he said, "The guards at the main door seem to have a strong sense of duty. They haven't left their posts."

"Great diversion, Silk," Belgarath said sarcastically.

"Toth and I can deal with them," Durnik said confidently. He went to the box beside the fireplace and picked up a stout chunk of oak firewood.

"That might be just a bit direct, dear," Polgara murmured. "I'm sure you don't want to kill them, and sooner or later they'll wake up and run straight to Zakath. I think we'll need to come up with something a little more sneaky."

"I don't care much for that word, Pol," he said stiffly.

"Would 'diplomatic' put a better light on it?"

He thought about it. "No," he said, "not really. It means the same thing, doesn't it?"

"Well," she conceded, "yes, probably. But it sounds nicer, doesn't it?"

"Polgara," the smith said firmly. It was the first time Garion had ever heard him use her full name. "I'm not trying to be unreasonable, but how can we face the world if we lie and cheat and sneak every time we go around a corner? I mean— really, Pol."

She looked at him. "Oh, my Durnik," she said, "I love you." She threw her arms about her husband's neck with a sort of girlish exuberance. "You're too good for this world, do you know that?"

"Well," he said, slightly abashed by a show of affection that he obviously believed should be kept very private, "it's a matter of decency, isn't it?"

"Of course, Durnik," she agreed in an oddly submissive tone. "Whatever you say."

"What are we going to do about the guards?" Garion asked.

"I can manage them, dear." Polgara smiled. "I can arrange it so that they won't see or hear a thing. We'll be able to leave with no one the wiser—assuming that father knows what he's talking about."

Belgarath looked at her, then suddenly winked. "Trust me," he said. "Durnik, bring the horses inside."

"Inside?" the smith looked startled.

Belgarath nodded. "We have to take them down into the cellar."

"I didn't know that this wing had a cellar," Silk said.

"Neither does Zakath," Belgarath smirked. "Or Brador."

"Garion," Ce'Nedra said sharply.

Garion turned to see a shimmering in the center of the room. Then the blindfolded form of Cyradis appeared.

"Make haste," she urged them. "Ye must reach Ashaba 'ere the week is out."

"Ashaba?" Silk exclaimed. "We have to go to Calida. A man named Mengha is raising demons there."

"That is of no moment, Prince Kheldar. The demons are thy least concern. Know, however, that the one called Mengha also journeys toward Ashaba. He will be caught up in one of the tasks which must be completed 'ere the meeting of the Child of Light and the Child of Dark can come to pass in the Place Which Is No More." She turned her blindfolded face toward Garion. "The time to complete this task is at hand, Belgarion of Riva, and shouldst those of thy companions upon whom the task hath been laid fail in its accomplishment, the world is lost. I pray thee, therefore, go to Ashaba." And then she vanished.

There was a long silence as they all stared at the spot where she had stood.

"That's it, then," Belgarath said flatly. "We go to Ashaba."

"*If* we can get out of the palace," Sadi murmured.

"We'll get out. Leave that to me."

"Of course, Ancient One."

The old man led them out into the hallway, down the stairs, and along the main corridor toward the stout door leading to the rest of the palace.

"Just a moment, father," Polgara said. She concentrated for a moment, the white lock at her brow glowing. Then Garion felt the surge of her will. "All right," she said. "The guards are asleep now."

The old man continued on down the corridor. "Here we are," he said, stopping before a large tapestry hanging on the marble wall. He reached behind the tapestry, took hold of an age-blackened iron ring, and pulled. There was a squeal of protesting metal and then a solid-sounding clank. "Push on that side," he said, gesturing toward the far end of the tapestry.

Garion went on down a few steps and set his shoulder to the tapestry. There was a metallic shriek as the covered marble slab turned slowly on rusty iron pivots set top and bottom in its precise center.

"Clever," Silk said, peering into the dark, cobweb-choked opening beyond the slab. "Who put it here?"

"A long time ago one of the Emperors of Mallorea was a bit nervous about his position," the old man replied. "He wanted to have a quick way out of the palace in case things started to go wrong. The passageway's been forgotten, so nobody's likely to follow us. Let's go bring out our packs and other belongings. We won't be coming back."

It took about five minutes for them to pile their things in front of the tapestry-covered panel, and by then Durnik, Toth, and Eriond were leading the horses along the marble corridor with a great clatter of hooves.

Garion stepped to the corner and peered around it at the main door. The two guards were standing rigidly, their faces blank and their eyes glassy and staring. Then he walked back to join the others. "Someday you'll have to show me how to do that," he said to Polgara, jerking his thumb back over his shoulder toward the two comatose soldiers.

"It's very simple, Garion," she told him.

"For you, maybe," he said. Then a thought suddenly came to him. "Grandfather," he said with a worried frown, "if this passage of yours comes out in the city, won't we be worse off than we were here in the palace? There's plague out there, you know, and all the gates are locked."

"It doesn't come out inside Mal Zeth," the old man replied. "Or so I've been told."

Out on the palace grounds the sounds of fighting intensified.

"They seem very enthusiastic, don't they?" Sadi murmured in a self-congratulatory way.

"Well, now," a familiar lilting voice came up out of the cellar beyond the panel. "Will ye stand there for hours pattin' yerselves on the backs an' allowin' the night to fly by with nothin' more accomplished at all? We've miles and miles to go, don't y' know? An' we won't get out of Mal Zeth this month unless we make a start, now will we?"

"Let's go," Belgarath said shortly.

The horses were reluctant to enter the dark, musty place behind the marble panel, but Eriond and Horse confidently went through with Garion's big gray, Chretienne, close behind; and the other animals somewhat skittishly followed.

It was not really a cellar, Garion realized. A flight of shallow stairs led down to what could be more properly described as a rough stone passageway. The horses had some difficulty negotiating the stairs, but eventually, following Eriond, Horse, and Chretienne, they reached the bottom.

At the top of the stairs the giant Toth pushed the hidden panel shut again, and the latch made an omniously heavy clank as it closed.

"One moment, father," Polgara said. In the close and musty-smelling darkness, Garion felt the faint surge of her will. "There," she said. "The soldiers are awake again, and they don't even know that we've been here."

At the bottom of the stairs the comic juggler, Feldegast, stood holding a well-shielded lantern. "'Tis a fine night fer a little stroll," he observed. "Shall we be off, then?"

"I hope you know what you're doing," Belgarath said to him.

"How could ye possibly doubt me, old man?" the comedian said with an exaggerated expression of injury. "I'm the very

soul of circumspection, don't y' know." He made a faint gri-
mace. "There's only one teensy-weensy little problem. It
seems that a certain portion of this passageway collapsed in
on itself a while back, so we'll be forced to go through the
steets up above for a triflin' bit of a way."

"Just *how* triflin—trifling?" Belgarath demanded. He
glared at the impudent comedian. "I wish you'd stop that,"
he said irritably. "What possessed you to resurrect a dialect
that died out two thousand years ago?"

"'Tis a part of me charm, Ancient Belgarath. Any man at
all kin throw balls in the air an' catch 'em again, but it's the
way a performer talks that sets the tone of his act."

"You two have met before, I take it?" Polgara said with
one raised eyebrow.

"Yer honored father an' me are old, old friends, me dear
Lady Polgara," Feldegast said with a sweeping bow. "I know
ye all by his description. I must admit, however, that I'm
overcome altogether by yer unearthly beauty."

"This is a rare rogue you've found, father," she said with
a peculiar smile on her face. "I think I could grow to like
him."

"I don't really advise it, Pol. He's a liar and a sneak and
he has uncleanly habits. You're evading the question, Feldegast—if that's what you want to call yourself. How far do we
have to go through the streets?"

"Not far at all, me decrepit old friend—a half a mile perhaps until the roof of the passage is stout enough again to
keep the pavin' stones where they belong instead of on the
top of our heads. Let's press on, then. 'Tis a long, long way
to the north wall of Mal Zeth, an' the night is wearin' on."

"Decrepit?" Belgarath objected mildly.

"Merely me way of puttin' things, Ancient One," Feldegast
apologized. "Be sure that I meant no offense." He turned to
Polgara. "Will ye walk with me, me girl? Ye've got an absolutely ravishin' fragrance about ye that quite takes me breath

away. I'll walk along beside ye, inhalin' and perishin' with sheer delight."

Polgara laughed helplessly and linked her arm with that of the outrageous little man.

"I *like* him," Ce'Nedra murmured to Garion as they followed along through the cobwebby passageway.

"Yer supposed to, me girl," Garion said in a not altogether perfect imitation of the juggler's brogue. "'Tis a part of his charm, don't y' know?"

"Oh, Garion," she laughed, "I love you."

"Yes," he said. "I know."

She gave him an exasperated look and then punched him in the shoulder with her little fist.

"Ouch."

"Did I hurt you?" she asked, taking his arm in sudden concern.

"I think I can stand it, dear," he replied. "We noble heroes can bear all sorts of things."

They followed Feldegast's lantern for a mile or more with the horses clattering along behind them through the cobweb-draped passageway. Occasionally they heard the rumble of the dead-carts bearing their mournful freight through the streets above. Here in the musty darkness, however, there was only the sound of the furtive skittering of an occasional errant mouse and the whisperlike tred of watchful spiders moving cautiously across the vaulted ceiling.

"I hate this," Silk said to no one in particular. "I absolutely hate it."

"That's all right, Kheldar," Velvet replied, taking the little man's hand. "I won't let anything hurt you."

"Thanks awfully," he said, though he did not remove his hand from hers.

"Who's there?" The voice came from somewhere ahead.

"'Tis only me, good Master Yarblek," Feldegast replied. "Me an' a few lost, strayed souls tryin' to find their way on this dark, dark night."

"Do you really enjoy him all that much?" Yarblek said sourly to someone else.

"He's the delight of my life," Vella's voice came through the darkness. "At least with him I don't have to look to my daggers every minute to defend my virtue."

Yarblek sighed gustily. "I had a feeling that you were going to say something like that," he said.

"My lady," Vella said, making an infinitely graceful curtsy to Polgara as the sorceress and the juggler, arm in arm, moved up to the place where a moss-grown rockfall blocked the passageway.

"Vella," Polgara responded in an oddly Nadrak accent. "May your knives always be bright and keen." There was a strange formality in her greeting, and Garion knew that he was hearing an ancient ritual form of address.

"And may you always have the means at hand to defend your person from unwanted attentions," the Nadrak dancing girl responded automatically, completing the ritual.

"What's happening up above?" Belgarath asked the felt-coated Yarblek.

"They're dying," Yarblek answered shortly, "whole streets at a time."

"Have you been avoiding the city?" Silk asked his partner.

Yarblek nodded. "We're camped outside the gates," he said. "We got out just before they chained them shut. Dolmar died, though. When he realized that he had the plague, he got out an old sword and fell on it."

Silk sighed. "He was a good man—a little dishonest, maybe, but a good man all the same."

Yarblek nodded sadly. "At least he died clean," he said. Then he shook his head. "The stairs up to the street are over here," he said, pointing off into the darkness. "It's late enough so that there's nobody much abroad—except for the dead-carts and the few delirious ones stumbling about and looking for a warm gutter to die in." He squared his shoulders. "Let's go," he said. "The quicker we can get through those

225

streets up there, the quicker we can get back underground where it's safe."

"Does the passage go all the way to the city wall?" Garion asked him.

Yarblek nodded. "And a mile or so beyond," he said. "It comes out in an old stone quarry." He looked at Feldegast. "You never did tell me how you found out about it," he said.

"'Tis one of me secrets, good Master Yarblek," the juggler replied. "No matter how honest a man might be, it's always good to know a quick way out of town, don't y' know."

"Makes sense," Silk said.

"You ought to know," Yarblek replied. "Let's get out of here."

They led the horses to a flight of stone stairs reaching up into the darkness beyond the circle of light from Feldegast's lantern and then laboriously hauled the reluctant animals up the stairway, one step at a time. The stairway emerged in a rickety shed with a straw-littered floor. After the last horse had been hauled up, Feldegast carefully lowered the long trap door again and scuffed enough straw over it to conceal it. "'Tis a useful sort of thing," he said, pointing downward toward the hidden passage, "but a secret's no good at all if just anybody kin stumble over it."

Yarblek stood at the door peering out into the narrow alleyway outside.

"Anybody out there?" Silk asked him.

"A few bodies," the Nadrak replied laconically. "For some reason they always seem to want to die in alleys." He drew in a deep breath. "All right, let's go, then."

They moved out into the alley, and Garion kept his eyes averted from the contorted bodies of the plague victims huddled in corners or sprawled in the gutters.

The night air was filled with smoke from the burning city, the reek of burning flesh, and the dreadful smell of decay.

Yarblek also sniffed, then grimaced. "From the odor, I'd say that the dead-carts have missed a few," he said. He led the way to the mouth of the alley and peered out into the street. "It's clear enough," he grunted. "Just a few looters picking over the dead. Come on."

They went out of the alley and moved along a street illuminated by a burning house. Garion saw a furtive movement beside the wall of another house and then made out the shape of a raggedly dressed man crouched over a sprawled body. The man was roughly rifling through the plague victim's clothes. "Won't he catch it?" he asked Yarblek, pointing at the looter.

"Probably." Yarblek shrugged. "I don't think the world's going to miss him very much if he does, though."

They rounded a corner and entered a street where fully half the houses were on fire. A dead-cart had stopped before one of the burning houses, and two rough-looking men were tossing bodies into the fire with casual brutality.

"Stay back!" one of the men shouted to them. "There's plague here!"

"There's plague everywhere in this mournful city, don't y' know," Feldegast replied. "But we thank ye fer yer warnin' anyway. We'll just go on by on the other side of the street, if ye don't mind." He looked curiously at the pair. "How is it that yer not afraid of the contagion yerselves?" he asked.

"We've already had it," one replied with a short laugh. "I've never been so sick in my life, but at least I didn't die from it—and they say you can only catch it once."

"'Tis a fortunate man y' are, then," Feldegast congratulated him.

They moved on past the rough pair and on down to the next corner.

"We go this way," Feldegast told them.

"How much farther is it?" Belgarath asked him.

"Not far, an' then we'll be back underground where it's safe."

"*You* might feel safe underground," Silk said sourly, "but *I* certainly don't."

227

Halfway along the street Garion saw a sudden movement in one of the deeply inset doorways, and then he heard a feeble wail. He peered at the doorway. Then, one street over, a burning house fell in on itself, shooting flame and sparks high into the air. By that fitful light he was able to see what was in the shadows. The crumpled figure of a woman lay huddled in the doorway, and seated beside the body was a crying child, not much more than a year old. His stomach twisted as he started at the horror before his eyes.

Then, with a low cry, Ce'Nedra darted toward the child with her arms extended.

"Ce'Nedra!" he shouted, trying to shake his hand free of Chretienne's reins. "No!"

But before he could move in pursuit, Vella was already there. She caught Ce'Nedra by the shoulder and spun her around roughly. "Ce'Nedra!" she snapped. "Stay away!"

"Let me go!" Ce'Nedra almost screamed. "Can't you see that it's a baby?" She struggled to free herself.

Very coolly, Vella measured the little Queen, then slapped her sharply across the face. So far as Garion knew, it was the first time anyone had ever hit Ce'Nedra. "The baby's dead, Ce'Nedra," Vella told her with brutal directness, "and if you go near it, you'll die, too." She began to drag her captive back toward the others. Ce'Nedra stared back over her shoulder at the sickly wailing child, her hand outstretched toward it.

Then Velvet moved to her side, put an arm about her shoulders, and gently turned her so that she could no longer see the child. "Ce'Nedra," she said, "you must think first of your own baby. Would you want to carry this dreadful disease to him?"

Ce'Nedra stared at her.

"Or do you want to die before you ever see him again?"

With a sudden wail, Ce'Nedra fell into Velvet's arms, sobbing bitterly.

"I hope she won't hold any grudges," Vella murmured.

"You're very quick, Vella," Polgara said, "and you think very fast when you have to."

Vella shrugged. "I've found that a smart slap across the mouth is the best cure for hysterics."

Polgara nodded. "It usually works," she agreed approvingly.

They went on down the street until Feldegast led them into another smelly alley. He fumbled with the latch to the wide door of a boarded-up warehouse, then swung it open. "Here we are, then," he said, and they all followed him inside. A long ramp led down into a cavernous cellar, where Yarblek and the little juggler moved aside a stack of crates to reveal the opening of another passageway.

They led their horses into the dark opening, and Feldegast remained outside to hide the passage again. When he was satisfied that the opening was no longer visible, he wormed his way through the loosely stacked crates to rejoin them. "An' there we are," he said, brushing his hands together in a self-congratulatory way. "No man at all kin possibly know that we've come this way, don't y' know, so let's be off."

Garion's thoughts were dark as he trudged along the passageway, following Feldegast's winking lantern. He had slipped away from a man for whom he had begun to develop a careful friendship and had left him behind in a plague-stricken and burning city. There was probably very little that he could have done to aid Zakath, but his desertion of the man did not make him feel very proud. He knew, however, that he had no real choice. Cyradis had been too adamant in her instructions. Compelled by necessity, he turned his back on Mal Zeth and resolutely set his face toward Ashaba.

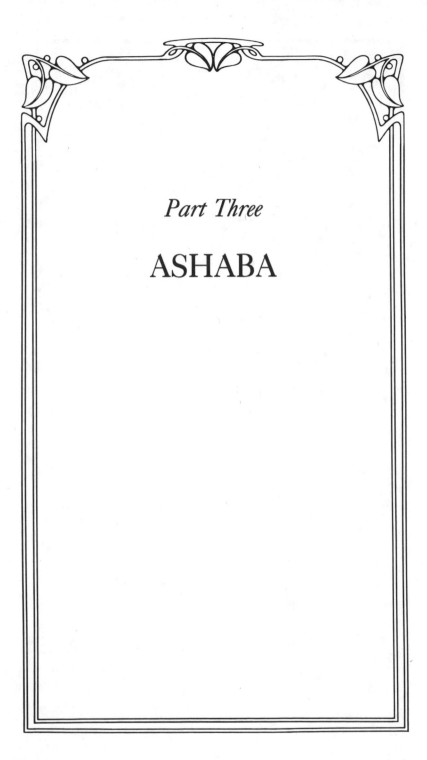

Part Three

ASHABA

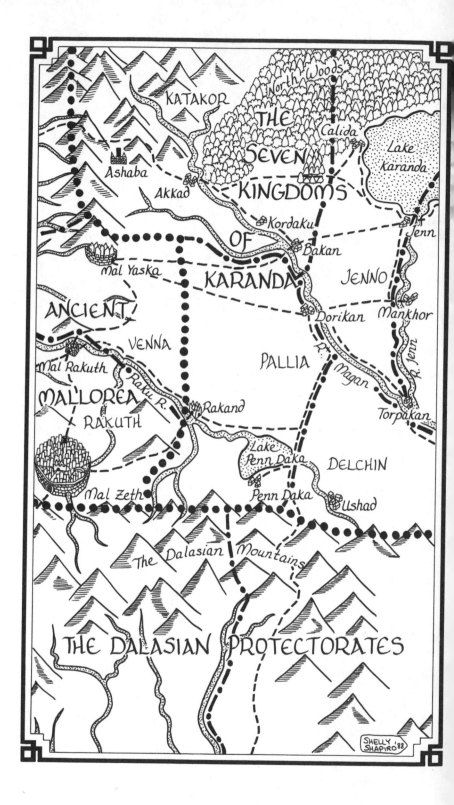

CHAPTER THIRTEEN

The road leading north from Mal Zeth passed through a fair, fertile plain where new-sprouted grain covered the damp soil like a low, bright green mist and the warm spring air was filled with the urgent scent of growth. In many ways, the landscape resembled the verdant plains of Arendia or the tidy fields of Sendaria. There were villages, of course, with white buildings, thatched roofs, and dogs that came out to stand at the roadside and bark. The spring sky was an intense blue dotted with puffy white clouds grazing like sheep in their azure pastures.

The road was a dusty brown ribbon laid straight where the

surrounding green fields were flat, and folded and curved where the land rose in gentle, rounded hills.

They rode out that morning in glistening sunshine with the sound of the bells fastened about the necks of Yarblek's mules providing a tinkling accompaniment to the morning song of flights of birds caroling to greet the sun. Behind them there rose a great column of dense black smoke, marking the huge valley where Mal Zeth lay burning.

Garion could not bring himself to look back as they rode away.

There were others on the road as well, for Garion and his friends were not the only ones fleeing the plague-stricken city. Singly or in small groups, wary travelers moved north, fearfully avoiding any contact with each other, leaving the road and angling far out into the fields whenever they overtook other refugees, and returning to the brown, dusty ribbon only when they were safely past. Each solitary traveler or each group thus rode in cautious isolation, putting as much empty air about itself as possible.

The lanes branching off from the road and leading across the bright green fields were all blocked with barricades of fresh-cut brush, and bleak-faced peasants stood guard at those barricades, awkwardly handling staffs and heavy, graceless crossbows and shouting warnings at any and all who passed to stay away.

"Peasants," Yarblek said sourly as the caravan plodded past one such barricade. "They're the same the world over. They're glad to see you when you've got something they want, but they spend all the rest of their time trying to chase you away. Do you think they actually believe that anybody would really *want* to go into their stinking little villages?" Irritably he crammed his fur cap down lower over his ears.

"They're afraid," Polgara told him. "They know that their village isn't very luxurious, but it's all they have, and they want to keep if safe."

"Do those barricades and threats really do any good?" he asked. "To keep out the plague, I mean?"

"Some," she said, "if they put them up early enough."

Yarblek grunted, then looked over at Silk. "Are you open to a suggestion?" he asked.

"Depends," Silk replied. The little man had returned to his customary travel clothing—dark, unadorned, and nondescript.

"Between the plague and the demons, the climate here is starting to turn unpleasant. What say we liquidate all our holdings here in Mallorea and sit tight until things settle down?"

"You're not thinking, Yarblek," Silk told him. "Turmoil and war are good for business."

Yarblek scowled at him. "Somehow I thought you might look at it that way."

About a half mile ahead, there was another barricade, this one across the main road itself.

"What's this?" Yarblek demanded angrily, reining in.

"I'll go find out," Silk said, thumping his heels against his horse's flanks. On an impulse, Garion followed his friend.

When they were about fifty yards from the barricade, a dozen mud-spattered peasants dressed in smocks made of brown sackcloth rose from behind it with leveled crossbows. "Stop right there!" one of them commanded threateningly. He was a burly fellow with a coarse beard and eyes that looked off in different directions.

"We're just passing through, friend," Silk told him.

"Not without paying toll, you're not."

"*Toll?*" Silk exclaimed. "This is an imperial highway. There's no toll."

"There is now. You city people have cheated and swindled us for generations and now you want to bring your diseases to us. Well, from now on, you're going to pay. How much gold have you got?"

"Keep him talking," Garion muttered, looking around.

"Well," Silk said to the wall-eyed peasant in the tone of voice he usually saved for serious negotiations, "why don't we talk about that?"

The village stood about a quarter of a mile away, rising dirty and cluttered-looking atop a grassy knoll. Garion concentrated, drawing in his will, then he made a slight gesture in the direction of the village. "Smoke," he muttered, half under his breath.

Silk was still haggling with the armed peasants, taking up as much time as he could.

"Uh—excuse me." Garion interrupted mildly, "but is that something burning over there?" He pointed.

The peasants turned to stare in horror at the column of dense smoke rising from their village. With startled cries, most of them threw down their crossbows and ran out across the fields in the direction of the apparent catastrophe. The wall-eyed man ran after them, shouting at them to return to their posts. Then he ran back, waving his crossbow threateningly. A look of anguish crossed his face as he hopped about in an agony of indecision, torn between his desire for money that could be extorted from these travelers and the horrid vision of a fire raging unchecked through his house and outbuildings. Finally, no longer able to stand it, he also threw down his weapon and ran after his neighbors.

"Did you really set their village on fire?" Silk sounded a little shocked.

"Of course not," Garion said.

"Where's the smoke coming from then?"

"Lots of places." Garion winked. "Out of the thatch on their roofs, up from between the stones in the streets, boiling up out of their cellars and granaries—lots of places. But it's only smoke." He swung down from Chretienne's back and gathered up the discarded crossbows. He lined them up, nose down, in a neat row along the brushy barricade. "How long does it take to restring a crossbow?" he asked.

"Hours." Silk suddenly grinned. "Two men to bend the

limbs with a windlass and another two to hook the cable in place."

"That's what I thought," Garion agreed. He drew his old belt knife and went down the line of weapons, cutting each twisted rope cable. Each bow responded with a heavy twang. "Shall we go, then?" he asked.

"What about this?" Silk pointed at the brushy barricade.

Garion shrugged. "I think we can ride around it."

"What were they trying to do?" Durnik asked when they returned.

"An enterprising group of local peasants decided that the highway needed a tollgate about there." Silk shrugged. "They didn't really have the temperament for business affairs, though. At the first little distraction, they ran off and left the shop untended."

They rode on past the now-deserted barricade with Yarblek's laden mules plodding along behind them, their bells clanging mournfully.

"I think we're going to have to leave you soon," Belgarath said to the fur-capped Nadrak. "We have to get to Ashaba within the week, and your mules are holding us back."

Yarblek nodded. "Nobody ever accused a pack mule of being fast on his feet," he agreed. "I'll be turning toward the west before long anyway. You can go into Karanda if you want to, but I want to get to the coast as quickly as possible."

"Garion," Polgara said. She looked meaningfully at the column of smoke rising from the village behind them.

"Oh," he replied. "I guess I forgot." He raised his hand, trying to make it look impressive. "Enough," he said, releasing his will. The smoke thinned at its base, and the column continued to rise as a cloud, cut off from its source.

"Don't overdramatize, dear," Polgara advised. "It's ostentatious."

"You do it all the time," he accused.

"Yes, dear, but I know how."

It was perhaps noon when they rode up a long hill, crested

it in the bright sunshine, and found themselves suddenly surrounded by mailed, red-tunicked Mallorean soldiers, who rose up out of ditches and shallow gullies with evil-looking javelins in their hands.

"You! Halt!" the officer in charge of the detachment of soldiers commanded brusquely. He was a short man, shorter even than Silk, though he strutted about as if he were ten feet tall.

"Of course, Captain," Yarblek replied, reining in his horse.

"What do we do?" Garion hissed to Silk.

"Let Yarblek handle it," Silk murmured. "He knows what he's doing."

"Where are you bound?" the officer asked when the rangy Nadrak had dismounted.

"Mal Dariya," Yarblek answered, "or Mal Camat—wherever I can hire ships to get my goods to Yar Marak."

The captain grunted as if trying to find something wrong with that. "What's more to the point is where you've come from." His eyes were narrowed.

"Maga Renn." Yarblek shrugged.

"Not Mal Zeth?" The little captain's eyes grew even harder and more suspicious.

"I don't do business in Mal Zeth very often, Captain. It costs too much—all those bribes and fees and permits, you know."

"I assume that you can prove what you say?" The captain's tone was belligerent.

"I suppose I could—if there's a need for it."

"There's a need, Nadrak, because, unless you can prove that you haven't come from Mal Zeth, I'm going to turn you back." He sounded smug about that.

"Turn back? That's impossible. I have to be in Boktor by midsummer."

"That's *your* problem, merchant." The little soldier seemed rather pleased at having upset the larger man. "There's plague in Mal Zeth, and *I'm* here to make sure that it doesn't spread." He tapped himself importantly on the chest.

"Plague!" Yarblek's eyes went wide, and his face actually paled. "Torak's teeth! And I almost stopped there!" He suddenly snapped his fingers. "So *that's* why all the villages hereabouts are barricaded."

"Can you prove that you came from Maga Renn?" the captain insisted.

"Well—" Yarblek unbuckled a well-worn saddlebag hanging under his right stirrup and began to rummage around in it. "I've got a permit here issued by the Bureau of Commerce," he said rather dubiously. "It authorizes me to move my goods from Maga Renn to Mal Dariya. If I can't find ships there, I'll have to get another permit to go on to Mal Camat, I guess. Would that satisfy you?"

"Let's see it." The captain held out his hand, snapping his fingers impatiently.

Yarblek handed it over.

"It's a little smeared," the captain accused suspiciously.

"I spilled some beer on it in a tavern in Penn Daka." Yarblek shrugged. "Weak, watery stuff it was. Take my advice, Captain. Don't ever plan to do any serious drinking in Penn Daka. It's a waste of time and money."

"Is drinking all you Nadraks ever think about?"

"It's the climate. There's nothing else to do in Gar og Nadrak in the wintertime."

"Have you got anything else?"

Yarblek pawed through his saddlebag some more. "Here's a bill of sale from a carpet merchant on Yorba Street in Maga Renn—pockmarked fellow with bad teeth. Do you by any chance know him?"

"Why would I know a carpet merchant in Maga Renn? I'm an officer in the imperial army. I don't associate with riffraff. Is the date on this accurate?"

"How should I know? We use a different calendar in Gar og Nadrak. It was about two weeks ago, if that's any help."

The captain thought it over, obviously trying very hard to find some excuse to exert his authority. Finally his expression became faintly disappointed. "All right," he said grudgingly, handing back the documents. "Be on your way. But don't make any side trips, and make sure that none of your people leave your caravan."

"They'd better not leave—not if they want to get paid. Thank you, Captain." Yarblek swung back up into his saddle.

The officer grunted and waved them on.

"Little people should never be given any kind of authority," the Nadrak said sourly when they were out of earshot. "It lies too heavily on their brains."

"*Yarblek!*" Silk objected.

"Present company excepted, of course."

"Oh. That's different, then."

"Ye lie like ye were born to it, good Master Yarblek," Feldegast the juggler said admiringly.

"I've been associating with a certain Drasnian for too long."

"How did you come by the permit and the bill of sale?" Silk asked him.

Yarblek winked and tapped his forehead slyly. "Official types are always overwhelmed by official-looking documents—and the more petty the official, the more he's impressed. I could have proved to that obnoxious little captain back there that we came from any place at all—Melcene, Aduma in the Mountains of Zamad, even Crol Tibu on the coast of Gandahar—except that all you can buy in Crol Tibu are elephants, and I don't have any of those with me, so that might have made even him a little suspicious."

Silk looked around with a broad grin. "Now you see why I went into partnership with him," he said to them all.

"You seem well suited to each other," Velvet agreed.

Belgarath was tugging at one ear. "I think we'll leave you after dark tonight," he said to Yarblek. "I don't want some

240

other officious soldier to stop us and count noses—or decide that we need a military escort."

Yarblek nodded. "Are you going to need anything?"

"Just some food is all." Belgarath glanced back at their laden pack horses plodding along beside the mules. "We've been on the road for quite some time now and we've managed to gather up what we really need and discard what we don't."

"I'll see to it that you've got enough food," Vella promised from where she was riding between Ce'Nedra and Velvet. "Yarblek sometimes forgets that full ale kegs are not the *only* things you need on a journey."

"An' will ye be ridin' north, then?" Feldegast asked Belgarath. The little comic had changed out of his bright-colored clothes and was now dressed in plain brown.

"Unless they've moved it, that's where Ashaba is," Belgarath replied.

"If it be all the same to ye, I'll ride along with ye fer a bit of a ways."

"Oh?"

"There was a little difficulty with the authorities the last time I was in Mal Dariya, an' I'd like to give 'em time t' regain their composure before I go back fer me triumphant return engagement. Authorities tend t' be a stodgy an' unfergivin' lot, don't y' know—always dredgin' up old pranks an' bits of mischief perpetrated in the spirit of fun an' throwin' 'em in yer face."

Belgarath gave him a long, steady look, then shrugged. "Why not?" he said.

Garion looked sharply at the old man. His sudden acquiescence seemed wildly out of character, given his angry protests at the additions of Velvet and Sadi to their party. Garion then looked over at Polgara, but she showed no signs of concern either. A peculiar suspicion began to creep over him.

As evening settled over the plains of Mallorea, they drew off the road to set up their night's encampment in a parklike grove of beech trees. Yarblek's muleteers sat about one campfire, passing an earthenware jug around and becoming increasingly rowdy. At the upper end of the grove, Garion and his friends sat around another fire, eating supper and talking quietly with Yarblek and Vella.

"Be careful when you cross into Venna," Yarblek cautioned his rat-faced partner. "Some of the stories coming out of there are more ominous than the ones coming out of Karanda."

"Oh?"

"It's as if a kind of madness has seized them all. Of course, Grolims were never very sane to begin with."

"Grolims?" Sadi looked up sharply.

"Venna's a Church-controlled state," Silk explained. "All authority there derives from Urvon and his court at Mal Yaska."

"It *used* to," Yarblek corrected. "Nobody seems to know *who's* got the authority now. The Grolims gather in groups to talk. The talk keeps getting louder until they're sceaming at each other, and then they all reach for their knives. I haven't been able to get the straight of it. Even the Temple Guardsmen are taking sides."

"The idea of Grolims cutting each other to pieces is one I can live with," Silk said.

"Truly," Yarblek agreed. "Just try not to get caught in the middle."

Feldegast had been softly strumming his lute and he struck a note so sour that even Garion noticed it.

"That string's out of tune," Durnik advised him.

"I know," the juggler replied. "The peg keeps slippin'."

"Let me see it," Durnik offered. "Maybe I can fix it."

"'Tis too worn, I fear, friend Durnik. 'Tis a grand instrument, but it's old."

"Those are the ones that are worth saving." Durnik took the lute and twisted the loose peg, tentatively testing the pitch of the string with his thumb. Then he took his knife and cut several small slivers of wood. He carefully inserted them around the peg, tapping them into place with the hilt of his knife. Then he twisted the peg, retuning the string. "That should do it," he said. He took up the lute and strummed it a few times. Then, to a slow measure, he picked out an ancient air, the single notes quivering resonantly. He played the air through once, his fingers seeming to grow more confident as he went along. Then he returned to the beginning again, but this time, to Garion's amazement, he accompanied the simple melody with a rippling counterpoint so complex that it seemed impossible that it could come from a single instrument. "It has a nice tone," he observed to Feldegast.

""Tis a marvel that ye are, master smith. First ye repair me lute, an' then ye turn around an' put me t' shame by playin' it far better than I could ever hope to."

Polgara's eyes were very wide and luminous. "Why haven't you told me about this, Durnik?" she asked.

"Actually, it's been so long that I almost forgot about it." He smiled, his fingers still dancing on the strings and bringing forth that rich-toned cascade of sound. "When I was young, I worked for a time with a lute maker. He was old, and his fingers were stiff, but he needed to hear the tone of the instruments he made, so he taught me how to play them for him."

He looked across the fire at his giant friend, and something seemed to pass between them. Toth nodded, reached inside the rough blanket he wore across one shoulder, and produced a curious-looking set of pipes, a series of hollow reeds, each longer than the one preceding it, all bound tightly together. Quietly, the mute lifted the pipes to his lips as Durnik returned again to the beginning of the air. The sound he produced from his simple pipes had an aching poignancy about it that pierced Garion to the heart, soaring through the intricate complexity of the lute song.

"I'm beginnin' t' feel altogether unnecessary," Feldegast said in wonder. "Me own playin' of lute or pipe be good enough fer taverns an' the like, but I be no virtuoso like these two." He looked at the huge Toth. "How is it possible fer a man so big t' produce so delicate a sound?"

"He's very good," Eriond told him. "He plays for Durnik and me sometimes—when the fish aren't biting."

"Ah, 'tis a grand sound," Feldegast said, "an' far to good t' be wasted." He looked across the fire at Vella. "Would ye be willin' t' give us a bit of a dance, me girl, t' sort of round out the evenin'?"

"Why not?" She laughed with a toss of her head. She rose to her feet and moved to the opposite side of the fire. "Follow this beat," she instructed, raising her rounded arms above her head and snapping her fingers to set the tempo. Feldegast picked up the beat, clapping his hands rhythmically.

Garion had seen Vella dance before—long ago in a forest travern in Gar og Nadrak—so he knew more or less what to expect. He was sure, however, that Eriond certainly—and Ce'Nedra probably—should not watch a performance of such blatant sensuality. Vella's dance began innocuously enough, though, and he began to think that perhaps he had been unduly sensitive the last time he had watched her.

When the sharp staccato of her snapping fingers and Feldegast's clapping increased the tempo, however, and she began to dance with greater abondon, he realized that his first assessment had been correct. Eriond should really not be watching this dance, and Ce'Nedra should be sent away almost immediately. For the life of him, however, he could not think of any way to do it.

When the tempo slowed again and Durnik and Toth returned to a simple restatement of the original air, the Nadrak girl concluded her dance with that proud, aggressive strut that challenged every man about the fire.

To Garion's absolute astonishment, Eriond warmly applauded with no trace of embarrassment showing on his young face. He knew that his own neck was burning and that his breath was coming faster.

Ce'Nedra's reaction was about what he had expected. Her

cheeks were flaming and her eyes were wide. Then she suddenly laughed with delight. "Wonderful!" she exclaimed, and her eyes were full of mischief as she cast a sidelong glance at Garion. He coughed nervously.

Feldegast wiped a tear from his eye and blew his nose gustily. Then he rose to his feet. "Ah, me fine, lusty wench," he said fulsomely to Vella, hanging a regretful embrace about her neck and—endangering life and limb just a little in view of her ever-ready daggers—bussing her noisily on the lips, "it's destroyed altogether I am that we must part. I'll miss ye, me girl, an' make no mistake about that. But I make ye me promise that we'll meet again, an' I'll delight ye with a few of me naughty little stories, an' ye'll fuddle me brains with yer wicked brew, an' we'll laugh an' sing together an' enjoy spring after spring in the sheer delight of each others' company." Then he slapped her rather familiarly on the bottom and moved quickly out of range before she could find the hilt of one of her daggers.

"Does she dance for you often, Yarblek?" Silk asked his partner, his eyes very bright.

"*Too* often," Yarblek replied mournfully, "and every time she does, I find myself starting to think that her daggers aren't really all *that* sharp and that a little cut or two wouldn't really hurt too much."

"Feel free to try at any time, Yarblek," Vella offered, her hand suggestively on the hilt of one of her daggers. Then she looked at Ce'Nedra with a broad wink.

"Why do you dance like that?" Ce'Nedra asked, still blushing slightly. "You *know* what it does to every man who watches."

"That's part of the fun, Ce'Nedra. First you drive them crazy, and then you hold them off with your daggers. It makes them absolutely wild. Next time we meet, I'll show you how it's done." She looked at Garion and laughed a wicked laugh.

Belgarath returned to the fire. He had left at some time during Vella's dance, though Garion's eyes had been too busy to notice. "It's dark enough," he told them all. "I think we can leave now without attracting any notice."

They all rose from where they had been sitting.

"You know what to do?" Silk asked his partner.

Yarblek nodded.

"All right. Do whatever you have to to keep me out of the soup."

"Why do you persist in playing around in politics, Silk?"

"Because it gives me access to greater opportunities to steal."

"Oh," Yarblek said. "That's all right then." He extended his hand. "Take care, Silk," he said.

"You, too, Yarblek. Try to keep us solvent if you can, and I'll see you in a year or so."

"If you live."

"There's that, too."

"I enjoyed your dance, Vella," Polgara said, embracing the Nadrak girl.

"I'm honored, Lady," Vella replied a bit shyly. "And we'll meet again, I'm sure."

"I'm certain that we will."

"Are ye sure that ye won't reconsider yer outrageous askin' price, Master Yarblek?" Feldegast asked.

"Talk to *her* about it," Yarblek replied, jerking his head in Vella's direction. "She's the one who set it."

"'Tis a hardhearted woman ye are, me girl," the juggler accused her.

She shrugged. "If you buy something cheap, you don't value it."

"Now that's the truth, surely. I'll see what I kin do t' put me hands on some money, fer make no mistake, me fine wench, I mean t' own ye."

"We'll see," she replied with a slight smile.

They went out of the circle of firelight to their picketed horses—and the juggler's mule—and mounted quietly. The moon had set, and the stars lay like bright jewels across the warm, velvet throat of night as they rode out of Yarblek's camp and moved at a cautious walk toward the north. When the sun rose several hours later, they were miles away, moving north-ward along a well-maintained highway toward Mal Rukuth, the Angarak city lying on the south bank of the Raku River, the stream that marked the southern border of Venna. The morning was warm, the sky was clear, and they made good time.

Once again there were refugees on the road, but unlike yesterday, significant numbers of them were fleeing toward the south.

"Is it possible that the plague has broken out in the north as well?" Sadi asked.

Polgara frowned. "It's possible, I suppose," she told him.

"I think it's more likely that those people are fleeing from Mengha," Belgarath disagreed.

"It's going to get a bit chaotic hereabouts," Silk noted. "If you've got people fleeing in one direction from the plague and people fleeing in the other from the demons, about all they'll be able to do is mill around out here on these plains."

"That could work to our advantage, Kheldar," Velvet pointed out. "Sooner or later, Zakath is going to discover that we left Mal Zeth without saying good-bye and he's likely to send troops out looking for us. A bit of chaos in this region should help to confuse their search, wouldn't you say?"

"You've got a point there," he admitted.

Garion rode on in a half doze, a trick he had learned from Belgarath. Though he had occasionally missed a night's sleep in the past, he had never really gotten used to it. He rode along with his head down, only faintly aware of what was happening around him.

He heard a persistent sound that seemed to nag at the edge of his consciousness. He frowned, his eyes still closed, trying to identify the sound. And then he remembered. It was a faint, despairing wail, and the full horror of the sight of the dying child in the shabby street in Mal Zeth struck him. Try though he might, he could not wrench himself back into wakefulness, and the continuing cry tore at his heart.

Then he felt a large hand on his shoulder, shaking him gently. Struggling, he raised his head to look full into the sad face of the giant Toth.

"Did you hear it, too?" he asked.

Toth nodded, his face filled with sympathy.

"It was only a dream, wasn't it?"

Toth spread his hands, and his look was uncertain.

Garion squared his shoulders and sat up in his saddle, determined not to drift off again.

They rode some distance away from the road and took a cold lunch of bread, cheese, and smoked sausage in the shade of a large elm tree standing quite alone in the middle of a field of oats. There was a small spring surrounded by a mossy rock wall not far away, where they were able to water the horses and fill their water bags.

Belgarath stood looking out over the fields toward a distant village and the barricaded lane which approached it. "How much food do we have with us, Pol?" he asked. "If every village we come to is closed up the way the ones we've passed so far have been, it's going to be difficult to replenish our stores."

"I think we'll be all right, father," she replied. "Vella was very generous."

"I like her." Ce'Nedra smiled. "Even though she does swear all the time."

Polgara returned the smile. "It's the Nadrak way, dear," she said. "When I was in Gar og Nadrak, I had to draw on my memories of the more colorful parts of my father's vocabulary to get by."

"Halloo!" someone hailed them.

"He's over there." Silk pointed toward the road.

A man who was wearing one of the brown robes that identified him as a Melcene bureaucrat sat looking at them longingly from the back of a bay horse.

"What do you want?" Durnik called to him.

"Can you spare a bit of food?" the Melcene shouted. "I can't get near any of these villages and I haven't eaten in three days. I can pay."

Durnik looked questioningly at Polgara.

She nodded. "We have enough," she said.

"Which way was he coming?" Belgarath asked.

"South, I think," Silk replied.

"Tell him that it's all right, Durnik," the old man said. "He can probably give us some recent news from the north."

"Come on in," Durnik shouted to the hungry man.

The bureaucrat rode up until he was about twenty yards away. Then he stopped warily. "Are you from Mal Zeth?" he demanded.

"We left before the plague broke out," Silk lied.

The official hesitated. "I'll put the money on this rock here," he offered, pointing at a white boulder. "Then I'll move back a ways. You can take the money and leave some food. That way neither one of us will endanger the other."

"Makes sense," Silk replied pleasantly.

Polgara took a loaf of brown bread and a generous slab of cheese from her stores and gave them to the sharp-faced Drasnian.

The Melcene dismounted, laid a few coins on the rock, and then led his horse back some distance.

"Where have you come from, friend?" Silk asked as he approached the rock.

"I was in Akkad in Katakor," the hungry man answered, eyeing the loaf and the cheese. "I was senior administrator there for the Bureau of Public Works—you know, walls, aqueducts, streets, that sort of thing. The bribes weren't spectacular, but I managed to get by. Anyway, I got out just a few hours before Mengha and his demons got there."

Silk laid the food on the rock and picked up the money. Then he backed away. "We heard that Akkad fell quite some time ago."

The Melcene almost ran to the rock and snatched up and bread and cheese. He took a large bite of cheese and tore a chunk off the loaf. "I hid out in the mountains," he replied around the mouthful.

"Isn't that where Ashaba is?" Silk asked, sounding very casual.

The Melcene swallowed hard and nodded. "That's why I finally left," he said, stuffing bread in his mouth. "The area's infested with huge wild dogs—ugly brutes as big as horses— and there are roving bands of Karands killing everyone they come across. I could have avoided all that, but there's something terrible going on at Ashaba. There are dreadful sounds coming from the castle and strange lights in the sky over it at night. I don't hold with the supernatural, my friend, so I bolted." He sighed happily, tearing off another chunk of bread. "A month ago I'd have turned my nose up at brown bread and cheese. Now it tastes like a banquet."

"Hunger's the best sauce," Silk quoted the old adage.

"That's the honest truth."

"Why didn't you stay up in Venna? Didn't you know that there's plague in Mal Zeth?"

The Melcene shuddered. "What's going on in Venna's even worse than what's going on in Katakor or Mal Zeth," he replied. "My nerves are absolutely destroyed by all this. I'm an engineer. What do I know about demons and new Gods and magic? Give me paving stones and timbers and mortar and a few modest bribes and don't even mention any of that other nonsense to me."

"New Gods?" Silk asked. "Who's been talking about new Gods?"

"The Chandim. You've heard of them?"

"Don't they belong to Urvon the Disciple?"

"I don't think they belong to anybody right now. They've gone on a rampage in Venna. Nobody's seen Urvon for more than a month now—not even the people in Mal Yaska. The Chandim are completely out of control. They're erecting altars out in the fields and holding double sacrifices—the first heart to Torak and the second to this new God of Angarak—and anybody up there that doesn't bow to *both* altars gets his heart cut out right on the spot."

"That seems like a very good reason to stay out of Venna," Silk said wryly. "Have they put a name to this new God of theirs?"

"Not that I ever heard. They just call him 'The new God of Angarak, come to replace Torak and to take dreadful vengeance on the Godslayer.'"

"That's you," Velvet murmured to Garion.

"Do you mind?"

"I just thought you ought to know, that's all."

"There's an open war going on in Venna, my friend," the Melcene continued, "and I'd advise you to give the place a wide berth."

"War?"

"Within the Church itself. The Chandim are slaughtering all the old Grolims—the ones who are still faithful to Torak. The Temple Guardsmen are taking sides and they're having pitched battles on the plains up there—that's when they're not marauding through the countryside, burning farmsteads, and massacring whole villages. You'd think that the whole of Venna's gone crazy. It's as much as a man's life is worth to go through there just now. They stop you and ask you which God you worship, and a wrong answer is fatal." He paused, still eating. "Have you heard about any place that's quiet—and safe?" he asked plaintively.

"Try the coast," Silk suggested. "Mal Abad, maybe—or Mal Camat."

"Which way are you going?"

"We're going north to the river and see if we can find a boat to take us down to Lake Penn Daka."

"It won't be safe there for very long, friend. If the plague doesn't get there first, Mengha's demons will—or the crazed Grolims and their Guardsmen out of Venna."

251

"We don't plan to stop," Silk told him. "We're going to cut on across Delchin to Maga Renn and then on down the Magan."

"That's a long journey."

"Friend, I'll go to Gandahar if necessary to get away from demons and plague and mad Grolims. If worse comes to worst, we'll hide out among the elephant herders. Elephants aren't all that bad."

The Melcene smiled briefly. "Thanks for the food," he said, tucking his loaf and his cheese inside his robe and looking around for his grazing horse. "Good luck when you get to Gandahar."

"The same to you on the coast," Silk replied.

They watched the Melcene ride off.

"Why did you take his money, Kheldar?" Eriond asked curiously. "I thought we were just going to give him the food."

"Unexpected and unexplained acts of charity linger in people's minds, Eriond, and curiosity overcomes gratitude. I took his money to make sure that by tomorrow he won't be able to describe us to any curious soldiers."

"Oh," the boy said a bit sadly. "It's too bad that things are like that, isn't it?"

"As Sadi says, I didn't make the world; I only try to live in it."

"Well, what do you think?" Belgarath said to the juggler.

Feldegast squinted off toward the horizon. "Yer dead set on goin' right straight up through the middle of Venna—past Mal Yaska an' all?"

"We don't have any choice. We've got just so much time to get to Ashaba."

"Somehow I thought y' might feel that way about it."

"Do you know a way to get us through?"

Feldegast scratched his head. "'Twill be dangerous, Ancient One," he said dubiously, "what with Grolims and Chandim and Temple Guardsmen an' all."

252

"It won't be nearly as dangerous as missing our appointment at Ashaba would be."

"Well, if yer dead set on it, I suppose I kin get ye through."

"All right," Belgarath said. "Let's get started then."

The peculiar suspicion which had come over Garion the day before grew stronger. Why would his grandfather ask these questions of a man they scarcely knew? The more he thought about it, the more he became convinced that there was a great deal more going on here than met the eye.

CHAPTER FOURTEEN

It was late afternoon when they reached Mal Ra-kuth, a grim fortress city crouched on the banks of a muddy river. The walls were high, and black towers rose within those walls. A large crowd of people was gathered outside, imploring the citizens to let them enter, but the city gates were locked, and archers with half-drawn bows lined the battlements, threatening the refugees below.

"That sort of answers that question, doesn't it?" Garion said as he and his companions reined in on a hilltop some distance from the frightened city.

Belgarath grunted. "It's more or less what I expected," he

said. "There's nothing we really need in Mal Rakuth anyway, so there's not much point in pressing the issue."

"How are we going to get across the river, though?"

"If I remember correctly, there be a ferry crossin' but a few miles upstream," Feldegast told him.

"Won't the ferryman be just as frightened of the plague as the people in that city are?" Durnik asked him.

"'Tis an ox-drawn ferry, Goodman—with teams on each side an' cables an' pulleys an' all. The ferryman kin take our money an' put us on the far bank an' never come within fifty yards of us. I fear the crossin' will be dreadful expensive, though."

The ferry proved to be a leaky old barge attached to a heavy cable stretched across the yellow-brown river.

"Stay back!" the mud-covered man holding the rope hitched about the neck of the lead ox on the near side commanded as they approached. "I don't want any of your filthy diseases."

"How much to go across?" Silk called to him.

The muddy fellow squinted greedily at them, assessing their clothing and horses. "One gold piece," he said flatly.

"That's outrageous!"

"Try swimming."

"Pay him," Belgarath said.

"Not likely," Silk replied. "I refuse to be cheated—even here. Let me think a minute." His narrow face became intent as he stared hard at the rapacious ferryman. "Durnik," he said thoughtfully, "do you have your axe handy?"

The smith nodded, patting the axe which hung from a loop at the back of his saddle.

"Do you suppose you could reconsider just a bit, friend?" the little Drasnian called plaintively to the ferryman.

"One gold piece," the ferryman repeated stubbornly.

Silk sighed. "Do you mind if we look at your boat first? It doesn't look all that safe to me."

"Help yourself—but I won't move it until I get paid."

Silk looked at Durnik. "Bring the axe," he said.

Durnik dismounted and lifted his broad-bladed axe from its loop. Then the two of them climbed down the slippery bank to the barge. They went up the sloping ramp and onto the deck. Silk stamped his feet tentatively on the planking. "Nice boat," he said to the ferryman, who stood cautiously some distance away. "Are you sure you won't reconsider the price?"

"One gold piece. Take it or leave it."

Silk sighed. "I was afraid you might take that position." He scuffed one foot at the muddy deck. "You know more about boats than I do, friend," he observed. "How long do you think it would take this tub to sink if my friend here chopped a hole in the bottom?"

The ferryman gaped at him.

"Pull up the decking in the bow, Durnik," Silk suggested pleasantly. "Give yourself plenty of room for a good swing."

The desperate ferryman grabbed up a club and ran down the bank.

"Careful, friend," Silk said to him. "We left Mal Zeth only yesterday, and I'm already starting to feel a little feverish—something I ate, no doubt."

The ferryman froze in his tracks.

Durnik was grinning as he began to pry up the decking at the frong of the barge.

"My friend here is an expert woodsman," Silk continued in a conversational tone, "and his axe is terribly sharp. I'll wager that he can have this scow lying on the bottom inside of ten minutes."

"I can see into the hold now," Durnik reported, suggestively testing the edge of his axe with his thumb. "Just how big a hole would you like?"

"Oh," Silk replied, "I don't know, Durnik—a yard or so square, maybe. Would that sink it?"

"I'm not sure. Why don't we try it and find out?" Durnik

pushed up the sleeves of his short jacket and hefted his axe a couple of times.

The ferryman was making strangled noises and hopping up and down.

"What's your feeling about negotiation at this point, friend?" Silk asked him. "I'm almost positive that we can reach an accommodation—now that you fully understand the situation."

When they were partway across the river and the barge was wallowing heavily in the current, Durnik walked forward to the bow and stood looking into the opening he had made by prying up the deck. "I wonder how big a hole it *would* take to sink this thing," he mused.

"What was that, dear?" Polgara asked him.

"Just thinking out loud, Pol," he said. "But do you know something? I just realized that I've never sunk a boat before."

She rolled her eyes heavenward. "Men," she sighed.

"I suppose I'd better put the planks back so that we can lead the horses off on the other side," Durnik said almost regretfully.

They erected their tents in the shelter of a grove of cedar trees near the river that evening. The sky, which had been serene and blue since they had arrived in Mallorea, had turned threatening as the sun sank, and there were rumbles of thunder and brief flickers of lightning among the clouds off to the west.

After supper, Durnik and Toth went out of the grove for a look around and returned with sober faces. "I'm afraid that we're in for a spell of bad weather," the smith reported. "You can smell it coming."

"I hate riding in the rain," Silk complained.

"Most people do, Prince Kheldar," Feldegast told him. "But bad weather usually keeps others in as well, don't y' know; an' if what that hungry traveler told us this afternoon be true, we'll not be wantin' t' meet the sort of folk that be abroad in Venna when the weather's fine."

"He mentioned the Chandim," Sadi said, frowning. "Just exactly who are they?"

"The Chandim are an order within the Grolim Church," Belgarath told him. "When Torak built Cthol Mishrak, he converted certain Grolims into Hounds to patrol the region. After Vo Mimbre, when Torak was bound in sleep, Urvon converted about half of them back. The ones who reassumed human form are all sorcerers of greater or lesser talent, and they can communicate with the ones who are still Hounds. They're very close-knit—like a pack of wild dogs—and they're all fanatically loyal to Urvon."

"An' that be much of the source of Urvon's power," Feldegast added. "Ordinary Grolims be always schemin' against each other an' against their superiors, but Urvon's Chamdim have kept the Mallorean Grolims in line fer five hundred years now."

"And the Temple Guardsmen?" Sadi added. "Are they Chandim, or Grolims, too?"

"Not usually," Belgarath replied. "There are Grolims among them, of course, but most of them are Mallorean Angaraks. They were recruited before Vo Mimbre to serve as Torak's personal bodyguard."

"Why would a God need a bodyguard?"

"I never entirely understood that myself," the old man admitted. "Anyway, after Vo Mimbre, there are still a few of them left—new recruits, veterans who'd been wounded in earlier battles and sent home, that sort of thing. Urvon persuaded them that *he* spoke for Torak, and now their allegiance is to him. After that, they recruited more young Angaraks to fill up the holes in their ranks. They do more than just guard the Temple now, though. When Urvon started having difficulties with the Emperors at Mal Zeth, he decided that he needed a fighting force, so he expanded them into an army."

"'Tis a practical arrangement," Feldegast pointed out. "The Chandim provide Urvon with the sorcery he needs t' keep the other Grolims toein' the mark, an' the Temple

Guardsmen provide the muscle t' keep the ordinary folk from protestin' their lot."

"These Guardsmen, they're just ordinary soldiers, then?" Durnik asked.

"Not really. They're closer to being knights," Belgarath replied.

"Like Mandorallen, you mean—all dressed in steel plate and with shields and lances and war horses and all that?"

"No, Goodman," Feldegast answered. "They're not nearly so grand. Lances an' helmets and shields they have, certainly, but fer the rest, they rely on chain mail. They be most nearly as stupid as Arends, however. Somethin' about wearin' all that steel empties the mind of every knight the world around."

Belgarath was looking speculatively at Garion. "How muscular are you feeling?" he asked.

"Not very—why?"

"We've got a bit of a problem here. We're far more likely to encounter Guardsmen than we are Chandim, but if we start unhorsing all these tin men with our minds, the noise is going to attract the Chandim like a beacon."

Garion stared at him. "You're not serious! I'm not Mandorallen, Grandfather."

"No. You've got better sense than he has."

"I will *not* stand by and hear my knight insulted!" Ce'Nedra declared hotly.

"Ce'Nedra," Belgarath said almost absently, "hush."

"Hush?"

"You heard me." He scowled at her so blackly that she faltered and drew back behind Polgara for protection. "The point, Garion," the old man continued, "is that you've received a certain amount of training from Mandorallen in this sort of thing and you've had a bit of experience. None of the rest of us have."

"I don't have any armor."

"You've got a mail shirt."

"I don't have a helmet—or a shield."

"I could probably manage those, Garion," Durnik offered.

Garion looked at his old friend. "I'm terribly disappointed in you, Durnik," he said.

"You aren't afraid, are you, Garion?" Ce'Nedra asked in a small voice.

"Well, no. Not really. It's just that it's so stupid—and it *looks* so ridiculous."

"Have you got an old pot I could borrow, Pol?" Durnik asked.

"How big a pot?"

"Big enough to fit Garion's head."

"Now that's going too far!" Garion exclaimed. "I'm not going to wear a kitchen pot on my head for a helmet. I haven't done that since I was a boy."

"I'll modify it a bit," Durnik assured him. "And then I'll take the lid and make you a shield."

Garion walked away swearing to himself.

Velvet's eyes had narrowed. She looked at Feldegast with no hint of her dimples showing. "Tell me, master juggler," she said, "how is it that an itinerant entertainer, who plays for pennies in wayside taverns, knows so very much about the inner working of Grolim society here in Mallorea?"

"I be not nearly so foolish as I look, me lady," he replied, "an' I do have eyes an' ears, an' know how t' use 'em."

"You avoided that question rather well," Belgarath complimented him.

The juggler smirked. "I thought so meself. Now," he continued seriously, "as me ancient friend here says, 'tis not too likely that we'll be encounterin' the Chandim if it rains, fer a dog has usually the good sense t' take t' his kennel when the weather be foul—unless there be pressin' need fer him t' be out an' about. 'Tis far more probable fer us t' meet Temple Guardsmen, fer a knight, be he Arendish or Mallorean, seems deaf t' the gentle patter of rain on his armor. I shouldn't wonder that our young warrior King over there be of sufficient might t' be a match fer any Guardsman we might meet alone, but there always be the possibility of comin' across 'em in groups. Should there be such encounters, keep yer wits about ye an' remember that once a knight has started his charge, 'tis very hard fer him t' swerve or change direction very much at all. A sidestep an' a smart rap across the back of the head be usually enough t' roll 'em out of the saddle, an' a man in armor—once he's off his horse—be like a turtle on his back, don't y' know."

"You've done it a few times yourself, I take it?" Sadi murmured.

"I've had me share of misunderstandin's with Temple Guardsmen," Feldegast admitted, "an' ye'll note that I still be here t' talk about 'em."

Durnik took the cast iron pot Polgara had given him and set it in the center of their fire. After a time, he pulled it glowing out of the coals with a stout stick, placed the blade of a broken knife on a rounded rock, and then set the pot over it. He took up his axe, reversed it, and held the blunt end over the pot.

"You'll break it," Silk predicted. "Cast iron's too brittle to take any pounding."

"Trust me, Silk," the smith said with a wink. He took a deep breath and began to tap lightly on the pot. The sound of his hammering was not the dull clack of cast iron, but the clear ring of steel, a sound that Garion remembered from his earliest boyhood. Deftly the smith reshaped the pot into a flat-topped helmet with a fierce nose guard and heavy cheek pieces. Garion knew that his old friend was cheating just a bit by the faint whisper and surge he was directing at the emerging helmet.

Then Durnik dropped the helmet into a pail of water, and it hissed savagely, sending off a cloud of steam. The pot lid that the smith intended to convert into a shield, however, challenged even *his* ingenuity. It became quite obvious that, should he hammer it out to give it sufficient size to offer protection, it would be so thin that it would not even fend off a dagger stroke, much less a blow from a lance or sword. He considered that, even as he pounded on the ringing lid. He shifted his axe and made an obscure gesture at Toth. The giant nodded, went to the river bank, returned with a pail full of clay, and dumped the bucket out in the center of the glowing shield. It gave off an evil hiss, and Durnik continued to pound.

"Un—Durnik," Garion said, trying not to be impolite, "a ceramic shield was not exactly what I had in mind, you know."

Durnik gave him a grin filled with surpressed mirth. "Look at it, Garion," he suggested, not changing the tempo of his hammering.

Garion stared at the shield, his eyes suddenly wide. The glowing circle upon which Durnik was pounding was solid, cherry-red steel. "How did you do that?"

"Transmutation!" Polgara gasped. "Changing one thing into something else! Durnik, where on earth did you ever learn to do that?"

"It's just something I picked up, Pol." He laughed. "As long as you've got a bit of steel to begin with—like that old knife blade—you can make as much more as you want, out of anything that's handy: cast iron, clay, just about anything."

Ce'Nedra's eyes had suddenly gone very wide. "Durnik," she said in an almost reverent whisper, "could you have made it out of gold?"

Durnik thought about it, still hammering. "I suppose I could have," he addmitted, "but gold's too heavy and soft to make a good shield, wouldn't you say?"

"Could you make another one?" she wheedled. "For me? It wouldn't have to be so big—at least not quite. Please, Durnik."

Durnik finished the rim of the shield with a shower of crimson sparks and the musical ring of steel on steel. "I don't think that would be a good idea, Ce'Nedra," he told her. "Gold is valuable because it's so scarce. If I started making

262

it out of clay, it wouldn't be long before it wasn't worth anything at all. I'm sure you can see that."

"But—"

"No, Ce'Nedra," he said firmly.

"Garion—" she appealed, her voice anguished.

"He's right, dear."

"But—"

"Never mind, Ce'Nedra."

The fire had burned down to a bed of glowing coals. Garion awoke with a start, sitting up suddenly. He was covered with sweat and trembling violently. Once again he had heard the wailing cry that he had heard the previous day, and the sound of it wrenched at his heart. He sat for a long time staring at the fire. In time, the sweat dried and his trembling subsided.

Ce'Nedra's breathing was regular as she lay beside him, and there was no other sound in their well-shielded encampment. He rolled carefully out of his blankets and walked to the edge of the grove of cedars to stare bleakly out across the fields lying dark and empty under an inky sky. Then, because there was nothing he could do about it, he returned to his bed and slept fitfully until dawn.

It was drizzling rain when he awoke. He got up quietly and went out of the tent to join Durnik, who was building up the fire. "Can I borrow your axe?" he asked his friend.

Durnik looked up at him.

"I guess I'm going to need a lance to go with all that." He looked rather distastefully at the helmet and shield lying atop his mail shirt near the packs and saddles.

"Oh," the smith said. "I almost forgot about that. Is one going to be enough? They break sometimes, you know—at least Mandorallen's always did."

"I'm certainly not going to carry more than one." Garion jabbed his thumb back over his shoulder at the hilt of his sword. "Anyway, I've always got this big knife to fall back on."

The chill drizzle that had begun shortly before dawn was the kind of rain that made the nearby fields hazy and indistinct. After breakfast, they took heavy cloaks out of their packs and prepared to face a fairly unpleasant day. Garion had already put on his mail shirt, and he padded the inside of his helmet with an old tunic and jammed it down on his head. He felt very foolish as he clinked over to saddle Chretienne. The mail already smelled bad and it seemed, for some reason, to attract the chill of the soggy morning. He looked at his new-cut lance and his round shield. "This is going to be awkward," he said.

"Hang the shield from the saddle bow, Garion," Durnik suggested, "and set the butt of your lance in the stirrup beside your foot. That's the way Mandorallen does it."

"I'll try it," Garion said. He hauled himself up into his saddle, already sweating under the weight of his mail. Durnik handed him the shield, and he hooked the strap of it over the saddle bow. Then he took his lance and jammed its butt into his stirrup, pinching his toes in the process.

"You'll have to hold it," the smith told him. "It won't stay upright by itself."

Garion grunted and took the shaft of his lance in his right hand.

"You look very impressive, dear," Ce'Nedra assured him.

"Wonderful," he replied dryly.

They rode out of the cedar grove into the wet, miserable morning with Garion in the lead, feeling more than a little absurd in his warlike garb.

The lance, he discovered almost immediately, had a stubborn tendency to dip its point toward the ground. He shifted his grip on it, sliding his hand up until he found its center of balance. The rain collected on the shaft of the lance, ran down across his clammy hand, and trickled into his sleeve. After a short while, a steady stream of water dribbled from his elbow. "I feel like a downspout," he grumbled.

"Let's pick up the pace," Belgarath said to him. "It's a long way to Ashaba, and we don't have too much time."

Garion nudged Chretienne with his heels, and the big gray moved out, at first at a trot and then in a rolling canter. For some reason that made Garion feel a bit less foolish.

The road which Feldegast had pointed out to them the previous evening was little traveled and this morning it was deserted. It ran past abandoned farmsteads, sad, bramble-choked shells with the moldy remains of their thatched roofs all tumbled in. A few of the farmsteads had been burned, some only recently.

The road began to turn muddy as the earth soaked up the steady rain. The cantering hooves of their horses splashed the mud up to coat their legs and bellies and to spatter the boots and cloaks of the riders.

Silk rode beside Garion, his sharp face alert, and just before they reached the crest of each hill, he galloped on ahead to have a quick look at the shallow valley lying beyond.

By midmorning, Garion was soaked through, and he rode on bleakly, enduring the discomfort and the smell of new rust, wishing fervently that the rain would stop.

Silk came back down the next hill after scouting on ahead. His face was tight with a sudden excitement, and he motioned them all to stop.

"There are some Grolims up ahead," he reported tersely.

"How many?" Belgarath asked.

"About two dozen. They're holding some kind of religious ceremony."

The old man grunted. "Let's take a look." He looked at Garion. "Leave your lance with Durnik," he said. "It sticks up too high into the air, and I'd rather not attract attention."

Garion nodded and passed his lance over to the smith, then followed Silk, Belgarath, and Feldegast up the hill. They dismounted just before they reached the crest and moved carefully to the top, where a brushy thicket offered some concealment.

The black-robed Grolims were kneeling on the wet grass before a pair of grim altars some distance down the hill. A limp, unmoving form lay sprawled across each of them, and there was a great deal of blood. Sputtering braziers stood at the end of each altar, sending twin columns of black smoke up into the drizzle. The Grolims were chanting in the rumbling groan Garion had heard too many times before. He could not make out what they were saying.

"Chandim?" Belgarath softly asked the juggler.

"'Tis hard t' say fer certain, Ancient One," Feldegast replied. "The twin altars would suggest it, but the practice might have spread. Grolims be very quick t' pick up changes in Church policy. But Chandim or not, 'twould be wise of us t' avoid 'em. There be not much point in engagin' ourselves in casual skirmishes with Grolims."

"There are trees over on the east side of the valley," Silk said, pointing. "If we stay in among them, we'll be out of sight."

Belgarath nodded.

"How much longer are they likely to be praying?" Garion asked.

"Another half hour at least," Feldegast replied.

Garion looked at the pair of altars, feeling an icy rage building up in him. "I'd like to cap their ceremony with a little personal visit," he said.

"Forget it," Belgarath told him. "You're not here to ride around the countryside righting wrongs. Let's go back and get the others. I'd like to get around those Grolims before they finish with their prayers."

They picked their way carefully through the belt of dripping trees that wound along the eastern rim of the shallow valley where the Grolims were conducting their grim rites and returned to the muddy road about a mile beyond. Again they set out at the same distance-eating canter, with Garion once more in the lead.

Some miles past the valley where the Grolims had sacrificed the two unfortunates, they passed a burning village that was spewing out a cloud of black smoke. There seemed to be no one about, though there were some signs of fighting near the burning houses.

They rode on without stopping.

The rain let up by midafternoon, though the sky remained overcast. Then, as they crested yet another hilltop in the rolling countryside, they saw another rider on the far side of the valley. The distance was too great to make out details, but Garion *could* see that the rider was armed with a lance.

"What do we do?" he called back over his shoulder at the rest of them.

"That's why you're wearing armor and carrying a lance, Garion," Belgarath replied.

"Shouldn't I at least give him the chance to stand aside?"

"To what purpose?" Feldegast asked. "He'll not do it. Yer very presence here with yer lance an' yer shield be a challenge, an' he'll not be refusin' it. Ride him down, young Master. The day wears on, don't y' know."

"All right," Garion said unhappily. He buckled his shield to his left arm, settled his helmet more firmly in place, and lifted the butt of his lance out of his stirrup. Chretienne was already pawing at the earth and snorting defiantly.

"Enthusiast," Garion muttered to him. "All right, let's go, then."

The big gray's charge was thunderous. It was not a gallop, exactly, nor a dead run, but rather was a deliberately implacable gait that could only be called a charge.

The armored man across the valley seemed a bit startled by the unprovoked attack, there having been none of the customary challenges, threats, or insults. After a bit of fumbling with his equipment, he managed to get his shield in place and his lance properly advanced. He seemed to be quite bulky, though that might have been his armor. He wore a sort of chain-mail coat reaching to his knees. His helmet was round and fitted with a visor, and he had a large sword sheathed at his waist. He clanged down his visor, then sank his spurs into his horse's flanks and also charged.

The wet fields at the side of the road seemed to blur as Garion crouched behind his shield with his lance lowered and aimed directly at his opponent. He had seen Mandorallen do this often enough to understand the basics. The distance between him and the stranger was narrowing rapidly, and Garion could clearly see the mud spraying out from beneath the hooves of his opponent's horse. At the last moment, just before they came together, Garion raised up in his stirrups as Mandorallen had instructed him, leaned forward so that his entire body was braced for the shock, and took careful aim with his lance at the exact center of the other man's shield.

There was a dreadful crashing impact, and he was suddenly surrounded by flying splinters as his opponent's lance shattered. His own lance, however, though it was as stout as that of the Guardsman, was a freshly cut cedar pole and it was quite springy. It bent into a tight arch like a drawn bow, then snapped straight again. The startled stranger was suddenly lifted out of his saddle. His body described a high, graceful arc through the air, which ended abruptly as he came down on his head in the middle of the road.

Garion thundered on past and finally managed to rein in his big gray horse. He wheeled and stopped. The other man lay on his back in the mud of the road. He was not moving. Carefully, his lance at the ready, Garion walked Chretienne back to the splinter-littered place where the impact had occurred.

"Are you all right?" he asked the Temple Guardsman lying in the mud.

There was no answer.

Cautiously, Garion dismounted, dropped his lance, and drew Iron-grip's sword. "I say, man, are you all right?" he asked again. He reached out with his foot and nudged the fellow.

The Guardsman's visor was closed, and Garion put the tip of his sword under the bottom of it and lifted. The man's eyes were rolled back in his head until only the whites showed, and there was blood gushing freely from his nose.

The others came galloping up, and Ce'Nedra flung herself out of the saddle almost before her horse and stopped and hurled herself into her husband's arms. "You were magnificent, Garion! Absolutely magnificent!"

"It did go rather well, didn't it?" he replied modestly, trying to juggle sword, shield, and wife all at the same time. He looked at Polgara, who was also dismounting. "Do you think he's going to be all right, Aunt Pol?" he asked. "I hope I didn't hurt him too much."

She checked the limp man lying in the road. "He'll be fine, dear," she assured him. "He's just been knocked senseless, is all."

"Nice job," Silk said.

Garion suddenly grinned broadly. "You know something," he said. "I think I'm starting to understand why Mandorallen enjoys this so much. It *is* sort of exhilarating."

"I think it has t' do with the weight of the armor," Feldegast observed sadly to Belgarath. "It bears down on 'em so much that it pulls all the juice out of their brains, or some such."

"Let's move on," Belgarath suggested.

By midmorning the following day, they had moved into the broad valley which was the location of Mal Yaska, the ecclesiastical capital of Mallorea and the site of the Disciple Urvon's palace. Though the sky remained overcast, the rain had blown on through, and a stiff breeze had begun to dry the grass and the mud which had clogged the roads. There were encampments dotting the valley, little clusters of people who had fled from the demons to the north and the plague to the south. Each group was fearfully isolated from its neighbors, and all of them kept their weapons close at hand.

Unlike those of Mal Rakuth, the gates of Mal Yaska stood open, though they were patrolled by detachments of mail-armored Temple Guardsmen.

"Why don't they go into the city?" Durnik asked, looking at the clusters of refugees.

"Mal Yaska's not the sort of place ye visit willin'ly, Goodman," Feldegast replied. "When the Grolims be lookin' fer people t' sacrifice on their altars, 'tis unwise t' make yerself too handy." He looked at Belgarath. "Would ye be willin' t' accept a suggestion, me ancient friend?" he asked.

"Suggest away."

"We'll be needin' information about what's happenin' up there." He pointed at the snow-capped mountains looming across the northern horizon. "Since I know me way about Mal Yaska an' know how t' avoid the Grolims, wouldn't ye say that it might be worth the investment of an hour or so t' have me nose about the central market place an' see what news I kin pick up?"

"He's got a point, Belgarath," Silk agreed seriously. "I don't like riding into a situation blind."

Belgarath considered it. "All right," he said to the juggler, "but be careful—and stay out of the alehouses."

Feldegast sighed. "There be no such havens in Mal Yaska, Belgarath. The Grolims there be fearful strict in their disapproval of simple pleasures." He shook the reins of his mule and rode on across the plain toward the black walls of Urvon's capital.

"Isn't he contradicting himself?" Sadi asked. "First he says it's too dangerous to go into the city and then he rides on in anyway."

"He knows what he's doing," Belgarath said. "He's in no danger."

"We might as well have some lunch while we're waiting, father," Polgara suggested.

He nodded, and they rode some distance into an open field and dismounted.

Garion laid aside his lance, pulled his helmet from his sweaty head, and stood looking across the intervening open space at the center of Church power in Mallorea. The city was large, certainly, though not nearly so large as Mal Zeth. The walls were high and thick, surmounted by heavy battlements, and the towers rising inside were square and blocky. There was a kind of unrelieved ugliness about it, and it seemed to exude a brooding menace as if the eons of cruelty and blood lust had sunk into its very stones. From somewhere near the center of the city, the telltale black column of smoke rose into the air, and faintly, echoing across the plain with its huddled encampments of frightened refugees, he thought he could hear the sullen iron clang of the gong coming from the Temple of Torak. Finally, he sighed and turned his head away.

"It will not last forever," Eriond, who had come up beside him, said firmly. "We're almost to the end of it now. All the altars will be torn down, and the Grolims will put their knives away to rust."

"Are you sure, Eriond?"

"Yes, Belgarion. I'm very sure."

They ate a cold lunch, and, not long after, Feldegast returned, his face somber. "'Tis perhaps a bit more serious than we had expected, Ancient One," he reported, swinging down from his mule. "The Chandim be in total control of the city, an' the Temple Guardsmen be takin' their orders directly from them. The Grolims who hold t' the old ways have all gone into hidin', but packs of Torak's Hounds be sniffin' out the places where they've hidden an' they be tearin' 'em t' pieces wherever they find 'em."

"I find it very hard to sympathize with Grolims," Sadi murmured.

"I kin bear their discomfort meself," Feldegast agreed, "but 'tis rumored about the market place that the Chandim an' their dogs an' their Guardsmen *also* be movin' about across the border in Katakor."

"In spite of the Karands and Mengha's demons?" Silk asked with some surprise.

"Now that's somethin' I could not get the straight of," the juggler replied. "No one could tell me why or how, but the Chandim an' the Guardsmen seem not t' be concerned about Mengha nor his army nor his demons."

"That begins to smell of some kind of accommodation," Silk said.

"There were hints of that previously," Feldegast reminded him.

"An alliance?" Belgarath frowned.

"'Tis hard t' say fer sure, Ancient One, but Urvon be a schemer, an' he's always had this dispute with the imperial throne at Mal Zeth. If he's managed t' put Mengha in his pocket, Kal Zakath had better look t' his defenses."

"Is Urvon in the city?" Belgarath asked.

"No. No one knows where he's gone fer sure, but he's not in his palace there."

"That's very strange," Belgarath said.

"Indeed," the juggler replied, "but whatever he's doin' or plannin' t' do, I think we'd better be walkin' softly once we cross the border into Katakor. When ye add the Hounds an' the Temple Guardsmen t' the demons an' Karands already there, 'tis goin' t' be fearful perilous t' approach the House of Torak at Ashaba."

"That's a chance we'll have to take," the old man said grimly. "We're going to Ashaba, and if anything—Hound, human, or demon—gets in our way, we'll just have to deal with it as it comes."

CHAPTER FIFTEEN

The sky continued to lower as they rode past the brooding city of the Grolim Church under the suspicious gaze of the armored Guardsmen at the gate and the hooded Grolims on the walls.

"Is it likely that they'll follow us?" Durnik asked.

"It's not very probable, Goodman," Sadi replied. "Look around you. There are thousands encamped here, and I doubt that either Guardsmen or Grolims would take the trouble to follow them all when they leave."

"I suppose you're right," the smith agreed.

By late afternoon they were well past Mal Yaska, and the snow-topped peaks in Katakor loomed higher ahead of them, starkly outlined against the dirty gray clouds scudding in from the west.

"Will ye be wantin' t' stop fer the night before we cross the border?" Feldegast asked Belgarath.

"How far is it to there from here?"

"Not far at all, Ancient One."

"Is it guarded?"

"Usually, yes."

"Silk," the old man said, "ride on ahead and have a look."

The little man nodded and nudged his horse into a gallop.

"All right," Belgarath said, signaling for a halt so that they could all hear him. "Everybody we've seen this afternoon was going south. Nobody's fleeing *toward* Katakor. Now, a man who's running away from someplace doesn't stop when the border's in sight. He keeps on going. That means that there's a fair chance that there's not going to be anybody within miles of the border on the Katakor side. If the border's not guarded, we can just go on across and take shelter for the night on the other side."

"And if the border *is* guarded?" Sadi asked.

Belgarath's eyes grew flat. "We're still going to go through," he replied.

"That's likely to involve fighting."

"That's right. Let's move along, shall we?"

About fifteen minutes later, Silk returned. "There are about ten Guardsmen at the crossing," he reported.

"Any chance of taking them by surprise?" Belgarath asked him.

"A little, but the road leading to the border is straight and flat for a half mile on either side of the guard post."

The old man muttered a curse under his breath. "All right then," he said. "They'll at least have time to get to their horses. We don't want to give them the leisure to get themselves set. Remember what Feldegast said about keeping your wits. Don't take any chances, but I want all of those Guardsmen on their backs after our first charge. Pol, you stay back with the ladies—and Eriond."

"But—" Velvet began to protest.

"Don't argue with me, Liselle—just this once."

"Couldn't Lady Polgara just put them to sleep?" Sadi asked. "The way she did with the spies back in Mal Zeth?"

Belgarath shook his head. "There are a few Grolims among the Guardsmen, and that particular technique doesn't work on Grolims. This time we're going to have to do it by main strength—just to be on the safe side."

Sadi nodded glumly, dismounted, and picked up a stout tree limb from the side of the road. He thumped it experimentally on the turf. "I want you all to know that this is not my preferred way of doing things," he said.

The rest of them also dismounted and armed themselves with cudgels and staffs. Then they moved on.

The border was marked by a stone shed painted white and by a gate consisting of a single white pole resting on posts on either side of the road. A dozen horses were tethered just outside the shed, and lances leaned against the wall. A single, mail-coated Guardsman paced back and forth across the road on the near side of the gate, his sword leaning back over his shoulder.

"All right," Belgarath said. "Let's move as fast as we can. Wait here, Pol."

Garion sighed. "I guess I'd better go first."

"We were hoping that you'd volunteer." Silk's grin was tight.

Garion ignored that. He buckled on his shield, settled his helmet in place, and once again lifted the butt of his lance out of his stirrup. "Is everybody ready?" he asked, looking around. Then he advanced his lance and spurred his horse into a charge with the others close on his heels.

The Guardsman at the gate took one startled look at the warlike party bearing down on him, ran to the door of the shed, and shouted at his comrades inside. Then he struggled into the saddle of his tethered horse, leaned over to pick up his lance, and moved out into the road. Other Guardsmen came boiling out of the shed, struggling with their equipment and stumbling over each other.

Garion had covered half the distance to the gate before more than two or three of the armored men were in their saddles, and so it was that the man who had been standing watch was forced to meet his charge alone.

The results were relatively predictable.

As Garion thundered past his unhorsed opponent, another Guardsman came out into the road at a half gallop, but Garion gave him no time to set himself or to turn his horse. The crashing impact against the unprepared man's shield hurled his horse from its feet. The Guardsman came down before the horse did, and the animal rolled over him, squealing and kicking in fright.

Garion tried to rein in, but Chretienne had the bit in his teeth. He cleared the pole gate in a long, graceful leap and charged on. Garion swore and gave up on the reins. He leaned forward and seized the big gray by one ear and hauled back. Startled, Chretienne stopped so quickly that his rump skidded on the road.

"The fight's back that way," Garion told his horse, "or did you forget already?"

Chretienne gave him a reproachful look, turned, and charged back toward the gate again.

Because of the speed of their attack, Garion's friends were on top of the Guardsmen before the armored men could bring their lances into play, and the fight had quickly turned ugly. Using the blunt side of his axe, Durnik smashed in one Guardsman's visor, denting it so severely that the man could no longer see. He rode in circles helplessly, both hands clutching at his helmet until he rode under a low-hanging limb, which smoothly knocked him off his horse.

Silk ducked under a wide, backhand sword stroke, reached down with his dagger, and neatly cut his attacker's girth strap.

The fellow's horse leaped forward, jumping out from under his rider. Saddle and all, the Guardsman tumbled into the road. He struggled to his feet, sword in hand, but Feldegast came up behind him and methodically clubbed him to earth again with an ugly lead mace.

It was Toth, however, who was the hardest pressed. Three Guardsmen closed on the giant. Even as Chretienne leaped the gate again, Garion saw the huge man awkwardly flailing with his staff for all the world like someone who had never held one in his hands before. When the three men came within range however, Toth's skill miraculously reemerged. His heavy staff whirled in a blurring circle. One Guardsman fell wheezing to earth, clutching at his broken ribs. Another doubled over sharply as Toth deftly poked him in the pit of the stomach with the butt of his staff. The third desperately raised his sword, but the giant casually swiped it out of his hand, then reached out and took the surprised man by the front of his mail coat. Garion clearly heard the crunch of crushed steel as Toth's fist closed. Then the giant looked about and almost casually threw the armored man against a roadside tree so hard that it shook the spring leaves from the highest twig.

The three remaining Guardsmen began to fall back, trying to give themselves room to use their lances, but they seemed unaware that Garion was returning to the fray—from behind them.

As Chretienne thundered toward the unsuspecting trio, a sudden idea came to Garion. Quickly he turned his lance sideways so that its center rested just in front of his saddlebow and crashed into the backs of the Guardsmen. The springy cedar pole swept all three of them out of their saddles and over the heads of their horses. Before they could stumble to their feet, Sadi, Feldegast, and Durnik were on them, and the fight ended as quickly as it had begun.

"I don't think I've ever seen anybody use a lance that way before," Silk said gaily to Garion.

"I just made it up," Garion replied with an excited grin.

"I'm sure that there are at least a half-dozen rules against it."

"We probably shouldn't mention it, then."

"I won't tell anybody if you don't."

Durnik was looking around critically. The ground was littered with Guardsmen who were either unconscious or groaning over assorted broken bones. Only the man Toth had poked in the stomach was still in his saddle, though he was doubled over, gasping for breath. Durnik rode up to him. "Excuse me," he said politely, removed the poor fellow's helmet, and then rapped him smartly on top of the head with the butt of his axe. The Guardsman's eyes glazed, and he toppled limply out of the saddle.

Belgarath suddenly doubled over, howling with laughter. *"Excuse me?"* he demanded of the smith.

"There's no need to be uncivil to people, Belgarath," Durnik replied stiffly.

Polgara came riding sedately down the hill, followed by Ce'Nedra, Velvet, and Eriond. "Very nice, gentlemen," she complimented them all, looking around at the fallen Guardsmen. Then she rode up to the pole gate. "Garion, dear," she said pleasantly, reining in her mount, "would you mind?"

He laughed, rode Chretienne over to the gate, and kicked it out of her way.

"Why on earth were you jumping fences in the very middle of the fight?" she asked him curiously.

"It wasn't altogether my idea," he replied.

"Oh," she said, looking critically at the big horse. "I think I understand."

Chretienne managed somehow to look slightly ashamed of himself.

They rode on past the border as evening began imperceptibly to darken an already gloomy sky. Feldegast pulled in beside Belgarath. "Would yer morals be at all offended if I was t' suggest shelterin' fer the night in a snug little smugglers' cave I know of a few miles or so farther on?" he asked.

Belgarath grinned and shook his head. "Not in the slightest," he replied. "When I need a cave, I never concern myself about the previous occupants." Then he laughed. "I shared quarters for a week once with a sleeping bear—nice enough bear, actually, once I got used to his snoring."

"'Tis a fascinatin' story, I'm sure, an' I'd be delighted t' hear it—but the night's comin' on, an' ye kin tell me about it over supper. Shall we be off, then?" The juggler thumped his heels into his mule's flanks and led them on up the rutted road in the rapidly descending twilight at a jolting gallop.

As they moved into the first of the foothills, they found the poorly maintained road lined on either side by mournful-looking evergreens. The road, however, was empty, though it showed signs of recent heavy traffic—all headed south.

"How much farther to this cave of yours?" Belgarath called to the juggler.

"'Tis not far, Ancient One," Feldegast assured him. "There be a dry ravine that crosses the road up ahead, an' we go up that a bit of a ways, an' there we are."

"I hope you know what you're doing."

"Trust me."

Somewhat surprisingly, Belgarath let that pass.

They pounded on up the road as a sullen dusk settled into the surrounding foothills and deep shadows began to gather about the trunks of the evergreens.

"Ah, an' there it is," Feldegast said, pointing at the rocky bed of a dried-up stream. "The footin' be treacherous here, so we'd best lead the mounts." He swung down from his mule and cautiously began to lead the way up the ravine. It grew steadily darker, the light fading quickly from the overcast sky. As the ravine narrowed and rounded a sharp bend, the juggler rummaged through the canvas pack strapped to the back of his mule. He lifted out the stub of a candle and looked at Durnik. "Kin ye be makin' me a bit of a flame, Goodman?" he asked. "I'd do it meself, but I seem t' have misplaced me tinder."

Durnik opened his pouch, took out his flint and steel and his wad of tinder, and, after several tries, blew a lighted spark into a tiny finger of fire. He held it out, shielded between his hands, and Feldegast lit his bit of candle.

"An' here we are now," the juggler said grandly, holding up his candle to illuminate the steep banks of the ravine.

"Where?" Silk asked, looking about in puzzlement.

"Well now, Prince Kheldar, it wouldn't be much of a hidden cave if the openin' was out in plain sight fer just anybody t' stumble across, now would it?" Feldegast went over to the steep side of the ravine to where a huge slab of water-scoured granite leaned against the bank. He lowered his candle, shielding it with his hand, ducked slightly, and disappeared behind it with his mule trailing along behind him.

The interior of the cave was floored with clean white sand, and the walls had been worn smooth by centuries of swirling water. Feldegast stood in the center of the cave holding his candle aloft. There were crude log bunks along the walls, a table and some benches in the center of the cave, and a rough fireplace near the far wall with a fire already laid. Feldegast crossed to the fireplace, bent, and lit the kindling lying under the split logs resting on a rough stone grate with his candle. "Well now, that's better," he said, holding his hands out to the crackling flames. "Isn't this a cozy little haven?"

Just beyond the fireplace was an archway, in part natural and in part the work of human hands. The front of the archway was closed off with several horizontal poles. Feldegast pointed at it. "There be the stable fer the horses, an' also a small spring at the back of it. 'Tis altogether the finest smugglers' cave in this part of Mallorea."

"A cunning sort of place," Belgarath agreed, looking around.

"What do they smuggle through here?" Silk asked with a certain professional curiosity.

"Gem stones fer the most part. There be rich deposits in the cliffs of Katakor, an' quite often whole gravel bars of the shiny little darlin's lyin' in the streams t' be had fer the trouble it takes t' pick 'em up. The local taxes be notorious cruel, though, so the bold lads in this part of these mountains have come up with various ways t' take their goods across the border without disturbin' the sleep of the hardworkin' tax collectors.''

Polgara was inspecting the fireplace. There were several iron pothooks protruding from its inside walls and a large iron grill sitting on stout legs to one side. "Very nice," she murmured approvingly. "Is there adequate firewood?"

"More than enough, me dear lady," the juggler replied. "'Tis stacked in the stable, along with fodder fer the horses."

"Well, then," she said, removing her blue cloak and laying it across one of the bunks, "I think I might be able to expand the menu I'd planned for this evening's meal. As long as we have such complete facilities here, it seems a shame to waste them. I'll need more firewood stacked here—and water, of course." She went to the pack horse that carried her cooking utensils and her stores, humming softly to herself.

Durnik, Toth, and Eriond led the horses into the stable and began to unsaddle them. Garion, who had left his lance outside, went to one of the bunks, removed his helmet and laid it, along with his shield, under the bunk, and then he began to struggle out of his mail shirt. Ce'Nedra came over to assist him.

"You were magnificent today, dear," she told him warmly.

He grunted noncommittally, leaning forward and extending his arms over his head so that she could pull the shirt off.

She tugged hard, and the mail shirt came free all at once. Thrown off balance by the weight, she sat down heavily on the sandy floor with the shirt in her lap.

Garion laughed and quickly went to her. "Oh, Ce'Nedra," he said, still laughing, "I do love you." He kissed her and then helped her to her feet.

"This is terribly heavy, isn't it?" she said, straining to lift the steel-link shirt.

"You noticed," he said, rubbing at one aching shoulder. "And here you thought I was just having fun."

"Be nice, dear. Do you want me to hang it up for you?"

He shrugged. "Just kick it under the bunk."

Her look was disapproving.

"I don't think it's going to wrinkle, Ce'Nedra."

"But it's untidy to do it that way, dear." She made some effort to fold the thing, then gave up, rolled it in a ball, and pushed it far back under the bunk with her foot.

Supper that evening consisted of thick steaks cut from a ham Vella had provided them, a rich soup so thick that it hovered on the very edge of stew, large slabs of bread that had been warmed before the fire, and baked apples with honey and cinnamon.

After they had eaten, Polgara rose and looked around the cave again. "The ladies and I are going to need a bit of privacy now," she said, "and several basins of hot water."

Belgarath sighed. "Again, Pol?" he said.

"Yes, father. It's time to clean up and change clothes—for all of us." She pointedly sniffed at the air in the small cave. "It's definitely time," she added.

They curtained off a portion of the cave to give Polgara, Ce'Nedra, and Velvet the privacy they required and began heating water over the fire.

Though at first reluctant even to move, Garion had to admit that after he had washed up and changed into clean, dry clothes, he did feel much better. He sat back on one of the bunks beside Ce'Nedra, not even particularly objecting to the damp smell of her hair. He had that comfortable sense of being clean, well fed, and warm after a day spent out of doors in bad weather. He was, in fact, right on the edge of dozing off when there echoed up the narrow ravine outside a vast bellow that seemed to be part animal and part human, a cry so dreadful that it chilled his blood and made the hair rise on the back of his neck.

"What's that?" Ce'Nedra exclaimed in fright.

"Hush now, girl," Feldegast warned softly. He jumped to his feet and quickly secured a piece of canvas across the opening of the fireplace, plunging the cave into near-darkness.

Another soulless bellow echoed up the ravine. The sound seemed filled with a dreadful malevolence.

"Can we put a name to whatever it is?" Sadi asked in a quiet voice.

"It's nothing I've ever heard before," Durnik assured him.

"I think I have," Belgarath said bleakly. "When I was in Morindland, there was a magician up there who thought it was amusing to turn his demon out at night to hunt. It made a sound like that."

"What an unsavory practice," the eunuch murmured. "What do demons eat?"

"You really wouldn't want to know," Silk replied. He turned to Belgarath. "Would you care to hazard a guess at just how big that thing might be?"

"It varies. From the amount of noise it's making, though, I'd say that it's fairly large."

"Then it wouldn't be able to get into this cave, would it?"

"That's a gamble I think I'd rather not take."

"It can sniff out our tracks, I assume?"

The old man nodded.

"Things are definitely going to pieces here, Belgarath. Can you do anything at all to drive it off?" The little man turned to Polgara. "Or perhaps you, Polgara. You dealt with the demon Chabat raised back in the harbor at Rak Urga."

"I had help, Silk," she reminded him. "Aldur came to my aid."

Belgarath began to pace up and down, scowling at the floor.

"Well?" Silk pressed.

"Don't rush me," the old man growled. "I *might* be able to do something," he said grudgingly, "but if I *do*, it's going to make so much noise that every Grolim in Katakor is going to hear it—and probably Zandramas as well. We'll have the

Chandim or her Grolims hot on our heels all the way to Ashaba."

"Why not use the Orb?" Eriond suggested, looking up from the bridle he was repairing.

"Because the Orb makes even more noise than I do. If Garion uses the Orb to chase off a demon, they're going to hear it in Gandahar all the way on the other side of the continent."

"But it *would* work, wouldn't it?"

Belgarath looked at Polgara.

"I think he's right, father," she said. "A demon *would* flee from the Orb—even if it were fettered by its master. An unfettered demon would flee even faster."

"Can you think of anything else?" he asked her.

"A God," she shrugged. "All demons—no matter how powerful—flee from the Gods. Do you happen to know any Gods?"

"A few," he replied, "but they're busy right now."

Another shattering bellow resounded through the mountains. It seemed to come from right outside the cave.

"It's time for some kind of decision, old man," Silk said urgently.

"It's the noise the Orb makes that bothers you?" Eriond asked.

"That and the light. That blue beacon that lights up every time Garion draws the sword attracts a lot of attention, you know."

"You aren't all suggesting that I fight a demon, are you?" Garion demanded indignantly.

"Of course not," Belgarath snorted. "Nobody fights a demon—nobody *can*. All we're discussing is the possibility of driving it off." He began to pace up and down again, scuffing his feet in the sand. "I hate to announce our presence here," he muttered.

Outside, the demon bellowed again, and the huge granite slab partially covering the cave mouth began to grate back and forth as if some huge force were rocking it to try to move it aside.

"Our options are running out, Belgarath," Silk told him. "And so is our time. If you don't do something quickly, that thing's going to be in here with us."

"Try not to pinpoint our location to the Grolims," Belgarath said to Garion.

"You really want me to go out there and do it?"

"Of course I do. Silk was right. Time's run out on us."

Garion went to his bunk and fished his mail shirt out from under it.

"You won't need that. It wouldn't do any good anyway."

Garion reached over his shoulder and drew his great sword. He set its point in the sand and peeled the soft leather sheath from its hilt. "I think this is a mistake," he declared. Then he reached out and put his hand on the Orb.

"Let me, Garion," Eriond said. He rose, came over, and covered Garion's hand with his own.

Garion gave him a startled look.

"It knows me, remember?" the young man explained, "and I've got a sort of an idea."

A peculiar tingling sensation ran through Garion's hand and arm, and he became aware that Eriond was communing with the Orb in a manner even more direct than he himself was capable of. It was is if during the months that the boy had been the bearer of the Orb, the stone had in some peculiar way taught him its own language.

There was a dreadful scratching coming from the mouth of the cave, as if huge talons were clawing at the stone slab.

"Be careful out there," Belgarath cautioned. "Don't take any chances. Just hold up the sword so that it can see it. The Orb should do the rest."

Garion sighed. "All right," he said, moving toward the cave mouth with Eriond directly behind him.

"Where are you going?" Polgara asked the blond young man.

"With Belgarion," Eriond replied. "We both need to talk with the Orb to get this right. I'll explain it later, Polgara."

The slab at the cave mouth was rocking back and forth again. Garion ducked quickly out from behind it and ran several yards up the ravine with Eriond on his heels. Then he turned and held up the sword.

"Not yet," Eriond warned. "It hasn't seen us."

There was an overpoweringly foul odor in the ravine, and then, as Garion's eyes slowly adjusted to the darkness, he saw the demon outlined against the clouds rolling overhead. It was enormous, its shoulders blotting out half the sky. It had long, pointed ears like those of a vast cat, and its dreadful eyes burned with a green fire that cast a fitful glow across the floor of the ravine.

It bellowed and reached toward Garion and Eriond with a great, scaly claw.

"Now, Belgarion," Eriond said quite calmly.

Garion lifted his arms, holding his sword directly in front of him with its point aimed at the sky, and then he released the curbs he had placed on the Orb.

He was not in the least prepared for what happened. A huge noise shook the earth and echoed off nearby mountains, causing giant trees miles away to tremble. Not only did the great blade take fire, but the entire sky suddenly shimmered an intense sapphire blue as if it had been ignited. Blue flame shot from horizon to horizon, and the vast sound continued to shake the earth.

The demon froze, its vast, tooth-studded muzzle turned upward to the blazing blue sky in terror. Grimly, Garion advanced on the thing, still holding his burning sword before him. The beast flinched back from him, trying to shield its face from the intense blue light. It screamed as if suddenly gripped by an intolerable agony. It stumbled back, falling and scrambling to its feet again. Then it took one more look at the blazing sky, turned, and fled howling back down the ravine with a peculiar loping motion as all four of its claws tore at the earth.

"*That* is your idea of quiet?" Belgarath thundered from the cave mouth. "And what's all that?" He pointed a trembling finger at the still-illuminated sky.

"It's really all right, Belgarath," Eriond told the infuriated old man. "You didn't want the sound to lead the Grolims to us, so we just made it general through the whole region. Nobody could have pinpointed its source."

Belgarath blinked. Then he frowned for a moment. "What about all the light?" he asked in a more mollified tone of voice.

"It's more or less the same with that," Eriond explained calmly. "If you've got a single blue fire in the mountains on a dark night, everybody can see it. If the whole sky catches on fire, though, nobody can really tell where it's coming from."

"It does sort of make sense, Grandfather," Garion said.

"Are they all right, father?" Polgara asked from behind the old man.

"What could possibly have hurt them? Garion can level mountains with that sword of his. He very nearly did, as a matter of fact. The whole Karandese range rang like a bell." He looked up at the still-flickering sky. "Can you turn that off?" he asked.

"Oh," Garion said. He reversed his sword and resheathed it in the scabbard strapped across his back. The fire in the sky died.

"We really had to do it that way, Belgarath," Eriond continued. "We needed the light and the sound to frighten off the demon and we had to do it in such a way that the Grolims couldn't follow it, so—" He spread both hands and shrugged.

"Did you know about this?" Belgarath asked Garion.

"Of course, Grandfather," Garion lied.

Belgarath grunted. "All right. Come back inside," he said.

Garion bent slightly toward Eriond's ear. "Why didn't you tell me what we were going to do?" he whispered.

"There wasn't really time, Belgarion."

"The next time we do something like that, *take* time. I almost dropped the sword when the ground started shaking under me."

"That wouldn't have been a good idea at all."

"I know."

A fair number of rocks had been shaken from the ceiling of the cave and lay on the sandy floor. Dust hung thickly in the air.

"What happened out there?" Silk demanded in a shaky voice.

"Oh, not much," Garion replied in a deliberately casual voice. "We just chased it away, that's all."

"There wasn't really any help for it, I guess," Belgarath said, "but just about everybody in Katakor knows that *something's* moving around in these mountains, so we're going to have to start being very careful."

"How much farther is it to Ashaba?" Sadi asked him.

"About a day's ride."

"Will we make it in time?"

"Only just. Let's all get some sleep."

Garion had the same dream again that night. He was not really sure that it was a dream, since dreaming usually involved sight as well as sound, but all there was to this one was that persistent, despairing wail and the sense of horror with which it filled him. He sat up on his bunk, trembling and sweat-covered. After a time, he drew his blanket about his shoulders, clasped his arms about his knees, and stared at the ruddy coals in the fireplace until he dozed off again.

It was still cloudy the following morning, and they rode cautiously back down the ravine to the rutted track leading up into the foothills of the mountains. Silk and Feldegast ranged out in front of them as scouts to give them warning should any dangers arise.

After they had ridden a league or so, the pair came back

down the narrow road. Their faces were sober, and they motioned for silence.

"There's a group of Karands camped around the road up ahead," Silk reported in a voice scarcely louder than a whisper.

"An ambush?" Sadi asked him.

"No," Feldegast replied in a low voice. "They're asleep fer the most part. From the look of things, I'd say that they spent the night in some sort of religious observance, an' so they're probably exhausted—or still drunk."

"Can we get around them?" Belgarath asked.

"It shouldn't be too much trouble," Silk replied. "We can just go off into the trees and circle around until we're past the spot where they're sleeping."

The old man nodded. "Lead the way," he said.

They left the road and angled off into the timber, moving at a cautious walk.

"What sort of ceremony were they holding?" Durnik asked quietly.

Silk shrugged. "It looked pretty obscure," Silk told him. "They've got an altar set up with skulls on posts along the back of it. There seems to have been quite a bit of drinking going on—as well as some other things."

"What sort of things?"

Silk's face grew slightly pained. "They have women with them," he answered disgustedly. "There's some evidence that things got a bit indiscriminate."

Durnik's cheeks suddenly turned bright red.

"Aren't you exaggerating a bit, Kheldar?" Velvet asked him.

"No, not really. Some of them were still celebrating."

"A bit more important than quaint local religious customs, though," Feldegast added, still speaking quietly, "be the peculiar pets the Karands was keepin'."

"Pets?" Belgarath asked.

"Perhaps 'tis not the right word, Ancient One, but sittin'

289

round the edges of the camp was a fair number of the Hounds—an' they was makin' no move t' devour the celebrants."

Belgarath looked at him sharply. "Are you sure?"

"I've seen enough of the Hounds of Torak t' recognize 'em when I see 'em."

"So there *is* some kind of an alliance between Mengha and Urvon," the old man said.

"Yer wisdom is altogether a marvel, old man. It must be a delight beyond human imagination t' have the benefit of ten thousand years experience t' guide ye in comin' t' such conclusions."

"*Seven* thousand," Belgarath corrected.

"Seven—ten—what matter?"

"*Seven* thousand," Belgarath repeated with a slightly offended expression.

CHAPTER SIXTEEN

They rode that afternoon into a dead wasteland, a region foul and reeking, where white snags poked the skeltonlike fingers of their limbs imploringly at a dark, roiling sky and where dank ponds of oily, stagnant water exuded the reek of decay. Clots of fungus lay in gross profusion about the trunks of long-dead trees and matted-down weeds struggled up through ashy soil toward a sunless sky.

"It looks almost like Cthol Mishrak, doesn't it?" Silk asked, looking about distastefully.

"We're getting very close to Ashaba," Belgarath told him. "Something about Torak did this to the ground."

"Didn't he know?" Velvet said sadly.

291

"Know what?" Ce'Nedra asked her.

"That his very presence befouled the earth?"

"No," Ce'Nedra replied, "I don't think he did. His mind was so twisted that he couldn't even see it. The sun hid from him, and he saw that only as a mark of his power and not as a sign of its repugnance for him."

It was a peculiarly astute observation, which to some degree surprised Garion. His wife oftentimes seemed to have a wide streak of giddiness in her nature which made it far too easy to think of her as a child, a misconception reinforced by her diminutive size. But he had frequently found it necessary to reassess this tiny, often willful little woman who shared his life. Ce'Nedra might sometimes behave foolishly, but she was never stupid. She looked out at the world with a clear, unwavering vision that saw much more than gowns and jewels and costly perfumes. Quite suddenly he was so proud of her that he thought his heart would burst.

"How much farther is it to Ashaba?" Sadi asked in a subdued tone. "I hate to admit it, but this particular swamp depresses me."

"You?" Durnik said. "I thought you liked swamps."

"A swamp should be green and rich with life, Goodman," the eunuch replied. "There's nothing here but death." He looked at Velvet. "Have you got Zith, Margravine?" he asked rather plaintively. "I'm feeling a bit lonesome just now."

"She's sleeping at the moment, Sadi," she told him, her hand going to the front of her bodice in an oddly protective fashion. "She's safe and warm and very content. She's even purring."

"Resting in her perfumed little bower." He sighed. "There are times when I envy her."

"Why, Sadi," she said, blushing slightly, lowering her eyes, and then flashing her dimples at him.

"Merely a clinical observation, my dear Liselle," he said to her rather sadly. "There are times when I wish it could be otherwise, but . . ." He sighed again.

"Do you really have to carry that snake there?" Silk asked the blond girl.

"Yes, Kheldar," she replied, "as a matter of fact, I do."

"You didn't answer my question, Ancient One," Sadi said to Belgarath. "How much farther is it to Ashaba?"

"It's up there," the old sorcerer replied shortly, pointing toward a ravine angling sharply up from the reeking wasteland. "We should make it by dark."

"A particularly unpleasant time to visit a haunted house," Feldegast added.

As they started up the ravine, there came a sudden hideous growling from the dense undergrowth to one side of the weedy track, and a huge black Hound burst out of the bushes, its eyes aflame and with foam dripping from its cruel fangs. "Now you are mine!" it snarled, its jaws biting off the words.

Ce'Nedra screamed, and Garion's hand flashed back over his shoulder; but quick as he was, Sadi was even quicker. The eunuch spurred his terrified horse directly at the hulking dog. The beast rose, its jaws agape, but Sadi hurled a strangely colored powder of about the consistency of coarse flour directly into its face.

The Hound shook its head, still growling horribly. Then it suddenly screamed, a shockingly human sound. Its eyes grew wide in terror. Then it began desperately to snap at the empty air around it, whimpering and trying to cringe back. As suddenly as it had attacked, it turned and fled howling back into the undergrowth.

"What did you do?" Silk demanded.

A faint smile touch Sadi's slender features. "When ancient Belgarath told me about Torak's Hounds, I took certain precautions," he replied, his head slightly cocked as he listened to the terrified yelps of the huge dog receding off into the distance.

"Poison?"

"No. It's really rather contemptible to poison a dog if you don't have to. The Hound simply inhaled some of that powder

I threw in its face. Then it began to see some very distracting things—*very* distracting." He smiled again. "Once I saw a cow accidentally sniff the flower that's the main ingredient of the powder. The last time I saw her, she was trying to climb a tree." He looked over at Belgarath. "I hope you didn't mind my taking action without consulting you, Ancient One, but as you've pointed out, your sorcery might alert others in the region, and I had to move quickly to deal with the situation before you felt compelled to unleash it anyway."

"That's quite all right, Sadi," Belgarath replied. "I may have said it before, but you're a very versatile fellow."

"Merely a student of pharmacology, Belgarath. I've found that there are chemicals suitable for almost every situation."

"Won't the Hound report back to its pack that we're here?" Durnik asked, looking around worriedly.

"Not for several days." Sadi chuckled, brushing off his hands, holding them as far away from his face as possible.

They rode slowly up the weed-grown track along the bottom of the ravine where mournful, blackened trees spread their branches, filling the deep cut with a pervading gloom. Off in the distance they could hear the baying of Torak's Hounds as they coursed through the forest. Above them, sooty ravens flapped from limb to limb, croaking hungrily.

"Disquieting sort of place," Velvet murmured.

"And *that* adds the perfect touch," Silk noted, pointing at a large vulture perched on the limb of a dead snag at the head of the ravine.

"Are we close enough to Ashaba yet for you to be able to tell if Zandramas is still there?" Garion asked Polgara.

"Possibly," she replied. "But even that faint a sound could be heard."

"We're close enough now that we can wait," Belgarath said. "I'll tell you one thing, though," he added. "If my great-grandson *is* at Ashaba, I'll take the place apart stone by stone until I find him and I don't care *how* much noise it makes."

Impulsively, Ce'Nedra pulled her horse in beside his,

leaned over, and locked her arms about his waist. "Oh, Belgarath," she said, "I love you." And she burrowed her face into his shoulder.

"What's this?" His voice was slightly surprised.

She pulled back, her eyes misty. She wiped at them with the back of her hand, then gave him an arch look. "You're the dearest man in all the world," she told him. "I might even consider throwing Garion over for you," she added, "if it weren't for the fact that you're twelve thousand years old, that is."

"Seven," he corrected automatically.

She gave him a sadly whimsical smile, a melancholy sign of her final victory in an on-going contest that no longer had any meaning for her. "Whatever," she sighed.

And then in a peculiarly uncharacteristic gesture, he enfolded her in his arms and gently kissed her. "My dear child," he said with brimming eyes. Then he looked back over his shoulder at Polgara. "How did we ever get along without her?" he asked.

Polgara's eyes were a mystery. "I don't know, father," she replied. "I really don't."

At the head of the ravine, Sadi dismounted and dusted the leaves of a low bush growing in the middle of the track they were following with some more of his powder. "Just to be on the safe side," he explained, pulling himself back into his saddle.

The region they entered under a lowering sky was a wooded plateau, and they rode on along the scarcely visible track in a generally northerly direction with the rising wind whipping at their cloaks. The baying of Torak's Hounds still sounded from some distance off, but seemed to be coming no closer.

As before, Silk and Feldegast raged out ahead, scouting for possible dangers. Garion again rode at the head of their column, his helmet in place and the butt of his lance riding in his stirrup. As he rounded a sharp bend in the track, he saw Silk and the juggler ahead. They had dismounted and were crouched behind some bushes. Silk turned quickly and motioned Garion back. Garion quickly passed on that signal and, step by step, backed his gray stallion around the bend again. He dismounted, leaned his lance against a tree, and took off his helmet.

"What is it?" Belgarath asked, also swinging down from his horse.

"I don't know," Garion replied. "Silk motioned us to stay out of sight."

"Let's go have a look," the old man said.

"Right."

The two of them crouched over and moved forward on silent feet to join the rat-faced man and the juggler. Silk put his finger to his lips as they approached. When Garion reached the brush, he carefully parted the leaves and looked out.

There was a road there, a road that intersected the track they had been following. Riding along that road were half-a-hundred men dressed mostly in furs, with rusty helmets on their heads and bent and dented swords in their hands. The men at the head of the column, however, wore mail coats. Their helmets were polished, and they carried lances and shields.

Tensely, without speaking, Garion and his friends watched the loosely organized mob ride past.

When the strangers were out of sight, Feldegast turned to Belgarath. "It sort of confirms yer suspicion, old friend," he said.

"Who were they?" Garion asked in a low voice.

"The ones in fur be Karands," Feldegast replied, "an' the ones in steel be Temple Guardsmen. 'Tis more evidence of an alliance between Urvon and Mengha, y' see."

"Can we be sure that the Karands were Mengha's men?"

"He's overcome Katakor altogether, an' the only armed Karands in the area be his. Urvon an' his Chandim control the Guardsmen—*an'* the Hounds. When ye see Karands an' Hounds together the way we did yesterday, it's fair proof of an alliance, but when ye see Karandese fanatics escorted by armed Guardsmen, it doesn't leave hardly any doubt at all."

"What *is* that fool up to?" Belgarath muttered.

"Who?" Silk asked.

"Urvon. He's done some fairly filthy things in his life, but he's never consorted with demons before."

"Perhaps 'twas because Torak had forbid it," Feldegast suggested. "Now that Torak's dead, though, maybe he's throwin' off all restraints. The demons would be a powerful factor if the final confrontation between the Church an' the imperial throne that's been brewin' all these years should finally come."

"Well," Belgarath grunted, "we don't have time to sort it out now. Let's get the others and move on."

They quickly crossed the road that the Karands and the Guardsmen had been following and continued along the narrow track. After a few more miles, they crested a low knoll that at some time in the past had been denuded by fire. At the far end of the plateau, just before a series of stark cliffs rose sharply up into the mountains, there stood a huge black building, rearing up almost like a mountain itself. It was surmounted by bleak towers and surrounded by a battlement-topped wall, half-smothered in vegetation.

"Ashaba," Belgarath said shortly, his eyes flinty.

"I thought it was a ruin," Silk said with some surprise.

"Parts of it are, I've been told," the old man replied. "The upper floors aren't habitable any more, but the ground floor's still more or less intact—at least it's supposed to be. It takes a very long time for wind and weather to tear down a house that big." The old man nudged his horse and led them down off the knoll and back into the wind-tossed forest.

It was nearly dark by the time they reached the edge of the clearing surrounding the House of Torak. Garion noted that the vegetation half-covering the walls of the black castle consisted of brambles and thick-stemmed ivy. The glazing in the windows had long since succumbed to wind and weather, and the vacant casements seemed to stare out at the clearing like the eye sockets of a dark skull.

"Well, father?" Polgara said.

He scratched at his beard, listening to the baying of the Hounds back in the forest.

"If yer open t' a bit of advice, me ancient friend," Feldegast said, "wouldn't it be wiser t' wait until dark before we go in? Should there be watchers in the house, the night will conceal us from their eyes. An' then, too, once it grows dark, there'll undoubtedly be lights inside if the house be occupied. 'Twill give us some idea of what t' expect."

"It makes sense, Belgarath," Silk agreed. "Walking openly up to an unfriendly house in broad daylight disturbs my sense of propriety."

"That's because you've got the soul of a burglar. But it's probably the best plan anyhow. Let's pull back into the woods a ways and wait for dark."

Though the weather had been warm and springlike on the plains of Rakuth and Venna, here in the foothills of the Karandese mountains there was still a pervading chill, for winter only reluctantly released its grip on these highlands. The wind was raw, and there were some places back under the trees where dirty windrows of last winter's snow lay deep and unyielding.

"Is that wall around the house going to cause us any problems?" Garion asked.

"Not unless someone's repaired the gates," Belgarath replied. "When Beldin and I came in here after Vo Mimbre, they were all locked, so we had to break them down to get in."

"Walkin' openly up to them gates might not be the best idea in the world, Belgarath," Feldegast said, "fer if the house do be occupied by Chandim or Karands or Guardsmen, 'tis certain that the gates are goin' t' be watched, an' there be a certain amount of light even on the darkest night. There be a sally port on the east side of the house though, an' it gives entry into an inner court that's sure t' be filled with deep shadows as soon as the night comes on.''

"Won't it be barred off?" Silk asked him.

"T' be sure, Prince Kheldar, it was indeed. The lock, however, was not difficult fer a man with fingers as nimble as mine.''

"You've been inside, then?"

"I like t' poke around in abandoned houses from time t' time. One never knows what the former inhabitants might have left behind, an' findin' is often times as good as earnin' or stealin'.''

"I can accept that," Silk agreed.

Durnik came back from the edge of the woods where he had been watching the house. He had a slightly worried look on his face. "I'm not entirely positive," he said, "but it looks as if there are clouds of smoke coming out of the towers of that place.''

"I'll just go along with ye an' have a bit of a look," the juggler said, and he and the smith went back through the deepening shadows beneath the trees. After a few minutes they came back. Durnik's expression was faintly disgusted.

"Smoke?" Belgarath asked.

Feldegast shook his head. "Bats," he replied. "Thousands of the little beasties. They be comin' out of the towers in great black clouds.''

"Bats?" Ce'Nedra exclaimed, her hands going instinctively to her hair.

"It's not uncommon," Polgara told her. "Bats need protected places to nest in, and a ruin or an abandoned place is almost ideal for them.''

"But they're so *ugly*!" Ce'Nedra declared with a shudder.

"'Tis only a flyin' mouse, me little darlin','' Feldegast told her.

"I'm not fond of mice, either."

"'Tis a very unforgivin' woman ye've married, young Master," Feldegast said to Garion, "brim-full of prejudices an' unreasonable dislikes."

"More important, did you see any lights coming from inside?" Belgarath asked.

"Not so much as a glimmer, Ancient One, but the house be large, an' there be chambers inside which have no windows. Torak was unfond of the sun, as ye'll recall."

"Let's move around through the woods until we're closer to this sally port of yours," the old man suggested, "before the light goes entirely."

They stayed back from the edge of the trees as they circled around the clearing with the great black house in its center. The last light was beginning to fade from the cloud-covered sky as they cautiously peered out from the edge of the woods.

"I can't quite make out the sally port," Silk murmured, peering toward the house.

"'Tis partially concealed," Feldegast told him. "If ye give ivy the least bit of a toe hold, it can engulf a whole buildin' in a few hundred years. Quiet yer fears, Prince Kheldar. I know me way, an' I kin find the entrance t' the House of Torak on the blackest of nights."

"The Hounds are likely to be patrolling the area around here after dark, aren't they?" Garion said. He looked at Sadi. "I hope you didn't use up all of your powder back there."

"There's more than enough left, Belgarion." The eunuch smiled, patting his pouch. "A light dusting at the entrance to Master Feldegast's sally port should insure that we won't be disturbed once we're inside."

"What do you think?" Durnik asked, squinting up at the dark sky.

"It's close enough," Belgarath grunted. "I want to get inside."

They led their horses across the weed-choked clearing until they reached the looming wall.

"'Tis this way just a bit," Feldegast said in a low voice as

300

he began to feel his way along the rough black stones of the wall.

They followed him for several minutes, guided more by the faint rustling sound of his feet among the weeds than by sight.

"An' here we are, now," Feldegast said with some satisfaction. It was a low, arched entrance in the wall, almost totally smothered in ivy and brambles. Durnik and the giant Toth, moving slowly to avoid making too much noise, pulled the obstructing vines aside to allow the rest of them and the horses to enter. Then they followed, pulling the vines back in place once again to conceal the entrance.

Once they were inside, it was totally dark, and there was the musty smell of mildew and fungus. "May I borrow yer flint an' steel an' tinder again, Goodman Durnik?" Feldegast whispered. Then there was a small clinking sound, followed by a rapid clicking accompanied by showers of glowing sparks as Feldegast, kneeling so that his body concealed even those faint glimmers, worked with Durnik's flint and steel. After a moment, he blew on the tinder, stirring a tiny flame to life. There was another clink as he opened the front of a square lantern he had taken from a small niche in the wall.

"Is that altogether wise?" Durnik asked doubtfully as the juggler lighted the candle stub inside the lantern and returned the flint and steel.

"'Tis a well-shielded little bit of a light, Goodman," Feldegast told him, "an' it be darker than the inside of yer boots in this place. Trust me in this, fer I kin keep it so well concealed that not the tiniest bit of a glow will escape me control."

"Isn't that what they call a burglar's lantern?" Silk asked curiously.

"Well, now." Feldegast's whisper sounded slightly injured. "I don't know that I'd call it that, exactly. 'Tis a word that has an unsavory ring t' it."

"Belgarath," Silk chuckled softly. "I think your friend here has a more checkered past than we've been led to believe. I wondered why I liked him so much."

Feldegast had closed down the tin sides of his little lantern, allowing only a single, small spot of light feebly to illuminate the floor directly in front of his feet. "Come along, then," he told them. "The sally port goes back a way under the wall here, an' then we come t' the grate that used t' close it off. Then it makes a turn t' the right an' a little farther on, another t' the left, an' then it comes out in the courtyard of the house."

"Why so many twists and turns?" Garion asked him.

"Torak was a crooked sort, don't y' know. I think he hated straight lines almost as much as he hated the sun."

They followed the faint spot of light the lantern cast. Leaves had blown in through the entrance over the centuries to lie in a thick, damp mat on the floor, effectively muffling the sounds of their horses' hooves.

The grate that barred the passageway was a massively constructed criss cross of rusty iron. Feldegast fumbled for a moment with the huge latch, then swung it clear. "An' now, me large friend," he said to Toth, "we'll be havin' need of yer great strength here. The gate is cruel heavy, let me warn ye, an' the hinges be so choked with rust that they'll not likely yield easily." He paused a moment. "An' that reminds me— ah, where have me brains gone? We'll be needin' somethin' t' mask the dreadful squeakin' when ye swing the grate open." He looked back at the others. "Take a firm grip on the reins of yer horses," he warned them, "fer this is likely t' give 'em a bit of a turn."

Toth place his huge hands on the heavy grate, then looked at the juggler.

"Go!" Feldegast said sharply, then he lifted his face and bayed, his voice almost perfectly imitating the sound of one of the great Hounds prowling outside, even as the giant slowly swung the grate open on shrieking hinges.

Chretienne snorted and shied back from the dreadful howl, but Garion held his reins tightly.

"Oh, that was clever," Silk said in quiet admiration.

"I have me moments from time to time," Feldegast admitted. "With all the dogs outside raisin' their awful caterwallin', 'tis certain that one more little yelp won't attract no notice, but the squealin' of them hinges could have been an altogether different matter."

He led then on through the now-open grate and on along the dank passageway to a sharp right-hand turn. Somewhat farther along, the passage bent again to the left. Before he rounded that corner, the juggler closed down his lantern entirely, plunging them into total darkness. "We be approachin' the main court now," he whispered to them. "'Tis the time for silence an' caution, fer if there be others in the house, they'll be payin' a certain amount of attention t' be sure that no one creeps up on 'em. There be a handrail along the wall there, an' I think it might be wise t' tie the horses here. Their hooves would make a fearful clatter on the stones of the court, an' we'll not be wantin' t' ride them up an' down the corridors of this accursed place."

Silently they tied the reins of their mounts to the rusty iron railing and then crept on quiet feet to the turn in the passageway. There was a lessening of the darkness beyond the turn—not light, certainly, but a perceptible moderation of the oppressive gloom. And then they reached the inside entrance to the sally port and looked out across the broad courtyard toward the looming black house beyond. There was no discernible grace to the construction of that house. It rose in blocky ugliness almost as if the builders had possessed no understanding of the meaning of the word beauty, but had striven instead for a massive kind of arrogance to reflect the towering pride of its owner.

"Well," Belgarath whispered grimly, "that's Ashaba."

Garion looked at the dark house before him, half in apprehension and half with a kind of dreadful eagerness.

Something caught his eye then, and he thrust his head out to look along the front of the house across the court. At the far end, in a window on a lower floor, a dim light glowed, looking for all the world like a watchful eye.

CHAPTER SEVENTEEN

"Now what?" Silk breathed, looking at the dimly lighted window. "We've got to cross that courtyard to get to the house, but we can't be sure if there's somebody watching from that window or not."

"You've been out of the academy for too long, Kheldar," Velvet murmured. "You've forgotten your lessons. If stealth is impossible, then you try boldness."

"You're suggesting that we just walk up to the door and knock?"

"Well, I hadn't planned to knock, exactly."

"What have you got in mind, Liselle?" Polgara asked quietly.

"If there are people in the house, they're probably Grolims, right?"

"It's more than likely," Belgarath said. "Most other people avoid this place."

"Grolims pay little attention to other Grolims, I've noticed," she continued.

"You're forgetting that we don't have any Grolim robes with us," Silk pointed out.

"It's very dark in that courtyard, Kheldar, and in shadows that deep, any dark color would appear black, wouldn't it?"

"I suppose so," he admitted.

"And we still have those green silk slavers' robes in our packs, don't we?"

He squinted at her in the darkness, then looked at Belgarath. "It goes against all my instincts," he said, "but it might just work, at that."

"One way or another, we've got to get into the house. We have to find out who's in there—and why—before we can decide anything."

"Would Zandramas have Grolims with her?" Ce'Nedra asked. "If she's alone in that house and she sees a line of Grolims walking across the courtyard, wouldn't that frighten her into running away with my baby?"

Belgarath shook his head. "Even if she does run, we're close enough to catch her—particularly since the Orb can follow her no matter how much she twists and dodges. Besides, if she's here, she's probably got some of her own Grolims with her. It's not really so far from here to Darshiva that she couldn't have summoned them."

"What about him?" Durnik whispered the question and pointed at Feldegast. "He hasn't got a slavers' robe."

"We'll improvise something," Velvet murmured. She smiled at the juggler. "I've got a nice dark blue dressing gown that should set off his eyes marvelously. We can add a kerchief to resemble a hood and we can slip him by—if he stays in the middle of the group."

"'Twould be beneath me dignity," he objected.

"Would you prefer to stay behind and watch the horses?" she asked pleasantly.

"'Tis a hard woman y' are, me lady," he complained.

"Sometimes, yes."

"Let's do it," Belgarath decided. "I've got to get inside that house."

It took only a few moments to retrace their steps to the place where the horses were tied and to pull the neatly folded slavers' robes from their packs by the dim light of Feldegast's lantern.

"Isn't this ridiculous, now?" the juggler grumbled indignantly, pointing down at the blue satin gown Velvet had draped about him.

"I think it looks just darling," Ce'Nedra said.

"If there are people in there, aren't they likely to be patrolling the corridors?" Durnik asked.

"Only on the main floor, Goodman," Feldegast replied. "The upper stories of the house be almost totally uninhabitable—on account of all the broken windows an' the weather blowin' around in the corridors fer all the world like they was part of the great outdoors. There be a grand staircase just opposite the main door, an' with just a bit of luck we kin nip up the stairs an' be out of sight with no one the wiser. Once we're up there, we're not likely t' encounter a livin' soul—unless ye be countin' the bats an' mice an' an occasional adventuresome rat."

"You absolutely had to say that, didn't you?" Ce'Nedra said caustically.

"Ah, me poor little darlin'." He grinned at her. "But quiet yer fears. I'll be beside ye an' I've yet t' meet the bat or mouse or rat I couldn't best in a fair fight."

"It makes sense, Belgarath," Silk said. "If we all go trooping through the lower halls, sooner or later someone's bound to notice us. Once we're upstairs and out of sight, though,

I'll be able to reconnoiter and find out exactly what we're up against."

"All right," the old man agreed, "but the first thing is to get inside."

"Let's be off, then," Feldegast said, swirling his dressing gown about him with a flourish.

"Hide that light," Belgarath told him.

They filed out through the entrance to the sally port and marched into the shadowy courtyard, moving in the measured, swaying pace Grolim priests assumed on ceremonial occasions. The lighted window at the end of the house seemed somehow like a burning eye that followed their every move.

The courtyard was really not all that large, but it seemed to Garion that crossing it took hours. Eventually, however, they reached the main door. It was large, black, and nail-studded, like the door of every Grolim temple Garion had ever seen. The steel mask mounted over it, however, was no longer polished. In the faint light coming from the window at the other end of the house, Garion could see that over the centuries it had rusted, making the coldly beautiful face look scabrous and diseased. What made it look perhaps even more hideous were the twin gobbets of lumpy, semiliquid rust running from the eye sockets down the cheeks. Garion remembered with a shudder the fiery tears that had run down the stricken God's face before he had fallen.

They mounted the three steps to that bleak door, and Toth slowly pushed it open.

The corridor inside was dimly illuminated by a single flickering torch at the far end. Opposite the door, as Feldegast had told them, was a broad staircase reaching up into the darkness. The treads were littered with fallen stones, and cobwebs hung in long festoons from a ceiling lost in shadows. Still moving at that stately Grolim pace, Belgarath led them across the corridor and started up the stairs. Garion followed close behind him with measured tread, though every nerve screamed at him to run. They had gone perhaps halfway up the staircase when they heard a clinking sound behind them, and there was a sudden light at the foot of the stairs. "What are you doing?" a rough voice demanded. "Who are you?"

Garion's heart sank, and he turned. The man at the foot of the stairs wore a long, coatlike shirt of mail. He was helmeted and had a shield strapped to his left arm. With his right he held aloft a sputtering torch.

"Come back down here," the mailed man commanded them.

The giant Toth turned obediently, his hood pulled far over his face with his arms crossed so that his hands were inside his sleeves. With an air of meekness he started down the stairs again.

"I mean all of you," the Temple Guardsman insisted. "I order you in the name of the God of Angarak."

As Toth reached the foot of the stairs, the Guardsman's eyes widened as he realized that the robe the huge man wore was not Grolim black. "What's this?" he exclaimed. "You're not Chandim! You're—" He broke off suddenly as one of Toth's huge hands seized him by the throat and lifted him off the floor. He dropped his torch, kicking and struggling. Then, almost casually, Toth removed his helmet with his other hand and banged his head several times against the stone wall of the corridor. With a shudder, the mail-coated man went limp. Toth draped the unconscious form across his shoulder and started back up the stairs.

Silk bounded back down to the corridor, picked up the steel helmet and extinguished torch, and came back up again. "Always clean up the evidence," he murmured to Toth. "No crime is complete until you've tidied up."

Toth grinned at him.

As they neared the top of the stairs, they found the treads covered with leaves that had blown in from the outside, and the cobwebs hung in tatters like rotted curtains, swaying in the wind that came moaning in from the outside through the shattered windows.

309

The hall at the top of the stairs was littered. Dry leaves lay in ankle-deep windrows on the floor, skittering before the wind. A large, empty casement at the end of the corridor behind them was half covered with thick ivy that shook and rustled in the chill night wind blowing down off the slopes of the mountains. Doors had partially rotted away and hung in chunks from their hinges. The rooms beyond those doors were choked with leaves and dust, and the furniture and bedding had long since surrendered every scrap of cloth or padding to thousands of generations of industrious mice in search of nesting materials. Toth carried his unconscious captive into one of those rooms, bound him hand and foot, and then gagged him to muffle any outcry, should he awaken before dawn.

"That light was at the other end of the house, wasn't it?" Garion asked. "What's at that end?"

"'Twas the livin' quarters of Torak himself," Feldegast replied, adjusting his little lantern so that it emitted a faint beam of light. "His throne room be there, an' his private chapel. I could even show ye t' his personal bedroom, an' ye could bounce up an' down on his great bed—or what's left of it— just fer fun, if yer of a mind."

"I think I could live without doing that."

Belgarath had been tugging at one earlobe. "Have you been here lately?" he asked the juggler.

"Perhaps six months ago."

"Was anybody here?" Ce'Nedra demanded.

"I'm afraid not, me darlin'. 'Twas as empty as a tomb."

"That was before Zandramas got here, Ce'Nedra," Polgara reminded her gently.

"Why do ye ask, Belgarath?" Feldegast said.

"I haven't been here since just after Vo Mimbre," Belgarath said as they continued down the littered hall. "The house was fairly sound then, but Angaraks aren't really notorious for the permanence of their construction. How's the mortar holding out?"

"'Tis as crumbly as year-old bread."

Belgarath nodded. "I thought it might be," he said. "Now, what we're after here is information, not open warfare in the corridors."

"Unless the one who's here happens to be Zandramas," Garion corrected. "If she's still here with my son, I'll start a war that's going to make Vo Mimbre look like a country fair."

"And I'll clean up anything he misses," Ce'Nedra added fiercely.

"Can't you control them?" Belgarath asked his daughter.

"Not under the circumstances, no," she replied. "I might even decide to join in myself."

"I thought that we'd more or less erased the Alorn side of your nature, Pol," he said to her.

"That's not the side that was just talking, father."

"My point," Belgarath said, "at least the point I was trying to make before everybody started flexing his—or her—muscles, is that it's altogether possible that we'll be able to hear and maybe even see what's going on in the main part of the house from up here. If the mortar's as rotten as Feldegast says it is, it shouldn't be too hard to find—or make—some little crevices in the floor of one of these rooms and find out what we need to know. If Zandramas is here, that's one thing, and we'll deal with her in whatever way seems appropriate. But if the only people down there are some of Urvon's Chandim and Guardsmen or a roving band of Mengha's Karandese fanatics, we'll pick up Zandramas' trail and go on about our business without announcing our presence."

"That sounds reasonable," Durnik agreed. "It doesn't make much sense to get involved in unnecessary fights."

"I'm glad that *someone* in this belligerent little group has some common sense," the old man said.

"Of course, if it *is* Zandramas down there," the smith added, "I'll have to take steps myself."

"You, too?" Belgarath groaned.

"Naturally. After all, Belgarath, right is right."

They moved on along the leaf-strewn corridor where the

311

cobwebs hung from the ceiling in tatters and where there were skittering sounds in the corners.

As they passed a large double door so thick that it was still intact, Belgarath seemed to remember something. "I want to look in here," he muttered. As he opened those doors, the sword strapped across Garion's back gave a violent tug that very nearly jerked him off his feet. "Grandfather!" he gasped. He reached back, instructing the Orb to restrain itself, and drew the great blade. The point dipped to the floor, and then he was very nearly dragged into the room. "She's been here," he exulted.

"What?" Durnik asked.

"Zandramas. She's been in this room with Geran."

Feldegast opened the front of his lantern wider to throw more light into the room. It was a library, large and vaulted, with shelves reaching from the floor to the ceiling and filled with dusty, moldering books and scrolls.

"So *that* was what she was looking for," Belgarath said.

"For what?" Silk asked.

"A book. A prophecy, most likely." His face grew grim. "She's following the same trail that I am, and this would probably be just about the only place where she could find an uncorrupted copy of the Ashabine Oracles."

"Oh!" Ce'Nedra's little cry was stricken. She pointed a trembling hand at the dust-covered floor. There were footprints there. Some of them had obviously been made by a woman's shoes, but there were others as well—quite tiny. "My baby's been here," Ce'Nedra said in a voice near tears, and then she gave a little wail and began to weep. "H-he's walking," she sobbed, "and I'll never be able to see his first steps."

Polgara moved to her and took her into a comforting embrace.

Garion's eyes also filled with tears, and his grip on the hilt of his sword grew so tight that his knuckles turned white. He felt an almost overpowering need to smash things.

Belgarath was swearing under his breath.

"What's the matter?" Silk asked him.

"That was the main reason I had to come here," the old man grated. "I need a clean copy of the Ashabine Oracles, and Zandramas has beaten me to it."

"Maybe there's another."

"Not a chance. She's been running ahead of me burning books at every turn. If there was more than one copy here, she'd have made sure that I couldn't get my hands on it. That's why she stayed here so long—ransacking this place to make sure that she had the only copy." He started to swear again.

"Is this in any way significant?" Eriond said, going to a table that, unlike the others in the room, had been dusted and even polished. In the precise center of that table lay a book bound in black leather and flanked on each side by a candlestick. Eriond picked it up, and as he did so, a neatly folded sheet of parchment fell out from between its leaves. The young man bent, picked it up, and glanced at it.

"What's that?" Belgarath demanded.

"It's a note," Eriond replied. "It's for you." He handed the parchment and the book to the old man.

Belgarath read the note. His face went suddenly pale and then beet red. He ground his teeth together with the veins swelling in his face and neck. Garion felt the sudden building up of the old sorcerer's will.

"Father!" Polgara snapped, "No! Remember that we aren't alone here!"

He controlled himself with a tremendous effort, then crumpled the parchment into a ball and hurled it at the floor so hard that it bounced high into the air and rolled across the room. He swung back the hand holding the book as if he were about to send it after the ball of parchment, but then seemed to think better of it. He opened the book at random, turned a few pages, and then began to swear sulfurously. He shoved the book at Garion. "Here," he said, "hold on to this." Then he began to pace up and down, his face as black as a thundercloud, muttering curses and waving his hands in the air.

Garion opened the book, tilting it to catch the light. He saw at once the reason for Belgarath's anger. Whole passages had been neatly excised—not merely blotted out, but cut entirely from the page with a razor or a very sharp knife. Garion also started to swear.

Silk curiously went over, picked up the parchment, and looked at it. He swallowed hard and looked apprehensively at the swearing Belgarath. "Oh, my," he said.

"What is it?" Garion asked.

"I think we'd all better stay out of your grandfather's way for a while," the rat-faced man replied. "It might take him a little bit to get hold of himself."

"Just read it, Silk," Polgara said. "Don't editorialize."

Silk looked again at Belgarath, who was now at the far end of the room pounding on the stone wall with his fist. "'Belgarath,'" he read. "'I have beaten thee, old man. Now I go to the Place Which Is No More for the final meeting. Follow me if thou canst. Perhaps this book will help thee.'"

"Is it signed?" Velvet asked him.

"Zandramas," he replied. "Who else?"

"That is a truly offensive letter," Sadi murmured. He looked at Belgarath, who continued to pound his fist on the wall in impotent fury. "I'm surprised that he's taking it so well—all things considered."

"It answers a lot of questions, though," Velvet said thoughtfully.

"Such as what?" Silk asked.

"We were wondering if Zandramas was still here. Quite obviously, she's not. Not even an idiot would leave that kind of message for Belgarath and then stay around where he could get his hands on her."

"That's true," he agreed. "There's no real point in our staying here, then, is there? The Orb has picked up the trail again, so why don't we just slip out of the house again and go after Zandramas?"

"Without findin' out who's here?" Feldegast objected. "Me curiosity has been aroused, an' I'd hate t' go off with it unsatisfied." He glanced across the room at the fuming Belgarath. "Besides, it's goin' t' be a little while before our ancient friend there regains his composure. I think I'll go along t' the far end of the hall an' see if I kin find a place where I kin look down into the lower part of the house—just t' answer some burnin' questions which have been naggin' at me." He went to the table and lighted one of the candles from his little lantern. "Would ye be wantin' t' come along with me, Prince Kheldar?" he invited.

Silk shrugged. "Why not?"

"I'll go, too," Garion said. He handed the book to Polgara and then pointedly looked at the raging Belgarath. "Is he going to get over that eventually?"

"I'll talk with him, dear. Don't be too long."

He nodded, and then he, Silk, and the juggler quietly left the library.

There was a room at the far end of the hall. It was not particularly large, and there were shelves along the walls. Garion surmised that it had at one time been a storeroom or a linen closet. Feldegast squinted appraisingly at the leaf-strewn floor, then closed his lantern.

The leaves had piled deep in the corners and along the walls, but in the sudden darkness a faint glow shone up through them, and there came the murmur of voices from below.

"Me vile-tempered old friend seems t' have been right," Feldegast whispered. "'Twould appear that the mortar has quite crumbled away along that wall. 'Twill be but a simple matter t' brush the leaves out of the way an' give ourselves some convenient spy holes. Let's be havin' a look an' find out who's taken up residence in the House of Torak."

Garion suddenly had that strange sense of reexperiencing

315

something that had happened a long time ago. It had been in King Anheg's palace at Val Alorn, and he had followed the man in the green cloak through the deserted upper halls until they had come to a place where crumbling mortar had permitted the sound of voices to come up from below. Then he remembered something else. When they had been at Tol Honeth, hadn't Belgarath said that most of the things that had happened while they were pursuing Zedar and the Orb were likely to happen again, since everything was leading up to another meeting between the Child of Light and the Child of Dark? He tried to shake off the feeling, but without much success.

They removed the leaves from the crack running along the far wall of the storeroom carefully, trying to avoid sifting any of them down into the room below. Then each of them selected a vantage point from which to watch and listen.

The room into which they peered was very large. Ragged drapes hung at the windows, and the corners were thick with cobwebs. Smoky torches hung in iron rings along the walls, and the floor was thick with dust and the litter of ages. The room was filled with black-robed Grolims, a sprinkling of roughly clad Karands, and a large number of gleaming Temple Guardsmen. Near the front, drawn up like a platoon of soldiers, a group of the huge black Hounds of Torak sat on their haunches expectantly. In front of the Hounds stood a black altar, showing signs of recent use, flanked on either side by a glowing brazier. Against the wall on a high dais was a golden throne, backed by thick, tattered black drapes and by a huge replica of the face of Torak.

"'Twas Burnt-face's throne room, don't y' know," Feldegast whispered.

"Those are Chandim, aren't they?" Garion whispered back.

"The very same—both human an' beast—along with their mail-shirted bully boys. I'm a bit surprised that Urvon has chosen t' occupy the place with his dogs—though the best use fer Ashaba has probably always been as a kennel."

It was obvious that the men in the throne room were expecting something by the nervous way they kept looking at the throne.

Then a great gong sounded from below, shimmering in the smoky air.

"On your knees!" a huge voice commanded the throng in the large room. "Pay obeisance and homage to the new God of Angarak!"

"*What?*" Silk exclaimed in a choked whisper.

"Watch an' be still!" Feldegast snapped.

From below there came a great roll of drums, followed by a brazen fanfare. The rotten drapes near the golden throne parted, and a double file of robed Grolims entered, chanting fervently, even as the assembled Chandim and Guardsmen fell to their knees and the Hounds and the Karands groveled and whined.

The booming of the drums continued, and then a figure garbed in cloth of gold and wearing a crown strode imperiously out from between the drapes. A glowing nimbus surrounded the figure, though Garion could clearly sense that the will that maintained the glow emanated from the gold-clad man himself. Then the figure lifted its head in a move of overweening arrogance. The man's face was splotched—some patches showing the color of healthy skin and others a hideous dead white. What chilled Garion's blood the most, however, was the fact that the man's eyes were totally mad.

"Urvon!" Feldegast said with a sudden intake of his breath. "You piebald son of a mangy dog!" All trace of his lilting accent had disappeared.

Directly behind the patch-faced madman came a shadowy figure, cowled so deeply that its face was completely obscured. The black that covered it was not that of a simple Grolim robe, but seemed to grow out of the figure itself, and Garion felt a cold dread as a kind of absolute evil permeated the air about that black shape.

Urvon mounted the dais and seated himself on the throne,

317

his insane eyes bulging and his face frozen in that expression of imperious pride. The shadow-covered figure took its place behind his left shoulder and bent forward toward his ear, whispering, whispering.

The Chandim, Guardsmen, and Karands in the throne room continued to grovel, fawning and whining, even as did the Hounds, while the last disciple of Torak preened himself in the glow of their adulation. A dozen or so of the black-robed Chandim crept forward on their knees, bearing gilded chests and reverently placing them on the altar before the dais. When they opened the chests, Garion saw that they were all filled to the brim with red Angarak gold and with jewels.

"These offerings are pleasing to mine eyes," the enthroned Disciple declared in a shrill voice. "Let others come forth to make also their offerings unto the new God of Angarak."

There was a certain amount of consternation among the Chandim and a few hasty consultations.

The next group of offerings were in plain wooden boxes; when they were opened, they revealed only pebbles and twigs. Each of the Chandim who bore those boxes to the alter surreptitiously removed one of the gilded chests after depositing his burden on the black stone.

Urvon gloated over the chests and boxes, apparently unable to distinguish between gold and gravel, as the line continued to move toward the altar, each priest laying one offering on the altar and removing another before returning to the end of the line.

"I am well pleased with ye, my priests," Urvon said in his shrill voice when the charade had been played out. "Truly, ye have brought before me the wealth of nations."

As the Chandim, Karands, and Guardsmen rose to their feet, the shadowy figure at Urvon's shoulder continued to whisper.

"And now will I receive Lord Mengha" the madman announced, "most favored of all who serve me, for he has de-

livered unto me this familiar spirit who revealed my high divinity unto me." He indicated the shadow behind him.

"Summon the Lord Mengha that he may pay homage to
the God Urvon and be graciously received by the new God
of Angarak." The voice that boomed that command was as
hollow as a voice issuing from a tomb.

From the door at the back of the hall came another fanfare
of trumpets, and another hollow voice responded. "All hail
Urvon, new God of Angarak," it intoned. "Lord Mengha ap-
proacheth to make his obeisance and to seek counsel with the
living God."

Again there came the booming of drums, and a man robed
in Grolim black paced down the broad aisle toward the altar
and the dais. As he reached the altar, he genuflected to the
madman seated on Torak's throne.

"Look now upon the awesome face of Lord Mengha, most
favored servant of the God Urvon and soon to become First
Disciple," the hollow voice boomed.

The figure before the altar turned and pushed back his hood
to reveal his face to the throng.

Garion stared, supressing a gasp of surprise. The man
standing before the altar was Harakan.

CHAPTER EIGHTEEN

"Belar!" Silk swore under his breath.

"All bow down to the First Disciple of your God!" Urvon declaimed in his shrill voice. "It is my command that ye honor him."

There was a murmur of amazement among the assembled Chandim, and Garion, peering down from above, thought that he could detect a certain reluctance on the faces of some of them.

"Bow to him!" Urvon shrieked, starting to his feet. "He is my Disciple!"

The Chandim looked first at the frothing madman on the

dais and then at the cruel face of Harakan. Fearfully they sank to their knees.

"I am pleased to see such willing obedience to the commands of our God," Harakan observed sardonically. "I shall remember it always." There was a scarcely veiled threat in his voice.

"Know ye all that my Disciple speaks with my voice," Urvon announced, resuming his seat upon the throne. "His words are my words, and ye will obey him even as ye obey me."

"Hear the words of our God," Harakan intoned in that same sardonic voice, "for mighty is the God of Angarak, and swift to anger should any fail to heed him. Know further that I, Mengha, am now the sword of Urvon as well as his voice, and that the chastisement of the disobedient is in *my* hands." The threat was no longer veiled, and Harakan swept his eyes slowly across the faces of the assembled priests as if challenging each of them to protest his elevation.

"Hail Mengha, Disciple of the living God!" one of the mailed Guardsmen shouted.

"Hail Mengha!" the other Guardsmen responded, smashing their fists against their shields in salute.

"Hail Mengha!" the Karands shrieked.

"Hail Mengha!" the kneeling Chandim said at last, cowed finally into submission. And then the great Hounds crept forward on their bellies to fawn about Harakan's feet and to lick his hands.

"It is well," the enthroned madman declared in his shrill voice. "Know that the God of Angarak is pleased with ye."

And then another figure appeared in the throne room below, coming through the same rotted drapes which had admitted Urvon. The figure was slender and dressed in a robe of clinging black satin. Its head was partially covered by a black hood, and it was carrying something concealed beneath its robe. When it reached the altar, it tipped back its head in a derisive laugh, revealing a face with at once an unearthly beauty and an unearthly cruelty all cast in marble white. "You poor fools," the figure rasped in a harsh voice. "Think you to raise a new God over Angarak without my permission?"

"I have not summoned thee, Zandramas!" Urvon shouted at her.

"I feel no constraint to heed thy summons, Urvon," she replied in a voice filled with contempt, "nor its lack. I am not thy creature, as are these dogs. I serve the God of Angarak, in whose coming shalt thou be cast down."

"*I* am the God of Angarak!" he shrieked.

Harakan had begun to come around the altar toward her.

"And wilt thou pit thy puny will against the Will of the Child of Dark, Harakan?" she asked coolly. "Thou mayest change thy name, but thy power is no greater." Her voice was like ice.

Harakan stopped in his tracks, his eyes suddenly wary.

She turned back to Urvon. "I am dismayed that I was not notified of thy deification, Urvon," she continued, "for should I have known, I would have come before thee to pay thee homage and seek thy blessing." Then her lip curled in a sneer that distorted her face. "Thou?" she said. "*Thou*, a God? Thou mayest sit upon the throne of Torak for all eternity whilst this shabby ruin crumbles about thee, and thou wilt never become a God. Thou mayest fondle dross and call it gold, and thou wilt never become a God. Thou mayest bask in the canine adulation of thy cringing dogs, who even now befoul thy throne room with their droppings, and thou wilt never become a God. Thou mayest hearken greedily to the words of thy tame demon, Nahaz, who even now whispers the counsels of madness in thine ear, and thou wilt never become a God."

"I *am* a God!" Urvon shrieked, starting to his feet again.

"So? It may be even as thou sayest, Urvon," she almost purred. "But if thou *art* a God, I must tell thee to enjoy thy Godhood whilst thou may, then, for even as maimed Torak, thou art doomed."

322

"Who hath the might to slay a God?" he foamed at her.

Her laugh was dreadful. "Who hath the might? Even he who reft Torak of *his* life. Prepare thyself to receive the mortal thrust of the burning sword of Iron-grip, which spilled out the life of thy master, for *thus* I summon the Godslayer!"

And then she reached forward and placed the cloth-wrapped bundle which she had been concealing beneath her robe on the black altar. She raised her face and looked directly at the crack through which Garion was staring in frozen disbelief. "Behold thy son, Belgarion," she called up to him, "and hear his crying!" She turned back the cloth to reveal the infant Geran. The baby's face was contorted with fear, and he began to wail, a hopeless, lost sound.

All thought vanished from Garion's mind. The wailing was the sound he had been hearing over and over again since he had left Mal Zeth. It was *not* the wail of that doomed child in those plague-stricken streets that had haunted his dreams. It was the voice of his own son! Powerless to resist that wailing call, he leaped to his feet. It was as if there were suddenly sheets of flame before his eyes, flames that erased everything from his mind but the desperate need to go to the child wailing on the altar below.

He realized dimly that he was running through the shadowy, leaf-strewn halls, roaring insanely even as he ripped Iron-grip's sword from its sheath.

The moldering doors of long-empty rooms flashed by as he ran full tilt along the deserted corridor. Dimly behind him, he heard Silk's startled cry. "Garion! No!" Heedless, his brain afire, he ran on with the great Sword of Riva blazing in his hand before him as he went.

Even years later, he did not remember the stairs. Vaguely, he remembered emerging in the lower hall, raging.

There were Temple Guardsmen and Karands there, flinching before him and trying feebly to face him, but he seized the hilt of his sword in both hands and moved through them like a man reaping grain. They fell in showers of blood as he sheared his way through their ranks.

The great door to the dead God's throne room was closed and bolted, but Garion did not even resort to sorcery. He simply destroyed the door—and those who were trying desperately to hold it closed—with his burning sword.

The fire of madness filled his eyes as he burst into the throne room, and he roared at the terrified men there, who gaped at the dreadful form of the Godslayer, advancing on them, enclosed in a nimbus of blue light. His lips were peeled back from his teeth in a snarl, and his terrible sword, all ablaze, flickered back and forth before him like the shears of fate.

A Grolim jumped in front of him with one arm upraised as Garion gathered his will with an inrushing sound he scarcely heard. Garion did not stop, and the other Grolims in the throne room recoiled in horror as the point of his flaming sword came sliding out from between the rash priest's shoulder blades. The mortally wounded Grolim stared at the sizzling blade sunk into his chest. He tried with shaking hands to clutch at the blade, but Garion kicked him off the sword and continued his grim advance.

A Karand with a skull-surmounted staff stood in his path, desperately muttering an incantation. His words cut off abruptly, however, as Garion's sword passed through his throat.

"Behold the Godslayer, Urvon!" Zandramas exulted. "Thy life is at an end, God of Angarak, for Belgarion hath come to spill it out, even as he spilled out the life of Torak!" Then she turned her back on the cringing madman. "All hail the Child of Light!" she announced in ringing tones. She smiled her cruel smile at him. "Hail, Belgarion," she taunted him. "Slay once again the God of Angarak, for that hath ever been thy task. I shall await thy coming in the Place Which Is No More." And then she took up the wailing babe in her arms, covered it with her cloak again, shimmered, and vanished.

Garion was suddenly filled with chagrin as he realized that

he had been cruelly duped. Zandramas had not actually been here with his son, and all his overpowering rage had been directed at an empty projection. Worse than that, he had been manipulated by the haunting nightmare of the wailing child which he now realized *she* had put into his mind to force him to respond to her taunting commands. He faltered then, his blade lowering and its fire waning.

"Kill him!" Harakan shouted. "Kill the one who slew Torak!"

"Kill him!" Urvon echoed in his insane shriek. "Kill him and offer his heart up to me in sacrifice!"

A half-dozen Temple Guardsmen began a cautious, clearly reluctant, advance. Garion raised his sword again; its light flared anew, and the Guardsmen jumped back.

Harakan sneered as he looked at the armored men. "Behold the reward for cowardice," he snapped. He extended one hand, muttered a single word, and one of the Guardsmen shrieked and fell writhing to the floor as his mail coat and helmet turned instantly white-hot, roasting him alive.

"Now obey me!" Harakan roared. "Kill him!"

The terrified Guardsmen attacked more fervently then, forcing Garion back step by step. Then he heard the sound of running feet in the corridor outside. He glanced quickly over his shoulder and saw the others come bursting into the throne room.

"Have you lost your mind?" Belgarath demanded angrily.

"I'll explain later," Garion told him, still half-sick with frustration and disappointment. He returned his attention to the armored men before him and began swinging his great sword in wide sweeps, driving them back again.

Belgarath faced the Chandim on one side of the central aisle, concentrated for an instant, then gestured shortly. Suddenly a raging fire erupted from the stones of the floor all along the aisle.

Something seemed to pass between the old man and Polgara. She nodded, and quite suddenly the other side of the aisle was also walled off by flame.

Two of the Guardsmen had fallen beneath Garion's sword, but others, accompanied by wild-eyed Karands, were rushing to the aid of their comrades, though they flinched visibly from the flames on either side of the aisle up which they were forced to attack.

"Combine your wills!" Harakan was shouting to the Chandim. "Smother the flames!"

Even as he closed with the Guardsmen and the Karands, beating down their upraised swords and hacking at them with Iron-grip's blade, Garion felt the rush and surge of combined will. Despite the efforts of Belgarath and Polgara, the fires on either side of the aisle flickered and grew low.

One of the huge Hounds came loping through the ranks of the Guardsmen facing Garion. Its eyes were ablaze, and its tooth-studded muzzle agape. It leaped directly at his face, snapping and growling horribly, but fell twitching and biting at the floor as he split its head with his sword.

And then Harakan thrust his way through the Guardsmen and Karands to confront Garion. "And so we meet again, Belgarion," he snarled in an almost doglike voice. "Drop your sword, or I will slay your friends—and your wife. I have a hundred Chandim with me, and not even you are a match for so many." And he began to draw in his will.

Then, to Garion's amazement, Velvet ran forward past him, her arms stretched toward the dread Grolim. "Please!" she wailed. "Please don't kill me!" And she threw herself at Harakan's feet, clutching at his black robe imploringly as she cringed and groveled before him.

Thrown off balance by this sudden and unexpected display of submissiveness, Harakan let his will dissipate and he backed away, trying to shake her hand from his robe and kicking at her to free himself. But she clung to him, weeping and begging for her life.

"Get her off me!" he snapped at his men, turning his head

slightly. And that briefest instant of inattention proved fatal. Velvet's hand moved so quickly that it seemed to blur in the air. She dipped swiftly into her bodice; when her hand emerged, she held a small, bright-green snake.

"A present for you, Harakan!" she shouted triumphantly. "A present for the leader of the Bear-cult from Hunter!" And she threw Zith full into his face.

He screamed once the first time Zith bit him, and his hands came up to claw her away from his face, but the scream ended with a horrid gurgle, and his hands convulsed helplessly in the air in front of him. Squealing and jerking, he reeled backward as the irritated little reptile struck again and again. He stiffened and arched back across the altar, his feet scuffing and scrabbling on the floor and his arms flopping uselessly. He banged his head on the black stone, his eyes bulging and his swollen tongue protruding from his mouth. Then a dark froth came from his lips, he jerked several more times, and his body slid limply off the altar.

"And *that* was for Bethra," Velvet said to the crumpled form of the dead man lying on the floor before the altar.

The Chandim and their cohorts again drew back in fear as they stared at the body of their fallen pack leader.

"They are few!" Urvon shrieked at them. "We are many! Destroy them all! Your God commands it!"

The Chandim gaped first at Harakan's contorted body, then at the crowned madman on the throne, then at the terrible little snake who had coiled herself atop the altar with her head raised threateningly as she gave vent to a series of angry hisses.

"That's about enough of this," Belgarath snapped. He let the last of the flames die and began to refocus his will. Garion also straightened, pulling in his own will even as he felt the frightened Chandim start to focus their power for a final, dreadful confrontation.

"What is all this now?" Feldegast laughed, suddenly coming forward until he stood between Garion and his foes. "Surely, good masters, we can put aside all this hatred and strife. I'll tell ye what I'll do. Let me give ye a demonstration of me skill, an' we'll laugh together an' make peace between us once an' fer all. No man at all kin keep so great a hatred in his heart while he's bubblin' with laughter, don't y' know.''

Then he began to juggle, seeming to pull brightly colored balls out of the air. The Grolims gaped at him, stunned by this unexpected interruption, and Garion stared incredulously at the performer, who seemed deliberately bent on self-destruction. Still juggling, Feldegast flipped his body onto the back of a heavy bench, holding himself upside down over it with one hand while he continued to juggle with his free hand and his feet. Faster and faster the balls whirled, more and more of them coming, it seemed out of thin air. The more the balls whirled, the brighter they became until at last they were incandescent, and the inverted little man was juggling balls of pure fire.

Then he flexed the arm that was holding him in place, tossing himself high over the bench. When his feet touched the floor, however, it was no longer Feldegast the juggler who stood there. In place of the roguish entertainer stood the gnarled, hunchbacked shape of the sorcerer Beldin. With a sudden evil laugh, he began to hurl his fireballs at the startled Grolims and their warriors.

His aim was unerring, and the deadly fireballs pierced Grolim robes, Guardsmen's mail coats, and Karandese fur vests with equal facility. Smoking holes appeared in the chests of his victims, and he felled them by the dozen. The throne room filled with smoke and the reek of burning flesh as the grinning, ugly little sorcerer continued his deadly barrage.

"You!" Urvon shrieked in terror, the sudden appearance of the man he had feared for so many thousands of years shocking him into some semblance of sanity, even as the terrified Chandim and their cohorts broke and fled, howling in fright.

"So good to see you again, Urvon," the hunchback said to him pleasantly. "Our conversation was interrupted the last time we were talking, but as I recall, I'd just promised to sink

a white-hot hook into your belly and yank out all your guts."
He held out his gnarled right hand, snapped his fingers, and
there was a sudden flash. A cruel hook, smoking and glowing,
appeared in his fist. "Why don't we continue with that line
of thought?" he suggested, advancing on the splotchy-faced
man cowering on the throne.

Then the shadow which had lurked behind the madman's
shoulder came out from behind the throne. "Stop," it said in
a voice that was no more than a crackling whisper. No human
throat could have produced that sound. "I need this thing,"
it said, pointing a shadowy hand in the direction of the gib-
bering Disciple of Torak. "It serves my purposes, and I will
not let you kill it."

"You would be Nahaz, then," Beldin said in an ominous
voice.

"I am," the figure whispered. "Nahaz, Lord of Demons
and Master of Darkness."

"Go find yourself another plaything, Demon Lord," The
hunchback grated. "This one is mine."

"Will you pit your will against mine, sorcerer?"

"If need be."

"Look upon my face, then, and prepare for death." The
demon pushed back its hood of darkness, and Garion recoiled
with a sharp intake of his breath. The face of Nahaz was
hideous, but it was not the misshapen features alone which
were so terrifying. There emanated from its burning eyes a
malevolent evil so gross that it froze the blood. Brighter and
brighter those eyes burned with evil green fire until their
beams shot forth toward Beldin. The gnarled sorcerer
clenched himself and raised one hand. The hand suddenly
glowed an intense blue, a light that seemed to cascade down
over his body to form a shield against the demon's power.

"Your will is strong," Nahaz hissed. "But mine is stronger."

Then Polgara came down the littered aisle, the white lock
at her brow gleaming. On one side of her strode Belgarath
and on the other Durnik. As they reached him, Garion joined

329

them. They advanced slowly to take up positions flanking
Beldin, and Garion became aware that Eriond had also joined
them, standing slightly off to one side.

"Well, Demon," Polgara said in a deadly voice, "will you
face us all?"

Garion raised his sword and unleashed its fire. "And *this* as
well?" he added, releasing all restraints on the Orb.

The Demon flinched momentarily, then drew itself erect
again, its horrid face bathed in that awful green fire. From
beneath its robe of shadow, it took what appeared to be a
scepter or a wand of some kind that blazed an intense green.
As it raised that wand, however, it seemed to see something
that had previously escaped its notice. An expression of sudden fear crossed its hideous face, and the fire of the wand
died, even as the intense green light bathing its face flickered
and grew wan and weak. Then it raised its face toward the
vaulted ceiling and howled—a dreadful, shocking sound. It
spun quickly, moving toward the terrified Urvon. It reached
out with shadowy hands, seized the gold-robed madman, and
lifted him easily from the throne. Then it fled, its fire pushing
out before it like a great battering ram, blasting out the walls
of the House of Torak as it went.

The crown which had surmounted Urvon's brow fell from
his head as Nahaz carried him from the crumbling house, and
it clanked when it hit the floor with the tinny sound of brass.

Part Four

THE MOUNTAINS
OF ZAMAD

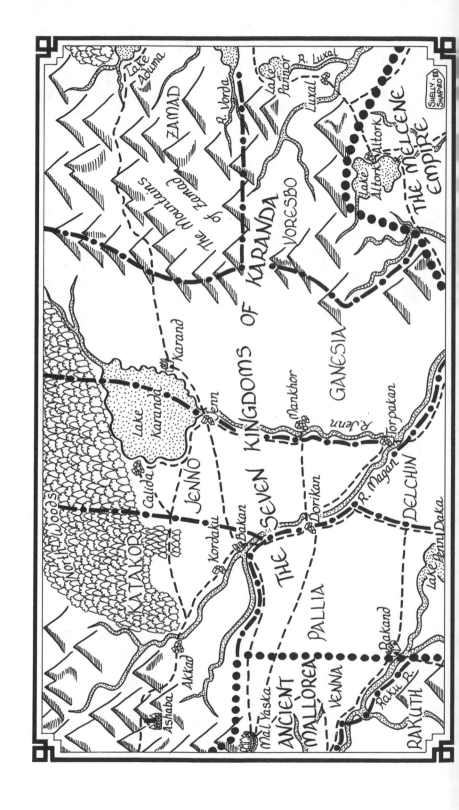

CHAPTER NINETEEN

Beldin spat out a rancid oath and hurled his glowing hook at the throne. Then he started toward the smoking hole the fleeing demon had blasted out through the wall of the throne room.

Belgarath, however, managed to place himself in front of the angry hunchback. "No, Beldin," he said firmly.

"Get out of my way, Belgarath."

"I'm not going to let you chase after a demon who could turn on you at any minute."

"I can take of myself. Now stand aside."

"You're not thinking, Beldin. There'll be time enough to

deal with Urvon later. Right now we need to make some decisions."

"What's to decide? You go after Zandramas and I go after Urvon. It's all pretty much cut and dried, isn't it?"

"Not entirely. In any event, I'm not going to let you chase after Nahaz in the dark. You know as well as I do that the darkness multiplies his power—and I haven't got so many brothers left that I can afford to lose one just because he's irritated."

Their eyes locked, and the ugly hunchback finally turned away. He stumped back toward the dais, pausing long enough to kick a chair to pieces on his way, muttering curses all the while.

"Is everyone all right?" Silk asked, looking around as he resheathed his knife.

"So it would seem," Polgara replied, pushing back the hood of her blue cloak.

"It was a bit tight there for a while, wasn't it?" The little man's eyes were very bright.

"Also unnecessary," she said, giving Garion a hard look. "You'd better take a quick look through the rest of the house, Kheldar. Let's make sure that it's really empty. Durnik, you and Toth go with him."

Silk nodded and started back up the blood-splashed aisle, stepping over bodies as he went, with Durnik and Toth close behind him.

"I don't understand," Ce'Nedra said, staring in bafflement at the gnarled Beldin, who was once again dressed in rags and had the usual twigs and bits of straw clinging to him. "How did you change places with Feldegast—and where is he?"

A roguish smile crossed Beldin's face. "Ah, me little darlin'," he said to her in the juggler's lilting brogue, "I'm right here, don't y' know. An' if yer of a mind, I kin still charm ye with me wit an' me unearthly skill."

"But I *liked* Feldegast," she almost wailed.

"All ye have t' do is transfer yer affection t' me, darlin'."

"It's not the same," she objected.

Belgarath was looking steadily at the twisted sorcerer. "Have you got any idea of how much that particular dialect irritates me?" he said.

"Why, yes, brother." Beldin grinned. "As a matter of fact I do. That's one of the reasons I selected it."

"I don't entirely understand the need for so elaborate a disguise," Sadi said as he put away his small poisoned dagger.

"Too many people know me by sight in this part of Mallore," Beldin told him. "Urvon's had my description posted on every tree and fence post within a hundred leagues of Mal Yaska for the last two thousand years, and let's be honest about it, it wouldn't be too hard to recognize me from even the roughest description."

"You are a unique sort of person, Uncle," Polgara said to him, smiling fondly.

"Ah, yer too kind t' say it, me girl," he replied with an extravagant bow.

"*Will* you stop that?" Belgarath said. Then he turned to Garion. "As I remember, you said that you were going to explain something later. All right—it's later."

"I was tricked," Garion admitted glumly.

"By whom?"

"Zandramas."

"She's still here?" Ce'Nedra exclaimed.

Garion shook his head. "No. She sent a projection here—a projection of herself and of Geran."

"Couldn't you tell the difference between a projection and the real thing?" Belgarath demanded.

"I wasn't in any condition to tell the difference when it happened."

"I suppose you can explain that."

Garion took a deep breath and sat down on one of the benches. He noticed that his bloodstained hands were shaking. "She's very clever," he said. "Ever since we left Mal Zeth, I've been having the same dream over and over again."

"Dream?" Polgara asked sharply. "What kind of dream?"

"Maybe dream isn't the right word," he replied, "but over and over again, I kept hearing the cry of a baby. At first I thought that I was remembering the cry of that sick child we saw in the streets back in Mal Zeth, but that wasn't it at all. When Silk and Beldin and I were in that room just above this one, we could see down into the throne room here and we saw Urvon come in with Nahaz right behind him. He's completely insane now. He think's he's a God. Anyway, he summoned Mengha—only Mengha turned out to be Harakan, and then—"

"Wait a minute," Belgarath interrupted him. "*Harakan* is Mengha?"

Garion glanced over at the limp form sprawled in front of the altar. Zith was still coiled atop the black stone, muttering and hissing to herself. "Well, he *was*," he said.

"Urvon made the announcement before all this broke out," Beldin added. "We didn't have the time to fill you in."

"That explains a great many things, doesn't it?" Belgarath mused. He looked at Velvet. "Did you know about this?" he asked her.

"No, Ancient One," she replied, "as a matter of fact, I didn't. I just seized the opportunity when it arose."

Silk, Durnik, and Toth came back into the body-strewn throne room. "The house is empty," the little man reported. "We've got it all to ourselves."

"Good," Belgarath said. "Garion was just telling us why he saw fit to start his own private war."

"Zandramas told him to." Silk shrugged. "I'm not sure why he started taking orders from her, but that's what happened."

"I was just getting to that," Garion said. "Urvon was down here telling all the Chandim that Harakan—Mengha—was going to be his first disciple. That's when Zandramas came in—or at least she seemed to. She had a bundle under her cloak. I didn't know it at first, but it was Geran. She and Urvon shouted at each other for a while, and Urvon finally insisted that he was a God. She said something like, 'All right. Then I will summon the Godslayer to deal with you.' That's when she put the bundle on the altar. She opened it, and it was Geran. He started to cry, and I realized all at once that it was *his* cry I'd been hearing all along. I just totally stopped thinking at that point."

"Obviously," Belgarath said.

"Well, anyway, you know all the rest." Garion looked around at the corpse-littered throne room and shuddered. "I hadn't altogether realized just how far things went," he said. "I guess I was sort of crazy."

"The word is berserk, Garion," Belgarath told him. "It's fairly common among Alorns. I'd sort of thought you might be immune, but I guess I was wrong."

"There was some justification for it, father," Polgara said.

"There's never a justification for losing your wits, Pol," he growled.

"He was provoked." She pursed her lips thoughtfully, then came over and lightly placed her hands on Garion's temples. "It's gone now," she said.

"What is?" Ce'Nedra sounded concerned.

"The possession."

"Possession?"

Polgara nodded. "Yes. That's how Zandramas tricked him. She filled his mind with the sound of a crying child. Then, when she laid the bundle that *seemed* to be Geran on the altar and Garion heard that same crying, he had no choice but to do what she wanted him to do." She looked at Belgarath. "This is very serious, father. She's already tampered with Ce'Nedra, and now it's Garion. She may try the same thing with others as well."

"What would be the point?" he asked. "You can catch her at it, can't you?"

"Usually, yes—*if* I know what's going on. But Zandramas is very skilled at this and she's very subtle. In many ways she's even better at it than Asharak the Murgo was." She looked around at them. "Now listen carefully, all of you," she told them. "If anything unusual begins to happen to you—dreams, notions, peculiar ideas, strange feelings—anything at all, I want you to tell me about it at once. Zandramas knows that we're after her and she's using this to delay us. She tried it with Ce'Nedra while we were on our way to Rak Hagga, and now—"

"Me?" Ce'Nedra said in amazement. "I didn't know that."

"Remember your illness on the road from Rak Verkat?" Polgara said. "It wasn't exactly an illness. It was Zandramas putting her hand on your mind."

"But nobody told me."

"Once Andel and I drove Zandramas away, there was no need to worry you about it. Anyway, Zandramas tried it first with Ce'Nedra and now with Garion. She could try it on any one of the rest of us as well, so let me know if you start feeling in the least bit peculiar."

"Brass," Durnik said.

"What was that, dear?" Polgara asked him.

He held up Urvon's crown. "This thing is brass," he said. "So's that throne. I didn't really think there'd be any gold left here. The house has been abandoned and wide open for looters for too many centuries."

"That's usually the way it is with the gifts of demons," Beldin told him. "They're very good at creating illusions." He looked around. "Urvon probably saw all this as unearthly splendor. He couldn't see the rotten drapes, or cobwebs, or all the trash on the floor. All he could see was the glory that Nahaz wanted him to see." The dirty, twisted man chuckled. "I sort of enjoy the idea of Urvon spending his last days as a raving lunatic," he added, "right up until the moment when I sink a hook into his guts."

Silk had been looking narrowly at Velvet. "Do you suppose you could explain something for me?" he asked.

"I'll try," she said.

"You said something rather strange when you threw Zith into Harakan's face."

"Did I say something?"

"You said, 'A present for the leader of the Bear-cult from Hunter.'"

"Oh, that." She smiled her dimples into life. "I just wanted him to know who was killing him, that's all."

He stared at her.

"You *are* getting rusty, my dear Kheldar," she chided him. "I was certain that you'd have guessed by now. I've done everything but hit you over the head with it."

"Hunter?" he said incredulously. *"You?"*

"I've been Hunter for quite some time now. That's why I hurried to catch up with you at Tol Honeth." She smoothed the front of her plain gray traveling gown.

"At Tol Honeth you told us that *Bethra* was Hunter."

"She *had* been, Kheldar, but her job was finished. She was supposed to make sure that we'd get a reasonable man as a successor to Ran Borune. First she had to eliminate a few members of the Honeth family before they could consolidate their positions, and then she made a few suggestions about Varana to Ran Borune while the two of them were—" She hesitated, glancing at Ce'Nedra, and then she coughed. "—ah—shall we say, entertaining each other?" she concluded.

Ce'Nedra blushed furiously.

"Oh, dear," the blond girl said, putting one hand to her cheek. "That didn't come out at all well, did it? Anyway," she hurried on, "Javelin decided that Bethra's task was complete and that it was time for there to be a new Hunter with a new mission. Queen Porenn was *very* cross about what Harakan did in the west—the attempt on Ce'Nedra's life, the murder of Brand, and everything that went on at Rheon—so she instructed Javelin to administer some chastisement. He selected me to deliver it. I was fairly sure that Harakan would come back to Mallorea. I knew that you were all coming here, too—eventually—so that's why I joined you." She looked over at the sprawled form of Harakan. "I was absolutely amazed when I saw him standing in front of the altar," she admitted, "but I couldn't allow an opportunity like that to slip by." She smiled. "Actually, it worked out rather well. I was just on the verge of leaving you and going back to Mal Yaska to look for him. The fact that he turned out to be Mengha, too, was just sort of a bonus."

"I thought you were tagging along to keep an eye on *me*."

"I'm very sorry, Prince Kheldar. I just made that up. I needed some reason to join you, and sometimes Belgarath can be very stubborn." She smiled winsomely at the old sorcerer, then turned back to the baffled-looking Silk. "Actually," she continued, "my uncle isn't really upset with you at all."

"But you said—" He stared at her. "You *lied*!" he accused.

"'Lie' is such an ugly word, Kheldar," she replied, patting his cheek fondly. "Couldn't we just say that I exaggerated a trifle? I wanted to keep an eye on you, certainly, but it was for reasons of my own—which had nothing whatsoever to do with Drasnian state policy."

A slow flush crept up his cheeks.

"Why, Kheldar," she exclaimed delightedly, "you're actually blushing—almost like a simple village girl who's just been seduced."

Garion had been struggling with something. "What was the point of it, Aunt Pol?" he asked. "What Zandramas did to me, I mean?"

"Delay," she replied, "but more importantly, there was the possibility of defeating us before we ever get to the final meeting."

"I don't follow that."

She sighed. "We know that one of us is going to die," she said. "Cyradis told us that at Rheon. But there's always a chance that in one of these random skirmishes, someone *else* could be killed—entirely by accident. If the Child of Light— you—meets with the Child of Dark and he's lost someone whose task hasn't been completed, he won't have any chance

340

of winning. Zandramas could win by default. The whole point of that cruel game she played was to lure you into a fight with the Chandim and Nahaz. The rest of us, quite obviously, would come to your aid. In that kind of fight, it's always possible for accidents to happen."

"Accident? How can there be accidents when we're all under the control of a prophecy?"

"You're forgetting something, Belgarion," Beldin said. "This whole business started with an accident. That's what divided the Prophecies in the first place. You can read prophecies until your hair turns gray, but there's always room for random chance to step in and disrupt things."

"You'll note that my brother is a philosopher," Belgarath said, "always ready to look on the dark side of things."

"Are you two really brothers?" Ce'Nedra asked curiously.

"Yes," Beldin told her, "but in a way that you could never begin to understand. It was something that our Master impressed upon us."

"And Zedar was *also* one of your brothers?" She suddenly stared in horror at Belgarath.

The old man set his jaw. "Yes," he admitted.

"But you—"

"Go ahead and say it, Ce'Nedra," he said. "There's nothing you can possibly say to me that I haven't already said to myself."

"Someday," she said in a very small voice, "someday when this is all over, will you let him out?"

Belgarath's eyes were stony. "I don't think so, no."

"And if he *does* let him out, I'll go find him and stuff him right back in again," Beldin added.

"There's not much point in chewing over ancient history," Belgarath said. He thought a moment, then said, "I think it's time for us to have another talk with the young lady from Kell." He turned to Toth. "Will you summon your mistress?" he asked.

341

The giant's face was not happy. When he finally nodded, it was obviously with some reluctance.

"I'm sorry, my friend," Belgarath said to him, "but it's really necessary."

Toth sighed and then he sank to one knee and closed his eyes in an oddly prayerful fashion. Once again, as it had happened back on the Isle of Verkat and again at Rak Hagga, Garion heard a murmur as of many voices. Then there came that peculiar, multicolored shimmering in the air not far from Urvon's shoddy throne. The air cleared, and the unwavering form of the Seeress of Kell appeared on the dais. For the first time, Garion looked closely at her. She was slender and somehow looked very vulnerable, a helplessness accentuated by her white robe and her blindfolded eyes. There was, however, a serenity in her face—the serenity of someone who has looked full in the face of Destiny and has accepted it without question or reservation. For some reason, he felt almost overcome with awe in her radiant presence.

"Thank you for coming, Cyradis," Belgarath said simply. "I'm sorry to have troubled you. I know how difficult it is for you to do this, but there are some answers I need before we can go any further."

"I will tell thee as much as I am permitted to say, Ancient One," she replied. Her voice was light and musical, but there was, nonetheless, a firmness in it that spoke of an unearthly resolve. "I must say unto thee, however, that thou must make haste. The time for the final meeting draws nigh."

"That's one of the things I wanted to talk about. Can you be any more specific about this appointed time?"

She seemed to consider it as if consulting with some power so immense that Garion's imagination shuddered back from the very thought of it. "I know not time in thy terms, Holy Belgarath," she said simply, "but only for so long as a babe lieth beneath his mother's heart remains ere the Child of Light and the Child of Dark must face each other in the Place Which Is No More, and my task must be completed."

"All right," he said. "That's clear enough, I guess. Now, when you came to us at Mal Zeth, you said that there was a task here at Ashaba that needed to be accomplished before we could move on. A great deal has happened here, so I can't pinpoint exactly what that task was. Can you be a bit more specific?"

"The task is completed, Eternal One, for the Book of the Heavens sayeth that the Huntress must find her prey and bring him low in the House of Darkness in the sixteenth moon. And lo, even as the stars have proclaimed, it hath come to pass."

The old man's face took on a slightly puzzled expression.

"Ask further, Disciple of Aldur," she told him. "My time with you grows short."

"I'm supposed to follow the trail of the Mysteries," he said, "but Zandramas cut certain key passages out of the copy of the Ashabine Oracles she left here for me to find."

"Nay, Ancient One. It was not the hand of Zandramas which mutilated thy book, but rather the hand of its author."

"Torak?" he sounded startled.

"Even so. For know thou that the words of prophecy come unbidden, and ofttimes their import is not pleasing unto the prophet. So it was with the master of this house."

"But Zandramas managed to put her hands on a copy that hadn't been mutilated?" he asked.

The seeress nodded.

"Are there any other copies that Burnt-face didn't tamper with?" Beldin asked intently.

"Only two," she replied. "One is in the house of Urvon the Disciple, but that one lieth under the hand of Nahaz, the accursed. Seek not to wrest it from him, lest ye die."

"And the other?" the hunchback demanded.

"Seek out the clubfooted one, for he will aid thee in thy search."

"That's not too helpful, you know."

"I speak to thee in the words that stand in the Book of the

Heavens and were written ere the world began. These words have no language but speak instead directly to the soul."

"Naturally," he said. "All right. You spoke of Nahaz. Is he going to line our path with demons all the way across Karanda?"

"Nay, gentle Beldin. Nahaz hath no further interest in Karanda, and his legions of darkness abide no longer there and respond to no summons, however powerful. They infest instead the plains of Darshiva where they do war upon the minions of Zandramas."

"Where is Zandramas now?" Belgarath asked her.

"She doth journey unto the place where the Sardion lay hidden for unnumbered centuries. Though it is no longer there, she hopes to find traces of it sunk into the very rocks and to follow those traces to the Place Which Is No More."

"Is that possible?"

Her face grew very still. "That I may not tell thee," she replied. Then she straightened. "I may say no more unto thee in this place, Belgarath. Seek instead the mystery which will guide thee. Make haste, however, for Time will not stay nor falter in its measured pace." And then she turned toward the black altar standing before the dais where Zith was coiled, still muttering and hissing in irritation. "Be tranquil, little sister," she said, "for the purpose of all thy days is now accomplished, and that which was delayed may now come to pass." She then seemed, even though blindfolded, to turn her serene face toward each of them, pausing briefly only to bow her head to Polgara in a gesture of profound respect. At last she turned to Toth. Her face was filled with anguish, but she said nothing. And then she sighed and vanished.

Beldin was scowling. "That was fairly standard," he said. "I *hate* riddles. They're the entertainment of the preliterate."

"Stop trying to show off your education and let's see if we can sort this out," Belgarath told him. "We know that this is all going to be decided one way or the other in nine more months. That was the number I needed."

Sadi was frowning in perplexity. "How did we arrive at that number?" he asked. "To be perfectly frank, I didn't understand very much of what she said."

"She said that we have only as much time as a baby lies in its mother's womb," Polgara explained. "That's nine months."

"Oh," he said. Then he smiled a bit sadly. "That's the sort of thing I don't pay too much attention to, I guess."

"What was that business about the sixteenth moon?" Silk asked. "I didn't follow that at all."

"This whole thing began with the birth of Belgarion's son," Beldin told him. "We found a reference to that in the Mrin Codex. Your friend with the snake had to be here at Ashaba sixteen moons later."

Silk frowned, counting on his fingers. "It hasn't been sixteen months yet," he objected.

"Moons, Kheldar," the hunchback said. "Moons, not months. There's a difference, you know."

"Oh. That explains it, I guess."

"Who's this clubfoot who's supposed to have the third uncorrupted copy of the Oracles?" Belgarath said.

"It rings a bell somehow," Beldin replied. "Let me think about it."

"What's Nahaz doing in Darshiva?" Garion asked.

"Apparently attacking the Grolims there," Belgarath replied. "We know that Darshiva is where Zandramas originally came from and that the church in that region belongs to her. If Nahaz wants to put the Sardion in Urvon's hands, he's going to have to stop her. Otherwise, she'll get to it first."

Ce'Nedra seemed to suddenly remember something. She looked at Garion, her eyes hungry. "You said that you saw Geran—when Zandramas tricked you."

"A projection of him, yes."

"How did he look?"

"The same. He hadn't changed a bit since the last time I saw him."

345

"Garion, dear," Polgara said gently. "That's not really reasonable, you know. Geran's almost a year older now. He wouldn't look the same at all. Babies grow and change a great deal during their first few years."

He nodded glumly. "I realize that now," he replied. "At the time, I wasn't really in any condition to think my way through it." Then he stopped. "Why didn't she project an image of him the way he looks now?"

"Because she wanted to show you something she was sure you'd recognize."

"Now you stop that!" Sadi exclaimed. He was standing near the altar and he had just jerked his hand back out of Zith's range. The little green snake was growling ominously at him. The eunuch turned toward Velvet. "Do you see what you've done?" he accused. "You've made her terribly angry."

"Me?" she asked innocently.

"How would *you* like to be pulled out of a warm bed and thrown into somebody's face?"

"I suppose I hadn't thought about that. I'll apologize to her, Sadi—just as soon as she regains her composure a bit. Will she crawl into her bottle by herself?"

"Usually, yes."

"That might be the safest course, then. Lay the bottle on the altar and let her crawl inside and sulk a bit."

"You're probably right," he agreed.

"Are any of the other rooms in the house habitable?" Polgara asked Silk.

He nodded. "More or less. The Chandim and the Guardsmen were staying in them."

She looked around at the corpse-littered throne room. "Why don't we move out of here, then?" she suggested to Belgarath. "This place looks like a battlefield, and the smell of blood isn't that pleasant."

"Why bother?" Ce'Nedra said. "We're leaving to follow Zandramas, aren't we?"

"Not until morning, dear," Polgara replied. "It's dark and cold outside, and we're all tired and hungry."

"But—"

"The Chandim and the Guardsmen ran away, Ce'Nedra— but we can't be at all sure how far they went. And, of course, there are the Hounds as well. Let's not make the mistake of blundering out into a forest at night when we can't see what might be hiding behind the first tree we come to."

"It makes sense, Ce'Nedra," Velvet told her. "Let's try to get some sleep and start out early in the morning."

The little Queen sighed. "I suppose you're right," she admitted. "It's just that—"

"Zandramas can't get away from me, Ce'Nedra," Garion assured her. "The Orb knows which way she went."

They followed Silk out of the throne room and along the blood-spattered corridor outside. Garion tried as best he could to shield Ce'Nedra from the sight of the crumpled forms of the Guardsmen and Karands he had killed in his raging dash to the throne room of Torak. About halfway down the corridor Silk pushed open a door and held up the guttering torch he had taken from one of the iron rings sticking out of the wall. "This is about the best I can do," he told Polgara. "At least someone made an effort to clean it up."

She looked around. The room had the look of a barracks. Bunks protruded from the walls and there was a long table with benches in the center. There was a fireplace at the far end with the last embers of a fire glowing inside. "Adequate," she said.

"I'd better go look after the horses," Durnik said. "Is there a stable anywhere on the grounds?"

"It's down at the far end of the courtyard," Beldin told him, "and the Guardsmen who were here probably put in a supply of fodder and water for their own mounts."

"Good," Durnik said.

"Would you bring in the packs with my utensils and the stores, dear?" Polgara asked him.

"Of course." Then he went out, followed by Toth and Eriond.

"Suddenly I'm so tired that I can barely stand," Garion said, sinking onto a bench.

"I wouldn't be at all surprised." Beldin grunted. "You've had a busy evening."

"Are you coming along with us?" Belgarath asked him.

"No, I don't think so," Beldin replied, sprawling on the bench. "I want to find out where Nahaz took Urvon."

"Will you be able to follow him?"

"Oh, yes." Beldin tapped his nose. "I can smell a demon six days after he passes. I'll trail Nahaz just like a bloodhound. I won't be gone too long. You go ahead and follow Zandramas, and I'll catch up with you somewhere along the way." The hunchback rubbed at his jaw thoughtfully. "I think we can be fairly sure that Nahaz isn't going to let Urvon out of his sight. Urvon is—or was—a Disciple of Torak, after all. Even as much as I detest him, I still have to admit that he's got a very strong mind. Nahaz is going to have to talk to him almost constantly to keep his sanity from returning, so if our Demon Lord went to Darshiva to oversee his creatures there, he's almost certain to have taken Urvon along."

"You *will* be careful, won't you?"

"Don't get sentimental on me, Belgarath. Just leave me some kind of trail I can follow. I don't want to have to look all over Mallorea for you."

Sadi came from the throne room with his red leather case in one hand and Zith's little bottle in the other. "She's still very irritated," he said to Velvet. "She doesn't appreciate being used as a weapon."

"I told you that I'd apologize to her, Sadi," she replied. "I'll explain things to her. I'm sure she'll understand."

Silk was looking at the blond girl with an odd expression.

"Tell me," he said. "Didn't it bother you at all the first time you put her down the front of your dress?"

She laughed. "To be perfectly honest with you, Prince Kheldar, the first time it was all I could do to keep from screaming."

CHAPTER TWENTY

At first light the following morning, a light that was little more than a lessening of the darkness of a sky where dense cloud scudded before the chill wind blowing down off the mountains, Silk returned to the room in which they had spent the night. "The house is being watched," he told them.

"How many are there?" Belgarath asked.

"I saw one. I'm sure there are others."

"Where is he? The one that you saw?"

Silk's quick grin was vicious. "He's watching the sky. At least he looks like he's watching. His eyes are open and he's lying on his back." He slid his hand down into his boot, pulled out one of his daggers, and looked sorrowfully at its once-keen edge. "Do you have any idea of how hard it is to push a knife through a chain-mail shirt?"

"I think that's why people wear them, Kheldar," Velvet said to him. "You should use one of these." From somewhere amongst her soft, feminine clothing she drew out a long-bladed poniard with a needlelike point.

"I thought you were partial to snakes."

"Always use the appropriate weapon, Kheldar. I certainly wouldn't want Zith to break her teeth on a steel shirt."

"Could you two talk business some other time?" Belgarath said to them. "Can you put a name to this fellow who's suddenly so interested in the sky?"

"We didn't really have time to introduce ourselves," Silk replied, sliding his jagged-edged knife back into his boot.

"I meant what—not who."

"Oh. He was a Temple Guardsman."

"Not one of the Chandim?"

"All I had to go by was his clothing."

The old man grunted.

"It's going to be slow going if we have to look behind every tree and bush as we ride along," Sadi said.

"I realize that," Begarath answered, tugging at one earlobe. "Let me think my way through this."

"And while you're deciding, I'll fix us some breakfast," Polgara said, laying aside her hairbrush. "What would you all like?"

"Porridge?" Eriond asked hopefully.

Silk sighed. "The word is gruel, Eriond. Gruel." Then he looked quickly at Polgara, whose eyes had suddenly turned frosty. "Sorry, Polgara," he apologized, "but it's our duty to educate the young, don't you think?"

"What I think is that I need more firewood," she replied.

"I'll see to it at once."

"You're too kind."

Silk rather quickly left the room.

"Any ideas?" the hunchbacked Beldin asked Belgarath.

"Several. But they all have certain flaws in them."

"Why not let me handle it for you?" The gnarled sorcerer asked, sprawling on a bench near the fire and scratching absently at his belly. "You've had a hard night, and a ten-thousand-year-old man needs to conserve his strength."

"You really find that amusing, don't you? Why not say twenty—or fifty? Push absurdity to its ultimate edge."

"My," Beldin said. "Aren't we testy this morning? Pol, have you got any beer handy?"

"Before breakfast, Uncle?" she said from beside the fireplace where she was stirring a large pot.

"Just as a buffer for the gruel," he said.

She gave him a very steady look.

He grinned at her, then turned back toward Belgarath. "Seriously, though," he went on, "why not let me deal with all the lurkers in the bushes around the house? Kheldar could dull every knife he's carrying, and Liselle could wear that poor little snake's fangs down to the gums, and you still wouldn't be sure if you'd cleaned out the woods hereabouts. I'm going off in a different direction anyway, so why not let me do something flamboyant to frighten off the Guardsmen and the Kanrands and then leave a nice, wide trail for the Chandim and the Hounds? They'll follow me, and that should leave you an empty forest to ride through."

Belgarath gave him a speculative look. "Exactly what have you got in mind?" he asked.

"I'm still working on it." The dwarf leaned back reflectively. "Let's face it, Belgarath, the Chandim and Zandramas already know that we're here, so there's not much point in tiptoeing around any more. A little noise isn't going to hurt anything."

"That's true, I suppose," Belgarath agreed. He looked at Garion. "Are you getting any hints from the Orb about the direction Zandramas took when she left here?"

"A sort of a steady pull toward the east is all."

Beldin grunted. "Makes sense. Since Urvon's people were

wandering all over Katakor, she probably wanted to get to the nearest unguarded border as quickly as possible. That would be Jenno."

"Is the border between Jenno and Katakor unguarded?" Velvet asked.

"They don't even know for sure where the border is." He snorted. "At least not up in the forest. There's nothing up there but trees anyway, so they don't bother with it." He turned back to Belgarath. "Don't get your mind set in stone on some of these things," he advised. "We did a lot of speculating back at Mal Zeth, and the theories we came up with were related to the truth only by implication. There's a great deal of intrigue going on here in Mallorea, so it's a good idea to expect things to turn out not quite the way you thought they would."

"Garion," Polgara said from the fireplace, "would you see if you can find Silk? Breakfast is almost ready."

"Yes, Aunt Pol," he replied automatically.

After they had eaten, they repacked their belongings and carried the packs out to the stable.

"Go out through the sally port," Beldin said as they crossed the courtyard again. "Give me about an hour before you start."

"You're leaving now?" Belgarath asked him.

"I might as well. We're not accomplishing very much by sitting around talking. Don't forget to leave me a trail to follow."

"I'll take care of it. I wish you'd tell me what you're going to do here."

"Trust me." The gnarled sorcerer winked. "Take cover someplace and don't come out again until all the noise subsides." He grinned wickedly and rubbed his dirty hands together in anticipation. Then he shimmered and swooped away as a blue-banded hawk.

"I think we'd better go back inside the house," Belgarath suggested. "Whatever he's going to do out here is likely to involve a great deal of flying debris."

They reentered the house and went back to the room where they had spent the night. "Durnik," Belgarath said, "can you get those shutters closed? I don't think we want broken glass sheeting across the room."

"But then we won't be able to see," Silk objected.

"I'm sure you can live without seeing it. As a matter of fact, you probably *wouldn't* want to watch, anyway."

Durnik went to the window, opened it slightly, and pulled the shutters closed.

Then, from high overhead where the blue-banded hawk had been circling, there came a huge roar almost like a continuous peal of swirling thunder, accompanied by a rushing surge. The House of Torak shook as if a great wind were tearing at it, and the faint light coming from between the slats of the shutters Durnik had closed vanished, to be replaced by inky darkness. Then there came a vast bellow from high in the air above the house.

"A demon?" Ce'Nedra gasped. "Is it a demon?"

"A *semblance* of a demon," Polgara corrected.

"How can anybody see it when it's so dark outside?" Sadi asked.

"It's dark around the house because the house is *inside* the image. The people hiding in the forest should be able to see it very well—too well, in fact."

"It's *that* big?" Sadi looked stunned. "But this house is enormous."

Belgarath grinned. "Beldin was never satisfied with halfway measures," he said.

There came another of those huge bellows from high above, followed by faint shrieks and cries of agony.

"Now what's he doing?" Ce'Nedra asked.

"Some kind of visual display, I'd imagine." Belgarath shrugged. "Probably fairly graphic. My guess is that everyone in the vicinity is being entertained by the spectacle of an illusory demon eating imaginary people alive."

"Will it frighten them off?" Silk asked.

"Wouldn't it frighten you?"

From high overhead, a dreadful booming voice roared. "Hungry!" it said. "Hungry! Want food! More food!" There came a ponderous, earthshaking crash, the sound of a titanic foot crushing an acre of forest. Then there was another and yet another as Beldin's enormous image stalked away. The light returned, and Silk hurried toward the window.

"I wouldn't," Belgarath warned him.

"But—"

"You don't want to see it, Silk. Take my word for it. You don't want to see it."

The gigantic footsteps continued to crash through the nearby woods.

"How much longer?" Sadi asked in a shaken voice.

"He said about an hour." Belgarath replied. "He'll probably make use of all of it. He wants to make a lasting impression on everybody in the area."

There were screams of terror coming from the woods now, and the crashing continued. Then there was another sound— a great roaring that receded off into the distance toward the southwest, accompanied by the fading surge of Beldin's will.

"He's leading the Chandim off now," Belgarath said. "That means he's already chased off the Guardsmen and the Karands. Let's get ready to leave."

It took them a while to calm the wild-eyed horses, but they were finally able to mount and ride into the courtyard. Garion had once again donned his mail shirt and helmet, and his heavy shield hung from the bow of Chretienne's saddle. "Do I still need to carry the lance?" he asked.

"Probably not," Belgarath replied. "We're not likely to meet anybody out there now."

They went through the sally port and into the brushy woods. They circled the black house until they reached the east side, then Garion drew Iron-grip's sword. He held it lightly and swept it back and forth until he felt it pull at his hand. "The trail's over there," he said, pointing toward a scarcely visible path leading off into the woods.

"Good," Belgarath said. "At least we won't have to beat our way through the brush."

They crossed the weed-grown clearing that surrounded the House of Torak and entered the forest. The path they followed showed little sign of recent use, and it was at times difficult to see.

"It looks as if some people left here in a hurry." Silk grinned, pointing at various bits and pieces of equipment lying scattered along the path.

They they came up over the top of a hill and saw a wide strip of devastation stretching through the forest toward the southwest.

"A tornado?" Sadi asked.

"No," Belgarath replied. "Beldin. The Chandim won't have much trouble finding his trail."

The sword in Garion's hand was still pointed unerringly toward the path they were following. He led the way confidently, and they increased their pace to a trot and pushed on through the forest. After a league or so, the path began to run downhill, moving out of the foothills toward the heavily forested plains lying to the east of the Karandese range.

"Are there any towns out there?" Sadi asked, looking out over the forest.

"Akkad is the only one of any size between here and the border," Silk told him.

"I don't think I've ever heard of it. What's it like?"

"It's a pigpen of a place," Silk replied. "Most Karandese towns are. They seem to have a great affinity for mud."

"Wasn't Akkad the place where the Melcene bureaucrat was from?" Velvet asked.

"That's what he said," Silk answered.

"And didn't he say that there are demons there?"

"There *were*," Belgarath corrected. "Cyradis told us that Nahaz has pulled all of his demons out of Karanda and sent them off to Darshiva to fight the Grolims there." He scratched at his beard. "I think we'll avoid Akkad anyway. The demons may have left, but there are still going to be Karandese fanatics there, and I don't think that the news of Mengha's death has reached them yet. In any event, there's going to be a fair amount of chaos here in Karanda until Zakath's army gets back from Cthol Murgos and he moves in to restore order."

They rode on, pausing only briefly for lunch.

By midafternoon, the clouds that had obscured the skies over Ashaba had dissipated, and the sun came back out again. The path they had been following grew wider and more well traveled, and it finally expanded into a road. They picked up the pace and made better time.

As evening drew on, they rode some distance back from the road and made their night's encampment in a small hollow where the light from their fire would be well concealed. They ate, and, immediately after supper, Garion sought his bed. For some reason he felt bone weary.

After half an hour, Ce'Nedra joined him in their tent. She settled down into the blankets and nestled her head against his back. Then she sighed disconsolately. "It was all a waste of time, wasn't it?" she said. "Going to Ashaba, I mean."

"No, Ce'Nedra, not really," he replied, still on the verge of sleep. "We had to go there so that Velvet could kill Harakan. That was one of the tasks that have to be completed before we get to the Place Which Is No More."

"Does all that really have any meaning, Garion?" she asked. "Half the time you act as if you believe it, and the other half you don't. If Zandramas had been there with our son, you wouldn't have just let her walk away because all the conditions hadn't been met, would you?"

"Not by so much as one step," he said grimly.

"The you *don't* really believe it, do you?"

"I'm not an absolute fatalist, if that's what you mean, but I've seen things come out exactly the way the Prophecy said they were going to far too many times for me to ignore it altogether."

"Sometimes I think that I'll never see my baby again," she said in a weary little voice.

"You mustn't ever think that," he told her. "We *will* catch up with Zandramas, and we *will* take Geran home with us again."

"Home," she sighed. "We've been gone for so long that I can barely remember what it looks like."

He took her into his arms, buried his face in her hair, and held her close. After a time she sighed and fell asleep. In spite of his own deep weariness, however, it was quite late before he himself drifted off.

The next day dawned clear and warm. They made their way back to the road again and continued eastward with Irongrip's sword pointing the way.

About midmorning, Polgara called ahead to Belgarath. "Father, there's someone hiding off to the side of the road just ahead."

He slowed his horse to a walk. "Chandim?" he asked tersely.

"No. It's a Mallorean Angarak. He's very much afraid—and not altogether rational."

"Is he planning any mischief?"

"He's not actually planning anything, father. His thoughts aren't coherent enough for that."

"Why don't you go flush him out, Silk?" the old man suggested. "I don't like having people lurking behind me—sane or not."

"About where is he?" the little man asked Polgara.

"Some distance back in the woods from that dead tree," she replied.

He nodded. "I'll go talk with him," he said. He loped his horse on ahead and reined in beside the dead tree. "We know you're back there, friend," he called pleasantly. "We don't mean you any harm, but why don't you come out in the open where we can see you?"

There was a long pause.

"Come along now," Silk called. "Don't be shy."

"Have you got any demons with you?" The voice sounded fearful.

"Do I look like the sort of fellow who'd be consorting with demons?"

"You won't kill me, will you?"

"Of course not. We only want to talk with you, that's all."

There was another long, fearful pause. "Have you got anything to eat?" The voice was filled with a desperate need.

"I think we can spare a bit."

The hidden man thought about that. "All right," he said finally. "I'm coming out. Remember that you promised not to kill me." Then there was a crashing in the bushes, and a Mallorean soldier came stumbling out into the road. His red tunic was in shreds, he had lost his helmet, and the remains of his boots were tied to his legs with leather thongs. He had quite obviously neither shaved nor bathed for at least a month. His eyes were wild and his head twitched on his neck uncontrollably. He stared at Silk with a terrified expression.

"You don't look to be in very good shape, friend," Silk said to him. "Where's your unit?"

"Dead, all dead, and eaten by the demons." The soldier's eyes were haunted. "Were you at Akkad?" he asked in a terrified voice. "Were you there when the demons came?"

"No, friend. We just came up from Venna."

"You said that you had something for me to eat."

"Durnik," Silk called, "could you bring some food for this poor fellow?"

Durnik rode to the pack horse carrying their stores and took out some bread and dried meat. Then he rode on ahead to join Silk and the fear-crazed soldier.

"Were *you* at Akkad when the demons came?" the fellow asked him.

359

Durnik shook his head. "No," he replied, "I'm with him." He pointed at Silk. Then he handed the fellow the bread and meat.

The soldier snatched them and began to wolf them down in huge bites.

"What happened at Akkad?" Silk asked.

"The demons came," the soldier replied, still cramming food into his mouth. Then he stopped, his eyes fixed on Durnik with an expression of fright. "Are you going to kill me?" he demanded.

Durnik stared at him. "No, man," he replied in a sick voice.

"Thank you." The soldier sat down at the roadside and continued to eat.

Garion and the others slowly drew closer, not wanting to frighten the skittish fellow off.

"What *did* happen at Akkad?" Silk pressed. "We're going in that direction, and we'd sort of like to know what to expect."

"Don't go there," the soldier said, shuddering. "It's horrible—horrible. The demons came through the gates with howling Karands all around them. The Karands started hacking people to pieces and then they fed the pieces to the demons. They cut off both of my captain's arms and then his legs as well, and then a demon picked up what was left of him and ate his head. He was screaming the whole time." He lowered his chunk of bread and fearfully stared at Ce'Nedra. "Lady, are you going to kill me?" he demanded.

"Certainly not!" she replied in a shocked voice.

"If you are, please don't let me see it when you do. And pleasy bury me someplace where the demons won't dig me up and eat me."

"She's not going to kill you," Polgara told him firmly.

The man's wild eyes filled with a kind of desperate longing. "Would *you* do it then, Lady?" he pleaded. "I can't stand the horror any more. Please kill me gently—the way my mother

would—and then hide me so that the demons won't get me."
He put his face into his shaking hands and began to cry.

"Give him some more food, Durnik," Belgarath said, his
eyes suddenly filled with compassion. "He's completely mad,
and there's nothing else we can do for him."

"I think I might be able to do something, Ancient One,"
Sadi said. He opened his case and took out a vial of amber
liquid. "Sprinkle a few drops of this on the bread you give
him, Goodman," he said to Durnik. "It will calm him and
give him a few hours of peace."

"Compassion seems out of character for you, Sadi," Silk
said.

"Perhaps," the eunuch murmured, "but then, perhaps you
don't fully understand me, Prince Kheldar."

Durnik took some more bread and meat from the pack for
the hysterical Mallorean soldier, sprinkling them liberally with
Sadi's potion. Then he gave them to the poor man, and they
all rode slowly past and on down the road. After they had gone
a ways, Garion heard him calling after them. "Come back!
Come back! Somebody—anybody—please come back and
kill me. Mother, please kill me!"

Garion's stomach wrenched with an almost overpowering
sense of pity. He set his teeth and rode on, trying not to listen
to the desperate pleas coming from behind.

They circled to the north of Akkad that afternoon, by-
passing the city and returning to the road some two leagues
beyond. The pull of the sword Garion held on the pommel
of his saddle confirmed the fact that Zandramas had indeed
passed this way and had continued on along this road toward
the northeast and the relative safety of the border between
Katakor and Jenno.

They camped in the forest a few miles north of the road
that night and started out once more early the following morning. The road for a time stretched across open fields. It was
deeply rutted and still quite soft at the shoulders.

361

"Karands don't take road maintenance very seriously," Silk observed, squinting into the morning sun.

"I noticed that," Durnik replied.

"I thought you might have."

Some leagues farther on, the road they were following reentered the forest, and they rode along through a cool, damp shade beneath towering evergreens.

Then, from somewhere ahead they heard a hollow, booming sound.

"I think we might want to go rather carefully until we're past that," Silk said quietly.

"What is that sound?" Sadi asked.

"Drums. There's a temple ahead."

"Out here in the forest?" The eunuch sounded surprised. "I thought that the Grolims were largely confined to the cities."

"This isn't a Grolim Temple, Sadi. It was nothing to do with the worship of Torak. As a matter of fact, the Grolims used to burn these places whenever they came across them. They were a part of the old religion of the area."

"Demon worship, you mean?"

Silk nodded. "Most of them have been long abandoned, but every so often you come across one that's still in use. The drums are a fair indication that the one just ahead is still open for business."

"Will we be able to go around them?" Durnik asked.

"It shouldn't be much trouble," the little man replied. "The Karands burn a certain fungus in their ceremonial fires. The fumes have a peculiar effect on one's senses."

"Oh?" Sadi said with a certain interest.

"Never mind," Belgarath told him. "That red case of yours has quite enough in it already."

"Just scientific curiosity, Belgarath."

"Of course."

"What are they worshiping?" Velvet asked. "I thought that the demons had all left Karanda."

362

Silk was frowning. "The beat isn't right," he said.

"Have you suddenly become a music critic, Kheldar?" she asked him.

He shook his head. "I've come across these places before, and the drumming's usually pretty frenzied when they're holding their rites. That beat up ahead is too measured. It's almost as if they're waiting for something."

Sadi shrugged. "Let them wait," he said. "It's no concern of ours, is it?"

"We don't know that for sure, Sadi," Polgara told him. She looked at Belgarath. "Wait here, father," she suggested. "I'll go on ahead and take a look."

"It's too dangerous, Pol," Durnik objected.

She smiled. "They won't even pay any attention to me, Durnik." She dismounted and walked a short way up the path. Then, momentarily, she was surrounded with a kind of glowing nimbus, a hazy patch of light that had not been there before. When the light cleared, a great snowy owl hovered among the trees and then ghosted away on soft, silent wings.

"For some reason that always makes my blood run cold," Sadi murmured.

They waited while the measured drumming continued. Garion dismounted and checked his cinch strap. Then he walked about a bit, stretching his legs.

It was perhaps ten minutes later when Polgara returned, drifting on white wings under the low-hanging branches. When she resumed her normal shape, her face was pale and her eyes were filled with loathing. "Hideous!" she said. "Hideous!"

"What is it, Pol?" Durnik's voice was concerned.

"There's a woman in labor in that temple."

"I don't know that a temple is the right sort of place for that, but if she needed shelter—" The smith shrugged.

"The temple was chosen quite deliberately," she replied. "The infant that's about to be born isn't human."

"But—"

"It's a demon."

Ce'Nedra gasped.

Polgara looked at Belgarath. "We have to intervene, father," she told him. "This *must* be stopped."

"How can it be stopped?" Velvet asked in perplexity. "I mean, if the woman's already in labor . . ." She spread her hands.

"We may have to kill her," Polgara said bleakly. "Even that may not prevent this monstrous birth. We may have to deliver the demon child and then smother it."

"No!" Ce'Nedra cried. "It's just a baby! You can't kill it."

"It's not that kind of baby, Ce'Nedra. It's half human and half demon. It's a creature of *this* world and a spawn of the other. If it's allowed to live, it won't be possible to banish it. It will be a perpetual horror."

"Garion!" Ce'Nedra cried. "You can't let her."

"Polgara's right, Ce'Nedra," Belgarath told her. "The creature can't be allowed to live."

"How many Karands are gathered up there?" Silk asked.

"There are a half dozen outside the temple," Polgara replied. "There may be more inside."

"However many they are, we're going to have to dispose of them," he said. "They're waiting for the birth of what they believe is a God, and they'll defend the newborn demon to the death."

"All right, then," Garion said bleakly, "let's go oblige them."

"You're not condoning this?" Ce'Nedra exclaimed.

"I don't like it," he admitted, "but I don't see that we've got much choice." He looked at Polgara. "There's absolutely no way it could be sent back to the place where demons originate?" he asked her.

"None whatsoever," she said flatly. "*This* world will be it's home. It wasn't summoned and it has no master. Within two years, it will be a horror such as this world has never seen. It *must* be destroyed."

"Can you do it, Pol?" Belgarath asked her.

"I don't have any choice, father," she replied. "I *have* to do it."

"All right, then," the old man said to the rest of them. "We have to get Pol inside that temple—and that means dealing with the Karands."

Silk reached inside his boot and pulled out his dagger. "I should have sharpened this," he muttered, looking ruefully at his jagged blade.

"Would you like to borrow one of mine?" Velvet asked him.

"No, that's all right, Liselle," he replied. "I've got a couple of spares." He returned the knife to his boot and drew another from its place of concealment at the small of his back and yet a third from its sheath down the back of his neck.

Durnik lifted his axe from its loop at the back of his saddle. His face was unhappy. "Do we really have to do this, Pol?" he asked.

"Yes, Durnik. I'm afraid we do."

He sighed. "All right, then," he said. "Let's go get it over with."

They started forward, riding at a slow walk to avoid alerting the fanatics ahead.

The Karands were sitting around a large, hollowed-out section of log, pounding on it with clubs in rhythmic unison. It gave forth a dull booming sound. They were dressed in roughly tanned fur vests and cross-tied leggings of dirty sackcloth. They were raggedly bearded, and their hair was matted and greasy. Their faces were hideously painted, but their eyes seemed glazed and their expressions slack-lipped.

"I'll go first," Garion muttered to the others.

"Shouting a challenge, I suppose," Silk whispered.

"I'm not an assassin, Silk," Garion replied quietly. "One or two of them might be rational enough to run, and that means a few less we'll have to kill."

"Suit yourself, but expecting rationality from Karands is irrational all by itself."

Garion quickly surveyed the clearing. The wooden temple was constructed of half-rotten logs, sagging badly at one end and surmounted along its ridgepole by a line of mossy skulls staring out vacantly. The ground before the building was hard-packed dirt, and there was a smoky firepit not far from the drummers.

"Try not to get into that smoke," Silk cautioned in a whisper. "You might start to see all sorts of peculiar things if you inhale too much of it."

Garion nodded and looked around. "Are we all ready?" he asked in a low voice.

They nodded.

"All right then." He spurred Chretienne into the clearing. "Throw down your weapons!" he shouted at the startled Karands.

Instead of obeying, they dropped their clubs and seized up a variety of axes, spears, and swords, shrieking their defiance.

"You see?" Silk said.

Garion clenched his teeth and charged, brandishing his sword. Even as he thundered toward the fur-clad men, he saw four others come bursting out of the temple.

Even with these reinforcements, however, the men on foot were no match for Garion and his mounted companions. Two of the howling Karands fell beneath Iron-grip's sword on Garion's first charge, and the one who tried to thrust at his back with a broad-bladed spear fell in a heap as Durnik brained him with his axe. Sadi caught a sword thrust with a flick of his cloak and then, with an almost delicate motion, dipped his poisoned dagger into the swordsman's throat. Using his heavy staff like a club, Toth battered two men to the ground, the sound of his blows punctuated by the snapping of bones. Their howls of frenzy turned to groans of pain as they fell. Silk launched himself from his saddle, rolled with the skill of an acrobat, and neatly ripped open one fanatic with one of his daggers while simultaneously plunging the other into the chest of a fat man who was clumsily trying to wield an axe. Chretienne whirled so quickly that Garion was almost thrown from his saddle as the big stallion trampled a Karand into the earth with his steel-shod hooves.

The lone remaining fanatic stood in the doorway of the crude temple. He was much older than his companions, and his face had been tattooed into a grotesque mask. His only weapon was a skull-surmounted staff, and he was brandishing it at them even as he shrieked an incantation. His words broke off suddenly, however, as Velvet hurled one of her knives at him with a smooth underhand cast. The wizard gaped down in amazement at the hilt of her knife protruding from his chest. Then he slowly toppled over backward.

There was a brief silence, punctuated only by the groans of the two men Toth had crippled. And then a harsh scream came from the temple—a woman's scream.

Garion jumped from his saddle, stepped over the body in the doorway, and looked into the large, smoky room.

A half-naked woman lay on the crude altar against the far wall. She had been bound to it in a spread-eagle position and she was partially covered by a filthy blanket. Her features were distorted, and her belly grossly, impossibly distended. She screamed again and then spoke in gasps.

"Nahaz! Magrash Klat Grichak! Nahaz!"

"I'll deal with this, Garion," Polgara said firmly from behind him. "Wait outside with the others."

"Were they any others in there?" Silk asked him as he came out.

"Just the woman. Aunt Pol's with her." Garion suddenly realized that he was shaking violently.

"What was that language she was speaking?" Sadi asked, carefully cleaning his poisoned dagger.

"The language of the demons," Belgarath replied. "She was calling out to the father of her baby."

"Nahaz?" Garion asked, his voice startled.

"She *thinks* it was Nahaz," the old man said. "She could be wrong—or maybe not."

From inside the temple the woman screamed again.

"Is anybody hurt?" Durnik asked.

"They are," Silk replied, pointing at the fallen Karands. Then he squatted and repeatedly plunged his daggers into the dirt to cleanse the blood off them.

"Kheldar," Velvet said in a strangely weak voice, "would you get my knife for me?" Garion looked at her and saw that her face was pale and that her hands were trembling slightly. He realized then that this self-possessed young woman was perhaps not quite so ruthless as he had thought.

"Of course, Liselle," Silk replied in a neutral tone. The little man quite obviously also understood the cause of her distress. He rose, went to the doorway, and pulled the knife out of the wizard's chest. He wiped it carefully and returned it to her. "Why don't you go back and stay with Ce'Nedra?" he suggested. "We can clean up here."

"Thank you, Kheldar," she said, turned her horse, and rode out of the clearing.

"She's only a girl," Silk said to Garion in a defensive tone. "She *is* good, though," he added with a certain pride.

"Yes," Garion agreed. "Very good." He looked around at the twisted shapes lying in heaps in the clearing. "Why don't we drag all these bodies over behind the temple?" he suggested. "This place is bad enough without all of this."

There was another scream from the temple.

Noon came and went unnoticed as Garion and the others endured the cries of the laboring woman. By midafternoon, the screams had grown much weaker, and as the sun was just going down, there came one dreadful last shriek that seemed to dwindle off into silence. No other sound came from inside, and after several minutes, Polgara came out. Her face was pale, and her hands and clothing were drenched with blood.

"Well, Pol?" Belgarath asked her.

"She died."

"And the demon?"

"Stillborn. Neither one of them survived the birth." She

looked down at her clothing. "Durnik, please bring me a blanket and water to wash in."

"Of course, Pol."

With her husband shielding her by holding up the blanket, Polgara deliberately removed all of her clothing, throwing each article through the temple doorway. Then she drew the blanket about her. "Now burn it," she said to them. "Burn it to the ground."

CHAPTER TWENTY-ONE

They crossed the border into Jenno about noon the following day, still following the trail of Zandramas. The experiences of the previous afternoon and evening had left them all subdued, and they rode on in silence. A league or so past the rather indeterminate border, they pulled off to the side of the road to eat. The spring sunlight was very bright and the day pleasantly warm. Garion walked a little ways away from the others and reflectively watched a cloud of yellow-striped bees industriously working at a patch of wild flowers.

"Garion," Ce'Nedra said in a small voice, coming up behind him.

"Yes, Ce'Nedra?" He put his arm around her.

"What really happened back there?"

"You saw about as much of it as I did."

"That's not what I mean. What happened inside the temple? Did that poor woman and her baby *really* just die—or did Polgara kill them?"

"Ce'Nedra!"

"I have to know, Garion. She was so grim about it before she went inside that place. She was going to kill the baby. Then she came out and told us that the mother and baby had both died in the birth. Wasn't that very convenient?"

He drew in a deep breath. "Ce'Nedra, think back. You've known Aunt Pol for a long time now. Has she ever told you a lie—ever?"

"Well—sometimes she hasn't told me the whole truth. She's told me part of it and kept the rest a secret."

"That's not the same as lying, Ce'Nedra, and you know it."

"Well—"

"You're angry because she said we might have to kill that thing."

"Baby," she corrected firmly.

He took her by the shoulders and looked directly into her face. "No, Ce'Nedra. It was a thing—half human, half demon, and all monster."

"But it was so little—so helpless."

"How do you know that?"

"All babies are little when they're born."

"I don't think that one was. I saw the woman for just a minute before Aunt Pol told me to leave the temple. Do you remember how big you were just before Geran was born? Well, that woman's stomach was at least five times as big as yours was—and she wasn't a great deal taller than you are."

"You aren't serious!"

"Oh, yes, I am. There was no way that the demon could have been born without killing its mother. For all I know, it might just simply have clawed its way out."

"It's own mother?" she gasped.

"Did you think it would love its mother? Demons don't know how to love, Ce'Nedra. That's why they're demons. Fortunately the demon died. It's too bad that the woman had to die, too, but it was much too late to do anything for her by the time we got there."

"You're a cold, hard person, Garion."

"Oh, Ce'Nedra, you know better than that. What happened back there was unpleasant, certainly, but none of us had any choice but to do exactly what we did."

She turned her back on him and started to stalk away.

"Ce'Nedra," he said, hurrying to catch her.

"What?" She tried to free her arm from his grasp.

"We didn't have any choice," he repeated. "Would you want Geran to grow up in a world filled with demons?"

She stared at him. "No," she firmly admitted. "It's just that . . ." She left it hanging.

"I know." He put his arms about her.

"Oh, Garion." She suddenly clung to him, and everything was all right again.

After they had eaten, they rode on through the forest, passing occasional villages huddled deep among the trees. The villages were rude, most of them consisting of a dozen or so rough log houses and surrounded by crude log palisades. There were usually a rather surprising number of hogs rooting among the stumps that surrounded each village.

"There don't seem to be very many dogs," Durnik observed.

"These people prefer pigs as house pets," Silk told him. "As a race, Karands have a strong affinity for dirt, and pigs satisfy certain deep inner needs among them."

"Do you know something, Silk," the smith said then. "You'd be a much more pleasant companion if you didn't try to turn everything into a joke."

"It's a failing I have. I've looked at the world for quite a

372

few years now and I've found that if I don't laugh, I'll probably end up crying."

"You're really serious, aren't you?"

"Would I do that to an old friend?"

About midafternoon, the road they were following curved slightly, and they soon reached the edge of the forest and a fork in the rutted track.

"All right. Which way?" Belgarath asked.

Garion lifted his sword from the pommel of his saddle and swept it slowly back and forth until he felt the familiar tug. "The right fork," he replied.

"I'm *so* glad you said that," Silk told him. "The left fork leads to Calida. I'd expect that news of Harakan's death has reached there by now. Even without the demons, a town full of hysterics doesn't strike me as a very nice place to visit. The followers of Lord Mengha might be just a bit upset when they hear that he's gone off and left them."

"Where does the right fork go?" Belgarath asked him.

"Down to the lake," Silk replied. "Lake Karanda. It's the biggest lake in the world. When you stand on the shore, it's like looking at an ocean."

Garion frowned. "Grandfather," he said, starting to worry, "Do you think that Zandramas knows that the Orb can follow her?"

"It's possible, yes."

"And would she know that it can't follow her over water?"

"I couldn't say for sure."

"But if she *does*, isn't it possible that she went to the lake in order to hide her trail from us? She could have sailed out a ways, doubled back, and come ashore just about anyplace. Then she could have struck out in a new direction, and we'd never pick up her trail again."

Belgarath scratched at his beard, squinting in the sunlight. "Pol," he said. "Are there any Gromlins about?"

She concentrated a bit. "Not in the immediate vicinity, father," she replied.

"Good. When Zandramas was trying to tamper with Ce'Nedra back at Rak Hagga, weren't you able to lock your thought with hers for a while?"

"Yes, briefly."

"She was at Ashaba then, right?"

She nodded.

"Did you get any kind of notion about which direction she was planning to go when she left?"

She frowned. "Nothing very specific, father—just a vague hint about wanting to go home."

"Darshiva," Silk said, snapping his fingers. "We know that Zandramas is a Darshivan name, and Zakath told Garion that it was in Darshiva that she started stirring up trouble."

Belgarath grunted. "It's a little thin," he said. "I'd feel a great deal more comfortable with some confirmation." He looked at Polgara. "Do you think you could reestablish contact with her—even for just a moment. All I need is a direction."

"I don't think so, father. I'll try, but . . ." she shrugged. Then her face grew very calm, and Garion could feel her mind reaching out with a subtle probing. After a few minutes, she relaxed her will. "She's shielding, father," she told the old man. "I can't pick up anything at all."

He muttered a curse under his breath. "We'll just have to go on down to the lake and ask a few questions. Maybe somebody saw her."

"I'm sure they did," Silk said, "but Zandramas likes to drown sailors, remember? Anyone who saw where she landed is probably sleeping under thirty feet of water."

"Can you think of an alternative plan?"

"Not offhand, no."

"Then we go on to the lake."

As the sun began to sink slowly behind them, they passed a fair-sized town set perhaps a quarter of a mile back from the road. The inhabitants were gathered outside the palisade surrounding it. They had a huge bonfire going, and just in front of the fire stood a crude, skull-surmounted altar of logs. A

374

skinny man wearing several feathers in his hair and with lurid designs painted on his face and body was before the altar, intoning an incantation at the top of his lungs. His arms were stretched imploringly at the sky, and there was a note of desperation in his voice.

"What's he doing?" Ce'Nedra asked.

"He's trying to raise a demon so that the townspeople can worship it," Eriond told her calmly.

"Garion!" She said in alarm. "Shouldn't we run?"

"He won't succeed," Eriond assured her. "The demon won't come to him any more. Nahaz has told them all not to."

The wizard broke off his incantation. Even from this distance, Garion could see that there was a look of panic on his face.

An angry mutter came from the townspeople.

"That crowd is starting to turn ugly," Silk observed. "The wizard had better raise his demon on the next try, or he might be in trouble."

The gaudily painted man with feathers in his hair began the incantation again, virtually shrieking and ranting at the sky. He completed it and stood waiting expectantly.

Nothing happened.

After a moment, the crowd gave an angry roar and surged forward. They seized the cringing wizard and tore his log altar apart. Then, laughing raucously, they nailed his hands and feet to one of the logs with long spikes and, with a great shout, they hurled the log up onto the bonfire.

"Let's get out of here," Belgarath said. "Mobs tend to go wild once they've tasted bloood." He led them away at a gallop.

They made camp that night in a willow thicket on the banks of a small stream, concealing their fire as best they could.

It was foggy the following morning, and they rode warily with their hands close to their weapons.

"How much farther to the lake?" Belgarath asked as the sun began to burn off the fog.

Silk looked around into the thinning mist. "It's kind of hard to say. I'd guess a couple more leagues at least."

Let's pick up the pace, then. We're going to have to find a boat when we get there, and that might take a while."

They urged their horses into a canter and continued on. The road had taken on a noticeable downhill grade.

"It's a bit closer than I thought," Silk called to them. "I remember this stretch of road. We should reach the lake in an hour or so."

They passed occasional Karands, clad in brown fur for the most part and heavily armed. The eyes of these local people were suspicious, even hostile, but Garion's mail shirt, helmet, and sword were sufficient to gain the party passage without incident.

By midmorning the gray fog had completely burned off. As they crested a knoll, Garion reined in. Before him there lay an enormous body of water, blue and sparkling in the mid-morning sun. It looked for all the world like a vast inland sea, with no hint of a far shore, but it did not have that salt tang of the sea.

"Big, isn't it?" Silk said, pulling his horse in beside Chretienne. He pointed toward a thatch and log village standing a mile or so up the lake shore. A number of fair-sized boats were moored to a floating dock jutting out into the water. "That's where I've usually hired boats when I wanted to cross the lake."

"You've done business around here, then?"

"Oh, yes. There are gold mines in the mountains of Zamad, and deposits of gem stones up in the forest."

"How big are those boats?"

"Big enough. We'll be a little crowded, but the weather's calm enough for a safe crossing, even if the boat might be a bit overloaded." Then he frowned. "What are *they* doing?"

Garion looked at the slope leading down to the village and saw a crowd of people moving slowly down toward the lake shore. There seemed to be a great deal of fur involved in their clothing in varying shades of red and brown, though many of them wore cloaks all dyed in hues of rust and faded blue. More and more of them came over the hilltop, and other people came out of the village to meet them.

"Belgarath," the little Drasnian called. "I think we've got a problem."

Belgarath came jolting up to the crest of the knoll at a trot. He looked at the large crowd gathering in front of the village.

"We need to get into that village to hire a boat," Silk told him. "We're well enough armed to intimidate a few dozen villagers, but there are two or three hundred people down there now. That could require some fairly serious intimidation."

"A country fair, perhaps?" the old man asked.

Silk shook his head. "I wouldn't think so. It's the wrong time of year for it, and those people don't have any carts with them." He swung down from his saddle and went back to the pack horses. A moment or so later, he came back with a poorly tanned red fur vest and a baggy fur hat. He pulled them on, bent over, and wrapped a pair of sack cloth leggings about his calves, tying them in place with lengths of cord. "How do I look?" he asked.

"Shabby," Garion told him.

"That's the idea. Shab's in fashion here in Karanda." He remounted.

"Where did you get the clothes?" Belgarath asked curiously.

"I pillaged one of the bodies back at the temple." The little man shrugged. "I like to keep a few disguises handy. I'll go find out what's happening down there." He dug his heels into his horse's flanks and galloped down toward the throng gathering near the lakeside village.

"Let's pull back out of sight," Belgarath suggested. "I'd rather not attract too much attention."

They walked their horses down the back side of the knoll and then some distance away from the road to a shallow gully that offered concealment and dismounted there. Garion climbed back up out of the gully on foot and lay down in the tall grass to keep watch.

About a half-hour later, Silk came loping back over the top of the knoll. Garion rose from the grass and signaled to him.

When the little man reached the gully and dismounted, his expression was disgusted. "Religion," he snorted. "I wonder what the world would be like without it. That gathering down there is for the purpose of witnessing the performance of a powerful wizard, who absolutely guarantees that he can raise a demon—despite the notable lack of success of others lately. He's even hinting that he might be able to persuade the Demon Lord Nahaz himself to put in an appearance. That crowd's likely to be there all day."

"Now what?" Sadi asked.

Belgarath walked down the gully a ways, looking thoughtfully up at the sky. When he came back, his look was determined. "We're going to need a couple more of those," he said, pointing at Silk's disguise.

"Nothing simpler," Silk replied. "There are still enough latecomers going down that hill for me to be able to waylay a few. What's the plan?"

"You, Garion, and I are going down there."

"Interesting notion, but I don't get the point."

"The wizard, whoever he is, is promising to raise Nahaz, but Nahaz is with Urvon and isn't very likely to show up. After what we saw happen at that village yesterday, it's fairly obvious that failing to produce a demon is a serious mistake for a wizard to make. If our friend down there is so confident, it probably means that he's going to create an illusion—since nobody's been able to produce the real thing lately. I'm good at illusions myself, so I'll just go down and challenge him."

"Won't they just fall down and worship *your* illusion?" Velvet asked him.

His smile was chilling. "I don't really think so, Liselle," he replied. "You see, there are demons, and then there are *demons*. If I do it right, there won't be a Karand within five leagues of this place by sunset—depending on how fast they can run, of course." He looked at Silk. "Haven't you left yet?" he asked pointedly.

While Silk went off in search of more disguises, the old sorcerer made a few other preparations. He found a long, slightly crooked branch to use as a staff and a couple of feathers to stick in his hair. Then he sat down and laid his head back against one of their packs. "All right, Pol," he instructed his daughter, "make me hideous."

She smiled faintly and started to raise one hand.

"Not *that* way. Just take some ink and draw some designs on my face. They don't have to be too authentic-looking. The Karands have corrupted their religion so badly that they wouldn't recognize authenticity if they stepped in it."

She laughed and went to one of the packs, returning a moment later with an inkpot and a quill pen.

"Why on earth are you carrying ink, Lady Polgara?" Ce'Nedra asked.

"I like to be prepared for eventualities as they arise. I went on a long journey once and had to leave a note for someone along the way. I didn't have ink with me, so I ended up opening a vein to get something to write with. I seldom make the same mistake twice. Close your eyes, father. I always like to start with the eyelids and work my way out."

Belgarath closed his eyes. "Durnik," he said as Polgara started drawing designs on his face with her quill, "you and the others will stay back here. See if you can find some place a little better hidden than this gully."

"All right, Belgarath," the smith agreed. "How will we know when it's safe to come down to the lake shore?"

"When the screaming dies out."

"Don't move your lips, father," Polgara told him, frowning in concentration as she continued her drawing. "Did you want me to blacken your beard, too?"

"Leave it the way it is. Superstitious people are always

impressed by venerablility, and I look older than just about anybody."

She nodded her agreement. "Actually, father, you look older than dirt."

"Very funny, Pol," he said acidly. "Are you just about done?"

"Did you want the death symbol on your forehead?" she asked.

"Might as well," he grunted. "Those cretins down there won't recognize it, but it looks impressive."

By the time Polgara had finished with her art work, Silk returned with assorted garments.

"Any problems?" Durnik asked him.

"Simplicity itself." Silk shrugged. "A man whose eyes are fixed on heaven is fairly easy to approach from behind, and a quick rap across the back of the head will usually put him to sleep."

"Leave your mail shirt and helmet, Garion," Belgarath said. "Karands don't wear them. Bring your sword, though."

"I'd planned to." Garion began to struggle out of his mail shirt. After a moment, Ce'Nedra came over to help him.

"You're getting rusty," she told him after they had hauled off the heavy thing. She pointed at a number of reddish-brown stains on the padded linen tunic he wore under the shirt.

"It's one of the drawbacks to wearing armor," he replied.

"That and the smell," she added, wrinkling her nose. "You *definitely* need a bath, Garion."

"I'll see if I can get around to it one of these days," he said. He pulled on one of the fur vests Silk had stolen. Then he tied on the crude leggings and crammed on a rancid-smelling fur cap. "How do I look?" he asked her.

"Like a barbarian," she replied.

"That was sort of the whole idea."

"I didn't steal you a hat," Silk was saying to Belgarath. "I thought you might prefer to wear feathers."

Belgarath nodded. "All of us mighty wizards wear feathers," he agreed. "It's a passing fad, I'm sure, but I always like to dress fashionably." He looked over at the horses. "I think we'll walk," he decided. "When the noise starts, the horses might get a bit skittish." He looked at Polgara and the others who were staying behind. "This shouldn't take us too long," he told them confidently and strode off down the gully with Garion and Silk close behind him.

They emerged from the mouth of the gully at the south end of the knoll and walked down the hill toward the crowd gathering on the lake shore.

"I don't see any sign of their wizard yet," Garion said, peering ahead.

"They always like to keep their audiences waiting for a bit," Belgarath said. "It's supposed to heighten the anticipation or something."

The day was quite warm as they walked down the hill, and the rancid smell coming from their clothing grew stronger. Although they did not really look that much like Karands, the people in the crowd they quietly joined paid them scant attention. Every eye seemed to be fixed on a platform and one of those log altars backed by a line of skulls on stakes.

"Where do they get all the skulls?" Garion whispered to Silk.

"They used to be head-hunters," Silk replied. "The Angaraks discouraged that practice, so now they creep around at night robbing graves. I doubt if you could find a whole skeleton in any graveyard in all of Karanda."

"Let's get closer to the altar," Belgarath muttered. "I don't want to have to shove my way through this mob when things start happening." They pushed through the crowd. A few of the greasy-haired fanatics started to object to being thrust aside, but one look at Belgarath's face with the hideous designs Polgara had drawn on it convinced them that here was a wizard of awesome power and that it perhaps might be wiser not to interfere with him.

Just as they reached the front near the altar, a man in a

black Grolim robe strode out through the gate of the lakeside village, coming directly toward the altar.

"I think that's our wizard," Belgarath said quietly.

"A Grolim?" Silk sounded slightly surprised.

"Let's see what he's up to."

The black-robed man reached the platform and stepped up to stand in front of the altar. He raised both hands and spoke harshly in a language Garion did not understand. His words could have been either a benediction or a curse. The crowd fell immediately silent. Slowly the Grolim pushed back his hood and let his robe fall to the platform. He wore only a loincloth, and his head had been shaved. His body was covered from crown to toe with elaborate tattoos.

Silk winced. "That must have *really* hurt," he muttered.

"Prepare ye all to look upon the face of your God," the Grolim announced in a large voice, then bent to inscribe the designs on the platform before the altar.

"That's what I thought," Belgarath whispered. "That circle he drew isn't complete. If he were *really* going to raise a demon, he wouldn't have made that mistake."

The Grolim straightened and began declaiming the words of the incantation in a rolling, oratorical style.

"He's being very cautious," Belgarath told them. "He's leaving out certain key phrases. He doesn't want to raise a *real* demon accidentally. Wait." The old man smiled bleakly. "Here he goes."

Garion also felt the surge as the Grolim's will focused and then he heard the familiar rushing sound.

"Behold the Demon Lord Nahaz," the tattooed Grolim shouted, and a shadow-encased form appeared before the altar with a flash of fire, a peal of thunder, and a cloud of sulfur-stinking smoke. Although the figure was no larger than an ordinary man, it looked very substantial for some reason.

"Not too bad, really," Belgarath admitted grudgingly.

"It looks awfully solid to me, Belgarath," Silk said nervously.

"It's only an illusion, Silk," the old man quietly reassured him. "A good one, but still only an illusion."

The shadowy form on the platform before the altar rose to its full height and then pulled back its hood of darkness to reveal the hideous face Garion had seen in Torak's throne room at Ashaba.

As the crowd fell to its knees with a great moan, Belgarath drew in his breath sharply. "When this crowd starts to disperse, don't let the Grolim escape," he instructed. "He's actually seen the real Nahaz, and that means that he was one of Harakan's cohorts. I want some answers out of him." Then the old man drew himself up. "Well, I guess I might as well get started with this," he said. He stepped up in front of the platform. "Fraud!" he shouted in a great voice. "Fraud and fakery!"

The Grolim stared at him, his eyes narrowing as he saw the designs drawn on his face. "On your knees before the Demon Lord," he blustered.

"Fraud!" Belgarath denounced him again. He stepped up onto the platform and faced the stunned crowd. "This is no wizard, but only a Grolim trickster," he declared.

"The Demon Lord will tear all your flesh from your bones," the Grolim shrieked.

"All right," Belgarath replied with calm contempt. "Let's see him do it. Here. I'll even help him." He pulled back his sleeve, approached the shadowy illusion hovering threateningly before the altar and quite deliberately ran his bare arm into the shadow's gaping maw. A moment later, his hand emerged, coming, or so it appeared, out of the back of the Demon Lord's head. He pushed his arm further until his entire wrist and forearm were sticking out of the back of the illusion. Then, quite deliberately, he wiggled his fingers at the people gathered before the altar.

A nervous titter ran through the crowd.

"I think you missed a shred or two of flesh, Nahaz," the old man said to the shadowy form standing before him.

"There still seems to be quite a bit of meat clinging to my fingers and arm." He pulled his arm back out of the shadow and then passed both hands back and forth through the Grolim's illusion. "It appears to lack a bit of substance, friend," he said to the tattooed man. "Why don't we send it back where you found it? Then I'll show you and your parishoners here a *real* demon."

He put his hands derisively on his hips, leaned forward slightly from the waist, and blew at the shadow. The illusion vanished, and the tattooed Grolim stepped back fearfully.

"He's getting ready to run," Silk whispered to Garion. "You get on that side of the platform, and I'll get on this. Thump his head for him if he comes your way."

Garion nodded and edged around toward the far side of the platform.

Belgarath raised his voice again to the crowd. "You fall upon your knees before the reflection of the Demon Lord," he roared at them. "What will you do when I bring before you the King of Hell?" He bent and quickly traced the circle and pentagram about his feet. The tattooed priest edged further away from him.

"Stay, Grolim," Belgarath said with a cruel laugh. "The King of Hell is always hungry, and I think he might like to devour you when he arrives." He made a hooking gesture with one hand, and the Grolim began to struggle as if he had been seized by a powerful, invisible hand.

Then Belgarath began to intone an incantation quite different from the one the Grolim had spoken, and his words reverberated from the vault of heaven as he subtly amplified them into enormity. Seething sheets of varicolored flame shot through the air from horizon to horizon.

"Behold the Gates of Hell!" he roared, pointing.

Far out on the lake, two vast columns seemed to appear; between them were great billowing clouds of smoke and flame. From behind that burning gate came the sound of a multitude of hideous voices shrieking some awful hymn of praise.

"And now I call upon the King of Hell to reveal himself!" the old man shouted, raising his crooked staff. The surging force of his will was vast, and the great sheets of flame flickering in the sky actually seemed to blot out the sun and to replace its light with a dreadful light of its own.

From beyond the gate of fire came a huge whistling sound that descended into a roar. The flames parted, and the shape of a mighty tornado swept between the two pillars. Faster and faster the tornado whirled, turning from inky black to pale, frozen white. Ponderously, that towering white cloud advanced across the lake, congealing as it came. At first it appeared to be some vast snow wraith with hollow eyes and gaping mouth. It was quite literally hundreds of feet tall, and its breath swept across the now-terrified crowd before the altar like a blizzard.

"Ye have tasted ice," Belgarath told them. "Now taste fire! Your worship of the false Demon Lord hath offended the King of Hell, and now will ye roast in perpetual flames!" He made another sweeping gesture with his staff, and a deep red glow appeared in the center of the seething white shape that even now approached the shore of the lake. The sooty red glow grew more and more rapidly, expanding until it filled the encasing white entirely. Then the wraithlike figure of flame and swirling ice raised its hundred-foot-long arms and roared with a deafening sound. The ice seemed to shatter, and the wraith stood as a creature of fire. Flames shot from its mouth and nostrils, and steam rose from the surface of the lake as it moved across the last few yards of water before reaching the shore.

It reached down one enormous hand, placing it atop the altar, palm turned up. Belgarath calmly stepped up onto that burning hand, and the illusion raised him high into the air.

"Infidels!" he roared at them in an enormous voice. "Pre-

385

pare ye all to suffer the wrath of the King of Hell for your foul apostasy!"

There was a dreadful moan from the Karands, followed by terrified screams as the fire-wraith reached out toward the crowd with its other huge, burning hand. Then, as one man, they turned and fled, shrieking in terror.

Somehow, perhaps because Belgarath was concentrating so much of his attention on the vast form he had created and was struggling to maintain, the Grolim broke free and jumped down off the platform.

Garion, however, was waiting for him. He reached out and stopped the fleeing man with one hand placed flat against his chest, even as he swept the other back and then around in a wide swing that ended with a jolting impact against the side of the tattooed man's head.

The Grolim collapsed in a heap. For some reason, Garion found that very satisfying.

CHAPTER TWENTY-TWO

"Which boat did you want to steal?" Silk asked as Garion dropped the unconscious Grolim on the floating dock that stuck out into the lake.

"Why ask me?" Garion replied, feeling just a bit uncomfortable with Silk's choice of words.

"Because you and Durnik are the ones who are going to have to sail it. I don't know the first thing about getting a boat to move through the water without tipping over."

"Capsizing," Garion corrected absently, looking at the various craft moored to the dock.

"What?"

"The word is 'capsize,' Silk. You tip over a wagon. You capsize a boat."

"It means the same thing, doesn't it?"

"Approximately, yes."

"Why make an issue of it, then? How about this one?" The little man pointed at a broad-beamed vessel with a pair of eyes painted on the bow.

"Not enough freeboard," Garion told him. "The horses are heavy, so any boat we take is going to settle quite a bit."

Silk shrugged. "You're the expert. You're starting to sound as professional as Barak or Greldik." He grinned suddenly. "You know, Garion, I've never stolen anything as big as a boat before. It's really very challenging."

"I wish you'd stop using the word 'steal.' Couldn't we just say that we're borrowing a boat?"

"Did you plan to sail it back and return it when we're finished with it?"

"No. Not really."

"Then the proper word is 'steal.' You're the expert on ships and sailing; I'm the expert on theft."

They walked farther out on the dock.

"Let's go on board this one and have a look around," Garion said, pointing at an ungainly-looking scow painted an unwholesome green color.

"It looks like a washtub."

"I'm not planning to win any races with it." Garion leaped aboard the scow. "It's big enough for the horses and the sides are high enough to keep the weight from swamping it." He inspected the spars and rigging. "A little crude," he noted, "but Durnik and I should be able to manage."

"Check the bottom for leaks," Silk suggested. "Nobody would paint a boat that color if it didn't leak."

Garion went below and checked the hold and the bilges. When he came back up on deck, he had already made up his mind. "I think we'll borrow this one," he said, jumping back to the pier.

"The term is still 'steal,' Garion."

Garion sighed. "All right, steal—if it makes you happy."

"Just trying to be precise, that's all."

"Let's go get that Grolim and drag him up here," Garion suggested. "We'll throw him in the boat and tie him up. I don't *think* he'll wake up for a while, but there's no point in taking chances."

"How hard did you hit him?"

"Quite hard, actually. For some reason he irritated me." They started back to where the Grolim lay.

"You're getting to be more like Belgarath every day," Silk told him. "You do more damage out of simple irritation than most men can do in a towering rage."

Garion shrugged and rolled the tattooed Grolim over with his foot. He took hold of one of the unconscious man's ankles. "Get his other leg," he said.

The two of them walked back toward the scow with the Grolim dragging limply along behind them, his shaved head bouncing up and down on the logs of the dock. When they reached the scow, Garion took the man's arms while Silk took his ankles. They swung him back and forth a few times, then lobbed him across the rail like a sack of grain. Garion jumped across again and bound him hand and foot.

"Here comes Belgarath with the others," Silk said from the dock.

"Good. Here—catch the other end of this gangplank." Garion swung the ungainly thing around and pushed it out toward the waiting little Drasnian. Silk caught hold of it, pulled it out farther, and set the end down on the dock.

"Did you find anything?" he asked the others as they approached.

"We did quite well, actually," Durnik replied. "One of those buildings is a storehouse. It was crammed to the rafters with food."

"Good. I wasn't looking forward to making the rest of this trip on short rations."

Belgarath was looking at the scow. "It isn't much of a boat, Garion," he objected. "If you were going to steal one, why didn't you steal something a little fancier?"

"You see?" Silk said to Garion. "I told you that it was the right word."

"I'm not stealing it for its looks, Grandfather," Garion said. "I don't plan to keep it. It's big enough to hold the horses, and the sails are simple enough so that Durnik and I can manage them. If you don't like it, go steal one of your own."

"Grumpy today, aren't we?" the old man said mildly. "What did you do with my Grolim?"

"He's lying up here in the scuppers."

"Is he awake yet?"

"Not for some time, I don't think. I hit him fairly hard. Are you coming on board, or would you rather go steal a different boat?"

"Be polite, dear," Polgara chided.

"No, Garion," Belgarath said. "If you've got your heart set on this one, then we'll take this one."

It took awhile to get the horses aboard, and then they all fell to the task of raising the boat's square-rigged sails. When they were raised and set to Garion's satisfaction, he took hold of the tiller. "All right," he said. "Cast off the lines."

"You sound like a real sailor, dear," Ce'Nedra said in admiration.

"I'm glad you approve." He raised his voice slightly. "Toth, would you take that boat hook and push us out from the pier, please? I don't want to have to crash through all these other boats to get to open water."

The giant nodded, picked up the long boat hook, and shoved against the dock with it. The bow swung slowly out from the dock with the sails flapping in the fitful breeze.

"Isn't the word 'ship,' Garion?" Ce'Nedra asked.

"What?"

"You called them boats. Aren't they called ships?"

He gave her a long, steady look.

"I was only asking," she said defensively.

"Don't. Please."

"What did you hit this man with, Garion?" Belgarath asked peevishly. He was kneeling beside the Grolim.

"My fist," Garion replied.

"Next time, use an axe or a club. You almost killed him."

"Would anyone else like to register any complaints?" Garion asked in a loud voice. "Let's pile them all up in a heap right now."

They all stared at him, looking a bit shocked.

He gave up. "Just forget that I said it." He squinted up at the sails, trying to swing the bow to the exact angle which would allow the sails to catch the offshore breeze. Then, quite suddenly, they bellied out and boomed, and the scow began to pick up speed, plowing out past the end of the pier and into open water.

"Pol," Belgarath said. "Why don't you come over here and see what you can do with this man? I can't get a twitch out of him, and I want to question him."

"All right, father." She went to the Grolim, knelt beside him, and put her hands on his temples. She concentrated for a moment, and Garion felt the surge of her will.

The Grolim groaned.

"Sadi," she said thoughtfully, "Do you have any nephara in that case of yours?"

The eunuch nodded. "I was just going to suggest it myself, Lady Polgara." He knelt and opened his red case.

Belgarath looked at his daughter quizzically.

"It's a drug, father," she explained. "It induces truthfulness."

"Why not do it the regular way?" he asked.

"The man's a Grolim. His mind is likely to be very strong. I could probably overcome him, but it would take time—and it would be very tiring. Nephara works just as well and it doesn't take any effort."

He shurgged. "Suit yourself, Pol."

Sadi had taken a vial of a thick green liquid from his case. He unstoppered it and then took hold of the Grolim's nose, holding it until the half-conscious man was forced to open his mouth in order to breathe. Then the eunuch delicately tilted three drops of the green syrup onto the man's tongue. "I'd suggest giving him a few moments before you wake him, Lady Polgara," he said, squinting clinically at the Grolim's face. "Give the drug time to take effect first." He restoppered the vial and put it back in his case.

"Will the drug hurt him in any way?" Durnik asked.

Sadi shook his head. "It simply relaxes the will," he replied. "He'll be rational and coherent, but very tractable."

"He *also* won't be able to focus his mind sufficiently to use any talent he may have," Polgara added. "We won't have to worry about his translocating himself away from us the moment he wakes up." She critically watched the Grolim's face, occasionally lifting one of his eyelids to note the drug's progress. "I think it's taken hold now," she said finally. She untied the prisoner's hands and feet. Then she put her hands on the man's temples and gently brought him back to consciousness. "How are you feeling?" she asked him.

"My head hurts," the Grolim said plaintively.

"That will pass," she assured him. She rose and looked at Belgarath. "Speak to him calmly, father," she said, "and start out with simple questions. With nephara it's best to lead them rather gently up to the important things."

Belgarath nodded. He picked up a wooden pail, inverted it, put it on the deck beside the Grolim, and sat on it. "Good morning, friend," he said pleasantly, "or is it afternoon?" He squinted up at the sky.

"You're not really a Karand, are you?" the Grolim asked. His voice sounded dreamy. "I thought you were one of their wizards, but now that I look at you more closely, I can see that you're not."

"You're very astute, friend," Belgarath congratulated him. "What's your name?"

392

"Arshag," the Grolim replied.

"And where are you from?"

"I am of the Temple at Calida."

"I thought you might be. Do you happen to know a Chandim named Harakan, by any chance?"

"He now prefers to be known as Lord Mengha."

"Ah, yes, I'd heard about that. That illusion of Nahaz you raised this morning was very accurate. You must have seen him several times in order to get everything right."

"I have frequently been in close contact with Nahaz," the Grolim admitted. "It was I who delivered him to Lord Mengha."

"Why don't you tell me about that? I'm sure it's a fascinating story and I'd really like to hear it. Take your time, Arshag. Tell me the whole story, and don't leave out any of the details."

The Grolim smiled almost happily. "I've been wanting to tell someone the story for a long time now," he said. "Do you really want to hear it?"

"I'm absolutely dying to hear it," Belgarath assured him.

The Grolim smiled again. "Well," he began, "It all started quite a number of years ago—not too long after the death of Torak. I was serving in the Temple at Calida. Though we were all in deepest despair, we tried to keep the faith alive. Then one day Harakan came to our temple and sought me out privately. I had journeyed at times to Mal Yaska on Church business and I knew Harakan to be of high rank among the Chandim and very close to the Holy Disciple Urvon. When we were alone, he told me that Urvon had consulted the Oracles and Prophecies concerning the direction the Church must take in her blackest hour. The Disciple had discovered that a new God was destined to rise over Angarak, and that he will hold Cthrag Sardius in his right hand and Cthrag Yaska in his left. And he will be the almighty Child of Dark, and the Lord of Demons shall do his bidding."

"That's a direct quotation, I take it?"

Arshag nodded. "From the eighth antistrophe of the Ashabine Oracles," he confirmed.

"It's a little obscure, but prophecies usually are. Go on."

Arshag shifted his position and continued. "The Disciple Urvon interpreted the passage to mean that our new God would have the aid of the demons in quelling his enemies."

"Did Harakan identify these enemies for you?"

Arshag nodded again. "He mentioned Zandramas—of whom I have heard—and one named Agachak, whose name is strange to me. He also warned me that the Child of Light would probably attempt to interfere."

"That's a reasonable assumption," Silk murmured to Garion.

"Harakan, who is the Disciple's closest advisor, had selected *me* to perform a great task," Arshag continued proudly. "He charged me to seek out the wizards of Karanda and to study their arts so that I might summon up the Demon Lord Nahaz and beseech him to aid the Disciple Urvon in his struggles with his enemies."

"Did he tell you how dangerous that task would be?" Belgarath asked him.

"I understood the perils," Arshag said, "but I accepted them willingly, for my rewards were to be great."

"I'm sure," Belgarath murmured. "Why didn't Harakan do it himself?"

"The Disciple Urvon had placed another task upon Harakan—somewhere in the West, I understand—having to do with a child."

Belgarath nodded blandly. "I think I've heard about it."

"Anyway," Arshag went on, "I journeyed into the forest of the north, seeking out the wizards who still practiced their rites in places hidden from the eyes of the Church. In time, I found such a one." His lip curled in a sneer. "He was an ignorant savage of small skill, at best only able to raise an imp or two, but he agreed to accept me as his pupil—and slave. It was he who saw fit to put these marks upon my body." He glanced with distaste at his tattoos. "He kept me in a kennel and made me serve him and listen to his ravings. I learned what little he could teach me and then I strangled him and went in search of a more powerful teacher."

"Note how deep the gratitude of Grolims goes," Silk observed quietly to Garion, who was concentrating half on the story and half on the business of steering the scow.

"The years that followed were difficult," Arshag continued. "I went from teacher to teacher, suffering enslavement and abuse." A bleak smile crossed his face. "Occasionally, they used to sell me to other wizards—as one might sell a cow or a pig. After I learned the arts, I retraced my steps and repaid each one for his impertinences. At length, in a place near the barrens of the north, I was able to apprentice myself to an ancient man reputed to be the most powerful wizard in Karanda. He was very old, and his eyes were failing, so he took me for a young Karand seeking wisdom. He accepted me as his appentice, and my training began in earnest. The raising of minor demons is no great chore, but summoning a Demon Lord is much more difficult and much more perilous. The wizard claimed to have done it twice in his life, but he may have been lying. He did, however, show me how to raise the *image* of the Demon Lord Nahaz and also how to communicate with him. No spell or incantation is powerful enough to *compel* a Demon Lord to come when he is called. He will come only if he *consents* to come—and usually for reasons of his own.

"Once I had learned all that the old wizard could teach me, I killed him and journeyed south toward Calida again." He sighed a bit regretfully. "The old man was a kindly master, and I was sorry that I had to kill him." Then he shrugged. "But he was old," he added, "and I sent him off with a single knife stroke to the heart."

"Steady, Durnik," Silk said, putting his hand on the angry smith's arm.

"At Calida, I found the Temple in total disarray," Arshag went on. "My brothers had finally succumbed to absolute despair, and the Temple had become a vile sink of corruption and degeneracy. I suppressed my outrage, however, and kept to myself. I dispatched word to Mal Yaska, advising Harakan that I had been successful in my mission and that I awaited his commands in the Temple at Calida. In time, I received a reply from one of the Chandim, who told me that Harakan had not yet returned from the West." He paused. "Do you suppose that I could have a drink of water?" he asked. "I have a very foul taste in my mouth for some reason."

Sadi went to the water cask in the stern and dipped out a tin cup of water. "No drug is *completely* perfect," he murmured defensively to Garion in passing.

Arshag gratefully took the cup from Sadi and drank.

"Go on with your story," Belgarath told him when he had finished.

Arshag nodded. "It was a bit less than a year ago that Harakan returned from the West," he said. "He came up to Calida, and he and I met in secret. I told him what I had accomplished and advised him of the limitations involved in any attempts to raise a Demon Lord. Then we went to a secluded place, and I instructed him in the incantations and spells which would raise an image of Nahaz and permit us to speak through the gate that lies between the worlds and communicate directly with Nahaz. Once I had established contact with the Demon Lord, Harakan began to speak with him. He mentioned Cthrag Sardius, but Nahaz already knew of it. And then Harakan told Nahaz that during the long years that Torak slept, and Disciple Urvon had become more and more obsessed with wealth and power and had at last convinced himself that he was in fact a demigod, and but one step removed from divinity. Harakan proposed an alliance between himself and Nahaz. He suggested that the Demon Lord nudge Urvon over the edge into madness and then aid him in defeating all the others who were seeking the hiding place of Cthrag Sardius. Unopposed, Urvon would easily gain the stone."

"I gather that you chose to go along with them—instead

of warning Urvon what was afoot? What did *you* get out of the arrangement?"

"They let me live." Arshag shrugged. "I think Harakan wanted to kill me—just to be safe—but Nahaz told him that I could still be useful. He promised me kindgoms of my own to rule—and demon children to do my bidding. Harakan was won over by the Demon Lord and he treated me courteously."

"I don't exactly see that there's much advantage to Nahaz in giving the Sardion to Urvon," Belgarath confessed.

"Nahaz wants Cthrag Sardius for himself," Arshag told him. "If Urvon has been driven mad, Nahaz will simply take Cthrag Sardius from him and replace it with a piece of worthless rock. Then the Demon Lord and Harakan will put Urvon in a house somewhere—Ashaba perhaps, or some other isolated castle— and they'll surround him with imps and lesser demons to blind him with illusions. There he will play at being God in blissful insanity while Nahaz and Harakan rule the world between them."

"Until the *real* new God of Angarak arises," Polgara added.

"There will *be* no new God of Angarak," Arshag disagreed. "Once Nahaz puts his hand on Cthrag Sardius—the Sardion—*both* Prophecies will cease to exist. The Child of Light and the Child of Dark will vanish forever. The Elder Gods will be banished, and Nahaz will be Lord of the Universe and Master of the destinies of all mankind."

"And what does Harakan get out of this?" Belgarath asked.

"Dominion of the Church—and the secular throne of all the world."

"I hope he got that in writing," Belgarath said dryly. "Demons are notorious for not keeping their promises. Then what happened?"

"A messenger arrived at Calida with instructions for Harakan from Urvon. The Disciple told him that there must be a disruption in Karanda so violent that Kal Zakath would have no choice but to return from Cthol Murgos. Once the Emperor was back in Mallorea, it would be a simple matter to have him killed, and once he is dead, Urvon believes that he can manipulate the succession to place a tractable man on the throne—one he can take with him when he goes to the place where the Sardion lies hidden. Apparently, this is one of the conditions which must be met before the new God arises."

Belgarath nodded. "A great many things are starting to fall into place." he said. "What happened then?"

"Harakan and I journeyed again in secret to that secluded place, and I once again opened the gate and brought forth the image of Nahaz. Harakan and the Demon Lord spoke together for a time, and suddenly the image was made flesh, and Nahaz himself stood before us.

"Harakan instructed me that I should henceforth call him by the name Mangha, since the name Harakan is widely known in Mallorea, and then we went again to Calida, and Nahaz went with us. The Demon Lord summoned his hordes, and Calida fell. Nahaz demanded a certain repayment for his aid, and Lord Mengha instructed me to provide it. It was then that I discovered why Nahaz had let me live. We spoke together, and he told me what he wanted. I did not care for the notion, but the people involved were only Karands, so—" He shrugged. "The Karands regard Nahaz as their God, and so it was not difficult for me to persuade young Karandese women that receiving the attentions of the Demon Lord would be a supreme honor. They went to him willingly, each one of them hoping in her heart to bear his offspring—not knowing, of course, that such a birth would rip them apart like fresh-gutted pigs." He smirked contemptuously. "The rest I think you know."

"Oh, yes, we do indeed." Belgarath's voice was like a nail scraping across a flat stone. "When did they leave? Harakan and Nahaz, I mean? We know that they're no longer in this part of Karanda."

"It was about a month ago. We were preparing to lay siege to Torpakan on the border of Delchin, and I awoke one morning to discover that Lord Mengha and the Demon Nahaz were gone and that none of their familiar demons were any longer with the army. Everyone looked to me, but none of my spells or incantations could raise even the least of demons. The army grew enraged, and I barely escaped with my life. I journeyed north again toward Calida, but found things there in total chaos. Without the demons to hold them in line, the Karands had quickly become unmanageable. I found that I *could*, however, still call up the *image* of Nahaz. It seemed likely to me that with Mengha and Nahaz gone, I could sway Karandese loyalty to me, if I used the image cleverly enough, and thus come to rule all of Karanda myself. I was attempting a beginning of that plan this morning when you interrupted."

"I see," Belgarath said bleakly.

"How long have you been in this vicinity?" Polgara asked the captive suddenly.

"Several weeks," the Grolim replied.

"Good," she said. "Some few weeks ago, a woman came from the west carrying a child."

"I pay little attention to women."

"This one might have been a bit different. We know that she came to that village back on the lake shore and that she would have hired a boat. Did any word of that reach you?"

"There are few travelers in Karanda right now," he told her. "There's too much turmoil and upheaval. There's only one boat that left that village in the past month. I'll tell you this, though. If the woman you seek was a friend of yours, and if she *was* on board that boat, prepare to mourn her."

"Oh?"

"The boat sank in a sudden storm just off the city of Karand on the east side of the lake in Ganesia."

"The nice thing about Zandramas is her predictability," Silk murmured to Garion. "I don't think we're going to have much trouble picking up her trail again, do you?"

Arshag's eyelids were drooping now, and he seemed barely able to hold his head erect.

"If you have any more questions for him, Ancient One, you

399

should ask them quickly," Sadi advised. "The drug is starting to wear off, and he's very close to sleep again."

"I think I have all the answers I need," the old man replied.

"And I have what I need as well," Polgara added grimly.

Because of the size of the lake, there was no possibility of reaching the eastern shore before nightfall, and so they lowered the sails and set a sea anchor to minimize the nighttime drift of their scow. They set sail again at first light and shortly after noon saw a low, dark smudge along the eastern horizon.

"That would be the east coast of the lake," Silk said to Garion. "I'll go up to the bow and see if I can pick out some landmarks. I don't think we'll want to run right up to the wharves of Karand, do you?"

"No. Not really."

"I'll see if I can find us a quiet cove someplace, and then we can have a look around without attracting attention."

They beached the scow in a quiet bay surrounded by high sand dunes and scrubby brush about midafternoon.

"What do you think, Grandfather?" Garion asked after they had unloaded the horses.

"About what?"

"The boat. What should we do with it?"

"Set it adrift. Let's not announce that we came ashore here."

"I suppose you're right." Garion sighed a bit regretfully. "It wasn't a bad boat, though, was it?"

"It didn't tip over."

"Capsize," Garion corrected.

Polgara came over to where they were standing. "Do you have any further need for Arshag?" she asked the old man.

"No, and I've been trying to decide what to do with him."

"I'll take care of it, father," she said. She turned and went back to where Arshag still lay, once more bound and half asleep on the beach. She stood over him for a moment, then raised one hand. The Grolim flinched wildly even as Garion felt the sudden powerful surge of her will.

"Listen carefully, Arshag," she said. "You provided the Demon Lord with women so that he could unloose an abomination upon the world. That act must not go unrewarded. This, then, is your reward. You are now invincible. No one can kill you—no man, no demon—not even you yourself. *But*, no one will ever again believe a single word that you say. You will be faced with constant ridicule and derision all the days of your life and you will be driven out wherever you go, to wander the world as a rootless vagabond. Thus are you repaid for aiding Mengha and helping him to unleash Nahaz and for sacrificing foolish women to the Demon Lord's unspeakable lust." She turned to Durnik. "Untie him," she commanded.

When his arms and legs were free, Arshag stumbled to his feet, his tattooed face ashen. "Who are you, woman?" he demanded in a shaking voice, "and what power do you have to pronounce so terrible a curse?"

"I am Polgara," she replied. "You may have heard of me. Now go!" She pointed up the beach with an imperious finger.

As if suddenly seized by an irresistible compulsion, Arshag turned, his face filled with horror. He stumbled up one of the sandy dunes and disappeared on the far side.

"Do you think it was wise to reveal your identity, my lady?" Sadi asked dubiously.

"There's no danger, Sadi." She smiled. "He can shout my name from every rooftop, but no one will believe him."

"How long will he live?" Ce'Nedra's voice was very small.

"Indefinitely, I'd imagine. Long enough, certainly, to give him time to appreciate fully the enormity of what it was that he did."

Ce'Nedra stared at her. "Lady Polgara!" she said in a sick voice. "How could you do it? It's horrible."

"Yes," Polgara replied, "it is—but so was what happened back at that temple we burned."

CHAPTER TWENTY-THREE

The street, if it could be called that, was narrow and crooked. An attempt had been made at some time in the past to surface it with logs, but they had long since rotted and been trodden into the mud. Decaying garbage lay in heaps against the walls of crudely constructed log houses, and herds of scrawny pigs rooted dispiritedly through those heaps in search of food.

As Silk and Garion, once again wearing their Karandese vests and caps and their cross-tied sackcloth leggings, approached the docks jutting out into the lake, they were nearly overcome by the overpowering odor of long-dead fish.

"Fragrant sort of place, isn't it?" Silk noted, holding a handkerchief to his face.

"How can they stand it?" Garion asked, trying to keep from gagging.

"Their sense of smell has probably atrophied over the centuries," Silk replied. "The city of Karand is the ancestral home of all the Karands in all the seven kingdoms. It's been here for eons, so the debris—and the smell—has had a long time to build up."

A huge sow, trailed by a litter of squealing piglets, waddled out into the very center of the street and flopped over on her side with a loud grunt. The piglets immediately attacked, pushing and scrambling to nurse.

"Any hints at all? Silk asked.

Garion shook his head. The sword strapped across his back had neither twitched nor tugged since the two of them had entered the city early that morning on foot by way of the north gate. "Zandramas might not have even entered the city at all," he said. "She's avoided populated places before, you know."

"That's true, I suppose," Silk admitted, "but I don't think we should go any farther until we locate the place where she landed. She could have gone in any direction once she got to this side of the lake—Darshiva, Zamad, Voresebo—even down into Delchin and then on down the Magan into Rengel or Peldane."

"I know," Garion said, "but all this delay is very frustrating. We're getting closer to her. I can feel it, and every minute we waste gives her that much more time to escape again with Geran."

"It can't be helped." Silk shrugged. "About all we can do here is follow the inside of the wall and walk along the waterfront. If she came through the city at all, we're certain to cross her path."

They turned a corner and looked down another muddy

street toward the lake shore where fishnets hung over long poles. They slogged through the mud until they reached the street that ran along the shoreline where floating docks reached out into the lake and then followed it along the waterfront.

There was a certain amount of activity here. A number of sailors dressed in faded blue tunics were hauling a large boat half-full of water up onto the shore with a great deal of shouting and contradictory orders. Here and there on the docks, groups of fishermen in rusty brown sat mending nets, and farther on along the street several loiterers in fur vests and leggings sat on the log stoop in front of a sour-smelling tavern, drinking from cheap tin cups. A blowzy young woman with frizzy orange hair and a pockmarked face leaned out of a second-storey window, calling to passersby in a voice she tried to make seductive, but which Garion found to be merely coarse.

"Busy place," Silk murmured.

Garion grunted, and they moved on along the littered street.

Coming from the other direction, they saw a group of armed men. Though they all wore helmets of one kind or another, the rest of their clothing was of mismatched colors and could by no stretch of the imagination be called uniforms. Their self-important swagger, however, clearly indicated that they were either soldiers or some kind of police.

"You two! Halt!" one of them barked as they came abreast of Garion and Silk.

"Is there some problem, sir?" Silk asked ingratiatingly.

"I haven't seen you here before," the man said, his hand on his sword hilt. He was a tall fellow with lank red hair poking out from under his helmet. "Identify yourselves."

"My name is Saldas," Silk lied. "This is Kvasta." He pointed at Garion. "We're strangers here in Karand."

"What's your business here—and where do you come from?"

"We're from Dorikan in Jenno," Silk told him, "and we're here looking for my older brother. He sailed out from the village of Dashun on the other side of the lake awhile back and hasn't returned."

The redheaded man looked suspicious.

"We talked with a fellow near the north gate," Silk continued, "and he told us that there was a boat that sank in a storm just off the docks here." His face took on a melancholy expression. "The time would have been just about right, I think, and the description he gave us of the boat matched the one my brother was sailing. Have you by any chance heard about it, sir?" The little man sounded very sincere.

Some of the suspicion faded from the red-haired man's face. "It seems to me that I heard some mention of it," he conceded.

"The fellow we talked with said that he thought there might have been some survivors," Silk added, "one that he knew of, anyway. He said that a woman in a dark cloak and carrying a baby managed to get away in a small boat. Do *you* by chance happen to know anything about that?"

The Karand's face hardened. "Oh, yes," he said. "We know about *her,* all right."

"Could you by any chance tell me where she went?" Silk asked him. "I'd really like to talk with her and find out if she knows anything about my brother." He leaned toward the other man confidentially. "To be perfectly honest with you, good sir, I can't stand my brother. We've hated each other since we were children, but I promised my old father that I'd find out what happened to him." Then he winked outrageously. "There's an inheritance involved, you understand. If I can take definite word back to father that my brother's dead, I stand to come into a nice piece of property."

The red-haired man grinned. "I can understand your situation, Saldas." he said. "I had a dispute with my *own* brothers about our patrimony." His eyes narrowed. "You say you're from Dorikan?" he asked.

"Yes. On the banks of the northern River Magan. Do you know our city?"

"Does Dorikan follow the teachings of Lord Mengha?"

"The Liberator? Of course. Doesn't all of Karanda?"

"Have you seen any of the Dark Lords in the last month or so?"

"The minions of the Lord Nahaz? No, I can't say that I have—but then Kvasta and I haven't attended any worship services for some time. I'm sure that the wizards are still raising them though."

"I wouldn't be all that sure, Saldas. We haven't seen one here in Karand for over five weeks. Our wizards have tried to summon them, but they refuse to come. Even the Grolims who now worship Lord Nahaz haven't been successful and they're all powerful magicians, you know."

"Truly," Silk agreed.

"Have you heard anything at all about Lord Mengha's whereabouts?"

Silk shrugged. "The last I heard, he was in Katakor someplace. In Dorikan we're just waiting for his return so that we can sweep the Angaraks out of all Karanda."

The answer seemed to satisfy the tall fellow. "All right, Saldas," he said. "I'd say that you've got a legitimate reason to be in Karand after all. I don't think you're going to have much luck in finding the woman you want to talk to, though. From what I've heard, she *was* on your brother's boat and she *did* get away before the storm hit. She had a small boat, and she landed to the south of the city. She came to the south gate with her brat in her arms and went straight to the Temple. She talked with the Grolims inside for about an hour. When she left, they were all following her."

"Which way did they go?" Silk asked him.

"Out the east gate."

"How long ago was it?"

"Late last week. I'll tell you something, Saldas. Lord Mengha had better stop whatever he's doing in Katakor and

406

come back to central Karanda where he belongs. The whole movement is starting to falter. The Dark Lords have deserted us, and the Grolims are trailing after this woman with the baby. All we have left are the wizards, and they're mostly mad, anyway."

"They always have been, haven't they?" Silk grinned. "Tampering with the supernatural tends to unsettle a man's brains, I've noticed."

"You seem like a sensible man, Saldas," the redhead said, clapping him on the shoulder. "I'd like to stay and talk with you further, but my men and I have to finish our patrol. I hope you find your brother." He winked slyly. "Or *don't* find him, I should say."

Silk grinned back. "I thank you for your wishes about my brother's growing ill health," he replied.

The soldiers moved off along the street.

"You tell better stories that Belgarath does," Garion said to his little friend.

"It's a gift. That was a very profitable encounter, wasn't it? Now I understand why the Orb hasn't picked up the trail yet. We came into the city by way of the north gate, and Zandramas came up from the south. If we go straight to the Temple, the Orb's likely to jerk you off your feet."

Garion nodded. "The important thing is that we're only a few days behind her." He paused, frowning. "Why is she gathering Grolims, though?"

"Who knows? Reinforcements maybe. She knows that we're right behind her. Or, maybe she thinks she's going to need Grolims who have training in Karandese magic when she gets home to Darshiva. If Nahaz has sent his demons down there, she's going to need all the help she can get. We'll let Belgarath sort it out. Let's go to the Temple and see if we can pick up the trail."

As they approached the Temple in the center of the city, the Orb began to pull at Garion again, and he felt a surge of exultation. "I've got it," he said to Silk.

"Good." The little man looked up at the Temple. "I see that they've made some modifications," he observed.

The polished steel mask of the face of Torak which normally occupied the place directly over the nail-studded door had been removed, Garion saw, and in its place was a red-painted skull with a pair of horns screwed down into its brow.

"I don't know that the skull is all that big an improvement," Silk said, "but then, it's no great change for the worse either. I was getting a little tired of that mask staring at me every time I turned around."

"Let's follow the trail," Garion suggested, "and make certain that Zandramas left the city before we go get the others."

"Right," Silk agreed.

The trail led from the door of the Temple through the littered streets to the east gate of the city. Garion and Silk followed it out of Karand and perhaps a half mile along the highway leading eastward across the plains of Ganesia.

"Is she veering at all?" Silk asked.

"Not yet. She's following the road."

"Good. Let's go get the others—and our horses. We won't make very good time on foot."

They moved away from the road, walking through knee-high grass.

"Looks like good, fertile soil here," Garion noted. "Have you and Yarblek ever considered buying farmland? It might be a good investment."

"No, Garion." Silk laughed. "There's a major drawback to owning land. If you have to leave a place in a hurry, there's no way that you can pick it up and carry it along with you."

"That's true, I guess."

The others waited in a grove of large old willows a mile or so north of the city, and their faces were expectant as Garion and Silk ducked in under the branches.

"Did you find it?" Belgarath asked.

Garion nodded. "She went east," he replied.

"And apparently she took all the Grolims from the Temple along with her," Silk added.

Belgarath looked puzzled. "Why would she do that?"

"I haven't got a clue. I suppose we could ask her when we catch up with her."

"Could you get any idea of how far ahead of us she is?" Ce'Nedra asked.

"Just a few days," Garion said. "With any luck we'll catch her before she gets across the Mountains of Zamad."

"Not if we don't get started," Belgarath said.

They rode on back across the wide, open field to the highway leading across the plains toward the up-thrusting peaks lying to the east. The Orb picked up the trail again, and they followed it at a canter.

"What kind of a city was it?" Velvet asked Silk as they rode along.

"Nice place to visit," he replied, "but you wouldn't want to live there. The pigs are clean enough, but the people are awfully dirty."

"Cleverly put, Kheldar."

"I've always had a way with words," he conceded modestly.

"Father," Polgara called to the old man, "a large number of Grolims have passed this way."

He looked around and nodded. "Silk was right, then," he said. "For some reason she's subverting Mengha's people. Let's be alert for any possible ambushes."

They rode on for the rest of the day and camped that night some distance away from the road, starting out again at first light in the morning. About midday they saw a roadside village some distance ahead. Coming from that direction was a solitary man in a rickety cart being pulled by a bony white horse.

"Do you by any change have a flagon of ale, Lady Polgara?" Sadi asked as they slowed to a walk.

"Are you thirsty?"

"Oh, it's not for me. I detest ale personally. It's for that carter just ahead. I thought we might want some information."

He looked over at Silk. "Are you feeling at all sociable today, Kheldar?"

"No more than usual. Why?"

"Take a drink or two of this," the eunuch said, offering the little man the flagon Polgara had taken from one of the packs. ".Not too much, mind. I only want you to *smell* drunk."

"Why not?" Silk shrugged, taking a long drink.

"That should do it," Sadi approved. "Now give it back."

"I thought you didn't want any."

"I don't. I'm just going to add a bit of flavoring." He opened his red case. "Don't drink any more from this flagon," he warned Silk as he tapped four drops of a gleaming red liquid into the mouth of the flagon. "If you do, we'll all have to listen to you talk for days on end." He handed the flagon back to the little man. "Why don't you go offer that poor fellow up there a drink," he suggested. "He looks like he could use one."

"You didn't poison it, did you?"

"Of course not. It's very hard to get information out of somebody who's squirming on the ground clutching at his belly. One or two good drinks from that flagon, though, and the carter will be seized by an uncontrollable urge to talk— about anything at all and to anybody who asks him a question in a friendly fashion. Go be friendly to the poor man, Kheldar. He looks dreadfully lonesome."

Silk grinned, then turned and trotted his horse toward the oncoming cart, swaying in his saddle and singing loudly and very much off-key.

"He's very good," Velvet murmured to Ce'Nedra, "but he always overacts his part. When we get back to Boktor, I think I'll send him to a good drama coach."

Ce'Nedra laughed.

By the time they reached the cart, the seedy-looking man in a rust-red smock had pulled his vehicle off to the side of the road, and he and Silk had joined in song—a rather bawdy one.

"Ah, there you are," Silk said, squinting owlishly at Sadi. "I wondered how long it was going to take you to catch up. Here—" He thrust the flagon at the eunuch. "Have a drink."

Sadi feigned taking a long drink from the flagon. Then he sighed lustily, wiped his mouth on his sleeve, and handed the flagon back.

Silk passed it to the carter. "Your turn, friend."

The carter took a drink and then grinned foolishly. "I haven't felt this good in weeks," he said.

"We're riding toward the east," Sadi told him.

"I saw that right off," the carter said. "That's unless you've taught your horses to run backward." He laughed uproariously at that, slapping his knee in glee.

"How droll," the eunuch murmured. "Do you come from that village just up ahead?"

"Lived there all my life," the carter replied, "and my father before me—and his father before him—and his father's father before that and—"

"Have you seen a dark-cloaked woman with a babe in her arms go past here within the last week?" Sadi interrupted him. "She probably would have been in the company of a fairly large party of Grolims."

The carter made the sign to ward off the evil eye at the mention of the word "Grolim." "Oh, yes. She came by all right," he said, "and she went into the local Temple here— if you can really call it a Temple. It's no bigger than my own house and it's only got three Grolims in it—two young ones and an old one. Anyway, this woman with the babe in her arms, she goes into the Temple, and we can hear her talking, and pretty soon she comes out with our three Grolims—only the old one was trying to talk the two young ones into staying, and then she says something to the young ones and they pull out their knives and start stabbing the old one, and he yells and falls down on the ground dead as mutton, and the woman takes our two young Grolims back out to the road, and they join in with the others and they all go off, leaving us only that old dead one lying on his face in the mud and—"

"How many Grolims would you say she had with her?" Sadi asked.

"Counting our two, I'd say maybe thirty or forty—or it could be as many as fifty. I've never been very good at quick guesses like that. I can tell the difference between three and four, but after that I get confused, and—"

"Could you give us any idea of exactly how long ago all that was?"

"Let's see." The carter squinted at the sky, counting on his fingers. "It couldn't have been yesterday, because yesterday I took that load of barrels over to Toad-face's farm. Do you know Toad-face? Ugliest man I ever saw, but his daughter's a real beauty. I could tell you stories about *her*, let me tell you."

"So it wasn't yesterday?"

"No. It definitely wasn't yesterday. I spent most of yesterday under a haystack with Toad-face's daughter. And I know it wasn't the day before, because I got drunk that day and I don't remember a thing that happened after midmorning." He took another drink from the flagon.

"How about the day before that?"

"It could have been," the carter said, "or the day before that."

"Or even before?"

The carter shook his head. "No, that was the day our pig farrowed, and I know that the woman came by after that. It had to have been the day before the day before yesterday or the day before that."

"Three or four days ago, then?"

"If that's the way it works out," the carter shrugged, drinking again.

"Thanks for the information, friend," Sadi said. He looked at Silk. "We should be moving on, I suppose," he said.

"Did you want your jar back?" the carter asked.

"Go ahead and keep it, friend," Silk said. "I think I've had enough anyway."

"Thanks for the ale—and the talk," the carter called after them as they rode away. Garion glanced back and saw that the fellow had climbed down from his cart and was engaging in an animated conversation with his horse.

"Three days!" Ce'Nedra exlaimed happily.

"Or, at the most, four," Sadi said.

"We're gaining on her!" Ce'Nedra said, suddenly leaning over and throwing her arms about the eunuch's neck.

"So it appears, your majesty," Sadi agreed, looking slightly embarrassed.

They camped off the road again that night and started out again early the following morning. The sun was just coming up when the large, blue-banded hawk came spiraling in, flared, and shimmered into the form of Beldin at the instant its talons touched the road. "You've got company waiting for you just ahead," he told them, pointing at the first line of foothills of the Mountains of Zamad lying perhaps a mile in front of them.

"Oh?" Belgarath said, reining in his horse.

"About a dozen Grolims," Beldin said. "They're hiding in the bushes on either side of the road."

Belgarath swore.

"Have you been doing things to annoy the Grolims?" the hunchback asked.

Belgarath shook his head. "Zamadramas has been gathering them as she goes along. She's got quite a few of them with her now. She probably left that group behind to head off pursuit. She knows that we're right behind her."

"What are we going to do, Belgarath?" Ce'Nedra asked. "We're so *close*. We can't stop now."

The old man looked at his brother sorcerer. "Well?" he said.

Beldin scowled at him. "All right," he said. "I'll do it, but don't forget that you owe me, Belgarath."

"Write it down with all the other things. We'll settle up when this is all over."

"Don't think I won't."

"Did you find out where Nahaz took Urvon?"

"Would you believe they went back to Mal Yaska?" Beldin sounded disgusted.

"They'll come out eventually," Belgarath assured him. "Are you going to need any help with the Grolims? I could send Pol along if you like."

"Are you trying to be funny?"

"No. I was just asking. Don't make too much noise."

Beldin made a vulgar sound, changed again, and swooped away.

"Where's he going?" Silk asked.

"He's going to draw off the Grolims."

"Oh? How?"

"I didn't ask him," Belgarath shrugged. "We'll give him a little while and then we should be able to ride straight on through."

"He's very good, isn't he?"

"Beldin? Oh, yes, very, very good. There he goes now."

Silk looked around. "Where?"

"I didn't see him—I heard him. He's flying low a mile or so to the north of where the Grolims are hiding, and he's kicking up just enough noise to make it sound as if the whole group of us are trying to slip around them without being seen." He glanced at his daughter. "Pol, would you take a look and see if it's working?"

"All right, father." She concentrated, and Garion could feel her mind reaching out, probing. "They've taken the bait," she reported. "They all ran off after Beldin."

"That was accommodating of them, wasn't it? Let's move on."

They pushed their horses into a gallop and covered the distance to the first foothills of the Mountains of Zamad in a short period of time. They followed the road up a steep slope and through a shallow notch. Beyond that the terrain grew more rugged, and the dark green forest rose steeply up the flanks of the peaks.

Garion began to sense conflicting signals from the Orb as he rode. At first he had only felt its eagerness to follow the trail of Zandramas and Geran, but now he began to feel a sullen undertone, a sound of ageless, implacable hatred, and at his back where the sword was sheathed, he began to feel an increasing heat.

"Why is it burning red?" Ce'Nedra asked from behind him.

"What's burning red?"

"The Orb, I think. I can see it glowing right through the leather covering you have over it."

"Let's stop awhile," Belgarath told them, reining in his horse.

"What is it, Grandfather?"

"I'm not sure. Take the sword out and slip off the sleeve. Let's see what's happening."

Garion drew the sword from its sheath. It seemed heavier than usual for some reason, and when he peeled off the soft leather covering, they were all able to see that instead of its usual azure blue, the Orb of Aldur was glowing a dark, sooty red.

"What is it, father?" Polgara asked.

"It feels the Sardion." Eriond said in a calm voice.

"Are we that close?" Garion demanded. "Is this the Place Which Is No More?"

"I don't think so, Belgarion," the young man replied. "It's something else."

"What is it, then?"

"I'm not sure, but the Orb is responding to the other stone in some way. They talk to each other in a fashion I can't understand."

They rode on, and some time later the blue-banded hawk came swirling in, blurred into Beldin's shape, and stood in

415

front of them. The gnarled dwarf had a slightly self-satisfied look on his face.

"You look like a cat that just got into the cream," Belgarath said.

"Naturally. I just sent a dozen or so Grolims off in the general direction of the polar icecap. They'll have a wonderful time when the pan ice starts to break up and they get to float around up there for the rest of the summer."

"Are you going to scout on ahead?" Belgarath asked him.

"I suppose so," Beldin replied. He held out his arms, blurred into feathers, and drove himself into the air.

They rode more cautiously now, climbing deeper and deeper into the Mountains of Zamad. The surrounding country grew more broken. The reddish-hued peaks were jagged, and their lower flanks were covered with dark firs and pines. Rushing streams boiled over rocks and dropped in frothy waterfalls over steep cliffs. The road, which had been straight and flat on the plains of Ganesia, began to twist and turn as it crawled up the steep slopes.

It was nearly noon when Beldin returned again. "The main party of Grolims turned south," he reported. "There are about forty of them."

"Was Zandramas with them?" Garion asked quickly.

"No. I don't think so—at least I didn't pick up the sense of anyone unusual in the group."

"We haven't lost her, have we?" Ce'Nedra asked in alarm.

"No," Garion replied. "The Orb still has her trail." He glanced over his shoulder. The stone on the hilt of his sword was still burning a sullen red.

"About all we can do is follow her," Belgarath said. "It's Zandramas we're interested in, not a party of stray Grolims. Can you pinpoint exactly where we are?" he asked Beldin.

"Mallorea."

"Very funny."

"We've crossed into Zamad. This road goes on down into Voresebo, though. Where's my mule?"

"Back with the pack horses," Durnik told him.

As they moved on, Garion could feel Polgara probing on ahead with her mind.

"Are you getting anything, Pol?" Belgarath asked her.

"Nothing specific, father," she replied. "I can sense the fact that Zandramas is close, but she's shielding, so I can't pinpoint her."

They rode on, moving at a cautious walk now. Then, as the road passed through a narrow gap and descended on the far side, they saw a figure in a gleaming white robe standing in the road ahead. As they drew closer, Garion saw that it was Cyradis.

"Move with great care in this place," she cautioned, and there was a note of anger in her voice. "The Child of Dark seeks to circumvent the ordered course of events and hath laid a trap for ye."

"There's nothing new or surprising about that," Beldin growled. "What does she hope to accomplish?"

"It is her thought to slay one of the companions of the Child of Light and thereby prevent the completion of one of the tasks which must be accomplished ere the final meeting. Should she succeed, all that hath gone before shall come to naught. Follow me, and I will guide you safely to the next task."

Toth stepped down from his horse and quickly led it to the side of his slender mistress. She smiled at him, her face radiant, and laid a slim hand on his huge arm. With no apparent effort, the huge man lifted her into the saddle of his horse and then took the reins in his hand.

"Aunt Pol," Garion whispered, "is it my imagination, or is she really there this time?"

Polgara looked intently at the blindfolded Seeress. "It's not a projection," she said. "It's much more substantial. I couldn't begin to guess how she got here, but I think you're right, Garion. She's really here."

They followed the Seeress and her mute guide down the

steeply descending road into a grassy basin surrounded on all sides by towering firs. In the center of the basin was a small mountain lake sparkling in the sunlight.

Polgara suddenly drew in her breath sharply. "We're being watched," she said.

"Who is it, Pol?" Belgarath asked.

"The mind is hidden, father. All I can get is the sense of watching—and anger." A smile touched her lips. "I'm sure it's Zandramas. She's shielding, so I can't reach her mind, but she can't shield out my sense of being watched, and she can't control her anger enough to keep me from picking up the edges of it."

"Who's she so angry with?"

"Cyradis, I think. She went to a great deal of trouble to lay a trap for us, and Cyradis came along and spoiled it. She still might try something, so I think we'd all better be on our guard."

He nodded bleakly. "Right," he agreed.

Toth led the horse his mistress was riding out into the basin and stopped at the edge of the lake. When the rest of them reached her, she pointed down through the crystal water. "The task lies there," she said. "Below lies a submerged grot. One of ye must enter that grot and then return. Much shall be revealed there."

Belgarath looked hopefully at Beldin.

"Not this time, old man," the drawf said, shaking his head. "I'm a hawk, not a fish, and I don't like cold water any more than you do."

"Pol?" Belgarath said rather plaintively.

"I don't think so, father," she replied. "I think it's your turn this time. Besides, I need to concentrate on Zandramas."

He bent over and dipped his hand into the sparkling water. Then he shuddered. "This is cruel," he said.

Silk was grinning at him.

"Don't say it, Prince Kheldar." Belgarath scowled, starting to remove his clothing. "Just keep your mouth shut."

They were perhaps all a bit surprised at how sleekly muscular the old man was. Despite his fondness for rich food and good brown ale, his stomach was as flat as a board; although he was as lean as a rail, his shoulders and chest rippled when he moved.

"My, my," Velvet murmured appreciatively, eyeing the loincloth-clad old man.

He suddenly grinned at her impishly. "Would you care for another frolic in a pool, Liselle?" he invited with a wicked look in his bright blue eyes.

She suddenly blushed a rosy red, glancing guiltily at Silk.

Belgarath laughed, arched himself forward, and split the water of the lake as cleanly as the blade of a knife. Several yards out, he broached, leaping high into the air with the sun gleaming on his silvery scales and his broad, forked tail flapping and shaking droplets like jewels across the sparkling surface of the lake. Then his dark, heavy body drove down and down into the depths of the crystal lake.

"Oh, my," Durnik breathed, his hands twitching.

"Never mind, dear." Polgara laughed. "He wouldn't like it at all if you stuck a fishhook in his jaw."

The great, silver-sided salmon swirled down and disappeared into an irregularly shaped opening near the bottom of the lake.

They waited, and Garion found himself unconsciously holding his breath.

After what seemed an eternity, the great fish shot from the mouth of the submerged cave, drove himself far out into the lake, and then returned, skipping across the surface of the water on his tail, shaking his head and almost seeming to balance himself with his fins. Then he plunged forward into the water near the shore, and Belgarath emerged dripping and shivering. "Invigorating," he observed, climbing back up onto the bank. "Have you got a blanket handy, Pol?" he asked, stripping the water from his arms and legs with his hands.

"Show-off," Beldin grunted.

419

"What was down there?" Garion asked.

"It looks like an old temple of some kind," the old man answered, vigorously drying himself with the blanket Polgara had handed him. "Somebody took a natural cave and walled up the sides to give it some kind of shape. There was an altar there with a special kind of niche in it—empty, naturally— but the place was filled with an overpowering presence, and all the rocks glowed red."

"The Sardion?" Beldin demanded intently.

"Not any more," Belgarath replied, drying his hair. "It *was* there, though, for a long, long time—and it had built a barrier of some kind to keep anybody from finding it. It's gone now, but I'll recognize the signs of it the next time I get close."

"Garion!" Ce'Nedra cried. "Look!" With a trembling hand she was pointing at a nearby crag. High atop that rocky promontory stood a figure wrapped in shiny black satin. Even before the figure tossed back its hood with a gesture of supreme arrogance, he knew who it was. Without thinking, he reached for Iron-grip's sword, his mind suddenly aflame.

But then Cyradis spoke in a clear, firm voice. "I am wroth with thee, Zandramas," she declared. "Seek not to interfere with that which must come to pass, lest I make my choice here and now."

"And if thou dost, sightless, creeping worm, then all will turn to chaos, and thy task will be incomplete, and blind chance will supplant prophecy. Behold, I am the Child of Dark, and I fear not the hand of chance, for chance is *my* servant even more than it is the servant of the Child of Light."

Then Garion heard a low snarl, a dreadful sound—more dreadful yet because it came from his wife's throat. Moving faster than he thought was possible, Ce'Nedra dashed to Durnik's horse and ripped the smith's axe from the rope sling which held it. With a scream of rage, she ran around the edge of the tiny mountain lake brandishing the axe.

"Ce'Nedra!" he shouted, lunging after her. "No!"

Zandramas laughed with cruel glee. "Choose, Cyradis!"

she shouted. "Make thine empty choice, for in the death of the Rivan Queen, I triumph!" and she raised both hands over her head.

Though he was running as fast as he could, Garion saw that he had no hope of catching Ce'Nedra before she moved fatally close to the satin-robed sorceress atop the crag. Even now, his wife had begun scrambling up the rocks, screeching curses and hacking at the boulders that got in her way with Durnik's axe.

Then the form of a glowing blue wolf suddenly appeared between Ce'Nedra and the object of her fury. Ce'Nedra stopped as if frozen, and Zandramas recoiled from the snarling wolf. The light around the wolf flickered briefly, and there, still standing between Ce'Nedra and Zandramas stood the form of Garion's ultimate grandmother, Belgarath's wife and Polgara's mother. Her tawny hair was aflame with blue light, and her golden eyes blazed with unearthly fire.

"You!" Zandramas gasped, shrinking back even further.

Poledra reached back, took Ce'Nedra to her side, and protectively put one arm about her tiny shoulders. With her other hand she gently removed the axe from the little Queen's suddenly nerveless fingers. Ce'Nedra's eyes were wide and unseeing, and she stood immobilized as if in a trance.

"She is under my protection, Zandramas." Poledra said, "and you may not harm her."

The sorceress atop the crag howled in sudden, frustrated rage. Her eyes ablaze, she once again drew herself erect.

"Will it be now, Zandramas?" Poledra asked in a deadly voice. "Is this the time you have chosen for our meeting? You know even as I that should we meet at the wrong time and in the wrong place, we will *both* be destroyed."

"I do not fear thee, Poledra!" the sorceress shrieked.

"Nor I you. Come then, Zandramas, let us destroy each other here and now—for should the Child of Light go on to the Place Which Is No More unopposed and find no Child of Dark awaiting him there, then *I* triumph! If this be the time

421

and place of your choosing, bring forth your power and let it happen—for I grow weary of you."

The face of Zandramas was twisted with rage, and Garion could feel the force of her will building up. He tried to reach over his shoulder for his sword, thinking to unleash its fire and blast the hated sorceress from atop her crag, but even as Ce'Nedra's apparently were, he found that his muscles were all locked in stasis. From behind him he could feel the others also struggling to shake free of the force which seemed to hold them in place as well.

"No," Poledra's voice sounded firmly in the vaults of his mind. "This is between Zandramas and me. Don't interfere."

"Well, Zandramas," she said aloud then, "what is your decision? Will you cling to life a while longer, or will you die now?"

The sorceress struggled to regain her composure, even as the glowing nimbus about Poledra grew more intense. Then Zandramas howled with enraged disappointment and disappeared in a flash of orange fire.

"I thought she might see it my way," Poledra said calmly. She turned to face Garion and the others. There was a twinkle in her golden eyes. "What took you all so long?" she asked. "I've been waiting for you here for months." She looked rather critically at the half-naked Belgarath, who was staring at her with a look of undisguised adoration. "You're as thin as a bone, Old Wolf," she told him. "You really ought to eat more, you know." She smiled fondly at him. "Would you like to have me go catch you a nice fat rabbit?" she asked. Then she laughed, shimmered back into the form of the blue wolf, and loped away, her paws seeming scarcely to touch the earth.

Here ends Book III of *The Malloreon*.
Book IV, *Sorceress of Darsheva*,
continues the search for Zandramas and for the Sardion,
which has been at many sites, but is now to be found
at the "Place Which Is No More"—whatever that means!

About the Author

David Eddings was born in Spokane, Washington, in 1931 and was raised in the Puget Sound area north of Seattle. He received a Bachelor of Arts degree from Reed College in Portland, Oregon, in 1954 and a Master of Arts degree from the University of Washington in 1961. He has served in the United States Army, worked as a buyer for the Boeing Company, has been a grocery clerk, and has taught English. He has lived in many parts of the United States.

His first novel, *High Hunt* (published by Putnam in 1973), was a contemporary adventure story. The field of fantasy has always been of interest to him, however, and he turned to *The Belgariad* in an effort to develop certain technical and philosophical ideas concerning that genre.

Eddings currently resides with his wife, Leigh, in the southwest.